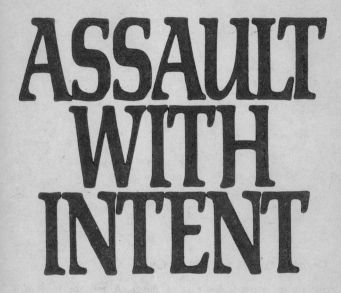

ASSAULT WITH INTENT

WILLIAM X. KIENZLE

BALLANTINE BOOKS • NEW YORK

Library of Congress Catalog Card Number: 82-1628

ISBN 0-345-30812-3

This edition published by arrangement with Andrews and McMeel, Inc.

Manufactured in the United States of America

First Ballantine Books Edition: April 1983

ASSAULT WITH INTENT

THE NEW FATHER KOESLER MYSTERY

Gratitude for technical advice to:

Inspector Robert Hislop, Commanding Officer, Crimes
   Against Persons, Sergeant Roy Awe, Homicide,
   Sergeant Mary Marcantonio, Office of Executive
   Deputy Chief, Sergeant Daniel McCarty, Homicide,
   Detroit Police Department
Ramon Betanzos, Professor of Humanities, Wayne
   State University
Margaret Cronyn, Editor, *The Michigan Catholic*
Lucille Duquette, Promotion Department, WXYZ-TV
Jim Grace, Detective, Kalamazoo Police Department
Donald Grimes, Director of Pharmacy, Deaconess
   Hospital
Sister Bernadelle Grimm, R.S.M., Pastoral Care
   Department, Samaritan Health Center
Timothy Kenny, Principal Trial Attorney, Wayne
   County Prosecuting Attorney's Office
Del Lewis, Secretary, St. John's Provincial Seminary
Sister Marian Mertz, R.S.M., Director of Patient
   Representatives, Mt. Carmel Mercy Hospital
Evelyn Orbach and Nancy Kelley, Station 12 Film
   Preproduction Company
Donald Olmsted, Ballistics Consultant
Thomas Petinga, M.D., Director of Emergency, Mt.
   Carmel Mercy Hospital
Neal Shine, Managing Editor, *Detroit Free Press*

Any technical error is the author's

For Fiona, *in saeculorum saecula*

1.

SEVERAL TEETH WERE MISSING FROM THE SKULL. The gaps gave the skull an even more eerie appearance. Not that it needed anything to amplify its stark and fearsome impact. The mere sight of a human skull is usually enough to make a reflective person more thoughtful. Not only does it punctuate mortal life; together with crossbones it signifies lethal poison. And the skull provides both home and protection for the brain, that organ which distinctly makes us human. Just whose brain had been enclosed in this skull was a mystery. For years, it, along with its accompanying male skeleton, had been the property of the Biology Department of Sacred Heart Seminary. However, when the seminary had discontinued teaching biology more than a decade before, the department's various properties had fallen into the hands of a few vulturine students and faculty members.

Father Leo Ward had gotten the skull. He had plans for it. For nearly fifty years, he had taught English to seminarians in all four years of college. His favorite subject was Shakespeare. He saw to it that the students who survived to college graduation had sampled all Shakespeare's plays and most of his sonnets.

But until he had managed to pluck the skull from

the moribund biology lab, Ward had never had a Yorick. Which is not to say he had a desperate need for a Yorick: along with no Yorick, he also had no other props called for by Shakespeare's plays. But Ward enjoyed keeping students off balance. Few undertakings were better suited to achieving this goal than compelling a young man to recite the wonders of Shakespeare's English—virtually a foreign tongue to late twentieth-century American college students—while clutching a skull.

Yorick was on Ward's crowded desk today because tomorrow the senior class was scheduled to begin reading act 4, scene 5 of *Hamlet*. Yorick did not appear until act 5, scene 1. But that was only a few pages away, and even if they didn't reach Yorick tomorrow, it would be delightful to have Yorick in the classroom so the students could contemplate the agony that would shortly befall one of them.

The only illumination in Ward's room came from a directional desk lamp. Against all four walls, from floor to ceiling, were wooden shelves filled with books. The faint light shed by the small lamp reflected off the glass doors fronting each shelf. Nearly every inch of floor space was heaped with books. This was the case not only in his sitting room but also in his bedroom: well-to-wall volumes with a narrow, mazelike path cleared for walking. Only Ward's bathroom was nonbooked. However, there was a stack of magazines near the toilet.

It was 9:00 P.M., October 31—Halloween. A party was in progress in the gymnasium. Faculty, students, employees, those who worked in the myriad organizations housed within the seminary walls, even some of the seminary's neighbors were at the party. But not Father Leo Ward.

He had been a recluse nearly all his life. Now, as he neared his eightieth birthday, his existence had become even more solitary. He lived almost exclusively for his students and his beloved Bard.

In tomorrow's reading of *Hamlet,* Ophelia, as she went mad, would croon her nonsensical ramblings. Ward plotted his own peculiar scenario. He wanted to make certain that William Zimmer, prime macho man of the senior class, would read the mad Ophelia role. Since readings were assigned daily in the order of the students' alphabetical seating arrangement, and since Ophelia would be the fourth character to speak in scene 5, Michael Totten would have to be the queen and Andrew Umberg the Gentleman; then Francis Wangler, Horatio and Mr. Zimmer, Ophelia. What fun!

Father Ward suppressed a smile. Any incipient laugh was always thus inhibited. His teeth, victims of determined neglect, were all but rotted. As a result, he tried never to let them show. On the rare occasion he was caught by surprise, usually by a ridiculous statement from a student, he would smile, but his lips, which he would shield with his hand, never parted. Occasionally, he would reflect that when it came his time to shuffle off this mortal coil, his skull would not look nearly as good as Yorick's.

All was now prepared for tomorrow, and he was an hour late for bed. He usually retired about eight so he could rise at five and prepare his usual side-altar Mass, the earliest by far in the seminary.

Daylight-Saving Time had ended the previous Sunday; it was now very dark. He had only one task remaining before sleep. He would deliver Yorick to the classroom where the students would find him bright and early tomorrow. He extinguished his cigar—his fifteenth of the day—stood, and arranged his simple black cassock so it was not bunched on his fragile frame.

With Yorick in his left hand and a large flashlight in his right, he managed to exit his quarters and close the door behind him. The corridor was long, narrow, and deserted. It was illuminated only dimly by the outside spotlights that shone on the seminary in hopes of discouraging break-and-enterers.

Ward switched on his flashlight and, in an enchanted mood, directed its beam onto Yorick. He began, softly, to intone Hamlet's monologue. *"Alas,"* Father Ward recited from impeccable memory, *"poor Yorick! I knew him, Horatio: a fellow of infinite jest, of most excellent fancy: he hath borne me on his back a thousand times: and now, how abhorred in my imagination it is! My gorge rises at it."*

Ward, as was his wont, was being carried away by the stunning beauty of Shakespeare's language. *"Here hung those lips that I have kist I know not how oft. Where be your gibes now*—uh-oh, I'm there already!"

Lost in Shakespearean declamation, Ward had reached the end of the rear corridor. To his right was the hall that led to the front of the building and then, immediately, a stairway that he intended to take down to his first-floor classroom.

Suddenly, a figure stepped from the shadows near the porch at his left.

The presence so startled him that only later could Ward fix such details as the person's height—approximately five-feet-five; voice—male, but rather high-pitched; and attire—a black cloak and hat and something—perhaps a stocking—over his face that distorted his features.

But right now, Ward was mainly conscious of the long, menacing knife in the figure's upraised hand. The blade caught and reflected an edge of Ward's flashlight beam.

"Oh! Oh! Oh! Oh, for heaven's sake!" Ward exclaimed. "What's going on here?"

Instinctively, in an attempt to keep his assailant at a safe distance, Ward had begun to paw the air in a dog-paddle motion while backing away from the fray. Each time Ward's hands passed each other in midair, the beam of the flashlight in his right hand shone full upon the skull in his left.

As he advanced on the retreating Ward, the assailant caught sight of Yorick. "What the hell! What in hell! WHAT THE HELL!" The man's voice rose in pitch with each intonation. Now, mirroring Ward's gestures, his gloved hands began to paw the air. In the fluctuating flashlight beam, the two appeared to be engaged in some sort of hitherto uninvented disco step.

Actually, the assailant was trying to knock the flashlight and the skull from Ward's hands. After some dozen pawings, he succeeded. The flashlight plunked down and the skull flew up.

Ward lost his balance and toppled backward. The flashlight, Ward, and the skull hit the floor in that order. However, as Ward spun heels over head, one foot caught the assailant's knife hand, catapulting the weapon into the hall's darkness. The knife thunked into the soft wood of a lavatory door and stuck there. Out of sight but not out of mind.

"Now, where the hell did the damn thing go?" wailed the assailant, looking at his now empty hand. "What the hell! You'd think I could at least . . ." The sentence trailed off as the figure turned abruptly and disappeared, stumbling noisily down the unlit staircase.

"Great Caesar's ghost!" Father Ward sat upright on the floor, rubbing his head and trying to slow his rapidly beating heart and bring down his blood pressure.

No doubt it had been a student.

But which one? Ward hadn't a clue. Well, he pondered. Halloween pranks were all well and good in moderation, but this was going a bit too far, thank you!

As his adrenal glands settled, he assessed the damage. Nothing in or on his person seemed broken. He retrieved his spectacles. The wire frame was bent, but that was easily straightened. He picked up his sturdy flashlight and shone it about. The beam found the knife, imbedded in the door not three feet above his head. He shuddered.

Finally, the flashlight found Yorick. He had lost two more teeth. Ward briefly contemplated the loss. It made Yorick definitely more rakish, he concluded. And, after tonight's brush with injury, possibly death, definitely more fearsome.

"The Enlightenment? Eh . . . eh . . . I don't see what the Enlightenment has to do with it," said Father Phil Merrit.

"It's pretty clear, Phil," Father Paul Burk rejoined. "The Age of Enlightenment in the eighteenth century pretty well marked the beginning of the end of the contemplative approach to reality in Western civilization."

"That statement is about as clear as this alleged pea soup," said Merrit, aiming his spoon at his bowl.

Sacred Heart Seminary's faculty and staff, along with others who worked in the building, as well as visitors, dined in what had been an open second-floor brick porch. The arches had been spanned with Thermopane to close in the area.

The luncheon diners had begun to assemble. Some were already eating; others were waiting their turns at the serving tables. Two white-jacketed seminarians were on hand to serve beverages or cater to special needs. Except for that, seminary meals were normally cafeteria-style.

Merrit taught English. Burk not only taught philosophy, he was close to being a philosopher.

"Look at it historically, man," Merrit continued. "The golden age of contemplation in the West was the twelfth century. Why . . . eh . . . eh . . . we in the West began to lose our intuitive values as early as the fourteenth century."

"Which is not to say there have been no contemplatives in recent times," contributed Father Robert Koesler. "There's Thomas Merton, of course; C.S. Lewis, Thoreau, and T.S. Eliot, among others."

Koesler was not a full-time member of the faculty. He taught a single course in communications. The instruction stemmed from his twelve years of experience as editor of the *Detroit Catholic,* the weekly newspaper of the Archdiocese of Detroit. However, Koesler was no longer in that assignment. For the past several years he had been pastor of St. Anselm's parish in suburban Dearborn Heights.

Koesler never ceased to marvel at the general headiness of conversations at seminary meals. Though he was fairly conversant with Western contemplative history, amid these experts Koesler felt he was close to being out of his depth in this discussion.

"Quite right, Bob." Burk gestured vigorously with his fork. A flourish that made his companions a whit nervous. "And," he turned to Merrit, who leaned defensively away from the fork, "I wouldn't argue over your citation of the twelfth and fourteenth centuries. But it was the Enlightenment and its consequences— Scientism and the Industrial Revolution—that put an empirical end to the contemplative view of reality."

"Oh, well . . . eh . . . eh . . . if you're going to look at it that way . . ."

"What do you mean by Scientism?" Koesler asked.

"In the sense that science is the exclusive source for the answers to all humanity's problems." No longer in argumentation, Burk, now the teacher, lowered his fork. "Scientism fostered the Industrial Revolution. And its material success reinforced Scientism's claims. Ever since, we in the West have been asking only 'how to' and hardly ever considering 'what for.' And we've been getting away with it, until fairly recently when we began to run out of energy, power, and moral integrity."

During this conversation, Father Edmund Sklarski joined the group. He listened with little interest or comprehension. His sole intention was to enter into and, if he were at all lucky, dominate the conversation. He never played the silent guest.

"It's been my experience," Sklarski pontificated, "that while the pen is mightier than the sword . . ." he hesitated, searching for some port in the storm, "faith comes by hearing," he concluded with an air of triumph.

An uncomfortable silence ensued.

Sklarski had recently been called out of retirement—a clear indication of the priest shortage—to teach public speaking at the seminary. While he did have one or two helpful theories regarding the composition and delivery of homilies, Sklarski tended to be vague about almost everything else. He was a man almost totally governed by mood. Students diligently tried to keep him in a good humor. The alternative could be terrifying.

Burk's open-mouthed puzzlement over Sklarski's non sequitur dissolved into a hearty laugh. "Absolutely, Ed. Faith comes by hearing. And Catholics in this archdiocese are not going to hear unless you teach these youngsters to speak up."

Burk had accurately picked up Sklarski's cue. Now Sklarski was part of the conversation. Never again, at this sitting, would the topic under discussion soar to the level of contemplation.

"Went in the drugstore the other day," Sklarski edged toward the interlocutor's position, "went in the drugstore, yes, walked up to the pharmacy counter and ordered a bottle of rubbing alcohol. And then, I don't know why, just for the hell of it," he paused for effect—he had everyone's attention—"I winked.

"Well, the clerk grinned from ear to ear, and winked back. So I just waited. And, sure enough, he came back with a fifth of Canadian Club. Well, I blew my cork. 'How dare you, sir!' I said. 'Here I want a bottle of rubbing alcohol for my poor sick father. And you, sir, you bring me an intoxicant! And me, sir, me a man of the cloth!' Well, the other customers stopped what they were doing and watched what was going on. The clerk spent half his time apologizing and the rest of the time trying to quiet me. And do you know what the upshot was?"

His audience collectively acknowledged ignorance.

"He gave me the C.C. *and* the rubbing alcohol free!"

All laughed.

"The perqs never quit, do they?" observed Koesler.

Sklarski noticed a large pitcher filled with a dark liquid on the serving table. It was fruit juice. But what kind? He beckoned one of the student waiters to the table.

"Uh . . ." Sklarski knew almost no one's name.

"Leonard Marks," the pudgy student replied.

"Ah, yes—Marks. What kind of fruit juice do we have today?"

Marks glanced at the pitcher. He had no idea what the juice was. But it looked like grape juice.

"Grape juice," Marks said decisively.

"Ah, yes, good. I'll just have some, Leonard."

Marks carefully poured a large glass full of loganberry juice and presented it to Sklarski, who downed it in one significant chugalug.

Sklarski's expression went from pleasure to surprise to anger.

"This is not grape juice," Sklarski fairly shouted as he banged the glass to the table, "this is *gall!* From now on, Mr. uh . . ."

"Marks," came the shaken clarification.

"Marks, you have my permission to taste the juice beforehand so that this disaster will not be repeated!"

"Yes, sir . . . uh . . . yes, your grace . . . uh . . . yes, Father."

How quickly things change. A pall settled on the gathering.

Koesler, finished with his light lunch, noticed Father Leo Ward sitting at a small table by himself. Nothing unusual about that. Most of the faculty and staff acknowledged Ward's Garboesque desire to be alone. Koesler, on the other hand, correctly perceived Ward's hermitlike life as the defense of a very shy man. He excused himself and moved to Ward's table.

"Quite a display." He nodded toward the still fuming Sklarski.

Ward glanced at the younger priest who now sat opposite him. A look of welcome flickered in his steel-gray eyes. "Yes, I should say." Ward was by no means reluctant to publicly castigate a student. But he was not fond of Sklarski, who, admittedly, was scarcely an academician. "However," Ward added, "he *is* a stupid boy."

"Marks?"

"Yes. He simply cannot do anything right. Years ago, he would not have lasted more than a semester or two. Now, there are so few candidates for the priest-hood . . ."

The sentence did not need completion. The virtually worldwide shortage in Catholic religious vocations was due not so much to priests, nuns, and brothers leaving as to the remarkably few young people entering.

"It's a buyer's market," Koesler agreed. He reflected on his own time in the seminary, back in the forties and fifties—a time when priests were portrayed by such macho actors as Pat O'Brien, Gregory Peck, and Humphrey Bogart. When seminaries were packed and only a small percentage of those who entered in the ninth grade persevered through the four years of high school, four of college, and the final four years of theology.

Now, Sacred Heart Seminary had closed its high school; there were fewer than forty students in its college and fewer than that at St. Joseph's Theological Seminary.

Now priests, when they did appear in films, were portrayed as confused, doubt-ridden men who were losing their vocation or faith, or both. In an explosively changing world, few things had changed as much as the image of the Catholic priest.

Ward had no sooner finished eating when Marks' companion student-waiter deftly removed his plate and quickly returned with coffee.

"Then on the other hand," said Ward, as the young man went back to his post, "there are seminarians like William Zimmer. He is almost enough to restore one's faith in the future of the priesthood."

"Yes, he is kind of special, isn't he?" Koesler glanced across the dining room at Zimmer, standing tall and alert next to the rattled Marks.

"Comes from a fine family," said Ward, "an excellent student, a fine cut of a man."

"Good voice, better-than-average musician," Koesler continued the paean, "good athlete, becomingly modest. And the other students recognize his specialness, don't they? I mean, there is no jealousy, is there?"

"None that I'm aware of. They seem to confide in him. He probably knows more about what goes on here than the entire faculty put together. He will make a fine priest."

As Koesler's gaze turned from the young man in question to his tablemate, for the first time he noticed a slight bruise on Ward's forehead, as well as a skew in his eyeglass frame.

"Say," Koesler's tone was clearly solicitous, "what happened to you, Father? Didn't walk into a door, did you?"

Ward flushed slightly. He did not enjoy being the center of attention. Almost apologetically, he recounted his hairy Halloween adventure.

"Have you told anyone about this?" Koesler asked.

"Well, no. I didn't want to bother anyone. After all, nothing really happened. That is, no one was seriously hurt."

"Seriously hurt! Why, it sounds like an attempt at murder!"

Ward hesitated, as if weighing his words. "I am not afraid to die," he said finally.

Koesler reflected that anyone who could make such a statement after having come so close to a violent death must sincerely mean it.

"Supposing," Koesler offered, "whoever attacked you did not intend you to be his victim? Suppose he was just waiting in the hall for anyone who came along? Suppose he tries it again? Suppose he actually kills someone?"

"I hadn't thought about it that way."

Koesler was reluctant to invade this very private man's life, but was genuinely shocked that anyone would attack a harmless old priest.

"You have no idea who it was?"

"No, none. There was so little light. I couldn't see very well. And then when my glasses fell off . . ."

"Is there anyone who might have a grudge against you? Or against any other faculty member that you know of?"

"A grudge? No, I can't think of anyone. Of course," he hesitated, "there are always students who become angry with their teachers. But that has been going on since the first lesson ever taught. And there are employees who are angry at the way they are treated or because they are dismissed. But I know of no one who bears me a grudge.

"Of course," another slight pause, "I can't speak for any of the others on the faculty."

"Well," Koesler prodded, "has anything like this happened before? I mean, to you, or to others, to your knowledge? Angry words? A threatening gesture? Anything this side of a physical attack?"

Ward reflected. "No. I don't believe so. No, nothing that would hint at violence."

Koesler, normally slow to jump to conclusions or act precipitately, was clearly concerned.

"Frankly, Father, I'm worried. Someone lay in wait for you—or at least for some faculty member. Someone armed with a lethal weapon. His attack was unprovoked. It's likely he would have actually killed you but for a series of extraordinary accidents. Whoever this character is, he's obviously got a problem, and he's still out there—and he very well might try again.

"I think we should go to the police about this," Koesler concluded. "Would you mind, Father, if I contacted them in your behalf?"

"If you thing it best, Father . . . all right." Again the elderly priest hesitated. "There wouldn't have to be any publicity, would there?"

"I don't think so. I have a few friends on the force; I'll ask them to keep it as quiet as possible."

With that, Koesler excused himself and set out for downtown Detroit and police headquarters. He feared that no one at Sacred Heart Seminary was safe with what might well be a homicidal maniac on the loose.

2.

FATHER KOESLER SAT ON A BENCH IN THE HALL ON
the fifth floor of police headquarters. His mind wan-
dered in a stream of consciousness. There were times
he was convinced he had mastered the art of daydreaming.

He wondered where the city had found these uncomfortable wooden benches that were distributed
throughout the building. He could think of no source
other than some church that had decided to be kind to
its parishioners and replace its pews with something
more comfortable. A blunder. A decided blunder. He
visualized a series of men and children in the congregation drifting off to sleep. Women, in Koesler's experience, seldom went to sleep in church. From time
to time he wondered how they managed that.

A large, well-dressed black man strode by. He wore
a plasticized police department I.D.; Koesler assumed
he was a detective. The man glanced at Koesler in
passing. He carried a dark attaché case. On it was en-
graved, in gold, the single name, "Tibbs."

Koesler pondered that. He had seen two movies in
which Sidney Poitier had portrayed a brilliant police
detective named Tibbs. Koesler decided the Detroit
officer must be kidding. Here was a clear indication

that even members of the Homicide Division had a sense of humor.

Gradually, Koesler became aware of a beehive of police and civilians passing to and fro. It was a busy and constant procession. It brought to mind a couple of observations he had made at Tiger Stadium.

The first had been made many years before when it had fallen Koesler's lot to chaperone his parish Boy Scout troop at a Tigers-Red Sox game. During the entire game, Koesler had sat sidesaddle while an endless series of little boys passed before him, en route to or from the restroom, souvenir seller, refreshment stand—or just to keep moving. At game's end, he could not tell which team had won—though he was fairly certain Ted Williams had hit a couple of homers and had bunted successfully down the third-base line against the Williams shift.

The second had occurred when he got a reserved seat at a subsequent Saturday afternoon game. Having experienced life in the left-field bleachers, now Koesler had an excellent vantage behind first base. He gazed for many minutes at the throng of youngsters in the bleachers. It resembled an anthill. At no time during the game was a majority seated. He thought he might have discovered the epitome of perpetual motion.

Koesler was many months and some miles away when he became conscious of a massive man standing next to the bench, patiently awaiting the priest's return from distraction land.

"Father Koesler," said a beaming Inspector Walter Koznicki, "how did you know my day was going so badly that I needed you to lighten it?"

Koesler rose to greet the Inspector. Koznicki was one or two inches taller than the priest's six-foot-three, but bigger-boned. Larger than life, while a cliché, aptly described Walter Koznicki.

"Been having a particularly bad day?" Koesler asked as he was ushered into Koznicki's busy office.

"We've just found another murdered coed." Koznicki was referring to a current series of homicides that was being spotlighted and graphically labeled by the news media, who had applied their own lurid epithet to the killings.

"Are you sure this is another one of them?"

"It's 'the Ripper' all right. There's no doubt."

Koesler knew better than to ask what the calling card might be that enabled the police to identify the work as that of the Ripper. That would be strictly a police affair, at least until the case was solved and closed.

"But what brings you here, Father?"

"I'm almost embarrassed to tell you. It seems inconsequential compared with the horrible death of that poor woman."

Koznicki waved his hand as if clearing his desk. "Perfectly all right, Father. We are geared to handle more than one investigation at a time." He paused. "I assume you've come on a professional matter."

Koesler and Koznicki had become fast friends during several Detroit criminal investigations involving the Catholic community. Thus, the priest's visit could well have been merely sociable, though this was unlikely in the headquarters setting.

"Oh, yes," Koesler hastened to assure. "In any case, I think I've come to the right place."

"If you have any doubt, Father, tell me what is on your mind and let me be the judge."

Koesler related the story Father Leo Ward had told a few hours before. During the narration, Koznicki sat back in his suitably large chair, fingers entwined over ample abdomen. Only his eyes, alert and occasionally darting from the desk surface to the priest's face, betrayed his growing interest in and understanding of the matter.

At length, Koesler concluded a fairly faithful rendition of the assault upon Father Ward and Yorick.

"When did this happen, Father?"

"A couple of evenings ago—Halloween, to be exact."

"And this has not been reported to date?"

"No." Koesler hesitated. It would have helped if Koznicki knew what sort of person Ward was. "You see, Father Ward is a most private person. It's probably difficult to understand, but . . . he just didn't want to be a bother to anyone."

"Be a bother!" Koznicki arched an eyebrow. For him, an emphatic expression. "Is it probable it could be one of the students?"

"Father has no idea."

"What do *you* think?"

"*I* have no idea."

"There's no way this could have been just a prank—a Halloween joke? You're satisfied the attack was in earnest?"

"I know only that Father Ward's face is bruised; his eyeglass frame is bent . . . and that, according to Father Ward, who is not given to hyperbole, a dangerously sharp knife found itself embedded in the woodwork too near Father Ward's head—a knife that, unlike the vision that Lady Macbeth imagined, is all too real."

The Inspector nodded, acknowledging the reality.

"How is security at the seminary?"

"Not bad, I suppose. There are guards day and night. They try to make sure the doors and windows are locked. But the neighborhood is so crime-ridden, and there are so many doors and windows accessible . . ." Koesler's voice trailed off.

"Well, Father, it seems we have something here that falls somewhere between felonious assault and attempted murder. It also seems that you are in the wrong place. This sort of investigation should at least begin at the precinct level." Koznicki took a chart from his desk drawer. "Let me see—the corner of Chicago Boulevard and Linwood, isn't it? Just on the fringe of the '67 riot?"

Koesler nodded.

Koznicki's searching finger settled on a spot adjacent to the map's near west side. "That would be Precinct Ten. I know the officers; there are some excellent people there. I can give you a reference, make a phone call—"

"I was hoping," Koesler interrupted diffidently, "I mean . . . I didn't know whose jurisdiction this might fall under . . . I guess I just instinctively came here. It seems clear to me that someone tried to kill Father Ward. And you're in charge of Homicide. And Father Ward is such a tender person. I was hoping you might see your way clear to . . ." Koesler's voice trailed off. It was getting to be a habit.

Koznicki smiled and waved his magic hand again. "Good friends need only to ask, Father. Of course we can handle it. If you will wait just a minute, I will call the precinct and inform them we are beginning this investigation. I think Lieutenant Harris is available. We will just get our coats and go right over with you."

"With *me*?"

"Of course. We are about to begin an investigation that involves a seminary, the very hub of Catholic life. You have had more experience than most priests in the hows and whys Catholics murder or are murdered in Detroit. You surely do not want to be excluded from the investigation, do you?"

"I certainly do. In the words of the late Sam Goldwyn, 'Include me out.' I want no part in another murder investigation. Or even an attempted-murder investigation. I'll be glad to introduce you to Father Ward. But then I will head out to my rustic little parish where I will take care of the sacraments while you solve the crimes."

"That is too bad." Koznicki smiled.

"Why's that?"

"Lieutenant Harris will be so disappointed you are not part of the team."

"I'll bet," Koesler retorted, recalling Harris' studied

lack of enthusiasm over having a priest as excess baggage in a murder investigation. "I'll just bet."

Father Phil Merrit almost literally steamed down the corridor. He stepped along at a brisk pace, puffing furiously on a cigarette, the hem of his cassock fluttering out behind him. His passage suggested that of an animated locomotive.

Father Merrit hated afternoon classes. The students were groggy after a steady stream of morning classes followed by lunch. Added to that, afternoon was usually when his ulcer most pained him. Yet here he was, hurrying to a class in which he would try to teach English to a group of young men many of whom thought their ability to merely speak the language, however indifferently, entitled them to a passing grade.

He passed through the doorway at the moment the bell sounded. Twin jets of smoke escaped his nostrils. He butted the cigarette in the ashtray on his desk. "In the name of the Father, and of the Son, and of the Holy Spirit. . . ."

Merrit led prayer as if he were angry with the Lord. But then the aura of anger was as mother's milk to him.

Prayer completed, the students sat down and quietly arranged their books and papers. There was little sense of frivolity in a Merrit-taught class.

"Gentlemen." Merrit's square face appeared to compress as if it were a TV image and someone were fooling with the horizontal button. "Gentlemen . . . eh . . . eh . . . I believe the assignment was to write a poem."

Rustling sounds as students searched through their papers for their homework. Several scrunched down, each hoping he would not be called to give a verbal report.

"Eh . . . eh . . . Wygoski . . ."

He had hit on one of the scrunchers.

". . . read your poem."

Herbert Wygoski stood reluctantly, clutching a paper that betrayed a slight tremor of his hands.

"Eh . . . what's the title of your poem, Wygoski?"

" 'Taps Are Like the Sound of Night.' "

A slight pause. "Eh . . . dammit, Wygoski, is it 'Taps *is*' or 'Taps *are*'?"

"Well, I suppose it's 'Taps *is*,' but I thought 'Taps *are*' sounded better."

Another slight pause. "Eh . . . dammit, Wygoski, how far can poetic license go!" Obvious disgust. "Read the poem, Wygoski."

Wygoski read his two-stanza poem. An extended silence followed.

"Gentlemen . . . eh . . . that was a perfect example of doggerel." More disgust. "Sit down, Wygoski."

Red-faced, a thoroughly mortified Wygoski resumed his seat.

And that bastard probably expects me to write another poem someday, he moped.

"I will not speak with her," Michael Totten read.

Father Leo Ward did not mind afternoon classes. He also liked morning classes. By now, teaching was his life. Just a few more lines from *Hamlet* and he would euchre William Zimmer into reading the role of the mad Ophelia.

"She is importunate, indeed distract;/Her mood will needs be pitied," read Andrew Umberg.

The students knew what Ward had in mind. They had been through similar setups too many times. They knew Zimmer was a particular favorite of Ward's. But while Ward's wrath could cut through a sluggard or laggard student, being among the brightest also had its drawbacks. The best and brightest were frequently singled out to prepare reports. Or they were singled out for outrageous roles such as that of the forthcoming mad Ophelia.

"Let her come in," read Totten.

Reading the part of Ophelia would not embarrass

Zimmer. He would do so with good grace. Father Ward had few enough gratifications. If Ward got his jollies by maneuvering Zimmer into the Ophelia role, the seminarian was willing to cooperate.

"To my sick soul, as sin's true nature is,
Each toy seems prologue to same great amiss:
So full of artless jealousy is guilt,
It spills itself in fearing to be spilt," Totten pressed on.

It was time for Ophelia's entrance. Going along with the mood, Wangler, as Horatio, walked over to escort Zimmer to center classroom. All—even Zimmer—but Ward smiled.

At that moment, a student knocked, entered the room, and gave Father Ward a message: Father Koesler and two police officers were waiting to see Father, now if possible.

Drat! Ward hated to postpone Zimmer's reading of Ophelia even for a day, but there was no helping it.

"Study the next act," he commanded. "Quietly," he added.

He hoped this would not take much time. After all, nobody had been hurt.

Punctuated by static, the off-and-on drone of the police radio held all the charm of a dripping faucet. Brian Fogerty, one of the *Free Press* reporters assigned to police headquarters, was fighting slumber. He decided a stroll was the only way of averting going to sleep on the job.

He started his tour on the third floor, where most of the police brass were. All present and accounted for. And nothing much going on. He climbed two flights to the fifth floor, where Homicide, among other departments, was located. Beginning, as was his wont, at the top, he checked Inspector Koznicki's office. Nobody home.

"Where's Koznicki?" Fogerty asked an officer in the adjacent office.

Fogerty, of course, was not interested in talking with Koznicki, just in his whereabouts. You never knew where an innocent question might lead.

"He and Harris went with . . . uh, what's his name . . . Koesler—Father Koesler. Seems someone tried to stab a priest at Sacred Heart Seminary." It was an unusually comprehensive reply.

Stab a priest, Fogerty pondered. That was a little out of the ordinary. He checked the seminary's location. Precinct Ten. Using a nearby pay phone, he called the Tenth Precinct. No, no one there was investigating an attempted stabbing at the seminary. Odd, again.

He decided to call his city desk.

"Kane," barked *Free Press* city editor Nelson Kane.

Flatly, Fogerty reported what he had learned.

"No record at the precinct, eh?"

"None. Listen, Nellie, this may be a dead end. But there's something else I want to check out here. And if you've got somebody loose there, you might want to cover this."

Kane surveyed the city room. All the staffers seemed busy, some programming into the VDTs, others on the phone. With one notable exception: Seated two desks removed from Kane was Joe Cox, reading a book.

"Yeah," Kane said conspiratorially, "I've got somebody loose.

"Cox." Kane growled just loudly enough for the reporter to hear.

Cox closed the book and circled to Kane's desk. He received the assignment, returned to his desk, and picked up his notepad. He started to leave, then turned back to Kane. "Did you say the priest's name was Koesler?"

"Yeah, Koesler. Why?"

"Nothing. It just seems that every year or so we keep running into him."

As Father Ward came around the bend in the corridor, he saw three men silhouetted outside the door to his suite. From a distance they did not appear very large. But, as he neared them, he realized it was because all of them were so very near the same height that none appeared outstanding. Close-up, they were.

Koesler made the introductions. Ward led them to the spot in the hallway where the assault had taken place and told the story in his characteristic unemotional manner. Then it was question and answer time.

"Let me get this straight, Father," said Lieutenant Harris. "Why were you carrying a skull?"

Father Ward looked at the tall, well-dressed black detective appraisingly. "It was for my class. A prop for my class on *Hamlet*."

"I thought I'd heard everything"—Harris could scarcely conceal his amusement—"but I never heard of a mugger attacking somebody who was carrying a skull. In this dark hallway and on Halloween, it must have scared the sh - - pants off him."

"Well," said Koznicki, "it seems to have confused him sufficiently to have caused him to fail.

"You say he escaped down this staircase, Father?" Ward nodded.

"He seems to have planned his attack with a handy escape route in mind," Harris observed.

"Excuse me, Lieutenant," Koesler interrupted, "but did you say 'mugger'? Aren't we talking about attempted murder?"

"We don't know yet what we're talking about," Harris replied. "It could be an attempted mugging or attempted murder . . . or"—he shook his head— "possibly even a Halloween prank that went awry."

"But you will continue your investigation?" Koesler persisted anxiously.

"For the time being at least," Koznicki replied. "This patch of floor where the attack occurred"—he indicated the spot—"it has been mopped?"

A large clean area where the men were standing

was framed by a thin layer of dust that ran the length of the corridor in both directions.

"I did fall down," Father Ward cast about for some explanation, "and I had to struggle to get to my feet."

"No, this area is too large for just your activity, and it seems well scrubbed," said Koznicki. He turned to Harris. "Have them look into this, will you, Ned?"

"Sure thing."

"And the knife used in the attack, Father; where is it now?" Koznicki asked.

"In my apartment."

"We will take it with us and see if there are any fingerprints on it. Other than yours, Father." Koznicki seemed disappointed at the dearth of evidence.

The four turned to go back to Father Ward's suite.

"Well," Harris said, as a figure appeared at the end of the corridor, "it wouldn't be the scene of a crime without the presence of the press."

"The press!" Ward was startled.

"That is the bad news, Father," said Koznicki. "The good news is that this is Joe Cox, one of the more competent reporters in the city. If your story must be told, better it be told accurately."

As the reporter approached, Koznicki made a mental note to find out just who or what had put Cox on the trail so quickly.

"Just give him your story as we walk along," Harris advised Father Ward. "Hopefully you'll be finished with him by the time we leave."

"Leave?"

"Yes, Father. We would like you to come to headquarters and enter a preliminary complaint report," Koznicki explained. "It will take only a short time."

"I don't understand all this fuss," said Ward. "After all, nobody wast hurt."

Joe Cox was wrapping up his report to Nelson Kane on the attempted knifing.

"Do you want to go with it?" Cox concluded.

"Sure. Give me eight or nine 'grafs. We'll tuck it inside Section A somewhere. Hang it on the 'Is nothing sacred?' hook.

"Any idea who did it?"

"None."

"Motive?"

"Not yet. But Harris said one guess could be robbery."

"Not a bad guess for that neighborhood." Kane knew the characteristics of the various sections of Detroit as well as anyone in the city. "Strange place, actually," Kane reflected. "Used to be heavily Jewish. In fact, at one time there was a synagogue kitty-cornered from the seminary. Now the neighborhood's almost completely black, but an odd mixture. A lot of wealthy blacks on the boulevards—Chicago and Boston. Very few middle-class in the neighborhood. Most of the rest—white or black—are dirt poor. Almost everybody's got weapons. B and Es and armed robbery are a way of life there."

Cox was mildly surprised at the city editor's rambling discourse. Kane rarely used two words if he could think of one, especially when his audience was a staff writer who had just been ordered to write eight or nine paragraphs on deadline. Cox's surprise mounted slightly because Kane was not finished with his off-the-cuff assessment of the crime and its scene.

"Yeah, robbery would be a good guess. Especially when the victim is a parish priest. All the seminary priests are diocesan. And all muggers know that parish priests do not take a vow of poverty." Kane tucked tongue firmly in cheek: "Now, if the guy had mugged a Jesuit at U. of D., all he'd have got was a bag of golf clubs . . . and they would have belonged to the order."

Cox was uncertain whether to laugh or gravely agree. Instead, he asked a question. "When did you become a talking encyclopedia on priests?"

"I'm a Catholic. Born and raised. Even parochial school," Kane acknowledged.

This exposition genuinely surprised Cox. "I'll be damned. All these years I never knew you were Catholic. You mean you actually go to church?"

"Every goddamn Sunday."

Cox departed to deposit in the VDT eight or nine paragraphs that would speak to such vital points as who, what, why, when, where, and how.

"Sporting Goods," blinked the neon sign atop the unpretentious building. Another sign, this one hand-painted and mounted in the front window, read, "Gun Shop." The store was empty of customers. It was near closing time.

For the past quarter of an hour, a man had been standing outside, looking through the window, studying the interior. Finally, with but a few minutes till closing, he entered. He made his way directly to the "Gun Shop" at the rear of the store, where he proceeded to study a limited variety of handguns in the display case.

"May I help you?" The clerk would not have approached a customer this quickly except that it was so near closing time.

"I . . . I want to buy some bullets."

The clerk noted the man was approximately five-feet-five, with a rather high-pitched voice.

"What kind of bullets?"

"For a gun."

The clerk sighed. "What kind of gun?"

"What?"

"Is it an automatic or a revolver?"

"I'm not sure."

The clerk pointed to an automatic—"Does it look like this?"—then to a revolver, "or this?"

"Like that." The man indicated the revolver. In gesturing, he tipped over a full ashtray. Cigarette and cigar butts and ashes cascaded over the counter onto the floor.

The clerk sighed again.

"Sorry," said the man.

"It's O.K.," said the clerk without the slightest sincerity. "What caliber?"

"What?"

"Caliber. What caliber ammunition do you want?"

For less than two cents, the clerk would have shot him.

"Oh, caliber." Comprehension lit up the man's eyes. "Just a minute." He left the counter and moved to the pay phone on the nearby wall. He fumbled with a change purse, extricated two dimes, and put them in the slot. He again delved into the purse, displacing several coins, which dropped on the floor. As they rolled in several directions, the man seemed to be performing an odd dance. Finally, he succeeded in stepping on one of the errant coins, picked it up, and inserted it in the slot.

Shooting was too good, the clerk decided. The store stocked ropes and knives. Perhaps hanging, drawing, and quartering. . . .

The man returned. ".38 caliber," he ordered.

"Very good."

In a few more moments, prolonged somewhat by the man's attempts to corral his change, dump the coins into his change purse, and stuff the bills into his wallet, the sale was completed.

The clerk, teeth clenched, locked the door after his departed customer, cleaned up the ashtray debris, and hammered a punching bag for a few minutes. He did not want to carry all this pent-up rage home to his wife.

In 1960, ground was broken for Cardinal Mooney Latin School. In 1965, the Second Vatican Council was concluded. In 1967, Detroit experienced fearsome riots that resulted in forty-three deaths, extensive looting, and the burning of wide areas of the black ghetto to the ground.

The three events bore an odd correlation for Detroit's Catholic community.

In the early sixties, seminary enrollment continued to climb. Not realizing it had crested in Detroit, the Archdiocese erected a separate high school building on the campus of Sacred Heart Seminary. This was in addition to the mammoth structure which for nearly half a century had been more than sufficient to house the seminary's high school and college students. Also at this time, serious consideration was given to building a second gymnasium.

In the middle sixties, Vatican Council II was convoked by Pope John XXIII and concluded by Pope Paul VI. Among the many consequences of the Council was that for the first time in centuries, Catholics were encouraged, or at least permitted, to question Church doctrines, morality, and law. Prior to this, Catholics, including the clergy and religious, had been expected to learn, not question. Change was everywhere—most notably in the ancient Latin liturgy, which now was permitted in the vernacular. As one thoughtful conservative observed at the introduction of the vernacular, "Change one word of that Latin Mass and the whole thing will fall apart." He may have been right.

In any case, one of the most prominent phenomena of the postconciliar Church was the return to lay life of thousands of priests and nuns. These left a vocation which hitherto had been unfailingly lifelong, if not eternal. Concurrently, the number of young Catholics entering the seminary or convent began to decline dramatically.

In 1967, the area surrounding Sacred Heart Seminary erupted in a riot that in less than a week spread to other areas and drastically changed the character of the city. Gangs, spawned or emboldened during the riot, began to escalate terrorism. Young white boys were mugged while waiting for buses near the seminary. The area was no longer safe for blacks or whites. The blacks who lived there could not afford to leave. Whites who had a choice decided, in great numbers, not to travel into trouble from their enclaves on the fringes of the city or from the suburbs.

Each of these factors, singly or in conjunction, contributed toward leading Detroit to near missionland status.

These factors also helped explain why the two detectives assigned to this case by Lieutenant Harris had a much easier time than they anticipated. They did have to interrogate thirty-eight students. But, though thirty-eight was not an insignificant number, it was far less than the hundreds they might have expected.

Each of the students could account for his whereabouts at the time of the attack on Father Ward. Most had been at the Halloween party. Three had been in the infirmary. Several had gone home to be with their families.

Sergeant Marge Morris, an attractive black woman, and Sergeant Dean Patrick, a salt-and-pepper-haired white veteran, were nearing the end of the second day of this investigation. Both were members of Homicide Squad Six.

They were walking down the seminary corridor leading to the southeast wing, a two-story structure that once had served as convent and infirmary. With nuns no longer serving or residing in the seminary, the infirmary had been relocated and the building rented to two archidocesan departments, the Hispanic Office and the *Detroit Catholic,* the archdiocesan newspaper.

The seminary department, once the raison d'être of the entire campus, had withdrawn into one small section of the building. A case of circling the wagons ever more tightly.

"Ever seen so many blind alleys?" Morris asked.

"Everybody's got an alibi." Patrick smiled, the corners of his eyes crinkling into well-worn crow's-feet.

"I've never seen a place like this, where everybody knows everybody."

"One big, happy family."

"Maybe not so happy." Morris pointed to the door leading into the southeast wing. "One of them might have tried to murder that old priest."

"Or not. It could just as easily have been someone from outside. It's almost impossible to make this place secure, even with guards. My best count so far says there are nearly twenty outside doors, and hundreds of windows in both the basement and first floor. It's a sieve."

"That's true. And this is a rough neighborhood. Did you see the record on this building over in the Tenth?"

"Yeah. These people don't have to host an open house; most of the neighbors seem to have toured the place after breaking and entering."

"On top of that"—Morris stepped back to allow Patrick to open the door—"the night of the attack the entire neighborhood actually had been invited in for the Halloween party."

"Lots of suspects, huh?" Patrick smiled again.

"If we ever finish this internal investigation, we can check with the neighbors who were here for the party."

"At least the ones who bothered to sign in."

Morris raised her eyes heavenward, whence, she was growing certain, the next lead would have to come.

They decided to begin at the rear of the wing with the *Detroit Catholic,* and work forward to the Hispanic Office. Consulting their list, they determined that Irene Casey, the editor, would be the appropriate person with whom to begin.

They introduced themselves. Mrs. Casey seemed flustered. Most people were when meeting homicide detectives.

"How many employees do you have, Mrs. Casey?" Patrick asked.

"Let's see, twelve, including me."

"Do you know the whereabouts of any of them on the evening of Halloween last?" Experience prompted Morris to cut right to the heart of the matter.

"Yes. As a matter of fact, all of us were at the Halloween party."

"All of you?"

"All of us."

"Did anyone leave around 9:00 P.M.?"

"No, no one left at any time during the evening. All of us were here from beginning to end."

Morris glanced heavenward once more. Still no singular help.

Outwardly, Father Phil Merrit was behaving no differently than any of the others of the seminary faculty. Each had put on a brave front. However, Merrit was frightened. He wondered how many others felt this fear.

The way he figured it, one of their number had been viciously, if unsuccessfully, attacked. And none of them could feel secure until Father Ward's assailant was apprehended. From all he could learn, the police were getting nowhere in their investigation. And they had been at it for more than a week.

It was a few minutes past six on this November morning. The weathercaster had predicted another relatively mild day. Detroit's winter had not yet gotten serious. It would.

Merrit was readying himself for his regular trip to nearby Saint Gregory parish, where he would offer the 6:45 Mass, as he had for the past several years. Most of the priest-faculty assisted in parishes with daily Mass as well as weekend liturgies.

Merrit tried to distract himself from the disquieting thoughts of the attack on Ward. As he shaved, he considered the scene that would shortly greet him as he entered Saint Gregory's.

Four or five pious souls would be scattered in

various sections of the darkened church. In the sacristy to the right, where the priests vested for Mass, old Father Wonski, the pastor, would be yelling across the sanctuary toward the sacristy on the left, where three or four small boys would be either getting into their cassocks and surplices or fooling around. The shouted threats never changed. They were always in roughly the same vein.

"Hey, you boys over by that other sacristy there! How do you mean fooling around when there are the candles for you to light and the wine and water and the chalice over by the safe for you to get out and get over by the altar! Yes, and that includes you, Tyrone Jones, with your fooling around! Do you want to lose that mouth!"

Once, only once, Merrit had stayed after Mass to breakfast with Wonski. Merrit had requested a couple of poached eggs on toast. The housekeeper had served them on a plate that was superheated. The eggs, of course, had continued to cook aboard the hot plate. In consideration of the rubbery eggs, Merrit had decided on the spot he would never eat there again.

However, it was on that occasion that Wonski had confided in Merrit. He had given a brief history of his star-crossed ecclesiastical career. It seems that from the very beginning of his priesthood, the bishop had given him one rotten assignment after another. "Until, finally," said Wonski, "I told the bishop to go to hell."

"And," Merrit replied in jest, "did he?"

"No," said Wonski, "he sent me."

To know all is to forgive all.

Bundled against the cold of even this mild November day, Merrit descended to the first floor whence he would exit through the back door, descend two short flights of steps to ground level and enter his car parked nearby.

He opened the heavy oak door, stepped outside, and paused. A premonition? All seemed deathly still. Not even any traffic sounds from adjacent streets.

A light fog hovered. The weathercaster hadn't mentioned that.

The feeling of nameless dread was so palpable he almost turned to go back to his room and phone in some excuse to the parish. But, what the hell; only women live their lives based on intuition. It was not the part of a macho man to fear the unknown.

Bracing, he descended the first flight of steps. As he reached the first landing, he thought he heard a click. As he turned to investigate, he was stopped by an explosive roar. He dropped as if poleaxed.

In a split second, a series of thoughts popped through his mind: This is what it is like to die. How long before I meet God? What will judgment be like? Will my father and mother greet me? Oh, my God, what if there is nothing!

Suddenly, a new and significant thought occurred: Nothing hurts.

He hadn't been hit. The close sound of gunfire, combined with his premonition of doom had caused him to collapse.

What happens now? Will he fire again?

Father Merrit flipped over on his back and peered up into the mist. A man stood inside the low railing of the porch. He was dressed entirely in black. His right wrist seemed bent at an unnatural angle. In his right forearm crooked close to his body he cradled a large, shiny revolver that seemed to have exploded.

As if in delayed action and slow motion, the man let out an excruciating cry—a howl of agony and frustration. Then, using his left hand as support, he clumsily vaulted the railing, as windows all about that section of the seminary were thrown open. He limped appreciably as he made his way to a nearby car, awkwardly entered it and, after a stretch of time, necessitated by having to turn the key and shift with his left hand, started it and drove off into the fog.

Heads bobbed and swiveled, as the onlookers at the

open windows gaped at the scene and each other in startled disbelief.

Merrit took stock. His clothes were soiled from rolling on the tile. His glasses had broken when he fell. Otherwise, no damage that he could ascertain.

Phil Merrit, he thought, this may have frightened a few years off your life, but, by and large, you are a lucky bastard.

Then he recalled that moment when he had thought he was dying, and had doubted, just for an instant, that immortality followed this life.

He breathed a prayer of faith just as he was being encircled by people who wanted only to help.

"Can you give any kind of physical description, Father?"

Father Merrit, since the attack earlier in the day, had been visited by several solicitous colleagues, the rector of the seminary, and his doctor—who had pronounced him alive, the possessor of soaring blood pressure, and on the verge of hyperventilating. Sergeant Patrick, with all this in mind, was trying not to pressure him.

"I'm afraid not, officer. I was on the ground, and there was all that fog."

"Let's give it a try, anyway, Father. Now, recall the incident. You say you saw no one as you descended the stairs to the first level. Did you see him at all before he fired?"

"No . . . eh . . . no." Merrit lit his fresh cigarette from his expiring one. He had been a heavy smoker for as long as his confreres could remember. But it had been many years since he had chain-smoked. "I heard a sound . . . a click. I suppose he was . . . eh . . . cocking the gun. I . . . eh . . . don't have much experience in that sort of thing.

"Anyway, I was just turning when he fired . . . or tried to. Then I fell to the ground. I don't know why. Just instinctive . . . I suppose it was the combination of the noise . . . the sound of that explosion, along with my premonition."

"You had a premonition?"

"Yes . . . I'm not sure why; maybe it's just—well, it's just that with what happened to Father Ward and all. . . ."

"I understand," Patrick reassured him. "What did you do when you realized you hadn't been hit?" Patrick was taking notes.

"Well, mostly . . . eh . . . I remember the gun. I couldn't take my eyes off it. It was shiny, metallic—steel, I guess. It was a revolver and it had evidently exploded. That must have saved my life."

"Did you see the man's face?"

"No, uh, yes. Yes, I did glance at him, now that I think of it, when he shrieked. But I couldn't see it very clearly . . . couldn't see his features. There was this fog, and . . ." Merrit paused. "No, eh . . . there was something more—something that distorted his features."

"Like a mask? Or a woman's stocking?"

"A stocking; yes, that was it."

"Could you tell his height or weight? His age?"

"That's difficult. I was on the ground looking up. I think he was wearing all black. I know he had on a black overcoat. He seemed stocky, as I recall . . . but not muscular. More like flabby. And he was not tall. He didn't appear to be anywhere near six feet. I couldn't possibly tell about his age, except that he didn't move like an older person. He could have been young, but then he did move kind of awkwardly. . . ."

Patrick noticed that Merrit's hands had begun to tremble. Ashes were falling to the floor from his cigarette.

"That's enough for now, Father. We'll contact you again, soon. In the meantime, if you remember any more details, please give us a call." He handed his card to the priest, who looked relieved. Patrick then stood and exited into the corridor, where his partner, Sergeant Morris, approached.

"Did you check everybody?" Patrick asked.

"Yes. Did you get much of a description from Father Merrit?"

"No. He's still pretty shook up. Understandable. We may get more from him later. He does think the guy had a stocking over his face. That would jibe with the M.O. of the guy who attacked Father Ward."

"That's not all that jibes," said Morris as they headed out to continue their investigation in the neighborhood.

"Naturally, not all the witnesses saw the same thing. But consensus has it that the guy was approximately five-five, -six, or -seven. Shoes, trousers, overcoat, and hat were black. All the witnesses saw him from the rear, so we have no facial description. He limped to his car, so he probably injured his leg when he jumped from the porch.

"For being roused from a sound sleep and with all that fog, I think that's a pretty good description."

"Not bad at all," Patrick agreed. "But who wears black?"

"Undertakers."

"Gary Player."

"A member of rock group."

"Priests."

"Priests! It couldn't be another priest, could it?"

"If it is, he picked a dilly of a disguise."

"I have it," said Morris, as they were about to enter their car, "the Bad Guy."

The shades had been lowered, making the small room nearly dark.

"Now look at the fine mess you've gotten us into," said the First Man.

"It couldn't be helped," said the Second Man, as he extinguished his cigarette. In the dimness, he missed the ashtray, butting the cigarette on the table.

"Watch it!" stage-whispered the Third Man. "Do you want to set the place on fire!"

"Don't be so hard on him," said the Fourth Man. "He tried."

"Tried!" stage-whispered the Third. "Tried! So did Squeaky Fromme! With about the same results."

"Who is Squeaky Fromme?" asked the Fourth.

"She tried to assassinate Ronald Reagan," answered the Third, "but her gun wouldn't go off."

"Gerald Ford," said the First.

"Gerald Ford?" asked the Third.

"Ford was the one Squeaky Fromme tried to assassinate," the First clarified.

"Whatever," commented the Third.

"What I want to know," said the First Man, "is how you could possibly bungle your attack on Father Ward."

"That skull shook me up," the Second Man whined, "and then things sort of fell apart."

"Yorick?" the Third Man scoffed. "Yorick was the basis of our plan! Ward never leaves his room at night except once a year to deliver Yorick to the classroom. You had to know he'd have Yorick with him!"

"I know, I know," the Second Man pouted, "but this was the first time I've ever physically attacked anyone, let alone tried to kill somebody. I was under a lot of stress, you know. And all that tension . . . and in the excitement . . . and in the dark with the flashlight shining on that freaky skull . . . well, it just shook me up."

"It wasn't going to bite you," the First Man observed.

"Well," said the Fourth Man, "it would have startled anyone." In his attempt at a conciliatory gesture, he knocked the ashtray off the table.

"First him, now you," said the Third Man. "Are you guys studying to be arsonists? Why don't we try to *burn* somebody up? It's about all you guys are good at!"

"Oh, come off it," said the Second Man, huffily. "Anyone can have an accident.

"Besides, it wasn't just the skull. I couldn't stay on my feet. Neither could Ward, for that matter. The floor must have been waxed."

"There are times," observed the First Man, "when you couldn't keep your feet if they were nailed to the floor."

"And furthermore," said the Third, "what about this morning? We had that so carefully planned. Do you realize how much time we spent setting up Merrit?"

The Second nodded.

The Third continued regardless. "We spent weeks in surveillance. We figured out that his early morning trip to Saint Gregory's was our best bet. And what happens? You blow it!" He made his way cautiously to the wet bar against the wall. He poured a jigger of scotch. In the dark, he missed the glass, pouring the whiskey onto the counter. He wiped it up surreptitiously.

"What actually happened?" asked the Fourth Man.

"Defective powder," answered the Second.

"Defective powder!" exclaimed the First.

"Yes," said the Second. "I called the store where I bought the bullets. They said it happens every now and again. There's nothing they can do about it."

"Could we sue?" asked the Fourth.

"Oh sure; with everybody and his brother looking for a gun that exploded," rejoined the First. "That suggestion sure makes a lot of sense." His voice dripped sarcasm.

He leaned back in his chair—too far. He would have fallen flat on his back if the chair hadn't been so close to the wall. As it was, he barely kept his balance. He tried to cover his bungle, but the others noticed.

"So, here I am," the Second Man reproached, "through no fault of my own. Probably fractured or broke my wrist. The same probably for my ankle. They both hurt like hell." As if to reinforce his state-

ment, he took a tablet from a bottle labeled Empirin
Codeine and popped it into his mouth. "And how can
I get medical help without appearing suspicious?"

"What you're overlooking," noted the Fourth Man,
"is that at least we've gotten their attention. We may
have had a run of bad luck. But it hasn't been a total
waste. Two of our targets have at least been almost
scared to death. That's not insignificant."

"Well," asked the Third, "where do we go from
here?"

"That's what we're gathered to discuss. I suggest the
meeting come to order," said the Fourth. He picked up
an ancient-looking gavel and whacked it against the
table top. The handle split; the head flew into a corner.

"I've got to hand it to you, Nellie," said Joe Cox.
"When it comes to weeping statues, or the image of
Christ on a tortilla, your sense of news value is
unerring."

"A gift," Nelson Kane acknowledged.

The two were lunching at the Money Tree, a popular
albeit expensive downtown restaurant.

"I mean the way you latched onto that initial attack.
The *News* missed it entirely. But they can't overlook
it now that the story's got TV and radio coverage.
They're going to have to play catch-up.

"Did you have any idea there would be another assault at the seminary?"

"Of course," Kane lied.

"Seriously?"

"Seriously? Of course not. But I'm not surprised.
It's a high crime area and anything can happen.
They've had plenty of B and Es. But I'm pretty certain no one has been attacked inside the building or
on the campus till now."

"No, if I had given it any thought, from the M.O. of
the first attack, I would have guessed another attempt
on the first guy—Father Ward."

"Ward?"

"Yeah."

"I wouldn't think so."

Kane looked up from his soup in mild surprise. Staffers rarely disagreed with him. Not because he was reluctant to argue a point. Rather because the more experience the reporters gained, the more they learned that he usually was correct in his appreciation of news stories.

"Walking the corridors at night was not one of Ward's practices," Cox said. "In fact, he usually had tucked himself in by nine. I think the guy was lying in wait for the first one who looked like he had a wallet to come by. Intent: robbery. Victim: anybody."

Kane paused, soup-filled spoon suspended between bowl and mouth. His eyes twinkled.

"And what was it this morning?" he challenged. "Intent: robbery? Victim: the first one out that door?"

"Well, why not?"

"You're overlooking a couple of things. And you'd better damn well not overlook them when you develop this story.

"First, if someone wanted to badly enough, he could have plotted to attack Ward specifically. According to your own notes, Ward uses that crazy prop once every year when Hamlet mourns Yorick's loss. Ward always brings the skull to the classroom the night before that particular reading is scheduled. Ward's current class was about to reach that passage. Thus, Ward walks down corridor leading to classroom on what turns out to be a lucky break for the attacker: Halloween night with a big party going on and security at its worst."

Cox thought for a moment. "Then why was the guy apparently scared off?"

"Spooky place, spooky night, spooky business and, from all indications in both these encounters, a guy who is easily spooked."

"And today?"

"Even more cleverly planned. A guy is waiting in

darkness and fog at a perfect spot for an ambush at just the moment when Father Whatzisname—Merrit—leaves the building. And, need I remind you, you don't have to shoot a guy to rob him. You just walk up behind him and say something clever like, 'This is a stick-up.' "

"You may be right."

"I'm right. Someone wanted to kill first Ward, then Merrit. He failed. Will he be back? Will he go after the same priests? Will he try for someone else? And the biggie: Who is he and why is he doing this?"

"Those are just some of the questions we pay you so handsomely to find answers to."

"Not me, Nellie; it's the police who are paid to find the answers."

"And we're paying you to dig until you find the police who have those answers."

"O.K., O.K., right after this quiche," temporized Cox, as he ate more rapidly than he cared to. Lunch with Kane was seldom leisurely. "Oh, by the way, I forgot to mention: Father Merrit's string of luck was *all* bad."

"Why? What else happened?"

"Somebody stole the battery from his car."

Kane smiled and shook his head. "So he couldn't have gone anywhere anyway."

"Right. They got the batteries from four of the six cars parked in the same area as Merrit's."

"The other two?"

"Hoods locked."

"Told you it was a rough neighborhood."

Kane had finished his soup. Cox knew if he didn't finish his quiche in the next sixty seconds he would be left alone with the check.

"Blind luck, I say," said Bob Ankenazy, news editor at the *Detroit News*.

"I'd have to agree," agreed managing editor Leon London.

"It never seems to fail: Just when you think you've got that upstart *Free Press* by the balls, she gets lucky," Ankenazy elaborated, badly mixing the gender of his metaphor.

"Yup. Any other time and that first mugging would have been just an isolated incident. But the Freep lucks into a beat on the story and we lie back rather than come in late, and now look: a second attack on a priest."

"Only hindsight could prove you were wrong in that decision, Leon."

"But now they have a print exclusive with TV and radio coverage and we're forced to play catch-up."

"It's not the first time. As a matter of fact, with our staff and resources, we're rather good at it."

"That's true," London affirmed. "I'd hate to be at the *Free Press* if our present roles were reversed.

The two stood in the *News* city room near the coffee-maker, though only London held a cup.

"Well, we'd better get on it," said Ankenazy. "Any suggestions on who you'd like to send?"

"Pat Lennon, of course."

"Geez, I've already got her on the slush fund story. And nobody covers Mayor Cobb better than Lennon. You sure you want to go with our top staffer?"

"Yup. They've got Cox on it and he's their Numero Uno. We've got to respond in kind."

"I couldn't dissuade you by reminding you that Cox is Lennon's live-in?"

"Why would you think that might change my mind? They've been living together for—what, now?—six, seven years or so? This wouldn't be the first time they've been on the same beat."

"O.K." Ankenazy smiled and shook his head. "You want our top card, you've got her."

Ankenazy made his way toward Lennon. All he could see of her over the CRT was a gentle flow of auburn hair cascading over the phone receiver pressed against her ear. For at least the foreseeable future, she would have to divide her time between Maynard Cobb and the strange goings-on at Sacred Heart Seminary.

3.

WITH ONLY THREE DAYS UNTIL CHRISTMAS VACATION, both faculty and students at Sacred Heart Seminary succumbed to the holiday spirit. The only pall darkening the festive season was the awareness of the attacks on two of the faculty.

It had been weeks since the assault on Father Merrit. Since a few days after the initial splash, the news media had virtually forgotten the incident. For three consecutive days, the *News* and the *Free Press* had run banner page one stories on the assaults under the bylines of Patricia Lennon and Joe Cox respectively. TV stations had featured the story for only one evening. Nothing is as old as yesterday's news. Especially to the news media.

By no means had the police investigation been closed. Sergeants Morris and Patrick had been busy screening those who, for their own pathological reasons, insisted on confessing to the crime though they had had nothing to do with it. The police also followed numerous leads that took them up one blind alley after another. Lately, though, more and more of the two detectives' time was being spent on more current homicides.

At the seminary itself, though academic business

continued as usual, the recent violence was never very far from everyone's mind.

Father Edmund Sklarski's temper tantrums were a phenomenon to behold. An objective party would see them as adolescently humorous. But from the students' viewpoint, they could be terrifying.

On mornings they were scheduled to endure a Sklarski class, students would pray that the weather be bright and beautiful, for a bleak atmosphere often would engender a corresponding mood in their preceptor. And so they would laugh inordinately at Sklarski's opening statement, regardless of its significance. Laughter frequently got things off on the right foot. But not always. There was no way of knowing; one played the percentages.

"Well, boys," Sklarski announced as he swept into the room, "this is our last class before vacation."

Uproarious laughter.

Michael Totten raised his hand.

"Yes . . ." Sklarski rarely recalled the name of any of his students.

"Totten—Michael Totten," Totten helped.

"Yes, of course, Totten."

"Father, we are about to go into the world for an extended period," Totten exaggerated, "and we'd like a few instructive words from you. We sort of look upon you as our second spiritual director."

The seminary's spiritual director was Father Burk. As far as the students were concerned, if there had been nine spiritual directors, Sklarski would have been tenth on the list. But, anything to get matters off to a good start.

"Well, yes. Now that you ask, of course." Sklarski lacked the good grace to doubt the student's sincerity. "Yes, boys, out there it is a jungle. A cesspool filled with temptation. Scarlet women eager to snatch from you your sacred, pure, priestly vocation. Avoid them, boys, avoid them. Take it for granted you would like women if you tried them. As far as you aspiring clergymen are concerned, the motto is 'Look but don't touch.' "

Armed with this selfsame advice, many previous students of Sklarski's had become skilled lookers, almost to the point of becoming voyeurs.

"Yes, boys: women . . . sex . . ." Sklarski permitted the ideas to roll around his imagination briefly. "A comfort to you married men, and a relief of concupiscence. But not for you, boys. Not for you.

"And books, boys. Careful of the books. Drugstores, supermarkets, shopping centers, bookracks, lascivious stuff, boys; girlie magazines, paperbacks. Pictures, stories. Not for you, boys.

"Too many books anyway, boys. Too many books. I see you reading them all the time. Never outside playing football, baseball, hockey, basketball. Always inside reading books."

It was difficult to imagine Sklarski's corpulent though surprisingly agile body engaged in athletics.

"There's only one of you I ever see out there exercising. You there, behind—what's your name?"

"Francis Wangler, Father."

"Behind Francis Wangler. What's your name?"

"Zimmer, William Zimmer, Father."

"Yes. Zimmer. The only one among you who even looks like an athlete.

"No, no, boys. Too many books. Makes Jack a dull boy. Why all the books, boys? Why read all those books? Good God, there are only twenty-six letters in the alphabet!"

Unfortunately for him, Leonard Marks found that remark risible. And, unfortunately, he laughed aloud and alone. That, frequently, was a serious mistake. As it now was.

"Think that's funny, do you . . . uh . . . uh . . ." Sklarski groped for a name.

"Leonard Marks, Father," the round young man quaked.

"Ah, yes, Marks! It's not enough that you try to poison me, now you laugh at your second spiritual director! I suppose you enjoy those girlie magazines, those paperbacks!"

Once under attack there was no alternative but to absorb the bombardment in silence.

"I know your type, Marks, I know your type! You, Marks, are a rabble-rouser!"

An ambience had been destroyed. For the next forty minutes the day would go downhill.

Father Koesler's head turned toward the door at the abrupt albeit muffled sound. Apparently, it came from a classroom down the corridor. Someone was shouting.

"Are they still getting worked up at the Albigensian heresy?" Koesler asked quizzically.

"I think," volunteered one of his students, "that is the wrath of Father Sklarski."

All of them were painfully familiar with Sklarski's emotional eruptions.

"Someone must have denied papal infallibility," Koesler mused.

"Or Sklarski's infallibility," a student observed, sotto voce.

"Or maybe it snowed last night," another student suggested.

"Well, gentlemen," Koesler leaned back against the blackboard, thus getting his jacket chalk-dusty, "let's get back to the business of communication, which very definitely puts us in the present day.

"As I was saying, the parish bulletin can be an effective means of communication or it can become the weekly throwaway. Face it: if you are ordained, there's a parish bulletin in your future. All parishes have them. Like as not, you're going to be the editor. Nowhere in the rubrics does it say, 'Can Father write?' or, 'Is it safe to let Father be editor?' It just says, 'Father is editor.' You'd be wise to get ready for that moment.

"Let me tell you of an incident that took place years ago when I was editing my first parish bulletin.

"Our printer was a budding entrepreneur whose office was pretty much in his hat. He made lots of mistakes, but we tried to overlook most of them. I was accustomed to give him more than enough copy for each issue, including little Catholic jokes that could be used for fillers.

"One week he used one of those little Catholic jokes. On page two of the bulletin at the bottom of column one, he had, 'A catechist in China was teaching a group of prospective converts about hell. He told them hell was a place of unending suffering where there would be weeping and gnashing of teeth. One old man asked, "What about people who have no teeth?"'

"That was it: just that; no explanation, no punchline.

"I must confess, I was annoyed. Then, on page three of the same issue, on the bottom of column four, I came across, with no preface or introduction whatsoever, the single line, 'Teeth will be provided.'"

Laughter.

"The point to remember, gentlemen, is that when dealing with a publication such as the parish bulletin, Murphy's is the law of the land; if anything can go wrong, it will.

"You should expect misspellings, transpositions, and a goodly but ungodly number of typos. So, when the copy leaves your hand, it should be in tiptop shape for its journey into print. And remember: no one *has* to read what you write; even Father has to entice readers.

"Now, the papers you turned in last week were good, generally. But many of you—and I noted this on the copy—need to improve your leads. Remember, you've got to grab the reader. If you don't grab the reader with the first paragraph, you've lost him or her for the entire piece."

The bell sounded.

The students began shuffling papers and books. Most of them appreciated Koesler's class and benefited from it. He made the subject matter seem relevant. And he, unlike a majority of the faculty, treated them as adults.

The seminary's exercise wing comprised six enclosed courts. For decades they had been used exclusively for handball. Those were the years before racquetball became de rigueur. Those also were the years during which long lines of seminarians waited their turns at the courts. Now, nonseminarians were permitted to use them.

Two firm black rubber balls thudded against the front wall and bounced around the court with no particular rhythm. Four young men, swinging racquets, seemed to be giving the little balls inordinate concentration.

"Ouch!"

"What is it, Lennie?" asked a concerned Bill Zimmer. "Is it your wrist, or that ankle again?"

"Neither," answered Marks, rubbing the small of his back. "I got hit." One of the balls tapped a decreasing tattoo at his feet.

"Oh, that won't hurt you." Zimmer smiled.

"Tell that to my back," Marks grimaced.

Marks, one of the world's classic accident-prone people, was forever getting hurt.

For whatever unknown reason, Zimmer had adopted Marks' cause shortly after they had met as fledgling seminarian-classmates.

The two could hardly have been more dissimilar. Zimmer, tall, athletic, accomplished, bright, and a winner, provided an existential contrast to Marks, pudgy, clumsy, unimaginative, inept, and a loser. Somehow, they had become inseparable friends, although the contributions in their relationship usually moved from Zimmer toward Marks, rather like the relationship of Moriarty and De Niro in *Bang the Drum Slowly*.

"I don't know why I let you talk me into this," Marks complained.

"Lennie, you've got to get exercise," Zimmer admonished, scooping up the now dormant ball and whacking it toward the wall. "You can't spend your life in a chair or you'll grow up to enjoy a heart attack."

"I could be studying," Marks groused.

"We'll study together later, Lennie." Zimmer smiled. He knew that, left to his own resources, Marks would be reading *Time* or *Newsweek* at best.

"How about it?" called out Frank Wangler. "You guys ready?"

"Ready as we'll ever be." Zimmer answered for himself and his inevitable partner.

Zimmer and Marks won the volley for service. Or, rather, Zimmer did.

Marks served weakly, and Mike Totten came back with a kill shot that was somehow saved by Zimmer. The volley continued at a furious pace between Totten, Wangler, and Zimmer. Finally, Zimmer shot the ball to the spot where walls met floor. The ball skidded back with hardly a bounce. Unreturnable.

"I think I've got this figured out," said Marks, looking up at Zimmer. "I'll serve and then try to stay the hell out of the way."

Faculty meetings were not what they once were. But then, what is what it once was? The meetings were held in the faculty lounge, a commodious room dotted with couches and chairs, most of them overstuffed, and several tables. An upright piano stood in one corner, a color TV in another; a third corner held a kitchenette.

Faculty meetings had been held in this lounge as far back as anyone could remember. But in the last decade and more, there had been a fundamental change in their character.

Up through the 1960s, during these meetings the

lounge had qualified as a certified smoke-filled room. Almost every one of the all-clergy faculty smoked either pipe, cigars, or cigarettes; many alternated between two, a few smoked all three forms of the tobacco products. Through this decade, the atmosphere also had been filled with tension as the faculty argued heatedly over the merits or lack of promise of various students.

The upshot of these arguments was by no means inconsequential. Each student desperately desired to become a priest. Whether this desire would be fulfilled depended, to a great extent, on the faculty consensus. Whether one considered the priesthood a career or a sacred vocation, the fact that certain young men wanted to give their lives to it made it of vital importance. The faculty members of old, by and large, acknowledged this importance.

All this had changed during the seventies. Most seminarians, if pressed, would be reluctant to claim their commitment to be lifelong. What was these days? Not marriage, not most occupations. Midlife career change was a recent phenomenon.

Instead of an all-clerical faculty, now easily half the members were laity. And there was even a nun who coordinated efforts at social service. Lay members tended to be less forceful and outspoken than the clergy. The laity depended on their jobs as teachers in the seminary for their livelihood and that of their families. The clergy, whether they accepted or sought a different assignment, would still receive the same remuneration. Of the priests, only the rector, Monsignor Albert Martin, felt compelled to keep the seminary functioning as such. A la Churchill, Martin had not become rector to preside over the dissolution of Sacred Heart Seminary. As for the nun, she was relevant.

And, with one or two exceptions, none of today's faculty smoked.

Shortly after the close of Christmas vacation, the first semester would end, which explained the faculty meeting now in progress.

"And, in conclusion," Father Burk summarized, "I think Bill Zimmer is not only an exemplary student; I believe he will become a priest of whom we all will be proud."

"All right, Father," Monsignor Martin commented tersely, "but we're not here to award medals of commendation, just to check on the students' progress or lack of it."

Father Louis Grandville finished writing on a small piece of notepaper, folded it, wrote Sister Ann's name on the outside, and asked his neighbor to pass it on. The note would have to traverse the entire room to reach Sister.

Grandville was one of the joys of the seminary faculty. Truly a blithe spirit, he was frequently ingenuously vulgar, always dependable, an excellent teacher with a compassionate temperament.

"Next." Martin consulted his list. "Mr. Michael Totten." He waited. A hand was raised. "Father Ward?"

"Oh, certainly this student is no better than mediocre. His grades are all Cs and Ds. I believe he could do better. He is not giving maximum effort. If not dismissed, I think, at very least, he should be warned."

"Father Sklarski?"

"I didn't have my hand up."

"Father Burk?"

"I agree with Father Ward in that Mike is not giving us his best. But I differ with Father in that I think the challenge is ours to inspire this kid to put out. I think the failure is more ours than his."

"Father Merrit?"

"Eh . . . eh . . . *pia stercora!* That is a . . . eh . . . eh . . . bleeding heart statement. If Totten fails, he ruins *his* vocation, not ours. His obligation is to learn."

"And ours is to teach," Burk offered in challenge.

"Fathers, Fathers," Martin moderated, "let's not get personal. Since there is a difference of opinion, we'll let the matter remain in status quo."

It was Martin's latest artifice to keep from decimating the already endangered species of seminarian. Martin seldom called for a vote of the faculty. If one or two members spoke in favor of a student, the status quo was preserved.

"Next." Martin winced imperceptibly. He feared they would lose this next student. "Mr. Leonard Marks."

Hands shot up.

"Father Merrit?"

"This *student,* if I may . . . eh . . . eh . . . debase the term by applying it to him, should not be allowed to use good air that the rest of us need. He is . . . eh . . . a complete fool!"

"Father Sklarski?"

"He is a rabble-rouser!"

"Father Ward?"

"He really is a disgrace. His marks are Ds and Fs. And, unlike Mr. Totten, Mr. Marks is doing his utmost. And none of it is right. Why, if this were only a few years ago, we would not even be considering him for the priesthood. That he was even allowed to *enter* this institution was a gross error; that he *remains* in this institution would be laughable if it were not so tragic."

"Father Koesler?"

"I will not argue that Lennie is very witty, quick, or even coordinated. Nor will I argue that he would have lasted long in yesterday's seminary. But I do question those very standards. After all, Jesus called twelve very ordinary men to be His Apostles. Somehow, I don't think Lennie would have been out of place in that group. And, if Jesus could choose Lennie, who are we to dismiss him?"

"Father Grandville?"

"I agree with Bob. Maybe there is an apostolate to the klutzes that we're overlooking."

"We won't overlook it any longer if we ordain that

. . . eh . . . eh . . . jerk!" Merrit commented acidu-
ously.

"Well, Fathers," Martin droned gratefully, "since
there is a difference of opinion, we'll let this matter
remain in status quo."

Father Grandville's note reached Sister Ann.
Slowly, she unfolded it. It was not signed. It didn't
have to be. She recognized both the handwriting and
the irreverence. It read, *Dear Sister Ann, I got the
hots for you.*

She shook her head, then rested it face down on the
tabletop.

The only pleasant feature connected with a faculty
meeting, in Father Koesler's view, was the soiree that
followed.

No sooner had Monsignor Martin closed the meeting with a prayer, than bottles of whiskey, scotch, ver-
mouth, gin, and vodka were brought from the liquor
cabinet to the wet bar. The brands were not the most
expensive, yet certainly not the cheapest. Routinely,
faculty members ambled to the bar and built drinks
for themselves.

Tonight's bash was special, a late celebration of the
feast of Saint Albert the Great, the patron saint of
Monsignor Albert Martin. In the Latin so favored by
the Monsignor, the saint was Albertus Magnus, or
Great Albert. Thus, the Monsignor was addressed,
especially by his cronies, as Big Al.

As part of the feast, huge bowls of jumbo shrimp
were placed on the table in the center of the lounge.
In honor of which event, Koesler whistled a few bars
of "Shrimp Boats Are a Comin'." The younger faculty
members had never heard of the song.

Koesler dropped a cherry into his thus completed
manhattan. He meandered, catching snatches of conversations.

"Of course he's just a puppy"—Sister Ann was de-
scribing her new dog to Father Merrit—"but I thought

nature took care of that sort of thing. I mean, for the first month or so, every time the dog wet, he squatted, instead of lifting his leg. Last week I gave him one more chance: If he didn't lift his leg, the next time I took him out I was going to tie a string around his rear leg and teach him. Fortunately, he came through."

"It is never easy growing up," observed Merrit, "no matter whether you're a ... eh ... eh ... child or a puppy."

Koesler moved on.

"So, I pick up the phone," Father Sklarski was telling a couple of the lay faculty, "and this voice says, 'Is this Father Sklarsk*a*?' Get it? 'sk*a*' not 'sk*i*.' So I say, 'Yes, this is *he*. This is *he*. That's good English. I don't suppose you'd understand that!' And the voice says, 'Well, this is the Archbishop.' The Archbishop! Boys, boys, the moral of that story: Always find out who's on the phone before committing yourself."

Laughter.

Koesler moved to the shrimp-laden table. There was still plenty of shrimp but the sauce was low. At that moment, Bill Zimmer appeared with more sauce.

Wouldn't you know it, thought Koesler; the All-American Boy shows up with the hot sauce just in the nick of time.

As Zimmer turned to leave, he almost bumped into Koesler.

"Oops, sorry, Father."

"No damage."

"Oh, I've been meaning to ask you, Father: How's the investigation going?"

"Investigation?"

"Yes, into the muggings. You know—Fathers Ward and Merrit?"

"Oh." Koesler smiled. "I haven't the slightest idea. I'm not involved in that in any way."

"Oh, I thought . . . I mean, you've participated in

criminal investigations in the past. I thought with one going on right here in the seminary—"

"No, no," Koesler chuckled. "Father Brown I am not. Just your simple suburban parish priest. Those other things—just flukes."

As Zimmer moved away, he seemed disappointed.

If we ever do get another Father Brown, thought Koesler, it probably will be Father Zimmer, the All-American Priest. Whether it's time for the hot sauce or the solution to the crime, there will be Father Zimmer, Billy-on-the-spot.

Koesler paused at the table long enough to devour several jumbo shrimp. Then he moved on.

"The libido isn't everything," Father Burk was virtually instructing Father Grandville. "There are other motivating forces in life. Remember when Freud found himself in a group of psychoanalysts? Freud was preparing to smoke a cigar when he sensed his colleagues focusing inordinate attention on the object. And so, even Freud was forced to say, 'Gentlemen, it may be only a cigar.' "

"So what?" asked a distracted Grandville.

"So take that fork you're holding." Burk pointed at Grandville's shrimp fork. "Is that or is it not; is it existentially or is it ontologically a phallic symbol?"

"Oh, fork you!" Grandville laughed. So did Burk.

Koesler moved on.

"The apartment complex is in our parish, very near the church, as a matter of fact," Father Dave Smith, youngest of the priest faculty, was telling Father Ward. "As I was passing it the other day, I got to wondering, what would happen if they had a major fire there?"

Ward, barely opening his mouth, nibbled on the shrimp.

"I mean, what if they had a fire and I was called to it? Would my priesthood make it obligatory for me to enter that burning building and risk my life to give those people the sacraments?"

Ward sipped his martini. He was not looking at

Smith. Koesler wondered if the old man were even listening.

"Now, I don't want you to think I didn't try to solve this problem myself. I searched in Noldin and in Tanquerey, but I couldn't find the answer anywhere. So, I thought I'd bring the problem to you. I mean, with all your years of experience and your expertise in theology, I just knew you'd have the answer."

Ward, utterly expressionless, continued to sip his martini.

"So then, Father, how about it? This could become a very real problem. If there were a fire in that apartment complex, would I be bound by my priesthood to go in there to administer the sacraments at the risk of my life?"

"Of course not. Don't be a damn fool." Ward still did not look at Smith.

The overhead lights blinked twice. Time for dinner.

Koesler finished his manhattan and joined the group as all were exiting the lounge to dine. But something unexpected was happening.

Instead of continuing down the second-floor corridor toward the faculty dining room, the group was descending the stairs to the basement. Koesler was embarrassed to confess that he, apparently, was the only one who did not know what was going on. So he wordlessly followed the crowd.

They filed into the student refectory.

The student dining area! Koesler was stricken. He had nothing against young people. He just did not want to socialize with them. And he assumed that if they were normal kids they would not want to socialize with him, an adult. He felt trapped.

He looked across the table. Standing opposite was Father Grandville. They were surrounded by students. Grandville seemed as unhappy with this situation as was Koesler.

Silently but elaborately, Koesler's lips formed the word, *Carl's?* Grandville nodded. Immediately following premeal prayer, Koesler and Grandville departed for Carl's Chop House, where they enjoyed prime ribs and adult conversation.

"I don't know why I let you talk me into this," said Pat Lennon.

"I need you as an interpreter," Joe Cox replied. "Why, I didn't even know there was a uniform of the day."

"Joe, you don't go to a superconservative Catholic meeting dressed for a discotheque."

"How was I to know? Kane gave me this assignment just as we were closing shop. I never even heard of the Tridentine Society before. So I've got to depend on a good Catholic girl like yourself—what does that stand for, anyway, 'Tridentine Society'?"

"Comes from the Latin for Trent, the Council of Trent, convened in the middle of the sixteenth century. Very conservative Catholics figure nothing important has happened, or should have happened, since then.

"But, I've got to warn you about tonight. These Tridentines are not your run-of-the-mill conservative Catholics. Catholics United for the Faith is a legitimate organization for legitimate conservative opinion. These people tonight are wackos. So we are dressed rather conservatively. And remember: no notes. If they were to tumble to the fact that we're reporters, we could be in a lot of trouble."

"Really? Not physically?"

" 'fraid so."

"Why would anybody get physical about religion?"

"These people take it seriously. You'll see."

"O.K. We'll blend in. No one will notice us."

As Cox continued to drive toward the Knights of Columbus Hall where the meeting was to be held, he reflected that while no one might notice him, it would be a miracle if Pat Lennon went unnoticed. From the tip of her toes to the top of her titian hair. she was one of the most beautiful women he had ever met. And Cox kept rather careful note of such statistics. He glanced down and caught sight of one of her well-turned ankles. She couldn't hide her curves in a muu-muu. On top of it all, she was one of the most intelligent people he knew. And one hell of a reporter. But then, in all candor, so was he.

They had met while both were staff writers for the *Free Press*. The chemistry was nearly perfect; for all these years they had lived together. Both had been previously married. Neither had children. At one time they had investigated the possibility of marriage in the Catholic Church. But that had come to naught. Now they were content to live together and let live.

Several years ago, because of sexual harassment, Lennon had left the *Free Press* for the *News*. The problem had been caused by an executive manager who made trouble for nearly the entire staff. When he provoked a popular columnist into defecting to the *News,* his fate was ultimately sealed. Now he was gone.

Overtures for her reinstatement came from the *Free Press,* but Lennon now owed loyalty to the *News*. She and Cox shared everything but their place of employment.

The Knights of Columbus Hall had seen better days. Like the rest of the neighborhood, the building appeared to be in its final glide path. There were many parking spaces in the ample adjacent lot. Once upon a time, Cox surmised, this must have been a going concern.

As Cox stood by, Lennon was handed an armful of fliers.

There couldn't have been more than a hundred people in attendance in a hall that could hold easily eight times that number.

"The weirdo business is falling off," Cox observed.

"Shhhh!" Lennon whispered.

"Why are they all looking at us?" asked Cox as they took seats in the rear of the assembly.

"They haven't seen us before. We don't belong to the Old Faithful. They don't trust us."

"They make me feel creepy." Cox shivered slightly. "But you were right about the uniform. Almost everyone here is wearing some black."

"They're in mourning for the thirteenth century."

With no preamble, a tall, slender man stepped onto the dais, took his place behind the lectern, and banged a gavel, though there was little sound to silence. Definitely blue-collar, Cox decided. Probably works on the line at Ford or at some small tool shop.

The man did not identify himself. "Ordinarily, we begin with the recitation of the Rosary. But our first speaker must leave early tonight, so we will have the Rosary at the end of our meeting."

Evidently he was the head of the Tridentines. Or at least acting as chairman of this gathering.

"Although we have never had the honor of having our first speaker with us before, all of us,"—he looked with distrust at Cox and Lennon, who tried to look ultraconservative—"are familiar with him.

"He is,"—an almost imperceptible pause—"the Mayor of Tumerango."

"Where the hell is Tumerango?" whispered Cox.

Lennon consulted one of the fliers she had been handed at the door. "Colombia."

"British Columbia?"

"Colombia, South America."

"His Honor, Carlos Silvanos," the chairman went on, "has wonderful news. I know we are all eager to hear him. So here he is: the Mayor of Tumerango."

The applause was more than polite. For this group, one might even say it was enthusiastic.

A swarthy, heavyset man in a blue pinstripe stepped to the podium.

"My friends, I have wonderful news." The Mayor echoed the chairman's words. "They have seen her again."

More applause, even more enthusiastic.

"Who saw whom?" Cox as a lapsed Presbyterian, feared he was missing something.

"Wait," Lennon cautioned, "but I'll bet it's the Blessed Mother."

"The Blessed Mother," the Mayor confirmed, "has appeared to the three children again."

"Why does it always have to be three kids?" Lennon murmured.

"Evita, Elena, and José last saw Our Blessed Lady on November 29," the Mayor continued. "She showed them a vision of purgatory. They report it is rotten there. Lots of fire. The place is crawling with priests and nuns who were unfaithful to their vows. She told the children to tell the world to pray for priests and nuns. And she told them to have a beautiful cathedral built on that spot."

"How can we carry out Our Blessed Lady's wish when so few know about Tumerango?" asked a voice from the audience.

"That's the best part," the Mayor explained. "Our Blessed Lady has promised a miracle!"

"A miracle!" the audience echoed as one.

"Yes. Bigger than Lourdes or Fatima!"

"Bigger than Lourdes or Fatima!"

"Yes. And that's not all." He paused, portentously. His listeners hung on every breath. "There will be eight days' warning before the miracle."

"Eight days," Cox whispered. "Why, it'll be listed in *TV Guide*. 'Thursday night, live and in color: The Miracle of Tumerango.'"

"Yes," Lennon choked, "I can see it now: The producer yells at the director. 'Adjust the blue, Murray: the lady's cape has got to be blue!'"

"Nellie will love this!" Cox exulted.

"While we await the miracle," said the Mayor, "I've brought you something. I have branches from the willow over which Our Lady appears. You can see them in the rear of the auditorium."

All turned to look at the rear of the hall, where it seemed as if an entire willow had been sundered and heaped up.

"Plant them," said Cox in an undertone, "and enjoy visions in the comfort of your own backyard."

"Any donation you make," said the Mayor, "will go toward the future cathedral. And I urge you to come to us in Tumerango and talk with the children. Maybe you will be lucky enough to be there during a vision."

With that, the Mayor excused himself, saying he had several other gatherings to attend.

"I think," murmured Cox, "the Mayor doubles as Director of Tourism."

"Shhhh," shushed Lennon, "people are starting to look at us again."

The chairman returned to the podium. "After hearing what Mayor Silvanos just told us, it almost seems our next speaker must have been sent by Almighty God.

"It doesn't take much brains to figure out that these young priests and nuns are in a peck of trouble. Priests don't wear the collar, don't wear black, got hair growing all over them except where it should. They don't stay in their rectories like they used to. They're out on the streets in marches, counseling draft-dodgers, or chasing women.

"And look at the nuns! Miniskirts and low-cut blouses. They look more like women of easy virtue than the good old nuns we knew!"

All almost palpable air of total agreement rose from the assembly.

"Now we have the words of Our Blessed Lady herself that these priests and nuns are going to purgatory in a handbasket. Personally," he looked around meaningfully, "I thought they were going to hell. But who am I to contradict the Blessed Mother?

"Anyway, our second and last speaker of the evening is going to talk about this very thing. About how in the seminaries today everything is going to pot. Let's hear now from Brother Alphonsus."

A tall, slender man, perhaps in his forties, stood and approached the stage.

Applause. Not as enthusiastic as for His Honor, the Mayor, but sincere.

"Do you suppose he's a real brother?" Cox leaned toward Lennon. "I mean in a religious order?"

"Don't know. Maybe. It's probably not even his real name. These people are pretty paranoid."

"They don't need to be paranoid. People could really dislike them."

Brother Alphonsus reached the stage, tripped on the bottom step and fell forward, preventing prostration only by catching himself with his outstretched arms. He tried to make the movement seem to be some sort of religious ritual but did not carry it off.

The embarrassed silence was almost broken by a Cox guffaw that was stifled in the nick of time by a Lennon elbow.

Alphonsus made it to the podium without further mishap. He placed his notes on the lectern and tapped the microphone. There was no resonance.

Cox could not imagine why Alphonsus might suspect that in the short time it had taken him to reach the microphone it would go dead. But the Brother's suspicions were confirmed.

The chairman, together with a member of the audience who looked as if he might be an electrician in workaday life, fiddled with the mike. Their efforts were fruitless. Finally, the chairman gave Alphonsus a pat on the back and the encouraging word to speak loudly.

"Sex," Brother Alphonsus stated.

He had their attention.

"Sex is what they're teaching in the seminaries today," Alphonsus annunciated.

Members of the audience glanced at each other and nodded.

If it was possible to look shocked and gratified simultaneously, Cox thought, that would accurately describe the visage of most of Alphonsus' listeners.

"Not the way they taught it when I was in the seminary," Alphonsus went on. "In my day, sex was in a textbook and the textbook was in Latin!"

The way he said it, Latin sounded like a panacea, thought Cox.

"Let me tell you," said Alphonsus, "sex in Latin can be pretty dull."

Perhaps it *was* a panacea, thought Cox.

"It isn't dull anymore, let me tell you!"

Thank God, thought Cox.

"Nowadays, at both Sacred Heart and St. Joseph's seminaries, they show pictures. Motion pictures and still pictures. There is this pseudoscientific group that comes right into the seminaries—at the invitation of the faculties, mind you—and displays these pictures. And do you know what these pictures show?"

The audience was on the edge of its collective seat.

"Fornication!"

The audience experienced a sharp intake of breath.

"Masturbation!"

Another sharp inhalation.

"GROUP SEX!"

The audience exhaled so explosively it sounded like one great hiss.

"I have many of these pictures with me tonight. I am not at liberty to tell you how I obtained them. But any of you who wish to view them can see me after the meeting."

He would have many customers.

"That is not all. After they look at these pictures, they form small groups and talk dirty."

In the first row, Lennie Marks, dressed in black, was *kvelling*. Brother Alphonsus was Lennie's idol. Here was a man who was afflicted with many of the coordination problems that Marks himself experienced. Yet Alphonsus was a success: here he was, addressing a group who were not only listening to what he had to say; they were motivated by his words.

"I must tell you this also," said Alphonsus. "These sessions are open to the public. And," he paused for emphasis, "there are women present at these meetings. And some of them are nuns!"

Just then, the janitor opened a door at one side of the stage, creating a draft. Alphonsus' notes and pictures blew off the lectern. Several members of the audience, including Marks, scrambled to help retrieve them.

"I ask you"—Alphonsus had recovered himself and his documents—"what can we do about this? What are *you* going to do about it? We cannot depend on the hierarchy for help. The bishops know what's going on, but they do nothing. What are *we* going to do? This is mortal sin we're talking about! The seminaries are leading their students into mortal sin! What are we going to do?"

"We've got to do something!" yelled one woman.

"Withhold our contributions!" shouted another.

"We could nuke them!" shouted a burly man.

"Hey," Cox had to speak in a normal voice for Pat to hear him amidst all the noise, "this is losing its humor. This is pretty inflammatory. I see what you meant by their getting physical."

"We've got to do something!" Alphonsus made a sweeping gesture—and knocked over the lectern. He righted it, collected his pictures and notes and, amid the confusion, resumed his seat.

The chairman returned to the podium and called for order. The microphone was operating.

"Friends," said the chairman, as order was restored, "I guess we can all be very grateful for Brother Alphonsus' vigilance. We will go into this further at our next meeting. Now we will close by saying the Rosary together. And remember, any of you who want to view the evidence that Brother Alphonsus brought tonight, see him after the Rosary. I know I surely want to see it. In the name of the Father and the Son and the Holy Ghost . . ."

Beads rattled.

"Let's get out of here," Cox urged.

"Are you kidding? Leave during the Rosary? These people have smelled blood! Holy Mary, Mother of God, pray for us sinners now and at the hour of our Death. Amen."

"Oh, God!" Cox lowered his head in misery.

It was an odd sound. Many would have to confess they had never heard it before. Some claimed no one had ever heard it before. A few maintained it was unique.

Nelson Kane was laughing out loud.

What had begun as a couple of snorts and escalated to a low chuckle was now a wheezy, staccato laugh.

Kane sat before the VDT reading Joe Cox's account of the meeting of the Tridentine Society.

Damn, thought Kane, say what you will about Cox, the sonuvabitch can really write. Whether it was an investigative report, a straight news story, or piece of fluff like this one on the Tridentines, Cox could crank it out with the best of them.

The chemistry between Kane and Cox was such that their relationship was settled and cemented. Kane played the stern, gruff demanding father to Cox's prodigal son. Both found the relationship productive.

Both had won Pulitzer Prizes, Kane for his coverage of Detroit's 1967 riots; Cox, a decade later, for his investigative account of a series of crimes known as the Rosary Murders.

No one enjoyed the spectacle of a laughing Kane more than Cox. He decided to approach Kane's desk. Who knows; this might develop into a propitious time to ask for a merit increase.

"Like it?" he asked, needlessly.

"Better than a goddamn weeping statue." Kane rubbed tears from his eyes. "The nice thing about you,

Cox, is that you know when to quit. Most writers would be jabbing the reader in the ribs pointing out what was bizarre about this bunch. But you know a fruitcake when you see one. Just tell it the way it happened when the crazies are doing their thing. Funny! Funny!"

"It's strange, though, Nellie; I got the distinct impression these people could be dangerous."

"You bet your sweet ass they can be dangerous. They're a giant step from the type who would send a nasty letter to an editor. They'd send a bomb."

"I was thinking I'd stay on this group. They probably won't get any funnier than they were last night, but something might develop anyway. You know, they could get physical."

"Wait a minute," cautioned Kane, "haven't you blown your cover? You and Lennon were the only outsiders at last night's meeting, weren't you? And now your story appears in the *Free Press*. I mean, even the Tridentines can add two and two."

"Yeah, but Nellie, remember that diet doctor's murder trial? The *Time*s quoted the daughter of the jury foreman as saying that her father never read a newspaper. You know, one of those people that even Cronkite used to complain get all their news from TV? This bunch strikes me as being in the same category: If any of them do read, it's just conservative parochial publications. They're so busy figuring out what's going wrong in the Church that they don't even bother to find out what's going on in the world.

"Besides," he grinned, "if I'm wrong, you'll have an even better page one head: REPORTER PUMMELED IN PURSUIT OF TRUTH."

"Yeah, well, be careful." Kane wedged an unlit cigar between his teeth. "But you're right; sticking with them might be a good idea. How often do they meet?"

"Irregularly, I'd guess. Last night's meeting was

advertised in the *Detroit Catholic*. They always advertise their meetings in the *Catholic*.

"I didn't know you get the *Detroit Catholic*."

"Pat does."

"Oh." Kane did not enjoy thinking of Pat Lennon. Contemplating what the *Free Press* might be able to accomplish with Cox and Lennon as its one-two punch was too painful, since it would never happen.

Cox, about to leave, hesitated.

"No," said Kane.

"No?"

"No, this would not be a good time to ask for a merit increase."

Father Koesler always pitied everyone who was not a parish priest on Christmas Eve.

The emotion recurred as he vested for Midnight Mass. Oh, sure, Christmas was for children and there were no kids in the rectory. But much of that element of the season was commercial. And that had been going on since well before Thanksgiving Day. Families would be together. And, generally everyone was in his or her best mood of the entire year.

But Christmas was especially wonderful for the parish priest.

There would be record crowds at all the Masses. At Christmas and Easter, the regulars were always augmented by the twice-a-year seasonal Catholics. Some priests found this discouraging; they vented their ire at such times by delivering caustic homilies.

But Koesler was always gladdened when people came to church, for whatever reason. He thought that having a packed congregation for all the Masses must match the feeling parents have when all their children and grandchildren are home for the holidays. Or the contented feeling experienced by that proverbial Biblical shepherd when all his sheep are present and accounted for.

Whenever he managed to deliver a particularly

inspiring homily, he always experienced an outstanding ebullience. But Christmas, perhaps because of the crowds, always brought a special high.

Everything seemed right and ready. A little more than a dusting of fresh snow covered the ground. The choir was beautifully rendering familiar Christmas hymns. The church was filled to standing-room-only. Everyone Koesler knew was at least relatively healthy and happy. The trouble at the seminary seemed to be over.

God was no longer in His heaven. He had come down to this beautful planet. And all was well with the earth.

4.

THE MAN SAT WAITING HIS TURN IN THE EMERGENCY room of Detroit's Henry Ford Hospital. Others who were waiting, most of them black, drifted in and out between this and an adjoining waiting room. Or they sat impassively, shifting periodically, in long rows of straightback chairs.

This was the post-Christmas rush expected by hospitals. Treatment for physical complaints that were more elective than emergency in nature was postponed from the pre-Christmas season until after the holidays. Now, in the beginning of the New Year, the hospitals were doing land-office business.

The man did not seem to fit in with the others. Since he was dressed entirely in black—shoes, trousers, overcoat, and hat—one might have expected a roman collar to complete his garb. But his coat, opened at the throat, revealed a conventional white shirt and a dark blue tie. He appeared agitated. He fiddled with the buttons of his coat, the crease in his trousers, the arm of his chair.

Finally, the man's name was called. He followed the nurse into a narrow cubicle. She gave the form he had filled out to the doctor, who was elderly, bearded, and unkempt. He seemed rather stern as he cursorily scanned the form. The nurse left the cubicle.

"Well," said the doctor, "what's wrong? What can we do for you?"

"Doctor, I'll come right to the point. I'm an alcoholic and I've been on Antabuse. And now I've run out of it and I'm afraid I'm going to take another drink. I need a prescription for more of the drug."

"Hmmm," the doctor pondered, "how long have you been on it?"

"Two months."

"And you haven't had a drink in that time?"

"No."

"What makes you think you need to continue with Antabuse?"

"I almost had one last night. And I'm sure I'll start drinking before the day is out if I don't get back on it."

"I see."

The doctor began writing on his prescription pad. "Now I must warn you, this is not a plaything or a panacea. It's a dangerous drug. Antabuse is just a contrived name. Its generic name is disulferam, and frankly, it could kill you. Now you know that under no circumstances are you to ingest any alcohol while you're taking this drug. Not even a cough medicine that contains alcohol."

The man nodded.

"You can have this filled at the pharmacy down the hall." The doctor ripped the page he had been writing on from the pad. "Is this going to be Blue Cross?"

"No; I'll pay cash."

"Very well." He handed the man the prescription. "The nurse will take care of it. Mind you, now: not a drop of alcohol. Or the next time I see you, I'll be closing your eyes."

The man nodded and departed.

Father Sklarski did not like it. He had not liked it when the faculty had voted for it back in September. He had neither the desire nor the ambition to direct another student play. Further, there were only a few more than thirty students in the entire college. Where could one find talent with so few from which to choose? And, additionally, the play must feature an all-male cast!

As far as Sklarski knew, there were precious few of that type. There was *Brother Orchid* and *Career Angel* and *Twelve Angry Men*. But those called for relatively large casts. And he just did not have the numbers.

Then he remembered Sir Arthur Sullivan's *Cox and Box*. A short musical comedy for three male characters. The musical aspect might cause some problems. But the numbers were right. And there were no royalties to pay.

Since returning from Christmas vacation, Sklarski had been busy directing; three students were busy learning their roles, and others were busy with the lighting, the staging, the props, and other technical aspects of the production. Leonard Marks was in charge of the props. The props were in trouble.

It was late in the evening when they began rehearsal on page 34. Just about everything that could go wrong had. They were now on page 43 and Sklarski was still waiting for some indication that this was not going to be one of the more serious blunders of his long clerical career.

Cox: Penelope Ann?

Box: Penelope Ann!

Cox: Originally widow of William Wiggins?

Box: Widow of William Wiggins!

Cox: Proprietor of bathing machines?

Box: Proprietor of bathing machines!

Cox: At Margate?

Box: At Ramsgate!

Cox: It must be she! And you sir—you are Box—the lamented, long lost Box!

Box: I am!

The stage was bathed in red light.

"Red lights!" Sklarski bellowed from the dark depths of the empty auditorium. "Why red lights? Please God, why red lights? Marks!" During the course of these rehearsals, he had used Marks' name in vain so often that this was one student whose name Sklarski now remembered. "Marks! Why red lights?"

"My hand slipped." A meek voice curled around the side of the stage.

"Your hand slips one more time," Sklarski threatened, "and I shall cut it off. Better you should go through life mutilated than that I should lose my mind. Continue!"

Cox: And I was about to marry the interesting creature you so cruelly deceived.

Box: Ah! Then you are Cox!

Cox: I am!

Box: I heard of it, I congratulate you—I give you joy! And now, I think I'll go and take a stroll.

Box rattled the door in the set. And rattled and rattled it. The door would not open. The two players on stage began to choke back laughter.

"Now the door won't open!" Sklarski shouted. "And you two ninnies think it's funny!

"Marks! Marks! Why won't the door open? Make the door open, Marks!"

After a few seconds, the door began rattling from the other side. Marks was apparently trying to open it from the back of the set. Soon the entire rear section of the set was shaking. A final wrench not only opened the door, but brought Marks tumbling through it to fall flat on his face at approximately center stage.

Cox and Box turned to face the rear. Their shoulders were quivering.

"Marks!" Sklarski bellowed. "Get off stage! Get off stage! If that door ever sticks again, I will personally see to it that you become a gelding! Continue!"

Cox: No you don't. I'll not lose sight of you till I've restored you to the arms of your intended.

Box: My intended? You mean your intended!

Cox: No sir, yours!

Box: How can she be my intended, now that I am drowned?

The door that Marks had shut behind him as he left the stage opened of its own accord, slowly and squeakily. Cox and Box broke up, utterly.

"All right!" Sklarski shouted, "that does it! Turn the house lights up!"

The auditorium went black.

"Marks!" Sklarski bellowed, "I said turn the house light *up,* not out!"

The house lights lit.

"Everybody out here in the aisle!"

All lined up in the center aisle in front of Sklarski.

"All right, as a penance we will say the Rosary! Marks, you lead us."

Marks led the introductory prayers and then announced: "The Joyful Mysteries."

Under these circumstances. the Sorrowful Mysteries might have been appropriate. Certainly not the Joyful Mysteries. There was something about the Joyful Mysteries, especially as introduced by Marks, that gave this evening its final magic touch. Everyone except Sklarski and, of course, Marks, was convulsed.

"All right," Sklarski said in his sharpest menacing tone, "to bed! Everyone to bed! I will give you fifteen minutes to be in bed! And I am going to check!"

Cast and crew scurried from the auditorium. Now was not the time for bluff-calling.

Fifteen minutes later, a still fuming Sklarski was storming through the residence halls in search of a telltale light peeking over a transom.

He found one. He threw open the door to Francis Wangler's room. Wangler was clad only in pajama tops. The crotch of his bottoms was ripped and he was sewing the tear. Wangler, not even in the play, knew of no reason why Father Sklarski should be glowering in his doorway.

"I said to bed!" Sklarski roared.

"But . . . I . . ." Wangler pointed at the open crotch with needle and thread sticking out of it.

"I said GET TO BED!"

Such was the priest's power of persuasion that Wangler pulled on his bottoms, needle and all, and burrowed under the covers.

"I was only a young seminarian when it happened." Father Burk smiled at the memory.

He was seated with Monsignor Martin and Fathers Koesler and Smith for a Friday dinner at Sacred Heart Seminary. The conversation had mellowed into nostalgia. This pretty much left Smith out of the conversational flow. He was too young to have much to remember. So he contented himself with listening and learning about the good old days.

The subject now was old Father John Fitzpatrick, who had taught at the seminary in its earliest days and through the twenties and thirties. A legend any way one wished to look at him, Fitz had had a memorable career. Now that Father Smith was hearing the Fitz stories, they would be passed on to another generation.

"We were on a streetcar headed for downtown," Burk was saying. "Fitz, of course, was wearing his clericals and I was dressed in a black suit. So we were rather conspicuous among all these ordinary citizens— and the streetcar was packed. There was a distinct air of hostility toward us on the part of many of our fellow passengers."

"Probably damn Protestants," Martin interjected.

"Undoubtedly." Burk wanted to go on with his story. "If I had been able to dig a hole and crawl in, I would have. But that's asking a lot of a streetcar. Anyway, about the time I was beginning to feel a bit more composed—or perhaps I was just numb— doesn't Fitz throw back his big head and start singing, 'Tantum ergo, sacramentum' at the top of his lungs. Well, I liked to died. I wiggled away from him as far as I could and still stay on the same bench. He looked at me with the contempt only *he* could muster, and said, 'What's the matter, you ashamed of your religion?' "

Laughter.

"Bob," Martin addressed Koesler, "you must remember how old Fitz hated the *Detroit Catholic*."

Koesler nodded. Ordinarily, during the week he would not have been at the seminary at dinner hour. But Fridays he taught a late afternoon class and regularly stayed rather than fight rush-hour traffic to the western suburbs.

"Yes," Martin continued, "Fitz used to call the *Detroit Catholic* 'that impediment to thought.' "

"In fairness," said Koesler, "that was before *I* edited it."

"That," said Martin, "was before you were *born.*"

"In any case, Fitz died. It was the custom in those days to bury a priest with his chalice."

"With a chalice?" Smith marveled. "There must be a literal gold mine in priests' burial plots."

"Undoubtedly." Martin did not suffer interruptions lightly. "Anyway, when it came time to display him, the mortician couldn't get Fitz's hand to stay holding the chalice. His belly was too big. So, underneath the coffin lining they had to stuff something to prop up his arms so he could hold the chalice."

"Don't tell me," said Smith: "Copies of the *Detroit Catholic*?"

Martin nodded. "And so, Fitz and that 'impediment to thought' went off together into eternity."

Laughter.

"Speaking of dead priests," said Koesler, "have any of you heard the story of what happened after old Monsignor Vismara died years ago?"

The three looked at him expectantly.

"Well," said Koesler, "some time after Vismara's death, an elderly man stopped in at St. Elizabeth's rectory and asked for Vis. The priest said, 'Oh, I'm

sorry, but Monsignor Vismara died five years ago.'
And the old gentleman replied, 'Oh, thatsa too bad
. . . he wasa my regular confessor.' "

Laughter.

They had finished their food, drunk their coffee and
told their stories. They rose, said a brief prayer and
strolled down the corridor to the front of the building.
They reached the row of mailboxes and, routinely,
each checked his box to see if there were any mail or
messages.

Koesler, with a puzzled expression, extracted a bottle of gin from his box.

"Well," exclaimed Martin, "a fifth of Beefeaters!
Someone likes teacher inordinately."

"Any name with it?" Smith asked.

"Not that I can see." Koesler turned the bottle in
his hand, examining it thoroughly.

"How about it?" asked Burk. "Going to share the
largess with your colleagues?"

Koesler seemed lost in thought.

"I think I'll do us all a favor," he said at length,
"and give none of us a drink. See, here: The seal is
broken."

Each in turn scrutinized the seal. It had indeed been
broken and very carefully reglued. None of the three
considered this sufficient reason not to have a drink.

"Look," Koesler continued, shaking the bottle
slightly, "there's some sediment."

Minute crystals danced near the bottom of the
bottle.

"I think," Koesler concluded, "I'm going to ask
the police to have this analyzed and see if we have
something more than gin here."

The four, mesmerized, stared at the bottle as if it
were about to do something. It did nothing. Even the
crystals settled again.

"In any case, you would have been a very, very sick
man," said Inspector Koznicki.

The Inspector, Sergeants Morris and Patrick, and Father Koesler were seated in the living room of St. Anselm's rectory. Koesler felt queasy. Not since his rather extensive career in amateur athletics had anyone tried to hurt him physically. But that had been man to man. Now, a faceless someone had tried to hurt him, possibly kill him. It was unsettling. The someone had failed, but the someone was still out there somewhere

As a priest, Koesler had been in the presence of death countless times. Frequently, because no one had thought to call a priest while the individual was merely ill, he was called to anoint a dead person. He also had been involved in the investigation of two series of murders—violent deaths. But it was a new ball game now that he himself had become a target.

"You mean," Koesler finally managed to stammer out, "this stuff wouldn't have killed me?"

"It could have," Koznicki assured him, "but that is unlikely. You are a healthy man, so the result undoubtedly would not have been fatal. But if you had drunk that gin, you would have remembered these next few days for the rest of your life."

"Antabuse is a prescription drug," Patrick explained. "It's usually given to alcoholics to deter them from drinking. If they are taking this drug and they fall off the wagon, they get so very sick they may never try mixing the two again."

"But if it wouldn't have killed me, why would anyone want to adulterate a perfectly good bottle of gin and slip it into my mailbox?"

"That's a good question," Morris acknowledged. "But you see, a lot of people think Antabuse is lethal. It's kind of routine for clinic directors or pharmacists or even doctors to exaggerate the effect of Antabuse— to try to frighten the user into staying on the wagon."

"Yes," Patrick affirmed, "I've actually heard staff people at alcoholism centers do it. They'll come right out with it to a patient—tell him if he dares take anything alcoholic it'll kill him."

"There is the likely scenario, Father," said Koznicki. "Probably your would-be poisoner was under the misconception that in mixing Antabuse with alcohol he was concocting a fatal dose. The intent was there. Thank God the attempt on your life failed."

Koesler mulled over the situation. There had been an apparent attempt on his life. In all probability, this was another in the recent series of assaults on the seminary faculty. But why would anyone assault Fathers Ward and Merrit and himself? If there was a common denominator in all this, he could not find it. He was baffled and bewildered.

"I think, considered in the present light," Koznicki said, "it would be good for you, Father, to reevaluate your position in this case."

"What?" Koesler's contemplation was broken.

"When we began this investigation," Koznicki explained, "I invited your participation. We are, after all, at the threshold of the inner sanctum, as it were, of the Catholic Church. The investigation is taking place within a seminary. Catholic priests are being assaulted. You have collaborated in previous police investigations where the Church was intimately involved. And your collaboration, I might remind you, has been most productive."

"You mean, do I want in on this one?"

Koznicki nodded.

"Yes. I'm already in. I might just as well try to discover who wants to kill me." Even as Koesler committed himself, he shuddered.

"But, how can he . . .?" Morris began to voice amazement that a priest should participate in a homicide investigation.

"I'll explain it all on our way back to headquarters." Patrick had been among those police who had worked with Koesler in the past. He and Morris excused themselves and left the rectory.

"May I get you some coffee?" asked Koesler.

"No. Oh, no!"

Both Koesler and Koznicki smiled; both were all too familiar with Koesler's peculiar notoriety with even instant coffee.

"One thing in this latest development surprises me, Father." Koznicki leaned back, filling the ample chair. "How did you happen to notice the seal on the bottle had been tampered with?"

"Not characteristic of me to notice the little things, is it?" Koesler acknowledged perhaps his principal failing as an investigator.

"Frankly, no."

"I think it was more a coincidence than anything else."

"Oh?"

"At dinner, just before I discovered the gin, we were sort of lost in nostalgia, telling stories about the good old days and the priests who went with that time.

"Well, we were talking about old Father Fitzpatrick, one of the most colorful of an almost extinct breed. The others at table told a couple of stories about Fitz. But there was one thing that happened to Fitz that, although it is storied, was not mentioned. I was about to bring it up, but the meal was over.

"It involved something that happened during Prohibition. Some of the then priest faculty somehow got hold of a fifth of Irish whiskey. They carefully removed the seal and replaced a small portion of the whiskey with human urine. Then they reglued the seal and put the bottle in Father Fitzpatrick's mailbox.

"After dinner, Fitz found the whiskey, and said enthusiastically, 'Isn't this nice, now? The Little Sisters of the Poor are going to enjoy this. They need it, you know, for the old ones they care for.' With that, Fitz headed for his room. Those who were in on the plot simply stood there . . . waiting.

"Well, sir, within five minutes, old Fitz came barreling out of his room, clutching at his throat, and roaring, 'I've been poisoned! It's a Masonic plot!' "

Both laughed.

"So that was it," Koznicki said.

"Yes. A remarkable coincidence. I was just remembering Fitz finding the bottle of whiskey in his mailbox, when what is waiting in mine but a bottle of fine gin. I was almost compelled to check it carefully. Then I noticed the fine line across the seal. And then I noticed the sediment."

"That was most fortunate."

"Yes, or I would have been that very sick man you described."

"Heaven forbid any worse."

"Have you been able to trace the Antabuse?"

"We're giving it a try. But it is the proverbial needle in the haystack. There are clinics, pharmacies, emergency rooms all over town—and that includes only the corporate limits of the city of Detroit. Thousands more as we move into suburbia."

"Well," Koesler assured, "we'll come up with something soon."

"What makes you think so?"

"We've got prayer on our side now."

"I see," said Koznicki, smiling, "more things happen through prayer than, etc."

The doorbell rang. Mary O'Connor, St. Anselm's secretary, answered it.

"It's a young lady for you, Father," Mary announced from the living room doorway. "A Patricia Lennon from the *Detroit News*."

Koznicki, promising to be in touch soon, excused himself. Koesler accompanied him to the door. It was, indeed, Pat Lennon. She would be followed in twenty minutes by Joe Cox.

Bob Ankenazy slowly shook his head as he studied the CRT. The screen displayed the text of Pat Lennon's story. Lennon, in turn, studied Ankenazy.

It was a scene played out in newsrooms around the world. As often as a writer chanced upon an editor scanning that writer's copy, the watching game was on. It was only natural. One liked to know where one's story was going—all the possibilities from page one to the spike.

It was rare that any editor shook his head over a Lennon story. She strolled to Ankenazy's side.

"Something wrong?"

"This, here." Ankenazy pointed. "Don't you think it a bit precious referring to Koesler as a priest-sleuth?"

"I don't think so. He joins the ranks of hyphenated priests. Like the banjo-playing priest, the hoodlum-priest, the sociologist-priest. As a matter of fact, Koesler *re*joins those ranks: He used to be a priest-editor."

"I don't question the hyphen. My problem is with the 'sleuth.' I mean, he's not Father Brown. He's just a simple priest in a simple suburban parish."

"Oh, I'll grant you he's not Father Brown." Lennon was becoming defensive. "But neither is he an unknown Father Smith. He's worked with the police on at least three criminal investigations. And a couple of times, he's actually come up with the solution."

"Yes, but when was the most recent one . . . a couple of years ago?"

"More like a year and a half. But the public hasn't forgotten. Trust me."

"Really feel strong about this 'sleuth' bit?"

"Absolutely."

"O.K., we'll let it stand."

They walked toward the wire copy machines.

"What about the Antabuse? Do you really think whoever put it in the gin thought it was lethal?" asked Ankenazy.

"Oh, yes. I think it's a perfectly reasonable explanation. I talked to a couple of alcoholics. They both recalled times when someone who was dispensing Antabuse warned them that mixing the drug with alcohol would be fatal."

"I wonder how the guy feels now that he knows he's failed."

"That's three failures in as many tries."

"Yeah, that's right." Ankenazy stroked his beard. "Remarkable coincidence."

"What's next?"

"The Tridentines have another meeting tomorrow night. I thought I'd go. They're a violent lot. I wouldn't be overly surprised if they had something to do with all this."

"Any facts to substantiate that?"

"Nope, just intuition."

"Go with it."

"By the way, Joe will be with me tomorrow night."

"Collaboration with the enemy?"

"Not really." Lennon laughed. "Joe doesn't understand things Catholic as well as I do. I've had to translate for him. And now he's in trouble."

"How's that?"

"His translator just quit."

"This meeting of the Tridentine Society will come to order." The chairman gave the lectern a resounding whack with the gavel.

Apparently, Cox's surmise was correct. Either none of the Tridentines read the newspapers or at least none read the *Free Press*. Cox and Lennon had been greeted with a touch less hostility than before. If he had been recognized as a reporter who made them seem ridiculous simply by recording what they did and said, neither Cox nor Lennon would have gotten past the door. Not only was his cover not blown; Cox felt that the slight lessening in overt hostility indicated the beginning of a grudging acceptance.

Tonight's meeting was in the basement of Immaculate Heart of Mary Church. Which indicated, Cox thought, that either the Tridentines were low on cash and had to take whatever was offered, or they didn't want to provide a stationary target—or both.

"Is there anything to report?" the chairman asked.

Hands shot up. The chairman began pointing at people, using no names. Perhaps he knew few if any names. He certainly did not know either Cox or Lennon.

"In my parish they had a Folk Mass at ten on Sunday morning, where they used to have the Latin High Mass," fumed a squat woman. It was not evident whether she had stood or was still seated. "And they sang 'Bridge Over Troubled Waters'!"

" 'Bridge Over Troubled Waters,' " the chairman repeated. "And what parish is that?"

"Shrine of the Little Flower."

"Holy God!" said the chairman, "old Father Charlie Coughlin will be spinning in his grave!"

Cox was not sure which, if any, law had been violated by singing "Bridge Over Troubled Waters." He glanced at Lennon. A smile just this side of a smirk played at the corners of her mouth. For once, he envied her her Catholic background. Obviously, these proceedings held more significance for her than for him.

"I was at old St. Mary's downtown last Sunday at the Latin High Mass—one of the few parishes left that has the guts to have a Latin Mass," a balding dumpy man contributed. "There was an ex-priest there, whispering to the woman he was with. And he was laughing during the sermon!"

"Probably thought he could get away with it because he was downtown," another man commented.

Cox noticed a woman in the front row taking notes furiously—a chapter-and-verse of other people's faults. Perhaps the Tridentines meted out punishments. For all Cox could ascertain, vengeance would clearly be in character for the Tridentines.

"Our parish council voted to close our parochial school," charged a tall, thin woman in a sensible hat. "Two years ago, they closed the high school and now they want to close the grade school."

"Which school is that?" the chairman asked after catching a frantically bewildered look on the part of the female note-taker.

"St. Ambrose," the tall woman replied.

"And didn't St. Ambrose used to have the best football teams in the city?" a chunky, well-built man observed. "Used to beat the damn public schools in the Soup Bowl every year. No matter how big the damn Protestants were."

"Seems like a step in the right direction to me," another voice was raised. "With what they're teaching in Catholic schools today. Not the holy nuns of old with their holy habits. And not the *Baltimore Catechism* any more either."

Things were beginning to get out of hand. The chairman pulled in the reins by recognizing another member with another report.

"We've got a young, upstart priest at our parish— Holy Redeemer, that is—hair all over his face; last Sunday, can you imagine"—the speaker was so bloated and red-faced he seemed about to explode—"he preached against the draft!"

The basement was filled with mixed sounds of disapproval.

"Can you imagine!" the red-faced man continued, "we are providing a shelter for young Commiesymps now! Have these young people never heard of the Holy Crusades? And who's paying for their keep?"

"We are!" Several replied as one to the rhetorical question.

"Well, I say," inveighed the red-faced one, "it's about time we stop paying their freight. They're not worthy of the roman collar they never wear. I say throw the bums out!"

"Did yez see TV last night?" The man wore a yellow bowling shirt with "Kominski's Sausage" lettered on the back and the word "Smaczne" beneath.

Everyone nodded an affirmative with respect to last night's TV viewing. Nielsen would have felt vindicated.

"Did yez see the late news?" asked the bowler. "They had that there party at the Ren Cen for Mayor Cobb. And that Father Cunneen was there. You know, that guy with his Project Faith? Well, he was there. And the camera caught him holding a drink and talking to a woman who had no back to her dress. And he was enjoying himself. He was laughing right into the camera!"

"Was he wearing his roman collar?" someone asked. "Yes."

"It's always the wrong ones wear them!"

It appeared to Cox that these people had an infinite list of things about which they were angry.

"I heard, I heard"—Even though he had been recognized by the chairman, the little man was forced to shout to be heard over the hubbub. "I heard they retired Father Schwartz!"

"Not the World War I Veteran, Retired!"

"That's the one."

"Why?"

"Age!"

"How old was he?"

"Seventy-four!"

"That was not old for Father Schwartz."

"He was among the last priests who were still fighting for our faith as it was handed down by the Apostles!"

At that moment, a TV crew entered the basement. An unkempt, unshaven young man balanced a TV camera on his shoulder. He was followed by the sound man carrying a microphone and looking about for the best place to aim it. They were followed by well-dressed, square-shaped Ven Marshall, Channel 7's longtime reporter.

Cox and Lennon feared they were about to witness a repeat of what ensued when the early Christians faced the lions. When this altercation concluded, the two reporters were certain, the score would read: Tridentines-3, TV Crew-0.

Oddly, just the opposite was happening. For the first time in the two meetings Cox and Lennon had attended, they saw smiles on a few faces. Tridentines self-consciously adjusted their clothing and posture. They were going to be on TV. This was Show Time!

The chairman began pounding the gavel for order, although with the advent of the TV crew he had more order than at any other time during the session.

The cameraman set up facing the chairman as Ven Marshall confidently took a seat at the far corner of the front row.

The chairman recommenced, "Well, members of the T.S."

Tough shit? the soundman wondered.

"The Tridentine Society . . ."

No.

". . . was founded to restore to the Church the richness of the sixteenth century—the greatest of centuries. As we can all see from the reports we have heard tonight, our major problem is with today's priests. Why, many of us still remember the hedonistic pictures brought to our last meeting by Brother Alphonsus . . ."

Yeah, where *is* Brother Alphonsus? Cox wondered. The good brother appeared not to have attended this meeting.

". . . and that most of us viewed afterward. This is what they are teaching today's seminarians. About group sex and single sex and the opposite sex. How can we expect to have any more priests like Father Schwartz with indoctrination like that in our seminaries?

"Probably all of you saw what happened to that priest at the seminary. Someone tried to poison him. I ask you, is that all bad? What can our seminary teachers expect when they lead our seminarians into mortal sin? It is about time someone got the attention of these Judases!"

"Excuse me, Mr. Chairman." Marshall's clipped tones were addressed jointly to the microphone in his hand and the chairman on the podium. "Do I understand you to say that the murder of a priest could be justified—even desirable?"

"There are worse things than death in this world, sir." The chairman was caught in the camera's zoom lens. "Mortal sin is the greatest evil in the world!"

"And wouldn't the killing of a priest be a mortal sin?" Marshall was aware that he was getting extraordinary, if outrageous, statements for quotation.

"There is such a thing as the lesser of two evils, sir!" the chairman shot back.

Cox and Lennon were exuberant. While TV would, of course, beat them chronologically, they would be able to talk to all these singular characters, write their stories, and be reasonably sure none of these people would read those stories. The Tridentines would be glued to their TV sets, watching themselves on Channel 7's newscast. But they would not read.

Cox and Lennon would live to fight another day.

"St. Anslem's." Koesler answered the rectory phone.

"Father Koesler, this is Inspector Koznicki. Do you have a few minutes?"

"Certainly, Inspector. We have a parish council meeting this evening. But that doesn't begin for half an hour."

"Fine. Have you read both the *Free Press* and *News* accounts of that Tridentine Society meeting?"

"Yes. Ordinarily, I wouldn't have paid much attention to something like that. Except that I was the priest the chairman happened to be referring to—and I don't regard myself as being as expendable as he does."

"Nor do I. Do you know anything of this group, Father?"

"Not an awful lot. There can't be many of them. They're sort of the lunatic fringe."

"You would not term them simply conservatives?"

"Oh, no. The stereotype of a Catholic conservative is a person who thinks the Church was from its very beginning the same as it was when he was growing up. So he deeply resents the drastic changes that have taken place in the Church since the Second Vatican Council. Most of this type have a peculiar notion of what we call the ordinary magisterium, or the ordinary teaching role of the Church. According to them, if a Catholic denies a noninfallible papal statement, the Catholic is not a heretic, he's just wrong.

"But people like the Tridentines have made up their own Church. They think they're Catholic but they are far too Catholic for the Catholic Church. Or am I telling you more than you ever wanted to know? That's a propensity of mine."

"No, no, Father. Never suppose that a police officer knows that much about religion. And knowledge of the Church will likely be an important element in the solution of this case.

"But tell me, Father: both Joseph Cox of the *Free Press* and Patricia Lennon of the *News* seem to believe that the Tridentines will not even read their stories in the newspapers, and that they will be able to continue covering this society with impunity. What do you think?"

"I'd have to agree. When I was editor of the *Detroit Catholic,* these people would often call to complain about something we had run—but they hadn't read it; others had told them about it. So I guess Joe and Pat are in the clear . . . unless someone tattles to the Tridentines.

"I take it you've talked to the reporters?"

"Yes, and to the chairman of the Tridentines—one Roman Kirkus. But it is next to impossible to pinpoint or identify the members. There are no lists or records. Even Mr. Kirkus claims to know not more than five members. It is one of the most secretive groups I have ever encountered."

"And you feel they could really be violent?"

"Oh, yes, Father. Trust me. This type can easily pass over the line between talk and action."

A chill passed down Koesler's spine.

He shook it off. "By the way, Inspector, I've been thinking. . . ."

"That's what we want you to do."

"Has it occurred to anyone that these attacks have taken place while all of the—us—were doing routine things?" It seemed strange to Koesler to include himself in the category of intended victim.

"Yes, it has, Father. You had finished your Friday dinner, the only dinner you regularly eat at the seminary. Father Merrit always travels to say Mass at the same time of the morning. And Father Ward each year takes the skull to his classroom just prior to the Yorick episode in *Hamlet*. Someone has done an excellent job of surveillance."

Silence. Koesler felt abashed; of course the police would notice such an obvious clue.

"But one final request, Father."

"What's that?"

"Keep thinking."

Each Friday afternoon at 3:30 during the school year, Father Sklarski took his week's dry cleaning to Robinson's Cleaners and picked up the previous week's supply. He found he had to establish a routine or he would forget for weeks at a time. Then he would find himself with a party to attend and no clean black suit in his closet.

Robinson's was only three blocks from the seminary, so Sklarski always walked.

At precisely 3:30 P.M. on a Friday in late January, Father Sklarski stepped gingerly out the seminary's front door.

It had snowed heavily earlier in the week. But two days of temperatures in the upper 40s had reduced the snow to slush. Long ago, Sklarski had grumpily concluded that Detroit's snow removal plan was called spring.

Walking in this neighborhood always made the priest

a bit uneasy. Say what you will, Sklarski would declaim, it's not a matter of racial prejudice: this was a damn dangerous neighborhood. And now, since the attacks on three faculty members, none of the remaining faculty could feel entirely safe ever. Walking the streets in this vicinity only heightened his apprehension.

He pretended to keep his gaze on the ground as he walked. But his eyes restlessly moved from side to side, catching as much as possible in peripheral view.

He breathed a sigh of relief as he reached the cleaners. Half the circuit completed without incident.

"Right on time, Father," said a cheerful Mr. Robinson.

"Yup. You can set your clock by me. It's nice to know there are some things in life that are dependable."

Robinson wrote up the current items Sklarski had brought in, then took his ticket and went to find last week's batch.

Fine, hard-working man, thought Sklarski. More blacks work that hard and the welfare rolls would be halved.

Sklarski paid his bill, hooked a pudgy finger under hangers holding a suit and an overcoat, and exited.

No sooner had the door closed behind him than the priest's heart skipped a beat. There was an unmistakable sound of violence.

"Help! Help! Help me!"

Sklarski dropped the suit and coat in the slush as his hands went up instinctively to protect himself. But the outcry came from across the wide street.

Four or five young blacks were mugging a white man. They had thrown him to the ground and were pummeling him.

"What's going on over there?" Sklarski shouted.

"What white mother wants to know?" one of the muggers shouted back, holding up an insolent finger.

Insult Sklarski, would they! He immediately reentered the cleaners and, using Robinson's personal phone, dialed 911. He then continued to watch the scuffle from the comparative safety of the cleaning establishment.

Finally, the muggee escaped from the muggers, who seemed to have acquired what they were after. Probably his wallet, thought Sklarski.

Just after the victim had broken away and run shrieking down a side street, the police arrived. The hoodlums scattered, but the police managed to nab two.

The excitement was over.

Sklarski glanced at his clothing, soiled by the slush. Robinson would have to begin anew with it.

Funny thing, now that he had the interval to think about it: the victim across the street had been wearing black too.

"My worst experience was with an Austrian," said Monsignor Martin. "Although I must confess, I made a major contribution to the mess."

It was Friday dinner at the seminary. Fathers Martin, Koesler, and Burk were seated at the same table. They, indeed, were the only faculty members dining at the seminary this evening. The topic of conversation had segued from the difficulty of teaching today's students a foreign language to problems they had experienced with foreign priests.

"Actually," Martin continued, "it was a bizarre combination of the initial blunder I made, coupled with the priest's unfamiliarity with English, and his Bavarian bullheadedness. It happened years ago, but I'll never forget it.

"It was a very busy Saturday morning. We had several weddings scheduled. Every hour on the hour from nine to noon. Which explains what the Austrian priest was doing among us: we needed help—anywhere we could get it.

"It began when I inadvertently gave him the wrong marriage license. He, of course, had never met the couple, so he had no way of knowing he had the wrong license."

Burk and Koesler began to grin, anticipating the chaos that was sure to follow.

"Well," Martin continued, "after the wedding party reached the altar, the priest consulted both the lectionary and the license and began with, 'Do you, John Smith'—whatever the names were; I've forgotten—'take Mary Brown, here present, to be your lawful wedded wife?'

"Well, the groom says, 'My name is not John Smith.' The priest says, 'Yes, it is. It must be. It says so right on the license.' 'Well, it's not John Smith,' the groom insists. So they argue awhile until the priest is convinced the groom must know his own name. 'So what is your name?' 'Joseph Doe,'—or something like that—the groom says. So the priest begins again, 'Do you, Joseph Doe, take Mary Brown, here present, for your lawful wife?' 'My name is not Mary Brown,' says the bride.

"Well, they went through the same process all over again, arguing whether the bride knew her own name in contrast to what the license said."

The three laughed heartily.

"That's pretty good, Al," said Burk, "but I think I can top that one. Or bottom it, depending on how you look at it.

"Our situation was similar to yours in that we ran short of priests. Only this was for Sunday Mass in the summer when one of our priests was on vacation and another fell ill.

"The only extra priest we could find was staying at a nearby monastery. Not only was he French, he had come to this country only a few months before. There was no problem with Mass, of course. It was in Latin then, and Latin with a French accent sounds better than Latin with an American accent.

"The problem was with the sermon. The French priest's fluency in English ran from poor to nonexistent.

We tried to assure him that one of us could handle the sermon and all he'd have to do was say Mass. But he wouldn't hear of it. He insisted upon preaching.

"Well, the Gospel text for that Sunday was the episode where Christ cures the ten lepers and only one of them returns to give thanks.

"To begin, the priest pronounced it 'leapers.' And in paraphrasing the Gospel's conclusion, he ' said, 'Christ cured ze ten leapers. And all of zem returned to give thanks except nine.' "

They laughed again.

While Burk had been telling his story, Father Sklarski had entered the dining room, helped himself from the serving table, and seated himself with the other three. He hadn't heard all of Burk's story but enjoyed the punch line regardless.

"Well, Ed, anything happen to you today?" asked Martin.

Whether or not anything had happened that day to Sklarski, the question was certain to launch his stream of consciousness.

"Did anything happen? Did anything happen!" Sklarski exclaimed. "Well, I should say. This day was like all other days except that I became part of the crime-fighting scene in our fair city."

He had their attention.

Sklarski told of his brief journey to the cleaners. He embellished the menace of the neighborhood needlessly. Each of them had walked the selfsame streets any number of times. They knew that while there was some danger, the neighborhood was not nearly as perilous, particularly in broad daylight, as Sklarski made out.

"Then," Sklarski continued, "as I was leaving Robinson's, I heard this piteous cry for help. I looked up keenly. Every nerve and sinew in my body was on the alert. The adrenalin coursed through my blood stream.

"It was across the street—across Linwood. Five or

six big black men had attacked one lonely white man. They had him on the ground and were killing him.

"What could I do? What could any one man do against such odds? I quickly crossed the street"—he would, he assured himself, have crossed the street if he had it to do over—"and confronted those hoodlums.

"Well, one of them turned on me and knocked my freshly cleaned suit and coat from my hands. I knew then I could not prevail alone. So I retreated to Robinson's and called the police."

"Did they come in time?" asked Burk.

"Promptly. Although not before the victim managed to struggle free of those vandals and run away. But the police caught a couple of them. One was the ringleader. The police were familiar with him. Then they took my statement and took the criminals into custody."

"Say, Ed," Martin observed, "that was pretty brave of you. I don't think I would have had the courage to charge into melee like that."

"Nor I," Burk agreed.

"If you're not part of the solution, you're part of the problem." Sklarski felt not a twinge of compunction.

"Funny thing, though," Sklarski continued, "as I told the police, the victim was dressed all in black. Black hat, coat, trousers, shoes . . . white socks though. You don't see that much anymore. Why, hell, you hardly see priests dressed that way anymore."

"Wait." Koesler had been listening intently. "The victim was dressed in black?"

"Why, yes."

"How big a man would you say he was?"

"Oh, I don't know. Not big. Maybe five-five, not an athletic figure at all. Oh, and he had a rather high-pitched voice. Maybe that was because he was frightened. And I don't blame him."

"And," Koesler continued his questioning, "this is something you do routinely, Ed? You go to the same cleaners at the same time each Friday?"

"Well, if I don't, I tend to forget about it and there you are, invited out to Grosse Pointe Farms with nothing to wear." Sklarski chuckled, joined by Martin and Burk.

"Part of your routine," Koesler mused as if he were alone, "the man is about five-five, pudgy, high voice, and dressed in black . . . hmmm.

"If you'll excuse me . . ." Koesler rose and quickly left the dining room.

He made his way to the room assigned for his use on the second floor. He found and dialed the number of Precinct Ten and spoke briefly with the inspector in charge.

Then he phoned Inspector Koznicki and told him what had happened, omitting the part about Sklarski's crossing the street and confronting the muggers. His call to the Tenth Precinct had revealed that part of Sklarski's tale to be a Walter Mittyism.

"I think, Inspector," Koesler concluded, "that the fact that the muggers robbed the victim of a loaded revolver makes it much more likely that he is our man. Same height, size, high voice, dressed in black. Add to this, Father Sklarski was doing what he routinely does each Friday.

"What do you think?"

"The coincidence is remarkable," Koznicki admitted at length.

"Too remarkable to be just coincidence, wouldn't you agree? Koesler pressed.

"Perhaps. Yes, I would agree. However, we are left with one inevitable conclusion."

"What's that?"

"We will not know, at least for the time being."

"Not know?"

"No. The victim escaped. And I do not think he will come claiming his revolver."

There was a pause.

"Keep in touch," said Koznicki. Then he added, "and keep thinking."

The shades had been lowered, making the small room nearly dark.

"Well, you did it again," said the First Man.

"I didn't hear you fighting for a chance to go into that neighborhood," said the Second Man. Hot ash had fallen from his cigarette, but in the dark he had not seen it. It was burning a hole in his trousers.

"You could have been mugged *after* you shot him," said the Third Man.

"Look," said the Second, "I didn't arrange for my mugging. Besides, if I had been mugged *after* the shooting, I'd have been caught by the cops."

"We're overlooking something," said the Fourth Man, "it was just an accident that the gang picked that moment to mug him. It could have happened to any one of us." He removed his glasses and laid them on the table.

"But it didn't happen to any one of us. It happened to *him*. It *always* happens to him," said the Third. He flicked the ashes from his cigarette in the general direction of the ashtray. They fell in his coffee.

"And on top of it all," said the First, "they got the gun."

"What do you mean, on top of it all?" said the Second. "They went right for it. Like they knew I was carrying it. They didn't even go for my wallet!"

"If they'd had the time, they would have taken your money too," said the Fourth. "But the cops came and you were able to escape. I'll wager if they'd had more time, they would've gone for your wallet."

"It's dark in here," said the First Man. He moved to the wall light switch, tripping on the rug's edge. He flipped on the switch. The bulb lit only a second, then with a pop!, burned out. "Ouch!" said the First Man.

"What's the matter?" asked the Fourth.

"I got a shock." He returned to the table, again tripping on the edge of the rug.

"What are we going to do about the gun?" asked the Second Man.

"What *can* we do about it?" said the Third. "It's gone. One gun explodes in your hand and you lose another. We are going to keep the gunmakers of America in business."

"Look," said the Second, "I feel bad enough without all of you rubbing it in. After all, *I'm* the one who got mugged."

"And this one was a complete waste," said the First. "We didn't even get his attention or scare him." He slammed his fist against the table, breaking the Fourth Man's glasses. "Sorry."

"It's all right; I always carry a spare pair."

"Yecch!" said the Third Man. "This coffee is terrible. Don't you filter the grounds?"

"There's nothing wrong with the coffee," the First Man assured. He took a sip of his just-poured coffee. "Arggh!" It burned his mouth.

"It's that neighborhood," the Fourth Man observed.

"Ow! Ow! Ow!" The Second Man jumped up from his chair, slapping at his trousers where the cigarette ash had burned through.

"The odds were against us from the beginning in that neighborhood," the Fourth Man continued. "We didn't stand a chance in that setting."

"Do you think it's time?" asked the Third.

"Yes, I think it is definitely time," said the Fourth Man. "But it must be clearly understood by all," he looked pointedly at the others, "that there never again can be a deviation from the plan such as we had a few weeks back. It is no longer important which of us was responsible for that. But it must never happen again.

"And finally, let's all remember what we learned in World War II: loose lips sink ships. We can't afford any more slipups. From now on, we tell no one about anything that goes on. Not colleagues, not friends, not coworkers. Is that understood?"

The other three nodded solemnly.

"Then, with these understandings, it is time we move into Phase Two."

5.

"AS FAR AS I'M CONCERNED," SAID FATHER LYR FEENY, "Pope John XXIII should have been strangled in his crib."

"Oh, that's going a bit far, don't you think, Ly?" asked Father Charles O'Dowd.

"Not quite far enough, really," Feeny replied. "Better that he should never have been born."

"Absolutely," Father Albert Budreau agreed. "Look what's happened to the Church as a result of John's *aggiornamento*. Look what's happened to the seminary!"

They were seated in the faculty dining room adjoining the student refectory at St. Joseph's Seminary.

"A shadow of its former self. A shadow!" Father Anthony Gennardo shook his head and snorted.

"A shallow? A shallow what?" Father George Dye was getting on in years and no longer heard as well as he had.

"A *shadow!*" Gennardo emphasized, and snorted.

"It's as Al says," said Feeny, "you all should remember, we were the pioneers of this seminary. Almost all of us are charter members of the founding faculty. We've suffered through the changes that have come spewing out of the Vatican Council."

"Absolutely," Budreau agreed. "Look at the syllabus. Compare that with the courses we offered years ago. Why, there's no comparision at all. We're offering fluff now."

"Oh, come now, Al," said O'Dowd, "it's not all that bad. The courses still have substance. We're still offering normal and dogmatic theology, scripture, canon law. The staples are still here."

"But in English! Everything's in English! Biblical Greek and Hebrew are electives. And not a word of Latin," Gennardo grumbled. "In the beginning here, we taught, questioned, answered, tested, thought in Latin. Now, not a word of it."

"And remember, Fathers," said Feeny, "Latin remains the official language of the Latin rite of the Catholic Church. A vernacular liturgy depends upon the official *Latin* text and may be used only with Rome's permission."

"Exactly," Budreau concurred. "Why, if you were to put a Latin missal in front of one of today's students, he wouldn't know what to do with it."

"It marks the death of the Latin liturgy," said Gennardo.

"The dearth of what?" Dye asked.

"Death! Death! Death of the Latin liturgy!" Gennardo almost shouted. Then he snorted.

"And the student body!" Budreau exclaimed. "As Tony suggested earlier, a shadow of its former self."

"What is this about a shallow?" asked Dye. "A shallow what? A shallow grave?"

"Years ago," Budreau ignored Dye, "we had students who were serious about the priesthood, ready to make a lifelong commitment. The young men we have now don't know the meaning of a lifelong commitment."

"Al," said O'Dowd, "you're just lonesome for a more innocent era. Those were the days when society demanded commitment until death. Today is a day of handy divorce and priests and nuns deciding on a different lifestyle. A midlife career change. Besides, there is not that much difference between the students of yesterday and today."

"I'm afraid I'll have to partially disagree," said Feeny. "There is some difference. Maybe mostly in quantity, and as a result the overall quality suffers. The parishes out there are running dry of priests. In effect, they are demanding that we supply priests in numbers. So, although we have a few good men and true with us now, the problem is that we do not dismiss obviously second-rate seminarians as we once did. Sending a seminarian back to the lay life has become a luxury."

"Well, then," said Budreau, "we are agreed on one point: Things are different than they were."

"But," added Dye, "you've got to know the territory."

The four looked at Dye in surprise. There were times when they wondered about him.

To train Detroit candidates for the Catholic priesthood, there were two seminary systems, a minor and a major.

Sacred Heart was the minor seminary. At one time, it had comprised both high school and college departments. A sharp drop in the student population had forced Sacred Heart to circle its wagons more tightly. Now, only the college department survived. and that, barely.

St. John's, located on the outskirts of the Michigan township of Plymouth, had been the major seminary. It had had the distinction of being the only provincial seminary in the United States. It served the Roman Catholic province of Michigan, which, in Church circles, corresponds with the State of Michigan.

Now, St. John's, as an institution, was no longer in operation. Its huge complex of buildings, nine-hole golf course, wooded area, apple orchard, and spring-fed lake had been bought by the estate of the late General Amos Motors, the automotive tycoon. The closing was the result of the incapability of the provincial minor seminaries to funnel sufficient students into St. John's.

The Archidocese of Detroit now had its own major seminary, St. Joseph's, on Schoolcraft at the city's northwest corner.

Though St. Joseph's had been built in recent years, it had already outgrown its student body. Both minor and major seminaries teetered on the brink of obsolescence. They were, in the words of Fathers Gennardo and Budreau, shadows of what they once had been—two rather peculiar white elephants.

It was impossible to fix the blame for this situation on any one cause in particular. In their day, the buildings had combined to make the institutions redundant.

One of the factors that had nearly emptied the seminaries was the significant number of priests who had resigned, particularly during the 1970s. An exodus that tended to create the impression that entering the seminary was tantamount to booking passage on the *Titanic*. Still another was a reluctance on the part of young men to make a long-term if not lifelong commitment to a clerical life in a celibate state.

The presenting problem was how to make these huge, near-empty structures relevant again.

Sacred Heart had addressed the problem by inviting other entities within its walls. Among these were the Department of Formation (of seminarians), the Office of Pastoral Ministry, the Hispanic Office, the *Detroit Catholic* newspaper, Michigan Welfare Reform, the New Center Academy, and Senior Citizens.

Clearly, there was no sense of purpose, plan, or homogeneity here. Just the need to fill up the corners.

Where Sacred Heart attempted to fill its empty spaces with other organizations, St. Joseph's banked on bodies.

Enrolled in various classes and programs at St. Joseph's were more than a hundred nonseminarian students. The presence of nearly two hundred bodies, even if far less than one hundred of them were actually studying for the priesthood, made it appear the seminary was functioning at full tilt, even if at the end of the tunnel there was little light and few ordinations.

The survival of the seminaries and the manner in which they conducted their affairs was of interest mainly to the Catholic community of Detroit—bishops, priests, nuns, and laity—including a watchdog Tridentine Society and four sinister men who met in a dark room.

The Catholic Archdiocese of Detroit could boast of many magnificent pulpits. Most of them, anachronistically, were in the wrong churches.

Enormous, vaulted, brick edifices stood throughout the inner city like relics, surrounded by decay, debris, and vacant land. They held magnificent pulpits. But, in most cases, the white parishioners who had built them were long gone. Now, only a relatively few black Catholics, with a sprinkling of whites, attended services. The era of these magnificent pulpits seemed to have perished. From time to time, Archbishop Mark Boyle could be heard to wish that these churches had been built on wheels, so they could be wheeled out to the suburbs.

For that—the suburbs—was where the magnificent crowds could be found. On weekends, suburban parishes regularly offered as many as five to seven Masses —all of them jam-packed. The magnificent crowds, however, had to be content with wood ranch-style churches with a most ordinary lectern for a pulpit.

Of course, it was possible to find places here and there where there were neither magnificent pulpits nor magnificent crowds.

Chief example of such was the Detroit House of Correction—known as DeHoCo. A large, sprawling complex, DeHoCo was designated as the prison for Detroit's convicts, although it sometimes housed county, state, and even, on occasion, federal prisoners. However, the general run of DeHoCo inmate was a vagrant, traffic offender, or wife-beater; the typical sentence ran from several months to several years.

Somehow, St. Joseph's Seminary had accepted responsibility, during the scholastic year, for providing Sunday Mass at DeHoCo.

Those seminarians who had been ordained to the deaconate order, one rung removed from the priesthood, were empowered to preach. The better preachers among the deacons were sent to preach at the better parishes. Those who had problems preaching were sent to problem parishes.

The Reverend Mr. Raphael Doody, a deacon for almost six months, had not yet been sent to preach anywhere. Today he would fulfill his first homiletic assignment: he would preach at DeHoCo. And, as his luck would have it, Father Anthony Gennardo would offer the Mass at which Deacon Doody would preach. Father Gennardo was acknowledged to be one of the faculty's Last Angry Men.

Other deacons, near the bottom of the homiletic barrel, who had had a crack at DeHoCo, warned Doody about the hazards of preaching there. However, they had not begun to plumb the depths of that experience.

The floor of DeHoCo's spacious gym was the nave; the gym's stage was the sanctuary. On the stage was a small table, draped with a white cloth. The makeshift altar bore two lighted candles. A smaller table carried wine and water cruets, a small dish, a lectionary, and the chalice. Two chairs were on the stage, one for the priest, the other for the deacon.

A few dozen gray folding chairs had been set up near the stage. Approximately twenty-five male prisoners were seated in no particular order. Many were stubble-bearded. Quite a few dozed. None seemed very interested in the religious ceremony. They were a captive audience in more than one sense.

It was time for the homily.

A very nervous Reverend Mr. Doody approached

center stage. For the first time as a preacher, he beheld a live congregation. Or rather, he almost beheld it. A basketball backboard directly in front of him hid part of his congregation. Struts connecting the backboard to the wall obscured the rest.

"Many centuries ago"—Doody cleared his throat; his voice was high from nervousness—"a man named Tall of Parsus . . . Paul of Tarsus gave a stirring sermon to the ancient pagans on the 'Unknowing God' . . . er . . . the 'Unknown God.'"

That guy and speech are enemies, thought Father Gennardo.

"Among the many . . . uh . . . wait . . ."—memory failed—"oh, yes, objects and idols worshiped by these pagans was an altar dedicated to the 'Unknown God.'"

Several dozing convicts slumped into deeper sleep as Doody's high-pitched voice droned on.

"With divorce, birth control, adultery, murder, and robbery so rampant, it would seem that we must be either atheists or insane!"

What was that? one of the few prisoners paying attention wondered. Divorce, birth control, adultery, murder, and robbery? Well, four out of five ain't bad.

"There have been parishes that had to cancel perpetual adoration because none of the laity would come to adore."

This guy should turn to a life of crime, thought another convict. He would be perfect in a lineup. Even after this exposure, I couldn't pick him out of a crowd of two.

"And thus we go to the altar, to worship the same God the ancient pagans worshiped under the title of . . . er . . . wait . . . oh, yes . . . the 'Unknown God.'

"In the name of the Father and the Son and the Holy Ghost . . . uh . . . er . . . Spirit. Amen."

The remainder of the Mass was uneventful if one chose to overlook the moment when Doody, who also acted as acolyte, dropped the water cruet. Oh well; at least he waited until it had been used for the final time before he dropped it.

Immediately after the Mass, Gennardo in silence drove Doody back to St. Joseph's.

Before they parted in the seminary vestibule, Doody hesitantly spoke.

"Was it all right?"

"Let me put it this way," said Gennardo, "in DeHo-Co I think you have found a home away from home."

And then he snorted.

It was just 11:30 A.M., the regular time for Father Gennardo's meditation. He entered the seminary's inner courtyard and began pacing the brown brick walkway. His path would take him around and around in a squared circle.

As he walked, he lit a cigarette and immediately thought of the old story of the Dominican and the Jesuit who were about to enter their periods of meditation. Each wanted to smoke; permission was required. The Dominican asked his superior if he might smoke while he meditated. Permission was refused. The Jesuit asked his superior if it were permissible to meditate while smoking. The superior allowed as how that seemed perfectly permissible.

Gennardo snorted, shrugged away the anecdote, and got down to some serious meditation.

"May I freshen the martini for you, Inspector?"

"No, thank you, Father; it is fine."

Walter Koznicki and his wife Wanda were seated in the small kitchen of St. Anselm's rectory. Father Koesler was preparing Sunday dinner. In recent years, the three had formed a habit of dining together at least once a month. Sometimes, particularly in good weather, more frequently.

Now that the Koznicki children were grown and on their own, the threesome's dinners had become movable feasts. At times, they ate at the Koznicki's, sometimes at a restaurant; occasionally, they supped at St. Anselm's, where Koesler prepared the simplest of meals.

Tonight, three steaks were broiling while frozen vegetables were thawing in boiling water. Koesler attacked head lettuce and spinach in the preparation of one of his few specialties—tossed salad.

"Still not drinking, Father?" Wanda Koznicki could not get used to a Koesler sans his usual preprandial bourbon manhattan.

"No, Wanda. Since that doctored gin, I'm still a bit queasy about alcohol."

"I don't blame you. I still get a shiver when I think of someone actually trying to kill you."

Koesler chuckled. "I shouldn't think you'd be disturbed by attempted murder after all the years you've spent looking over your husband's shoulder."

"Oh, but it's not the same. You know that, Bob." Wanda occasionally used Koesler's given name. Her husband always used the priest's title. "It's as different as night from day when the intended victim is a dear friend."

"She's right, Father," said Koznicki. "Even with my long experience in Homicide, I was shocked when we discovered the contents of that bottle."

"Well, so was I," Koesler acknowledged. "I guess I just never thought I was important enough to be the target of a murderer. I've had a number of extremely conservative adversaries—I wouldn't go so far as to call them enemies—when I was editor of the *Detroit Catholic*. But even that opposition never escalated beyond the medium of correspondence. I wrote editorials, and they wrote angry letters to the editor.

"But, then, I don't suppose many murder victims expect the attack, do they?"

"In most instances, I do not think so," Koznicki replied. "A goodly percentage of premeditated murders in this city are the result of organized crime. You might think that people engaged in such criminal activity might well anticipate a violent end. But most do not. Just as they do not anticipate being apprehended. They expect all that to happen to the other guy.

"Then there is the family homicide. It is rarely premeditated; generally it is provoked by a violent argument and abetted by the availability of a weapon, usually a gun.

"But now that you mention those conservative adversaries, have you been following the series on the Tridentine Society in the *Free Press* and the *News*?"

"Oh, Walt," said Wanda, "we shouldn't be talking business. This is a dinner party."

"It's a dinner party only if I don't foul it up." Koesler scraped the sliced radishes into the salad bowl. "And I don't mind talking about it. Actually, it helps.

"Yes, I followed them carefully, Inspector. I thought they were extremely well written, and showed the nicely contrasting styles of Joe Cox and Pat Lennon."

Koznicki smiled. "I did not intend to ask for a journalistic appraisal of the reporters' styles, Father. I meant, what do you think of the Tridentine Society and its members?"

"Well, it's rather too easy to find them laughable. Their positions and opinions are so extreme. This business of the Tumerango Visions, for instance . . ." Koesler checked the steaks; they were ready. He ladled the vegetables onto serving dishes. ". . . every responsible Church authority has disclaimed them. Yet the Tridentines are buying patches of Tumerango turf. They're even storing up branches from the tree over which all Church authorities agree the Blessed Mother has *not* appeared."

The Koznickis laughed

"But in all this humor, it's too easy to overlook the fact that some of these people can be dangerous." Koesler began to transfer the food to the dining room table. "They feel they have been virtually forsaken by their Church. And their Church, or the way they perceive their Church in retrospect, is of prime importance to them. They are humorless, aggrieved, abandoned people. Such people can be very dangerous."

Koesler invited the Koznickis to the dining room, led the before-meal grace, and poured three cups of coffee.

"I could not agree with you more, Father," said Koznicki. "And the present path of our investigation is in the direction of the very same Tridentine Society. But they are a slippery group."

Wanda hoped Koesler would have to return to the kitchen soon. She would take that opportunity, as she had on any number of occasions, to pour her coffee into the potted plant.

Dear, dear Father Koesler! He was such a sweet, good friend. But the poor man simply could not make a decent cup of coffee.

"I agree with you," said Sergeant Morris, "but with me it's more a matter of intuition."

Sergeant Patrick smiled broadly. "Just between the two of us, I'll go with your intuition every time. But, as we both know, intuition gets a rather unreceptive reaction in a court of law."

"Oh, I know. I know."

It was early Monday morning, and the two detectives were headed toward the far northeast section of Detroit. They were continuing their investigation into the disappearance of a twelve-year-old girl who, when last seen, had been selling Girl Scout cookies door-to-door.

"My intuition aside, what makes you think we should return to the Sommers' home?"

"Well," Patrick's brow furrowed, "first off, the Sommers' house is the last place we've been able to trace her. Sommers admits she called at his house and that he bought a box of cookies. But after that she just vanishes."

"Of course she could have been picked up by a motorist." Morris played devil's advocate. "Or something could have happened to her at the next house she called at. Wherever that might have been. Even though the Fifteenth Precinct team hasn't uncovered anything, it doesn't necessarily prove the girl didn't continue beyond the Sommers' home."

"I know, Marge. But there were all those cubbyholes that Sommers had recently built into the walls. I got to thinking about them last night. I could hardly sleep; I couldn't get them out of my mind."

"Well, we've got our search warrant. We'll soon see."

The two were silent for several minutes. The police radio crackled almost incessantly. But none of the calls related to them.

"It's a pity we had to put the seminary investigation on the back burner," reflected Morris. "It could happen again, you know."

"What?"

"I mean it's perfectly possible for another priest on the faculty to be attacked, maybe fatally."

"I know," said Patrick, "but the leads just petered out. We've looked just about everywhere. Besides, it's been a few weeks now since the last attempt. Maybe it's over. If it is, we're lucky no lives were lost."

There was another short period of silence.

"How about that Roman Kirkus, that head of the Tridentine Society?" Morris said. "Wasn't he something else!"

"Yeah." Patrick chuckled. "I think he might be able to wage a successful, if limited, war with that arsenal in his house."

"Yes, but everything's legal. Everything that needs registration is registered."

"Cocky son of a bitch, too." Patrick turned a corner and slowed the car. They were nearing the Sommers home. "He makes no bones about his hatreds. And all the while, he claims he's a good Catholic."

"More like Super Catholic."

"Yeah, with friends like Kirkus, the Catholics don't

need any enemies. The creepy thing is that a guy like Kirkus could be dangerously violent."

"Well, anyway, I hope the seminary caper is finished. I'd hate to imagine the event that would revive it."

"You mean another attack."

Patrick nodded. The car glided to a stop at the curb directly in front of the Sommers house.

The detectives climbed the front stairs. Morris stood to one side as Patrick rang the doorbell. Paul Sommers came to the door. Patrick presented and explained the warrant to Sommers, who seemed perturbed.

"Mr. Sommers," said Patrick, "I would like you to show us again those storage nooks you recently constructed."

Sommers began the tour on the first floor. As they made the rounds, Patrick carefully studied the man's demeanor. When they reached a large boarded-up storage space on the second floor, Sommers' agitation was obvious.

Wordlessly, Patrick looked around the room, then at Sommers. "Mr. Sommers, would you show us what is in that storage area?" Sommers did not answer, nor meet the policeman's gaze; his eyes were on a nearby hammer. Patrick picked up the hammer and pried a wall board loose. With some difficulty, he pulled himself through the narrow opening. In the dark interior, he smelled death. He switched on his flashlight. In the gloomy triangle formed by the eaves and the roof, something was wrapped in an old raincoat. Patrick pulled open the coat.

There lay the nude remains of a twelve-year-old who had wanted only to sell Girl Scout cookies.

Patrick worked himself out of the fetid hole. He nodded at Morris, looked impassively at Sommers, then removed a card from his wallet and began to read.

"You have the right to remain silent. . . ."

"Are you sure you want to be partners with Rafe?" asked Bill Zimmer.

"Yes, I really do," Lennie Marks replied. "That is, if you don't mind."

"Don't be silly; of course I don't mind. But it's apt to make the game a bit uneven."

"That's all right with me if it's O.K. with you."

Marks and Zimmer had arrived at St. Joseph's Seminary early for their scheduled racquetball game with Raphael Doody and Herb Wygoski. While waiting for the others, they were warming up in the indoor court.

While Marks almost worshiped Zimmer and literally owed what little academic success he had to Zimmer's tutoring, Lennie reserved a special admiration for two others: Brother Alphonsus, fellow member of, and frequent visitor to the Tridentine Society, and Raphael Doody, also a member of the Society and a deacon about to become a priest.

Alphonsus and Doody shared with Marks an innate awkwardness and a propensity to prove the omnipresence of Murphy's Law. On the positive side, Alphonsus and Doody were successful in fields usually beyond the attainment of the awkward of mind and body. The former was able to address and motivate the Tridentine Society; the latter would become a priest—if Murphy's Law were temporarily suspended.

Wygoski and Doody arrived almost simultaneously and climbed down the ladder into the court.

"Howdy," said Wygoski.

"What?" said Doody.

"Howdy Doody," said Wygoski, breaking himself, and no one else, up.

"Don't pick on him, Herb," Zimmer admonished.

"Why should I place myself outside the mainstream of American life?" retorted Wygoski.

"Leave him alone, Herb," said Marks. "After all, he's a deacon."

"I beg thy pardon, Reverend Mister Howdy Doody." Wygoski bowed.

"C'mon, get warmed up," Zimmer urged. "It's going to be you and I against Lennie and Rafe."

"You're kidding!" said Wygoski.

"No, that's it."

"The slaughter of the innocents."

Wygoski and Zimmer pounded the ball against the court's four walls. Marks and Doody found a corner at the rear of the court where Doody lectured his protege.

"This is a good idea, Lennie. You and Bill should keep coming out here to St. Joe's frequently. After all, you'll be students here next year and you should get used not only to the surroundings, but you should be familiar with the other students and the faculty. That way, when you get here next year—ouch!"

"Sorry, Rafe," said Wygoski, "but if you're going to just stand around in a racquetball court, odds are you're going to get hit with the ball."

"O.K., O.K.," said Doody, "it wasn't intentional. Let's get started."

"Don't you want to warm up?" asked Zimmer.

"I don't think that will be necessary," said Doody. "Let's go."

"Have it your way," said Wygoski. "You can have the starting service." It may be the last time you serve, he added under his breath.

Doody dropped the ball against the floor. As it bounded back for the serve, he missed it. He repeated this unusual feat several times. Wygoski fought for self-control. Finally, Doody successfully served. Wygoski played the ball off the rear wall and hit Marks squarely on the derriere.

"Ouch!" Marks rubbed his cheek.

"Hindrance!" Wygoski called.

Doody served again. Zimmer played it off the side wall and nailed it near the base of the front wall. The ball skittered along the floor, unplayable.

The two teams changed places.

Wygoski served; Doody missed with his forehand. Again, Marks missed a backhand. Again, Marks missed a forehand. Again, Doody missed a backhand.

With the score 4–0, Wygoski's next serve split the middle of the court, where Marks and Doody collided. They went down in a tangle of arms and legs.

"Are you hurt?" Zimmer ran solicitously to the heap of bodies.

"No, no, we're O.K.," said Doody as he tried to disentangle himself from Marks.

Wygoski served again. Marks' return barely made the front wall. But the ball was in play. Wygoski, surprised at this departure from routine failure, lunged for the weak spot, barely caught the ball after its first bounce and barely returned it to the wall.

Doody raced at top speed from the rear court. He missed the ball, but slammed into the wall. He staggered back three steps and collapsed.

"Is he all right? Are you all right?" shouted Marks. "Oh, I never should have returned that serve!"

"He's all right," Zimmer assured all after checking Doody. "He's just unconscious."

Wygoski shook his head. "All things considered, I guess that was about as long a game as we could have expected."

"This is one Fallopian tube," said Father Gennardo, as he drew two parallel lines on the chalkboard, "and this is the other Fallopian tube."

"They look like two-inch sewer pipe," whispered one student to his neighbor.

"I thought this was a course on the theology of human sexuality," whispered another, "and here the professor is drawing dirty pictures."

"If these are the dirtest pictures you ever saw," whispered the first, "you'll have to go through life in blinders."

"This is one ovary, and this is the other." Gennardo continued his diagraming.

"They look like eggs," quietly observed Lennie Marks, who was auditing the class.

"That's what they produce," replied Bill Zimmer, also auditing.

"Oh."

"This is the uterus, the cervix, and the vagina." Gennardo snorted. "Now, monthly, the ovary releases an egg, which is picked up by the Fallopian tube—"

"Excuse me, Father . . ." Raphael Doody raised his hand.

"Yes?"

"It doesn't look as if the ovary and the Fallopian tube are connected."

"They aren't."

"Then why doesn't the egg just fall in the woman's stomach?"

Laughter from the class.

"It doesn't." Was Gennardo blushing? With his swarthy complexion, it was difficult to tell. "Now, if the egg is penetrated by sperm while passing through the Fallopian tube, fertilization takes place. The fertilized egg implants itself in the lining—called the endometrium—of the womb, and the fetus begins to develop."

"Excuse me, Father."

Gennardo sighed. "What is it, Doody?"

"How does it get in there?"

"What?"

"The sperm."

Laughter from the class.

"Kulinski," Gennardo snorted and pointed simultaneously, "you seem to be laughing the hardest; why don't you explain for Doody?"

"The man screws his wife," Kulinski explained.

More laughter. The situation was getting away from Gennardo.

"Huh?" asked a bewildered Doody.

"Could you be less graphic and more technical?" asked Gennardo.

"He inserts his penis into her vagina and has an——"

"Oh, now I remember," Doody interrupted, "an organism."

"An orgasm!" Gennardo roared.

More laughter.

"Doody!" Gennardo called out over the laughter, "no more questions, or out on your ear you go.

"Now settle down!" He snorted.

"Now, then, fellas," he proceeded, "the important thing, theologically, is that nothing may interrupt or interfere with the integrity of this action. No mechanical or artificial means may be used to block the sperm from the tube, or to kill the sperm, nor may the sperm be ejaculated anywhere but in the vagina—yes, Kulinski?"

"Nobody believes that anymore."

"The Pope does, so you'd better too, Buster."

"It's not infallible."

"It's the ordinary magisterium."

"So if I don't believe it, I'm not a heretic."

"No; you're just wrong."

Kulinski shook his head.

"Doody?" It was more a threat than an invitation.

"I was wondering, Father: I have this problem at night occasionally. And when I wake up in the morning—"

"Doody!"

"I find that my pajamas—"

"Out, Doody!"

"—are wet, and—"

"OUT, Doody!"

Laughter.

The bell sounded. Gennardo fixed Doody with a furious gaze, lit a cigarette, snorted smoke through his nostrils, and angrily stamped out. A small group of students gathered in front of the room.

"I'm not surprised," said Zimmer. "I didn't think anybody still took artificial birth control seriously."

"Gennardo is antediluvian," Kulinski explained

"You mean Father is wrong?" Marks shook his head. "This is very confusing."

"It's just that Vatican II hit some of these older geezers pretty hard. A few were pretty crotchety to start with. The theology explosion just sent them off the deep end."

Kulinski led the foursome out of the room and into the inner courtyard, where they sat on a bench. The water in the pool in the center of the courtyard rippled occasionally as one or another of the large goldfish surfaced in search of food.

"Gennardo's not alone," Kulinski renewed the conversation. "Guys like Budreau, Dye, and O'Dowd—even Flinty Feeny—were here from the beginning of the forerunner to this seminary. For a lot of years, they taught a nineteenth-century theology. Things like 'probabilism' and 'intrinsic evil' and that crazy 'ordinary magisterium.' Well, it's like Bill here said, nobody believes in that stuff anymore . . . nobody, that is, with the exception of a few guys who should have been put on the shelf long ago. I don't know how they're able to coexist with the younger faculty members. By and large, the younger ones are up to date."

"Hey, wait a minute," said Zimmer, "that's a pretty full shelf you've got there, Dick. Not *all* the older guys belong in retirement, would you say?"

"Well, O.K.: O'Dowd tries to keep up. And Dye is, at most, harmless. And they are nice enough.

"But they certainly don't have the same fresh approach to theology that the younger faculty has."

"I'm with Lennie," said Doody. "I find this all very confusing."

"You didn't take those sex orientation classes, did you, Rafe?" asked Kulinski.

"No." Doody blushed.

"Too bad. You would have learned a lot about things like wet dreams," said Kulinski. "Come with me, Scooby-Dooby-Doody. I have some pictures in my room that will open up a whole new world for you."

"You'd better go too, Lennie," Zimmer urged Marks.

That very afternoon, Marks and Doody would learn what separates the boys from the girls. This information would have no effect whatsoever on the incidence of nocturnal pollution.

With the possible exception of the police chaplain, Father Koesler knew his way around police headquarters better than any other clergyman, indeed almost as well as any Detroit police officer. But his familiarity with the place was, as with St. Paul's call to apostleship, as one born out of due time.

The early years of his priesthood had been spent in an undistinguished manner. He had been ordained for parish service in the Archdiocese of Detroit. Over the following years, he had been assigned to several parishes as an assistant pastor. He had also concomitantly spent twelve of those years as editor-in-chief of the *Detroit Catholic*.

Late in his career as editor, he had incidentally become involved in the police investigation of a series of murders of area priests and nuns. Then, while pastor of St. Anselm's, he had been called upon by his friend, Inspector Koznicki, to participate in the investigation of two other homicide cases, each involving the local Catholic scene.

In the course of these investigations, Koesler had become conversant with police procedure, as well as the routine of police headquarters at 1300 Beaubien in the heart of downtown Detroit.

Koesler now strode confidently down the fifth floor corridor of headquarters until he reached the central office of the Homicide Division. He asked for Inspector Koznicki, then waited for the return of the sergeant who served as the Inspector's secretary. He was promptly ushered into his friend's office.

"I hope I'm not intruding. I was down at Ren Cen and decided to take a chance of finding you in."

"Not at all, Father. Always a pleasure to see you."

"I was wondering if there are any further developments in our seminary case."

"As a matter of fact, Father, yes. But we do not yet know what to make of it."

Koesler, immediately attentive, took a chair near Koznicki's desk.

"You will recall," Koznicki began, "the incident involving Father Sklarski outside Robinson's Cleaners . . . the one that may or may not be part of the series of attacks against seminary professors?"

Koesler nodded eagerly.

"Then you will recall that one of the people our men apprehended happens to be a neighborhood gang leader we have been after for a long time. We now have him on so many charges that he has decided to be somewhat cooperative in the hope of winning some concessions from the prosecutor's office.

"By the way, would you care for some coffee? Tea?"

Koesler shook his head.

"Well," Koznicki continued, "he swears—and I tend to believe him—that they had no intention of assaulting Father Sklarski. They are very aware of the routines followed by most of the priests at the seminary. But, by and large, they never considered the little they could hope to gain from the mugging of a priest worth the risk they would have to take of being apprehended."

"Then what—?"

"I come to that, Father. He claims that word was put out that 'a white dude' probably dressed in black would be in that vicinity and would have something on his person worth stealing. And, of course, a gun would be a desired object."

"But . . . who put out the word?"

"Unfortunately, the message had been passed through so many in the neighborhood that we have found it impossible to trace it to its source."

"Well," Koesler sat back with a bemused look, "isn't that interesting!"

"Yes, it is. But did you notice the mention of how

the neighborhood has taken cognizance of the routines followed by your priest faculty?"

Koesler nodded.

"And you will recall the importance we have placed on these very routines. These attacks have quite obviously been preceded by an enormous amount of surveillance. Who but someone who had spent hours planning would know, for example, that you always eat at the seminary on Friday evenings?"

"Certainly, Inspector, you have a point. I could not dispute it."

"Then, Father, it would stand to reason that, at least while this investigation continues, it would be well for the professors if they were to break their routines. Do things at unpredictable, unplanned, other-than-usual times."

Koesler began to laugh. Slowly, he brought himself back under control.

"Excuse me, Inspector," the priest shook out a clean handkerchief and began wiping his glasses, "but of all God's creatures, I believe we priests are among the most dedicated slaves to routine. At least priests of my generation and older. Our entire seminary training was planned to make us creatures of habit. 'Keep the rule and the rule will keep you.' We rose at the same time. Went to meditation and Mass at the same time. Dined —if you could call it that—went to class, studied, prayed, played, and retired at the same time every day. A bell ruled our lives.

"It was an ingenious system. And it produced slaves to routine: most of us still organize our lives compulsively in tight little routines. We say Mass at the same time every day. Arrange our class schedules for the same time. The second Tuesday of each month the parish council meets. The third Sunday of the month is for infant baptism. And on Friday evenings," Koesler paused and smiled as he put his glasses back on, "I eat dinner at the seminary.

"Some of the younger priests, especially those ordained in recent years, escaped our seminary regimen and can hang a bit more loose. But I assure you, Inspector, most of the priests now on the faculty of the seminary could break their habits of life as easily as a leopard could change its spots."

"Not even to save your lives?"

"Not for any reason. I firmly believe the formation of a habit-filled life is quite beyond our control. We must live with our habits."

"Apparently, Father, our assailant is aware of this and is taking advantage of it." Koznicki smoothed his bushy dark mustache with an index finger so large it seemed the equal of two fingers on anyone else's hand. "And that leaves us with one unpleasant if inescapable conclusion."

Koesler looked at Koznicki quizzically.

"We must become familiar with the routines of the seminary clerical faculty . . . at least as familiar with them as our assailant apparently is."

There was silence as the Inspector's words sank in.

"I'd better help you with this one," Koesler suggested. "I'll try to break this news to my confreres gently. I know from experience they will not take lightly what I am sure they will consider an invasion of their privacy."

"Then, that is a good idea, and I am grateful for your help, Father. Try to impress on the other Fathers that this is for their protection. An ounce of prevention, you know."

"*I* know. Now to convince *them*."

"Good luck, Father."

"Pray for me."

Koesler said it with a straight face. Koznicki smiled at the role reversal.

It was just 11:30 A.M., the regular hour for Father Gennardo's period of meditation. He entered the seminary's inner courtyard and began pacing the worn brick walkway.

The path would take him around and around in the squared circle.

The Gospel reading at this morning's Mass had been the Sermon on the Mount, or the Beatitudes. Gennardo decided, based on that reading, to meditate on the spirit of poverty.

Under the Sulpician method of meditation, he tried to conjure up an appropriate scene from the Gospels. He zeroed in on the Nativity. A traditional crèche came to mind. In his mind's eye he saw the mother and newborn child with Joseph protecting them. He saw the animals warming the three humans. He saw the snow. And, at this point, his stream of consciousness betrayed him.

The snow put him in mind of the light dusting of snow that had been added last night to the three inches already on the ground. It was only midday, but already it was trampled and gray.

This vision in turn led him to the memory of a time and place in his past wherein the snows of winter fell in unblemished blankets and remained white and smooth as a coverlet all season. That would have been at the erstwhile St. John's Seminary of happy memory. St. John's Seminary and the relatively uncluttered era of the 1950s and '60s. That was a time to remember!

The memories came flooding in. There was the beginning of it all on that bitter cold day in 1948 when Bishop Francis Haas of Grand Rapids dedicated the cornerstone. He had told a shivering crowd that this occasion marked "the Church's coming of age in Michigan."

If that were, indeed, the coming of age for the Catholic Church in Michigan, Gennardo meditated, maturation had peaked a bit early. For now, the Michigan Church was decidedly going downhill, at least as far as the clergy were concerned. Currently, there were not enough seminarians to keep even these modest buildings open. If not for the nonseminarian students, the

Archdiocese probably would have had to retrench again, and move into still less commodious buildings.

Lost in thought, Gennardo unconsciously quickened his pace.

He had completely lost his fanciful nativity scene. But the late St. John's Seminary was coming in clearly. He could almost smell the newness of the buildings.

For no particular reason, he recalled one early morning when the seminarian leading morning prayers turned too many pages just before the end, and concluded with the final words of evening prayers, "Let us offer up the sleep we are about to take in union with that which Jesus took while on earth." And that just prior to meditation period! It turned out that was just about the final straw for that young man. Stupid young man. It did not take us long to know that he did everything wrong. Nor did it take us long to dismiss him.

There was a loud 'ping'; a patch of plaster exploded just above Gennardo's head. Gennardo, lost in thought, paced on, accelerating ever so slightly.

Then there was the lad who broke everything—well, almost everything—he touched. Gennardo couldn't recall his name. But he could visualize the trail of demolished articles the seminarian had left in his wake. It had not taken the faculty long to advise him to look elsewhere for a career. Imagine! He would have been an absolute menace to any parish he might have been assigned to.

But that, of course, was another time and another faculty. The lout might even have been able to be ordained with the present faculty and today's need for priests. He could rely only on Ly Feeny and Al Budreau to join with him when it was time to stand firm for high standards for seminarians.

There was another loud 'ping' as something thwacked into the wood paneling just behind Gennardo. He turned briefly to look behind him. No one else was in the courtyard. He shrugged and continued pacing.

Of course, to be perfectly fair, we didn't catch all the loony tunes even back in the good old days, thought Gennardo. There was the young man who, just weeks before his scheduled ordination, sent a postcard, of all things, to the Chancery, addressed, "To whom it may concern," advising that he and his parents were planning a European trip after his ordination, and asking for an extended vacation before his first assignment. There had been some long, stormy faculty meetings attended by several priests from the Chancery regarding *that* young man. Eventually, he was ordained. And, while he *was* a priest, his career had been on the underside of mediocre.

There was another decidedly noticeable 'ping,' as a patch of gravel behind Father Gennardo's left heel kicked high into the air. Some of it splattered into the pool, startling the goldfish. Gennardo glanced at the water and noted its troubled surface. He looked up at the ceiling, but could see nothing indicating anything had fallen.

He lit a cigarette and continued pacing.

The pudgy man in black began to curse under his breath. How could he miss at this range? He stood in the shadows of the balcony overlooking the courtyard. He didn't know how many bullets he had left. He had been so proud of the silencer he had been able to purchase. But what good was it if he couldn't hit his target?

Maybe it was because he was using only one hand. Of course; that was it! He remembered all those TV movies: cops always held their weapon in both hands and stood with their feet apart, and then fired. They usually hit their target, too.

The man assumed the legendary stance, and waited for Gennardo to complete the square and come into view again.

Then there was the firebug, Gennardo mused. When he wasn't starting a blaze someplace in the seminary, he was pulling a false alarm. It had taken a goodly amount of time and effort to discover the culprit, but when we found him, out on his ear he went. Faster than he could strike a match. Of course, *he* wouldn't be kept in the seminary even today. There may be a drastic need for priests, and the present faculty may be lax when it comes to standards, but even today, no one would contend we should ordain a pyromaniac.

Another loud 'ping' and below the surface of the pool was a goldfish that would never flutter another gill. Gennardo looked up intently. At long last, still unable to detect any irregularity in the ceiling, he walked on.

Then there was the lad, Gennardo reminisced, who, during noon prayers, when the prayer-hall was crowded with seminarians, unleashed a mouse. The room was filled with squirming students—all trying to evade the scurrying little creature. Ly Feeny had been furious. We kept our eyes on *that* student and, eventually, had a sufficient case to get rid of him. Imagine what he might have done if we had let him loose in a parish! Probably done the same at a Rosary Altar meeting.

Poor ladies!

The little man in black was beside himself. He just couldn't go back to the group having failed again. They would remind him that his task was as simple as shooting fish in a barrel. And he would have to confess that that is exactly what he had accomplished. He looked at his weapon in disgust. He considered hitting it. He was, after all, a top-thumper: When things did not work—a normal experience in his life—he would usually thump them on the top.

Well, why not? He thumped the gun. It accidentally discharged.

Father Gennardo half spun and fell heavily to the ground. He did not move. Blood began to seep from his upper torso onto the bricks.

The little man could scarcely believe his eyes. He stared at Gennardo's inert form. He could not describe how he felt. Certainly not any single emotion. Some combination of exhilaration and shame. He had better put as much distance between himself and this scene in as brief a time as he possibly could. He separated the silencer from the pistol, pocketed both, and fled.

As far as could tell, no one had seen him.

As the EMS van sped along West Outer Drive toward Mt. Carmel, the driver phoned the hospital security guard, who, in turn, notified the emergency room. A Code One—gunshot—designation alerted the hospital's trauma team. Thus twelve medical attendants were on hand to greet Father Gennardo's unconscious form. Five doctors, five nurses, an anesthetist, and a respiratory care expert went to work on the priest.

They were followed by an agitated Father Albert Budreau, who had found Gennardo and had closely trailed the EMS van to the hospital. Now, violet stole over his left hand and a ball of cotton in his right, Budreau was trying to catch up with the gurney disappearing into the trauma room. Budreau scooted through the doors in the gurney's wake.

"Is it all right if I give him the Sacrament of the Sick?" Budreau felt a bit defensive.

"Yes, of course. But try to stay out of our way. We've got to find out what's wrong." Dr. Sam Blackford, chief resident surgeon, was, at best, an agnostic. On the odd occasion when a priest was a patient in emergency, Blackford was used to having several other priests attending to spiritual care. He didn't mind. If they believed in religion sufficiently to be priests, they deserved whatever consolation they got out of this blessing.

It still wasn't as bad as when a cop was admitted. Then there were so many other police in attendance, it was difficult for the trauma team to get close to the victim.

"Per istam sanctam unctionem et suam piisimam misericordiam, indulgeat tibi Dominus quidquid per visum deliquisti, Amen." Budreau made the sign of the

cross with the oil on both closed eyelids, then wiped away the oil with the cotton.

"The entrance was right here, under the scapular," said Blackford. "It looks like a small caliber."

"I'm giving Father the anointing in the old Latin. He would like that," Budreau gratuitously explained.

"That's nice," said Dr. Blackford.

Budreau traced a cross with oil on Gennardo's ears. *"Per istam sanctam unctionem et suam piisimam misericordiam, indulgeat tibi Dominus quidquid per auditum deliquisti, Amen."*

"We're in luck," said Blackford, "here's the exit just above the clavicle. But there's been a bit of exsanguination. Better get a tube in there."

"Exsanguination, Tony," Budreau explained, "that means bleeding."

"He can't hear you," said Blackford with some asperity, "he's in shock. Can you hurry it up, please!"

"Oh, certainly. Sorry." Budreau rapidly finished the anointing: *". . . atque Ecclesiae tuae sanctae, cum omni desiderata prosperitate restituas. Per Christum Dominum nostrum. Amen."*

Budreau left the trauma room. Several minutes later, Dr. Blackford emerged. It was his turn to be surprised. He had not expected to find a crowd waiting for word on his patient's condition. He recognized Inspector Koznicki, Sergeants Morris and Patrick, and Pat Lennon and Joe Cox. He noted Budreau, but did not know his name. And there was something vaguely familiar about the tall priest. Hadn't his picture been in the papers some time ago?"

"How is he?" asked Koznicki.

"Right now," said Blackford, "not bad, for having been shot."

"Thank God," said the tall priest, whom Blackford would later discover was Father Robert Koesler.

"He was exsanguinating," Budreau volunteered.

Blackford sighed. A little learning could be boresome.

"Was he actually shot?" Cox asked. "How many times?"

"One bullet entered his back just below the neck to the right of center. The exit was through the front of the right shoulder."

"How much trauma?" asked Lennon.

"One lung was collapsed. There was bleeding in the chest cavity. I'd say he lost about 600 ccs. But his respiration and blood pressure now are near normal."

"What's the treatment?" Lennon asked.

"We've inflated the lung and drained the blood. We've dressed the wounds. We're treating him for shock."

"What's the prognosis?" asked Cox.

"He'll be in ICU for at least the next couple of days. We'll be watching for pneumonia.

"All in all, he is a very fortunate man. Just about everything that might have gone wrong didn't."

"Murphy must have been asleep at the switch," murmured the tall priest.

"What's that?"

"Nothing."

"When can he be released?" asked Budreau.

"If there are no complications, I'd say in the next seven to nine days."

"You mean you won't have to operate?" Budreau enthused. "You mean his system will repair all that internal damage?"

"Remarkable instrument, the body, isn't it?" Blackford began edging away. Experience told him he had answered all the relevant questions.

"Inspector," Lennon turned her attention to Koznicki, "is this another in the series of assaults against seminary faculty members?"

"It is too early to say, Miss Lennon. But, for the time being, we are assuming it is."

"Any leads?" asked Cox. Both reporters had been writing assiduously in their notepads.

"Yes," said Koznicki, "several. I am not at liberty to discuss them."

"Any suspects?" asked Lennon.

"No. Not as yet. But," Koznicki saw a tall black officer advancing down the hall, "here is Lieutenant Harris. I believe he has just come from the scene of the crime."

'How's the priest?" Harris asked as he joined the group.

"He exsanguinated," Budreau noted.

"I beg your pardon?"

"He is one of our more fortunate gunshot victims, it seems," clarified Koznicki. "He should recover quite nicely."

"That's good. How many slugs did he take?"

"One."

"One? One! That courtyard back at the seminary looks like a shooting gallery. We found five slugs. We would have found only four, but then we spotted the floating fish."

"Floating fish?" Sergeant Patrick wondered aloud.

"Yeah . . . one of the bullets got a goldfish. Whoever did must've squeezed off five fast ones and didn't much care what he hit as long as one of them got the priest."

"What caliber?" asked Lennon.

".22. They're off at Ballistics now."

"Come on," Harris gestured to Patrick and Morris, "let's get back to the seminary and ask some more questions."

"Were there any eyewitnesses?" Koznicki asked as Harris turned to leave.

"Negative. It's a peculiar place . . . I'll have to talk to you about that later." Harris loped off to catch up with the other two detectives.

Cox and Lennon closed their notebooks. They too, would go to the scene of the crime, continuing to cover the story for their competing newspapers.

"Remarkable, that the human body can heal itself so well," Budreau mumbled as he departed.

Koznicki and Koesler were the only ones remaining.

"I think I know what Lieutenant Harris is going to tell you," said Koesler. "The problem that Sacred Heart Seminary presents is that crime is so rampant in that neighborhood that the attacks at the seminary simply fit in the general picture.

"Now, St. Joseph's Seminary is not located in a high crime neighborhood. But Sacred Heart has comparatively few students around, whereas St. Joseph's has about a hundred more students . . . though more than half are not studying for the priesthood. And they come in all sizes and shapes. Men, women, young, and old. It would be very easy for an intruder to blend into that potpourri."

"And you, Father, could you blend into that potpourri?"

"Me?"

"Yes. It seems that, for whatever reason, our assailant has moved his base of operations from Sacred Heart to St. Joseph's. It also seems that his pattern is such that none of the previous targets will be attacked again. If we are correct in our assessment, this affords you a sort of immunity. Is it possible for you to join the faculty at St. Joseph's Seminary and continue to be our special representative?"

Koesler pondered.

"Well, yes as a matter of fact. Father Feeny had asked me to teach a course in communications. I've been reluctant because of parish duties, and the course I teach at Sacred Heart uses up just about all my remaining time."

"As a special favor, could you stretch yourself a tad thinner?"

Koesler pondered a few more moments, then broke into a smile. "How could I resist your charm, Inspector?"

"How, indeed?" Koznicki's smile ran from ear to ear.

"You never stop plotting, do you, Inspector?"
"The Polish mind never rests."

Father Koesler was running behind. That sudden call earlier from Inspector Koznicki to meet at Mt. Carmel's emergency room had thrown a monkeywrench into his day. The time spent at the hospital had mangled his schedule. And Koesler was a scheduled man.

To cap the climax, he had just finished counseling a recently divorced parishioner. She had dropped in without an appointment, but he hadn't the heart to turn her away even though he was running so far behind.

She was an attractive blonde in her late thirties whose world had collapsed. She had been married nineteen years. Her husband, whose law career was climbing nicely, had fallen in love with a younger woman. Her image of her self-worth had disintegrated. She felt undesirable, unattractive, and worthless. Now, fifteen years out of the work force, she would have to find employment. The alimony would not cover her living expenses. Her fractured self-image was no help as she sought employment.

Koesler promised he would try to help her find a job. He tried to reassure her of her value as a still attractive and talented woman with much of her life still ahead.

It was one of those times when he hoped he had performed a service simply by listening sympathetically. Sometimes it helped when a troubled person was able to get it off his or her chest.

He put the leftover stew on the stove to heat while he showered and shaved preliminary to tonight's parish council meeting. Terminating this day's events with a parish council meeting insured that this would not be among his better evenings.

He ladled some stew onto a plate, turned on the TV, and sat down to try to enjoy a hurried dinner.

It was too late for the local news; only about fifteen minutes of the national remained.

Russia was still being cavalier with her satellites. Much of Asia and Africa went underfed. And many industries throughout the U.S. were still polluting the air, water, and earth.

Nothing had changed.

He wondered if the special talent needed for tele-news reporting might be the ability to write approximately the same thing day after day using only slightly different words.

Koesler's fork stopped midway between plate and mouth as his attention was grabbed by a familiar dateline.

"And in Detroit," Max Robinson, the network anchorman, was saying, "an all-too-common story—attempted murder. But an unlikely victim: A Catholic priest, a professor in a Catholic seminary. And, to make things worse, today's victim is only another in a series of priests as targets. In Detroit, WXYZ-TV's Ven Marshall has the story."

The serious, handsome face of Ven Marshall appeared onscreen.

"Four, perhaps five Detroit priests share a common and undesired distinction," the Ed Murrow sound-alike intoned, "each has been the target of what police describe as a bizarre murder plot.

"Until now, the attacks have been foiled by a series of odd circumstances. But today, the assailant's luck changed—at least slightly. Father Anthony Gennardo, professor of theology at Detroit's St. Joseph Seminary, was shot while praying in this inner courtyard."

The camera panned, showing viewers the courtyard, then returned to Marshall.

"Here with me now is the priest who discovered Father Gennardo's body, Father Albert Budreau."

The camera switched to an obviously perturbed Budreau.

"How did you happen to find the body, Father?"

"Well, when Tony—Father Gennardo—didn't show up for lunch—there are a group of us who ordinarily sit together—sort of charter members of the faculty of the major seminary—well, when he didn't show up, I got worried."

"But how did you happen to find the body?"

"Well, Father Gennardo has a habit of meditating in this courtyard for half an hour precisely—from 11:30 until noon. I was sure he would be here. But I had no notion what had happened to him."

"We should say, at this point, that Father Gennardo escaped serious permanent injury."

"Miraculously."

"Eh? Oh . . . yes. Doctors at Mt. Carmel Mercy Hospital report that Father Gennardo's condition is good. That he is improving and should be released within two weeks.

"How was he went you found him, Father?"

"Exsanguinating."

"What? I mean, was he conscious?"

"No, no. Unconscious."

"But is it your understanding that he has regained consciousness?"

"Oh, yes. But he said he didn't see his assailant."

The camera returned to Marshall, who looked as if Budreau had told him more than he wanted to know.

"Police state," Marshall concluded, "that they are following several leads in this series of attempts on the lives of priests in Detroit. However, they have no likely suspects as yet.

"This is Ven Marshall, Channel 7 Action News, in Detroit."

Koesler finished his stew, turned off the TV, and headed for his meeting.

Poor Detroit, he thought; so many good, hopeful things going on, but only our dirty linen makes the national news. It was always thus: no one cares about the millions of cats that do not get stuck in trees.

*   *   *

The shades had been lowered, making the small room nearly dark.

"The good news, I suppose, is that you hit him," said the First Man. "But did you have to shoot five times? It makes us look ridiculous."

"I was nervous," the Second Man mumbled.

"As far as I'm concerned," said the Third Man, menacingly, "there is no good news. Not only did you not kill him, you didn't even wound him seriously. Better *he* should have pulled the trigger and *you* should be slowly recovering."

"Now, now," said the Fourth Man soothingly, "let's not be too harsh. After all, for the first time we've drawn blood."

"That's just it," said the Second.

"What's it?" asked the Fourth.

"The blood," said the Second, "I don't know. It's . . . when I saw it . . . I mean, all the time we were planning this, and even in the first phase of our plan, everything seemed so—what?—clinical. So cut-and-dried. So removed from reality. I guess I just thought we would never actually harm anyone. You know how it is with us."

The other three shifted uncomfortably.

"But today," the Second continued, "when Father Gennardo fell and then I saw his blood flowing out of him, it dawned on me what we were doing. I'm still convinced we're justified. But I can't play the role of executioner anymore. I can't, I just can't pull another trigger."

"But you're still with us?" asked the Fourth Man.

"Yes, yes, of course I'm still with you."

"The question then," the Fourth said, "is who among us will carry on?"

"I will," said the First and Third Men simultaneously.

"That's good lads." The Fourth Man smiled. "But we can't have two. We'll have to draw lots." He nodded at the Second Man, who rose from his chair and walked to the closet, tripping over the floor lamp en route.

He returned with two broomstraws held in his right fist. The First Man, followed by the Third, pulled a straw. They compared straws. All sighed.

"They're the same size!" said the First Man disgustedly.

"Can't you do *anything* right?" asked the Third, rhetorically.

"They looked different when I pulled them from the broom." The Second Man sounded close to tears.

"That's all right . . . we'll draw cards." The Fourth Man reached for a deck of cards on a nearby end table. As he started to pick them up, the cards scattered to the floor. The First and Third Men hurried to retrieve them, bumping heads in the process.

"Why don't you look where you're going!" said the Third Man.

"I was here first," the First protested.

"That's all right," said the Fourth, "just give them to me."

The First and Third Men laid their separate piles on the table before the Fourth.

The Fourth shuffled the cards again and again, occasionally fumbling them, then scooping them up. Finally, he spread the cards face down on the table.

The First Man turned over a card. "The Ace of Spades." He smiled. "The Death Card."

With an air of desperation, the Third Man fingered another card and flipped it over. "The Ace of Spades," he said wonderingly.

There was silence.

"A pinochle deck!" the Second Man finally observed disgustedly.

"Damn!" commented the First.

"Draw again," the Fourth suggested.

The First Man drew. "The Queen of Hearts."

The Third Man drew. "The King of Clubs."

"Then it's done," said the Fourth. "But it must be clear that we are in this together. How say you?"

"Together," affirmed the First.

"Yes," said the Second.

"Of course: together," said the Third.

"Good," said the Fourth. "We may just need total collaboration to carry out our plan. It is very possible that the reason we have not yet been totally successful is because we have sent only one of our number into the field of battle."

"Wait," protested the Third Man, "I don't need any help. I can carry this out by myself."

"We know how you feel." The Fourth Man waved his hand. In doing so, he knocked over a glass. Fortunately, it was empty, yet the others momentarily recoiled as if to avoid the nonexistent liquid. In doing so, the Second Man's chair tipped, spilling him to the floor. He quickly righted the chair and seated himself again.

"But," the Fourth Man continued, "you must remember that humility is truth—and the truth is that we very often need help. I think we should make this a group effort even if one of our members must play the main role. How say you?"

"I agree," said the First Man.

"Yes, a group effort," said the Second.

"Oh, all right," said the Third.

"And," continued the Fourth, "while we are on the topic of doing things together, there is a meeting of the Tridentine Society next week. Will we all be there?" He gazed pointedly at the Second Man.

"I'm planning on it," said the First.

"So soon? I didn't know. But, yes, I'll be there," said the Third.

The Second Man was silent.

"Well?" asked the Fourth.

"I'm afraid not, if you don't mind," the Second said apologetically.

"Same old reason?"

"I just don't agree with the Society. Don't get me wrong: I believe in our cause. But the Tridentines sometimes oppose the Second Vatican Council."

"And well they should!" the Third Man snarled. "It was the work of the devil!"

"The work of the devil?" The Second Man verged on forcefulness. "It was called by a holy Pope of God!"

"John XXIII!" the Third exclaimed, "he should have been strangled in his crib!"

"You shouldn't say that about a holy Pope of God!"

"Now, now," the Fourth conciliated, "we do not have to agree in all things. Although," he nodded toward the Second Man, "we do hope you will join us in the Tridentine Society soon." He paused.

"I think this is a special moment. One that should be marked by our special ceremony. After all, we are about to collaborate in a more complete way than ever. Let us commingle our blood here in this sacred chalice we will never be able to use."

"Do you think it wise?" asked the Second Man. "The last time it was such a mess."

The Fourth Man smiled, then nodded.

The First Man rose and solemnly walked toward the bathroom. He reached inside the medicine cabinet. In doing so, he knocked over a bottle whose childproof cap had not been firmly affixed. Dozens of aspirins spilled over the sink and the floor.

Seemingly oblivious, he picked up an unused razor blade, closed the cabinet door, and returned to the table. On his way out of the bathroom, his shoes crushed several aspirins, leaving a powdery wake.

He took his place at the table, which was illuminated by a single candle, one dim light having been turned off.

All eyes were on him. Solemnly, he took the razor blade in his left hand and, holding his right hand over the chalice, made a small incision in his right wrist.

"Damn!"

"Oh, God!" said the Second Man, "he's cut a vein again!"

"Wait," said the Third, "I'll make a tourniquet with my tie."

"Heaven preserve us!" prayed the Fourth Man.

This was no casual visit. Father Koesler had been called by Inspector Koznicki, and asked to come see him as soon as possible.

The bad news was that this was in the heart of one of the seamier areas of downtown Detroit. The good news was the imposing presence of police head-quarters, as well as the Wayne County Sheriff's office across the street. Koesler had confidently left his car between two blue-and-white police cars in the nearby parking ramp.

As he walked briskly down the fifth floor corridor, the priest noted that the door to Squad Six's meeting room was open. Odd. Usually, the doors to all seven squadrooms were closed. Koesler assumed this open-door policy might have been because of the excessive heat. Like many older buildings, this one was either too hot or too cold during the winter.

Koesler's curiosity triumphed as his custody of the eyes faltered. He stopped and looked in the doorway. Sergeants Patrick and Morris were seated on either side of a small desk. Patrick was holding up a series of small cards—they appeared to be photos—while Morris appeared to be identifying them.

"Edward Maley," said Morris as she looked intently at the card Patrick held before her. "Not a seminarian. Student in the Morality of Christian Marriage class."

Patrick nodded and held up another card.

"Keaty, William," Morris identified, "custodian."

Patrick smiled and held up the next card.

"Schaaf, Eileen. Student in the Ascetical Theology class."

The two seemed oblivious to his presence, and Koesler had no wish to interrupt them. He continued down the hall, and was ushered into Koznicki's office, where he exchanged greetings with his friend.

"How is Father Gennardo coming along?" Koznicki leaned back in his chair, entwining thick fingers across his ample front.

"Doing very, very well. Just yesterday he returned to the seminary from the hospital. Of course, he'll be confined to bed rest for a while yet. But he is something of a hero."

Koznicki smiled. "Yes, I can understand that. He is probably the closest thing the seminary has to a martyr."

They laughed.

"And," Koznicki continued, "how are *you* doing with the new class in communications at St. Joseph's?"

"Pretty good." Koesler began to fiddle with a paperweight on Koznicki's desk. A former smoker, his hands had to keep occupied. "Of course it's a small class starting in midterm. The academic dean is making allowances for the telescoped time span." Koesler shook his head. "I find it difficult teaching young women in a seminary setting. There's nothing wrong with their being in a seminary classroom, of course. They ought to be welcomed into the priesthood if they want in. It's just that, with my background, it is strange once you get into the frame of mind of teaching young men to find yourself teaching young women. I suppose I'm a bridge over troubled waters—or over troubled centuries."

The priest laughed self-consciously. He hadn't intended to wax so philosophical. But he felt so at ease with his friend that it was natural to express what was on his mind.

"I'm sure you will adjust, Father. You always do."

Koznicki opened a manila folder and extracted a sheet of paper. "The reason I asked you down, Father, was to seek your assistance in our continuing investigation into these attacks on the seminary professors.

"Irene Casey of the *Detroit Catholic* has been most

helpful in going through back issues of her newspaper and gathering letters, published and unpublished, from readers who have expressed hostility toward the Church or the Catholic clergy.

"As you can see," Koznicki opened a box at one corner of his desk: newspaper clippings popped up like a jumping jack, "there are a significant number of such letters."

"I have had the names of these letter writers transcribed." He offered Koesler the list. "Father, I wonder if you would mind looking through this list. See if you recognize any of these people and can tell us anything about them."

As Koesler scanned the list, he began to smile. The smile grew into a chuckle.

"It's like meeting old friends. With most of them, I can remember editing their letters when I was at the newspaper. I've been more or less aware that they're still writing to the paper. But it's very impressive when you see them amassed like this."

"Do you know any of them personally?"

"Hmmm . . . most of them I couldn't pick out of a group of two. I'm just familiar with their penmanship and their opinions. Ah, here's one I know: Frank Crawford. He's head of the local chapter of Catholics United for the Faith, or CUF. He's also a former classmate."

"A priest?"

"No. He resigned while we were still in seminary. It was quite a shock for the rest of us. He was one of the most brilliant students we had. A good athlete. A strong spiritual life. Everybody thought he would have made an excellent priest. But, for some reason, he left. I think he quit sometimes after college . . . the first or second year of theology."

"Did he leave to marry?"

"No. To the best of my knowledge, he never married."

"Do you think he would be capable of violence, especially against a priest?"

"Oh, heavens, no. Frank is very cerebral. Given a couple of suppositions—as, for example, that the Pope, even when he is not being infallible, is always right—Frank's school of thought makes a lot of sense. Of course, that is a considerable supposition. One I would be unwilling to grant. But Frank is just not the physical type. He'll argue by the hour. But he would never be violent."

"How about the others?"

Koesler continued to study the list.

"Here's one. Conrad Nap. I've seen pictures of him . . . even met him a couple of times. I don't know for a fact, but I've heard he carries a gun, at least occasionally. And he is far to the right of someone like Frank Crawford and the CUF people.

"And here's another one. Roman Kirkus. If memory serves, he is just about as far out to the right as possible. He visited me several times after I began my assignment at the paper. Evidently, he concluded I was beyond the conservative's redemption. So, after a few very strong letters to the editor, he gave up completely on me and the *Detroit Catholic*."

"You think him capable of violence, Father?"

"Oh, yes, indeed. He has been violent in the past. Came near to inciting a couple of riots, as I recall. Yes, I could easily imagine a point beyond which he could turn to violence."

"Anyone else, Father?"

"Ah, yes, here's another leading candidate: the Archdiocese's most notorious conservative activist—Harold Langton. You remember him, Inspector; he was one of the early suspects in those Rosary Murders some years back. He's anti-feminist, anti-liberal, anti-busing, sex education, Vatican II, abortion, unions, birth control, altar girls, peace marches, charismatics, and folk masses. He is against priests being anywhere but in

Church, nuns being anywhere but in school, and bishops who don't enforce papal decrees.

"As a matter of fact, Harold is against so many things, I don't suppose anyone knows what, if anything, he is *for*."

Koesler cursorily went though the remainder of the names. "I don't see anyone else here that I know of who might be a violent person."

"Well, Father, we have several copies of this list. Why don't you take that copy and give it a little more consideration. Perhaps you may think of someone else.

"Oh, and by the way, Father," Koznicki said as Koesler rose preparatory to leaving, "there is a meeting tomorrow evening of the Tridentine Society. Kirkus is the head of that group."

"I know. That was some publicity the Tridentines got in the papers a while back."

"Yes. Well, I was wondering whether you would be interested in attending that meeting with me."

"Tomorrow evening? Yes, I think I can make it."

"Fine. I'll pick you up at St. Anselm's rectory at 7:30."

They exchanged a warm handshake and Koesler departed.

On a whim, he stepped into the Squad Six office. As he entered, Morris was holding up a card for Patrick.

"Shelby, Gloria," said Patrick, "kitchen crew and domestic help."

Suddenly, Patrick became aware of Koesler's presence. He looked up with a very winning Irish smile. "Oh, Father Koesler, Marge and I were just going over our flashcards."

"I haven't done anything like this since grade school." Morris seemed embarrassed.

"What's it all for?" the priest asked.

"It's for St. Joseph's Seminary," Patrick explained. "You see, the problem we faced in the investigation at Sacred Heart was the neighborhood. It was such a mixed bag that anybody could be at home there. Black, white, criminal, average citizen, derelict, unemployed, blue-collar. An assailant could disappear into the woodwork in such a setting.

"But now, at St. Joseph's we don't face a problem with the neighborhood. In fact, there is almost no neighborhood to speak of. At St. Joseph's, the mixed bag is the inhabitants of the place. Students, seminarians, nonseminarians, part-time and full-time students, men, women, faculty, staff. In such a situation almost anybody could slip in and go about pretty inconspicuously."

"So?"

"So," Morris explained, "we are getting to know everyone who has a legitimate reason to be in the building. Thus, the flashcards." She handed one to Koesler.

On one side was a head-and-shoulders photo. On the reverse were the individual's identification data.

"In addition, to familiarizing ourselves with the personnel, we have also beefed up security," Morris went on. "And the seminary is hiring additional guards. There are still a few holes to plug, but we're getting there."

"You certainly are." Koesler was impressed with their thoroughness. "I'd hate to try to get past all these security measures. For all our sakes, I wish you great good fortune."

Pat Lennon glanced about. The scene reminded her of the alleged makeup of the Ku Klux Klan in the sixties. During a nationwide investigation of the Klan, it was said that the group comprised more federal agents and infiltrators than authentic members.

She recalled the two previous meetings of the Tridentine Society she had attended. At each meeting, there couldn't have been more than a hundred people. However, at this meeting there was easily double that number here at the Knights of Columbus Hall.

This obviously had caught the society by surprise. As latecomers entered, they were forced to set up more folding chairs. It was well after the announced 8:00 P.M. starting time, but nothing had begun. Chairman Roman Kirkus stood at one side of the stage waiting for things to settle down.

Lennon and Joe Cox had arrived about half an hour early and had seated themselves in what was then the last row. But now, what with the goodly number of latecomers, the two found themselves in the middle of the audience.

While waiting for the meeting to open, Lennon tried as surreptitiously as possible to see if she could identify any familiar faces.

Of course there was Walt Koznicki. In any size crowd, he stood out like an elephant with a nosebleed in a snowbank. With him was Father Koesler, sans roman collar, but dressed in black. In any ordinary gathering, the black suit would have been a sore thumb. But with the Tridentines black was almost de rigueur.

Then there were Sergeants Patrick and Morris of Homicide. Lennon had known they were on this case. And there were two pudgy young men she thought she recognized from somewhere, possibly one of the seminaries, Scared Heart or St. Joseph's, she wasn't sure.

Lennon swiveled in her chair and faced front again. There was Roman Kirkus watching the gathering crowd rather contentedly. He was the only member of the society whose name she knew. There was Brother Alphonsus, and he was here tonight. But was that his real name? She did not know. And, seemingly, neither did any of the other members of the society. This was the most secretive bunch she had ever encountered.

There was no membership list. There were no dues, just free-will offerings at meetings. There were no mailings. No member knew any other member's name unless the information was spontaneously given on an individual basis, or unless they knew one another from work or residence neighborhood.

No doubt about it, as Cox had observed on numerous occasions, this was a weird group.

Tonight's audience included, in addition to the faithful, the police, and Koesler, several staff writers from metropolitan and suburban publications. But most of the newcomers, Pat surmised, were conservative Catholics whose curiosity had been aroused by publicity. She wondered how many of these would find the Tridentine viewpoints a bit too extreme.

As Kirkus moved toward the microphone, Lennon noticed several in the audience scowling at Sergeants Patrick and Morris. Suddenly she understood. The Tridentines did not know the couple were police officers. Society had pretty much come to accept racially mixed couples. But obviously not the Tridentines.

"This meeting will come to order," Kirkus announced several times. The microphone was operating sporadically. Only every other word was amplified.

Lennon wondered abstractedly why so many things seemed to go wrong for the Tridentines.

Gradually, the low cacophony of the audience subsided.

"This meeting will come to order," Kirkus repeated. There was no improvement in the microphone's operation.

"Oh, turn the damn thing off, Roman," someone shouted. "We can hear you O.K. without it."

Kirkus shrugged and flipped a switch at the side of the microphone. A spark arced to his finger.

"Damn!" Kirkus blurted.

Father Koesler, who had independently shared Pat Lennon's wonderment at the Tridentine penchant for being accident prone, wondered even more.

"We will begin this meeting," Kirkus said loudly without benefit of mike, "with the recitation of the holy Rosary."

This announcement was greeted by an audible groan from Cox immediately truncated by a Lennon elbow to the rib cage.

Ten minutes later, Rosary completed, Kirkus returned to the podium. He made a gesture toward the switch, then thought better of it.

"For the first point of business, does anyone have anything to report?"

Hands shot up.

Kirkus nodded at a woman in the first row. He appeared bored.

The woman stood. She was very tall, very thin, and her dress epitomized modesty. "A nun in our parish—"

"Louder," someone said.

She turned modestly and faced the audience. "A nun in our parish," she proceeded more loudly, "—she is the religious education coordinator—has announced her intention of running for city council."

"She can't do that!" someone shouted.

"The Pope said nuns can't run for office!" someone else shouted.

"Wasn't that priests who may not run?" Koznicki leaned over and asked Koesler. Smiling, Koesler nodded.

Shouted suggestions and sentiments came from various members of the audience.

"Remember Father Drinan? The Pope stopped him!"

"She should be in school teaching our children"

"Go see your pastor!"

"What good will that do? He's probably running for governor"

Laughter.

This was the first indication to Cox and Lennon that the group could laugh. But apparently only at their own jokes.

"People like her, you got to get their attention," said a short dark man, dourly.

"That is Conrad Nap," Koesler leaned over and said to Koznicki, who nodded.

"Is Frank Crawford here?" Koznicki asked.

Koesler shook his head. "This is simply not Frank's kind of crowd. And he would know enough about this

148 WILLIAM X. KIENZLE

organization not to bother coming to one of these meetings."

"How about Langton?"

"I don't see him, but I doubt that he'd be here. At one time, I believe he was a member, but then he branched off on his own and has been out beyond the fringes ever since. Besides, he's got his own jackal pack."

Kirkus' vigorous pounding of the gavel gradually quieted the audience.

"What parish is this you're talking about?" Kirkus asked.

"Our Lady Queen of Martyrs," the tall woman answered.

"That would be Father McNulty's parish." Kirkus paused. "He probably doesn't know what the nun is up to. I'd tell him if I were you. Likely enough he'll put a stop to it."

That problem having been given a Christian burial, Kirkus looked about for more upraised hands. They were there in abundance. He nodded at a nondescript, balding man in the fourth row. The man stood and positioned himself so he was facing the majority of the audience. His face was livid. He appeared on the verge of exploding.

"Did any of you see over the TV that our bishops approved of Michigan's sexual education plan?"

Heads nodded vigorously.

"The state," the man continued, "is going to bring sex right into the classroom, and with the blessings of our bishops, to top it all off! Well, I, for one, think this is a sin that cries to heaven for vengeance!"

Once again, the declamation provoked spontaneous individual reactions.

"That's right! The bishops are telling our children it's all right to go ahead and whore!"

Cox thought that might be a step in the right direction.

"They shouldn't be teaching children about sex. It's dirty! You should save it for the person you marry!"

"Yes, marriage is plenty of time to learn what you do in it!"

"And these are the same bishops who okayed all those sex classes and filthy pictures for those innocent seminarians!"

"Something ought to be done to them to get their attention!" said the short dark man.

"Nap seems to have a one-track mind," said Koznicki to Koesler.

"Kind of scary," Koesler murmured. He found this vehement outpouring overwhelming.

"Hit them where it hurts!" shouted an elderly woman. "The diocesan collection! Boycott it!"

There was so much uproar, Kirkus was forced to pound the gavel vigorously. The head of the gavel flew off and landed at the feet of a man in the first row. He picked it up and returned it to Kirkus, who screwed the two parts together.

"Murphy's Law seems to work overtime for these people," said Koesler to Koznicki.

With a semblance of order restored, Kirkus shouted that a boycott of diocesan collections throughout the state seemed the most effective course of action. He suggested that the society explore ways to publicize this action to get more broad-based support.

Just then, as if in answer to his prayer, there was a disturbance at the rear of the auditorium. Like a field of undulating grain, the audience swiveled to see what this disturbance was. It was television. The saving medium. The medium that would carry the Tridentine message as well as the Tridentine persona. It was Steve Schatz with the cameraman and soundman from WDIV-TV, the local NBC affiliate.

"That's Channel 4's crew," Cox said to Lennon. "Last time it was Channel 7. They must be taking turns."

"Look at that guy," Lennon stage-whispered, indicating Kirkus, "he's a true media creation."

Where Roman Kirkus had hitherto seemed to be slipping into ennui, now, conscious of the presence of a mobile camera, he had snapped to alertness and seemed eager to become the on-camera attraction.

"Does anyone want to make a motion to the effect that all Michigan Catholics be urged to boycott all diocesan collections until further notice?" This was Kirkus' first excursion into the realm of *Robert's Rules of Order.* He could think of no other way of bringing the subject to the TV reporter's attention.

"I'll make that motion," said somebody.

"Is there a second to the motion?"

"Second," said several voices.

"All those in favor?"

There was much clamor.

"Those opposed?"

Relative silence.

"Then the motion is passed," Kirkus concluded.

"Excuse me, sir," said Schatz, "but what was the motion related to? I mean, why do you want Catholics to boycott diocesan collections?"

"Because the Michigan bishops have come out in support of the state's sex education plan."

"I see."

"Aren't you going to turn on your camera?" Kirkus looked so disappointed he appeared on the verge of tears.

"Not yet. We'll get to that after the meeting."

If the meeting was all that was keeping him from being televised, there was a simple solution.

"If there is no further business," said Kirkus, ignoring the hands being raised all over the audience, "this meeting is concluded. Keep watching the *Detroit Catholic* for the time and place of our next meeting. The box for your free-will donations is over there at the corner of the stage."

Kirkus brought his gavel down hard to silence the

barely muted audience protest over the meeting's abrupt conclusion. Was it Koesler's imagination, or did he see the lectern split?

Just then, Ven Marshall and WXYZ-TV's crew entered the auditorium. Marshall paused to appraise the situation, then started for the front of the auditorium where Channel 4's crew was setting up. Soon, Kirkus became the center of more attention than he had dreamed possible.

Spotlights gave an unreal vividness to this section of the auditorium. Cameramen adjusted their gear. Soundmen seemed supremely bored. Two microphones, one with a number 7 affixed, the other with a number 4, were thrust close to Kirkus' face. Giving him their full attention were two handsome faces Kirkus had seen countless times on local TV.

There was no denying it: Roman Kirkus had become a celebrity. All those at work and in the rest of society who laughed at him and made jokes about his opinions and mistakes would have to heed his newfound fame. He would, indeed, have the last laugh.

"Mr. Kirkus—" said Marshall.

"Mr. Kirkus—" chorused Schatz.

"Mr. Kirkus—" Marshall prevailed; Kirkus knew that Channel 7 had higher ratings than Channel 4. "Mr. Kirkus, what is your position in the Tridentine Society?"

"I am chairman."

"And the purpose of the society?"

"To restore the Catholic Church to its divinely established purpose which it maintained before this Vatican II madness ran rampant."

"That's pretty ambitious, wouldn't you say?" said Schatz.

"Well, we're concentrating our efforts here in Detroit, mostly, and then the rest of Michigan. We figure if we can turn Detroit around, it will be example enough for other right-minded Catholics to do the same in their dioceses.

"Besides, you can never discount the power of prayer."

"You're dealing with something more tangible than prayer," Schatz interjected. "Your society just made a resolution to boycott all diocesan collections in the state. Did it not?"

"Yes."

Kirkus suddenly realized the truth of what he had just said about the power of prayer. Only minutes ago, the Tridentines were wondering how they were going to get their message across to the general public. Now, suddenly, two TV stations were recording the message for telecast at 11:00 P.M. God was mighty. And Kirkus was His prophet.

"What is it, specifically," Schatz asked, "that you object to that would cause you to resort to such an extreme stand?"

"The bishops' endorsement of Michigan's school sex education program."

"In a previous meeting," Marshall had the advantage, since he had covered the previous meeting, "you condemned the seminar in sexuality being offered at Detroit's two seminaries. Is there, do you think, any connection between that seminar and the present endorsement of the state's plan?"

"Of course there is," said Kirkus, who, until now, had not drawn any connection between the two. "It's another case of the hierarchy pandering to the public. There is no longer any question of right and wrong—it's all subjective morality. Before Vatican II, we Catholics knew that sex was for procreation and procreation alone. Now, the bishops and seminary professors want to have sex taught to children who are too young to do it, and seminarians who should never do it. Somebody is going to have to pay for this perversion of God's law!"

"When you say, 'somebody is going to have to pay,'" Schatz pressed, "are you alluding to eventual divine

retribution, or do you mean this as some sort of immediate physical threat?"

"Both. We are the tools God uses now in this world
to do His Holy Will."

"Are you then, Mr. Kirkus," Marshall asked,
"threatening the lives of the seminary professors and/
or the bishops of this state?"

"God does not always make His Will clear. And
neither will I."

Just beyond the TV crews, the print reporters, including Lennon and Cox, were taking notes incredu-
lously.

The two TV reporters had Kirkus pose with each
separately, this time filming from behind Kirkus, while
each reporter repeated and rephrased the questions
that had been asked. Then each reporter stood aside
and was recorded making an introduction to the tape,
and a wrap-up. The film would be edited at the studio.

Roman Kirkus had never been this high. He would
not sleep tonight. He would lie awake, planning.

At Inspector Koznicki's suggestion, he and Father
Koesler had stopped in at Topinka's for a nightcap.

They were seated on the first level of the nearly deserted restaurant. A small glass of port rested before
Koznicki; Koesler nursed a bourbon manhattan on the
rocks. He had sufficiently recovered from his brush with
Antabuse to return to his occasional drink.

"What did you make of it, Father?"

Koesler looked at his friend uncomprehendingly.

"The meeting," Koznicki clarified.

"I found it overwhelming. I mean, I knew there were
differences of opinion, but I have never heard them
aired with such vehemence. It was like concentrated
acid. Do you think it does them any good to get it out
of their system like that?"

"I do not really know, Father. There is a school that
claims that letting it all out, verbalizing one's hostile
feelings, is good for the psyche. Prevents their putting

their feelings into action . . . a safety spout to channel off violence."

"Like the hypothesis that voyeurism may appease a sex maniac . . . so that pornography is better than rape?"

"Exactly. On the other hand, there are those who argue that such inflammatory utterances can cause a borderline psychotic to pass over the threshold of violence."

"Ah . . ." Koesler thought a moment. "One such as Conrad Nap, perhaps."

"Yes, indeed. And as difficult as it it is to get any information about the Tridentines, we are conducting a rather thorough investigation of Mr. Nap and Mr. Kirkus.

"I must say, though, this society is among the most secretive I have ever encountered. We have not been able to obtain any information from inside the group. There is nothing to infiltrate. There may be an infra-structure—and I sense there is—but we have been unable to put our finger on it, much less penetrate it. We have been unable to detect a membership roster or a constitution. Nothing.

"But what continues to amaze me is that these people can become so worked up about a vernacular Mass or hymns or sex education."

"Well, Inspector, I think these people, if they were not hunting down what they consider to be a wayward theology, would be out beating the bushes for Communists. But then you ought to remember well the old Latin liturgy."

"Indeed I do. But what does that have to do with this?"

"Well, I think when one understands the Latin Mass —or, rather the Tridentine Mass, since there is a new Latin Mass—one can understand the rationale as well as the plight of today's conservative Catholic.

"The Mass you and I grew up with was formulated some time before the Council of Trent. But it was that council which sort of sunk that Latin Mass in cement with its reform of the *Missale Romanum* or Roman Missal. Which means that for approximately the past four hundred years that same Mass was offered unchanged all over the world in the Latin rite. We Catholics gloried in the notion that we could attend Mass in this country or in Japan or just about anywhere in the world, and the Mass would be the same, gesture for gesture, word for word. It was symbolic of the Church's universality."

"Yes," Koznicki interrupted, "but was not there an opposite opinion that having the Mass in Latin meant that a Catholic could misunderstand the Mass in his own country as well as he could misunderstand it in a foreign country?"

They laughed.

"That's true," Koesler admitted. With a finger, he stirred the ice in his drink. He was determined to have only one manhattan, no matter how long they remained at the restaurant.

"However," Koesler continued, "that objection was not raised popularly until about the time of the Second Vatican Council. In fact, there weren't many questions asked—except by the reformers—before Vatican II.

"But you see, Inspector, not only did we grow up with that Tridentine Mass, it had been around for nearly four hundred years! It's easy to see why Catholics, particularly those not only comfortable with the past but incorrectly convinced that nothing in the Church ever changes, would be shocked when the Tridentine Mass not only is altered but is abrogated!

"And all this takes place within a decade which, compared with its four-hundred-year history, seems almost to have happened overnight."

"Yes, I see."

"Of course, the transition was not without its light side. Something funny was bound to occur when you suddenly switch from a language few of your listeners understand to their vernacular. Mistakes in Latin cannot compare with bloopers in English.

"I have a friend—who shall remain nameless—who was chaplain at a girls' high school when we switched languages. He claims he was only vaguely aware that one of the seniors, named Linda, had developed magnificently and had a terrific figure . . . beautifully endowed. . . ."

"Yes, yes." Koznicki smiled in anticipation.

"Well, one day, while distributing communion, as this priest went along the railing, he was saying 'Gloria, the body of Christ,' to which she responded, 'Amen,' as she should. He continued, 'Mary, the body of Christ,' 'Susan, the body of Christ,' then, unwittingly, 'Christ, the body of Linda.' "

They laughed.

"And then there was the day I was standing in the rear of a suburban church during communion time. An usher, one of those who thought Vatican II might have been a major mistake, came back to talk to a few of his fellow ushers. Unaware of my presence, he said disgustedly, 'Some kid just peed on the altar rail.' And then he added, resignedly, 'Probably part of the new liturgy.' "

Koznicki shook his head in amusement.

"Now," Koesler went on, "I think those stories are intrinsically funny. But I doubt the average Tridentine Society member would laugh. They find no humor or joy in what has happened to the Mass. Nor to the new approach to moral theology, which they term 'situation ethics.' A term they intend as pejorative.

"Perhaps this is comparable to a form of psychopathology. We agree that abnormal behavior is an exaggeration of the normal. For instance, it is a normal reaction for many people to experience some fear of heights or closed-in areas. However, when this fear overcomes, immobilizes, paralyzes, then we have a neurosis or a psychosis.

"I think it well within the realm of normal behavior

to resist change, especially when one has good reason to. Few would argue that change is intrinsically good. But when you find a group like the Tridentines, you are no longer dealing with reason, logic, or normality.

"I don't think there are many of these people around. But when you do stumble across them, there's one thing you can bank on—they will be loud."

"And conceivably dangerous," Koznicki added.

"Do you really think the—our—assailant"— Koesler still had difficulty including himself in the intended victims—"might be one of the Tridentines?"

"Do you?"

"I don't know."

"At this point, Father, I would think it quite possible."

"Do you think you will discover whoever it is?"

"Oh, yes, I believe we will, Father. It is my hope we will do so in time?"

"In time?"

"Before he strikes again."

Koesler gulped, and drained the remainder of his manhattan. "On that awesome note, Inspector, I think we'd better call it day."

"Come on, Cox," Nelson Kane prodded, "what is it?"

Cox studied the eight-by-ten UPI photo Kane had handed him. The small building that took up most of the photo was being consumed by flames. That much was certain. Any further implication eluded Cox.

"It's a small building on fire," Cox said at length.

"It's more than that. Use your imagination."

Kane had taped over the caption. All that was visible was the dateline.

"South Billings Harbor," Cox read. "That's South Jersey, isn't it?"

Kane nodded encouragingly.

"Chickens," Cox said. "If it's South Jersey, it must have something to do with chickens."

Kane nodded again.

"Ummm," Cox made a meditative sound, "a chicken coop?"

Kane nodded enthusiastically.

"A burning chicken coop! What do I win?"

"That's not all."

"That's not all?"

"Look at it!"

Cox looked at it. He turned the photo sideways. He turned it upside down. He took his glasses from his shirt pocket, put them on, moved the photo close to his face, and studied it still further.

"It's a burning chicken coop," Cox pronounced flatly.

Kane, in a gesture reeking with disgust, tore the tape off the caption.

"Residents of South Billings Harbor see figure of Jesus in flames of burning chicken coop."

Kane picked up the photo. Cox circled to Kane's side of the desk.

"See it?" Kane's index finger traced the dark lines amid the flames engulfing the coop's doorway.

"Nellie, you've got one of the more overactive imaginations of all time."

"I should've known you wouldn't see it."

"That's right. I missed Christ in the tortilla and in the folds of the tabernacle veil. And I didn't see the tears of the Madonna in St. Elizabeth's church."

"You have no faith, Cox."

"That's all right; you have enough for all of us agnostics."

This was a peculiar side of Nelson Kane, thought Cox. Kane was an acknowledged professional from his soles to the top of his thinning hair. His news sense was unerring. But his fey sense of humor made him a hopeless patsy for the offbeat religious story or photo. From experience, Cox knew that Kane would throw all his considerable influence behind getting this burning chicken coop on page one of tomorrow's *Free Press*.

"But enough of Our Savior of the Chicken Coop." Kane crop-marked the photo for two columns, slugged it for page one and spun it into the copy basket. "How's the 'Is Nothing Sacred' story coming?"

"Dead in the water, I'm afraid. Unless the cops come up with a suspect, I think this thing will trickle into the unsolved cases file."

"You got any guesses?"

"Not really. If I had to drop a name, it would be that loony chairman of the Tridentines—whatzisname . . ." Cox consulted his notepad. "Roman Kirkus."

"Why him?"

"Just that he's the most conspicuous character I've come across in this crazy case."

"Oh?"

"We've all known people who come alive for the media. Pull out a pencil and pad and identify yourself as a reporter and this type grows about ten inches: 'Oh, boy! I'm gonna get my name in the papers.' But this guy Kirkus is almost entirely a creature of TV. He sort of slouches through a meeting—like he's lost interest in it. But let them turn on the lights and aim a TV camera at him and, bang, he comes to life. Add to that his professed philosophy—a little to the right of Attila the Hun—and he could fit the bill."

"Well, keep him in your back pocket. You never know when that story will pop again." Kane picked up a pile of letters from the corner of his desk.

"What happened?" Cox eyed the stack. "All my fans write in at the same time?"

"National Rifle Association. Fitzgerald had a column on gun control the other day."

"Yeah, I remember it. The NRA! I knew it had to be my fans or the NRA."

"These have already been entered in the VDT." Kane handed the letters to Cox. "Get in touch with some of these people. See if you can get an original idea. Then phone some of the gun control people for balance."

"That's different: doing an NRA story without an assassination or even a significant shooting. And we have Fitzgerald to thank."

"Only partly. The follow-up is Larry David's idea."

"The executive ed? Why the command from on high?"

"As you will see when you go through these letters, these people are threatening to withhold advertising."

"It is all very clear now." Cox bowed exaggeratedly in the general direction of the executive editor's office, then riffled through the letters as he returned to his desk.

"Hey, Lennon! C'mere a minute!"

Ordinarily, Pat Lennon would have ignored such a summons, particularly since it came from Pete Sands, the clown of the newsroom. But since she was only going to get a drink of water, she detoured to Sands' desk.

"You dabble in religion from time to time, don't you, Lennon?"

"As infrequently as possible."

"Well, you might be interested in the fact that the new Syrian bishop, who has not even officially taken over his Detroit diocese yet, granted me a telephone interview."

Lennon pursed her lips and nodded. She was impressed. No one else in the Detroit media had yet been able to speak with, let alone interview, the new bishop.

"Wanna hear it?" Sands prodded.

"Sure."

Sands' neighboring desk partner appeared to be interested at this point and moved his chair closer.

Sands depressed the rewind button on his tape recorder. The tape whirred madly to automatic cut-off. He pushed the play button. There were several scratchy sounds before a man—clearly Sands—began to speak.

"Bishop," Sands began, "now that you are coming into the Detroit diocese for the first time, I was wondering—and, by the way, thank you very much for this interview—"

" 'sallright," said a deep masculine voice with a heavy foreign accent.

"I was wondering, now that you are, in effect, sort of starting over—anew, as it were—I was wondering whether you expected that you might experience any change in your sexual fantasies?"

Lennon's mouth dropped open. "You didn't—"

She was interrupted by a nervous cough from the bishop. "Uh . . ." There was a long pause, then, "Jello."

"Jello?" Sands sounded surprised.

"Gelatin!"

"Gelatin?"

"In the bathtub!"

"In the bathtub?"

"Yes. You fill the bathtub with Jello. Then you get in."

"I see," said Sands. "And do you do this alone, bishop?"

Lennon, who had forgotten to close her mouth, reddened. "You didn't ask a bishop—!" She was again interrupted by another nervous cough.

"Uh . . ." Another long pause. "No; usually there are two, maybe three, secretaries. But sometimes—alone. Of course, it is more fun with secretaries. Not more than three, though."

Suddenly, the two recorded voices broke up in guffaws. Simultaneously, so did Sands and his desk partner. The live and taped sounds were identical.

Lennon eyed the two. Her mouth closed into a wry smile. "Did you guys write a script?"

"No," Sands replied, "I just turned on the recorder on the spur of the moment, and interviewed Roger here off the cuff. Pretty good, wouldn't you say? I mean, for extemporaneous?"

"Not bad. When can we expect to catch the two of you on the 'Comedy Shop'?" Lennon tried not to encourage this sort of thing. As she continued her quest for a simple glass of water, the boys were still snickering at their own prank.

Bob Ankenazy joined her at the water cooler.

"I've been meaning to ask you: Anything new with that seminary story?" Ankenazy filled his Styrofoam cup with water and watched, mesmerized by the bubble of air rising through the tank and popping at the water's surface.

"Nothing much. The investigation is continuing, but very low-key. The police are trying to beef up security at St. Joseph's. Of course, they're still looking into the attacks at Sacred Heart. But the cops seem to think that if there are going to be any more attacks the scene has shifted to St. Joe's."

"What do *you* think? *Will* there be any more attacks?"

"I'm not so sure. My intuition combined with a bit of logic tells me that whoever is responsible for these assaults isn't finished. There doesn't appear to be any rhyme or reason to them. I have a feeling there's a larger plan here somewhere.

"On the other hand, now that the police have seen to it that both seminaries have more security, maybe the assailant will be discouraged."

"The cops haven't any leads, have they?"

"No, not really. About the best bet is that crazy bunch of Tridentines."

"You think it's some sort of conspiracy?" Ankenazy refilled his cup and once more found the air bubble engrossing.

"Not, not a conspiracy. But I think it's very possible that one of them is the assailant. They're such a spooky bunch. Their paranoia is almost contagious. Every time I leave one of their meetings, I feel like putting more locks on my apartment door. And some of them seem so at ease with the idea of violence. Every so often, the subject of the seminary attacks comes up at their meetings. They just seem comfortable with—even in favor of—the attacks on those priests."

"Have you picked out a likely suspect?" Though he was smiling, Ankenazy was not laughing at Lennon. Experience had taught him to trust her journalistic instincts.

"If I had to pick one, it would be that creepy Conrad Nap. He seems addicted to violence as some people are hooked on smoking."

"Any proof?"

"Nope. Just a hunch."

"Well, this story's on a back burner now, right?"

"Yes, why?" She knew why: There was another assignment in the wings.

"Leon London has been . . . uh . . . urging me to give you another assignment."

"London! What's he doing on my case?"

"Nothing special. He was just aware that the seminary story was petering out and wanted you to get on something else." Ankenazy could not bring himself to explain to Lennon that since she was easily the most attractive female in the building, everyone was either consciously or subconsciously on her case.

"Before I suggest something," Ankenazy continued, "do you have anything started?"

"As a matter of fact, I do." Aware that assignments from above were usually dull, Lennon almost always had a story that interested her under way, or, at least researched.

"It's a pretty topical subject for the beginning of March: a bathhouse."

"A bathhouse!"

"Yup. The last of thirteen bathhouses that once operated in Detroit. It's called the Oakwood, and it's near the old Dodge plant on the east side."

"I know where it is." Ankenazy seemed surprised. "But it's for men only; how did you come across it?"

"It used to be male only. In the past year, they've begun a women's night."

"So you've already been there?"

"Yes. First they slather you all over with oil . . ."

Ankenazy allowed himself the luxury of picturing Lennon's body slathered with oil.

". . . then you go into a steam room where they bake your brains. That is immediately followed by being immersed in ice-cold water. One of their patrons committed suicide that way."

"How?"

"He kept taking these hot and cold treatments—they can't recall whether it was four or five times—until his heart gave out."

"He bathed himself to death!"

"Exactly. The place has a fantastc history. Detroit's old Purple Gang used to hang out there."

"We can get shots?"

"They agreed as long as we don't photograph any of the customers."

"O.K., go ahead."

"What about London?"

"I'll handle London."

"Hey, Bob! Ankenazy!" Pete Sands hollered across the newsroom. "C'mere a minute. I've got something you ought to hear!"

Lennon lingered at the water cooler so she could witness Ankenazy's expression when he heard one of his reporters question a Syrian bishop about his sexual fantasies.

The students and staff of St. Joseph's Seminary couldn't help noticing the changes. Immediately after the attack on Father Gennardo, the halls of St. Joe's began to be regularly patrolled by uniformed Detroit police officers. They had shortly been replaced by men from a private security firm.

Not only were all students, faculty, and staff required to wear an identifying tag on their outer clothing while on the premises, the front and rear main doors were guarded by uniformed security officers who monitored the parking areas as well as entrances to the building via closed circuit television.

Mere weeks ago, the seminary's policy had been, for all practical purposes, open-doored. Now, security measures, while not foolproof—many windows and some doors were impossible to secure—were nonetheless impressive.

Also impressive were the three people standing and conversing in the seminary's inner courtyard, the very place where Father Gennardo had been shot. The tallest, and by anyone's measure the largest, of the three was Inspector Walter Koznicki, a stranger to virtually all students and staff. A few recognized him from his infrequent appearances on TV newscasts or from his photo in the papers. During formidable or bizarre homicide investigations, the local media eventually gravitated to the Inspector.

The other two, Sergeants Patrick and Morris, were no longer strangers to the seminary population. Almost all of them had been interrogated by one or the other of the officers. And everyone, student and staff alike, was amazed that the two detectives knew each of them by name.

"Yes, Inspector," Patrick was replying to a Koznicki query, "we've run a check on both Conrad Nap and Roman Kirkus. Kirkus is clean as far as felony charges. A few traffic tickets. He appears to be quite an aggressive driver. Nap, on the other hand, has several disorderly conduct convictions, usually causing a disturbance during a religious or social rally or parade or the like. Once he pushed a priest down the steps of an east side church. He has a permit to own a gun. A .22 caliber automatic. We wanted to check it against the slugs we found in this courtyard, but Nap claims the gun was stolen recently and hasn't been recovered."

Koznicki nodded. "Then they remain our likeliest candidates?"

Patrick and Morris nodded.

"Are you satisfied with security?"

Morris shrugged. "I guess you'd have to say it's the best the seminary seems able to afford."

"Which company?" Koznicki feared the worst.

"Woods Security."

Fears confirmed, Koznicki shook his head.

"Mostly rejects from the police academies," Patrick commented. "A few pros, but not enough."

"The equipment is not bad though," said Morris. "The closed circuit TV surveillance is pretty sophisticated."

"If they stay awake to watch it," said Koznicki cynically.

"One thing we've got going for us is that Marge and I now know everyone here—students, faculty, and staff." Patrick was understandably pleased that they had accomplished so much in so short a time.

"Yes." Morris turned to look at some students crossing the courtyard. Classes were changing. "There, for example, is Eileen Schaaf, probably en route to Ascetical Theology class."

"So," Koznicki smiled as if he were the parent of two gifted children, "you know everyone!"

"Who the hell is that?" Patrick nudged Morris and pointed at a man who had just entered the courtyard and stood seemingly appraising the surroundings.

"And who's that with him?" Morris referred to the stranger's companion.

"You do not know who they are?" said Koznicki. "And they are not wearing identification! How did they get in here?"

"I don't know," said Patrick through clenched teeth, "but I'm going to find out in a hurry."

Patrick and Morris strode purposefully toward the two strangers. They were a study in contrasts. The taller, who appeared to be several inches short of six feet, wore a vicuna coat over a bright green silk suit. His dark brown patent leather shoes reflected up toward his green Homburg. He appeared not to have lost his baby fat.

The other, a slip of a man at about five-feet-five, slouched at his companion's side. His brown corduroy suit looked as if it had been slept in, not once but many times.

The taller man seemed absorbed in viewing the courtyard. The shorter man seemed ready to drift off into a needed nap.

"Who the hell are you?" Patrick challenged.

The smaller man looked up indifferently. "Who the hell wants to know?"

"I'm who the hell!" Patrick spat it out while removing a wallet from his jacket pocket. He displayed his identification. "Detective Sergeant Dean Patrick, Detroit Police, Homicide Division." It was enunciated meaningfully.

"Oh," said the smaller man, "that's who the hell."

"This," said the taller man, pointing to his companion, "is Herman Deutsch, the director and writer. And I," he almost bowed, "am Bruce Lauther, the executive producer."

"Director and producer of what?" Patrick was losing what small shred of patience he had worked up.

"Why the movie, of course. The made-for-TV movie."

"What made-for-TV movie?" It was Morris' turn to lose patience.

" 'Assault with Intent,' " Lauther explained, "a docudrama of these dastardly assaults against Detroit's innocent clergy!"

"I still don't like it, Bruce," Deutsch commented.

"Not here. Not now," Lauther quietly admonished.

"It's a lousy title," Deutsch insisted. "It should say 'Murder' or 'Mayhem' or 'Blood' or something violent. 'Assault with Intent' doesn't make it. It doesn't scare . . . it just doesn't scare."

"Herm," Lauther turned to his director, "everyone understands that 'Assault with Intent' is the beginning of a statement. Everyone is familiar with the phrase 'assault with intent to commit murder.' "

"I don't like it."

"Wait a minute! Wait a minute!" Patrick's growl was almost a shout. "How did you turkeys get in here? Where are your I.D. tags?"

"Yes, how did you get past the guard?" Morris demanded.

"Guard!" Deutsch snorted.

"By the very simple procedure of explaining to the guard just who we are and what we are about," said Lauther.

Morris glanced at Patrick, then raised her eyes to the heavens. "I'll take care of the guard." She headed for the main front door.

Koznicki, who, of course, had heard the entire exchange, approached and introduced himself.

"You must understand, gentlemen, that in the light of the shooting that occurred here, we are very concerned about security. Could you explain how you come to be here and what you intend to do?"

"Certainly." Lauther extracted business cards from his wallet and gave one each to Koznicki and Patrick. "Until recently, I was vice president in charge of production at a major TV network in Los Angeles. Naturally, the whole country is aware of your distressing situation here in Detroit with the attacks on priests in your seminaries. To be brief, I sold the idea of a docudrama on this tragedy to a rival network. While the iron is still hot, as it were."

"While the iron is still hot, indeed. You realize, of course, that this case is still under investigation," Koznicki emphasized. "We do not know, at this time, who is responsible for these assaults, nor, in fact, do we know whether there may be more. How do you expect to make—what did you term it?—a 'docudrama' when the real-life scenario has not been played out?"

"Ah, yes." Lauther patted his stomach. Koznicki wondered idly whether the producer could pat his stomach and rub his head simultaneously. "Well," Lauther continued, "we have obtained the services of an outstanding forensic psychiatrist to assist us in the workup and understanding of the characteristics of the assailant as well as his motivation."

"A local shrink." Deutsch's disgust was undisguised. Koznicki and Patrick exchanged glances.

"Not Dr. Fritz Heinsohn!" exclaimed Patrick.

"The same," Lauther confirmed. "We feel most confident in his ability."

"You shouldn't," Patrick muttered.

"I see," said Koznicki. "Well, whatever else you may be planning, I hope you do not intend to use these premises as a setting for your docudrama."

"That is precisely what we intend."

"That is out of the question."

"Not that far out." Lauther reached inside his jacket and removed a document, which he presented to Koznicki. "Our contract, Inspector, with the Archdiocese of Detroit, permitting us to use sections of St. Joseph's Seminary for four weeks, with an option for four more, to film 'Assault with Intent.' "

Koznicki studied the document briefly, then handed it to Patrick.

"I wonder if there's anything we can do about it," Patrick murmured.

"Perhaps," Koznicki touched his lips deliberatively, "in dealing with the Archdiocese, we might use the good offices of our friend Father Koesler. Dean, would you be so good as to see if Father is here? I believe he should be teaching a class now."

As Patrick left in search of Koesler, Koznicki studied the producer and the director.

"One thing occurs to me, now that I think of it," said the Inspector. "The contract with the Archdiocese calls only for the use of St. Joseph's Seminary. Yet three—perhaps four—of the attacks occurred at Sacred Heart Seminary. You do not intend to film at Sacred Heart?"

"No."

"Why not?"

"Dramatic license," Lauther explained.

"A nickle-and-dime budget," Deutsch grumbled.

Morris had returned by the time Patrick arrived with Koesler in tow. Koznicki explained to the priest why he had been summoned.

"Would you like me to check into this now?" Koesler asked.

"Please."

He left, and returned a few minutes later, shaking his head.

"Archbishop Boyle had nothing to do with this. Nor is he going to have anything to do with this. I talked with the Archdiocesan controller. He said Mr. Lauther offered the Archdiocese $5,000 for permission to use these facilities for four weeks."

"That's all?" Patrick exclaimed, "$5,000 to screw up our security!"

"You should talk to the controller," Koesler said. "Then you'd know how badly the Archdiocese needs $5,000. Especially when no one expected it. Talk about your pennies from heaven."

There was embarrassed silence during which Koesler crossed to Lauther's side.

"So you're going to make a movie about these attacks," he said, a smile playing at his lips. "Who's going to play the role of Father Koesler?"

"Father Who?"

"Father Koesler, the third priest in the case. The one who was almost poisoned."

"Oh. I don't know. You'd have to check with the production manager. Why do you ask?"

"Because he's Father Koesler," said a grinning Morris.

"No! Really?" Lauther backed away in surprise. "Say, I just got an idea! Father, how would you like to assist this project as a technical adviser? We could use your expertise, and it certainly wouldn't hurt publicity to have one of the victims as technical adviser. What do you say, Father? There'd be a modest honorarium." Lauther was enthusiastic.

"Oh, I don't think so," Koesler demurred.

"Father, could I speak with you for a moment?" Koznicki beckoned his friend aside.

"Father," he spoke just loudly enough to be heard by the priest, "there seems to be nothing we can do about the making of this film even though it will interfere with our investigation. It would be very helpful if we had one of our own—so to speak—on the scene to keep an eye on what they are doing, keep us informed . . . you know."

"Inspector, I have you to thank for this class I'm teaching here at St. Joe's. Now you want me to volunteer for an additional assignment . . . as a movie consultant!"

"Father . . ." Koznicki moved closer. Koesler feared he would find himself not only figuratively but literally in the Inspector's pocket. "Father, it is only for four weeks."

"Oh, all right, all right." Koesler laughed. "But I warn you: I may never be the same after Show Business!"

6.

THE SHADES HAD BEEN LOWERED, MAKING THE SMALL room nearly dark.

"I don't see how we can continue with our plan," said the First Man. "I think we are simply going to cut bait." He rose from his chair and made his way to the kitchenette. It was so dark that even though his eyes had become accustomed to the dimness, he had to grope along the wall until he felt the surface of the counter. He plugged in what he believed to be the coffeepot. In actuality, he plugged in a toaster. The plugs had lain side by side on the counter.

"I don't see why we should give up," said the Second Man, with a trace of a whine. "After all, we've come so far."

"You don't see why—!" En route back to his chair, the First Man tripped on the rug's edge. He almost fell, barely catching himself. "Why, it's as plain as the nose on your face. That is, if I could see your face. Why does it have to be so damn dark in here all the time?"

"Security," the Third Man responded. "You know we have to keep a tight lid on our meetings. Besides, I tend to agree. Even though this was supposed to be my ballgame now, I think we'd be smart to call off the whole project. Or at least postpone it for the immediate future."

"I think you're being premature," said the Fourth Man. "It may not be over yet." He occasionally made notes on a small pad. The others never understood how he could see enough to write anything.

"Of course it's off," said the Third Man angrily. "As soon as they decided to make a movie of our project, we were finished at St. Joseph's."

"Yes," the First Man agreed, "it'll be a three-ring circus now. Say, do you think the coffee's done?"

"Give it a little more time," the Fourth Man said. "I'll get the sugar." He rose and made his way cautiously to the kitchenette. There was the sound of sugar pouring into a bowl, followed by the sound of sugar overflowing onto the floor. The remainder of the Fourth Man's movements in the kitchenette sounded like a soft shoe dance.

"They'll be moving in technicians, cameramen, I-don't-know-whatall, to film this damn movie," said the Third Man. "We know for certain our original plan is completely out of the question now. What I'd like to know," he addressed the Fourth Man, who was trying to wipe sugar from his soles, "is just how you can hold out any hope?"

An odd popping noise cut through the gloom. The room was otherwise so quiet and the noise so unexpected that it sounded louder than it actually was.

The Fourth Man dove for the floor. The First and Third slithered under the table. The Second fell backward.

In sliding under the table, the Third Man had caught his cufflink on the tablecloth, jerking the linen to the floor with him.

"What the hell was that?"

"Any of you bring a gun with you?"

"No."

"No."

"No."

"Shhh . . . wait a few minutes," the Fourth Man cautioned from his prone position.

Deep silence ensued.

After a few minutes, the Fourth Man gingerly crawled across the floor in the direction the sound had come from.

He stood and groped about. His hand touched a warm toaster. "Who the hell turned on the toaster?"

Sheepish mumbling from the culprit. "Ummm . . . er . . . sorry; I must've mixed up the plugs."

All four brushed themselves off and returned to their chairs, the Third Man trying to be casual as he re-spread the cloth on the table.

"Now, where were we?" demanded the Fourth Man.

"I was asking," said the Third, "what in hell gave you the idea we weren't finished?"

"Well, I've done a little research. There will be as many as ten executives and technicians here from Los Angeles. Those, at least the technicians, will be complemented by local union people. There will also be the out-of-town and local actors and extras. There will be bedlam in the seminary. A perfect time to add a little chaos of our own. All we need is to adjust our plans ever so slightly."

"But how do we get on the set? We aren't technicians or actors. We're not even in any union. And even if they were to hire us as extras, we wouldn't know when we were going to be called. And we certainly wouldn't be there every day they were shooting!" The Second Man capped his harangue with one of his emphatic gestures.

"That's where my research paid off," the Fourth Man declared. "They also hire up to five or six local people they call production assistants. In reality, they're just general factotums—gofers. They need no special training. But they're on the set all the time."

The First Man got up and poured himself a cup of coffee. He tasted it. It was cold. "I believe our coffeepot is out of order."

The Fourth Man sighed. "I'll make a note to have it fixed." He made a notation on his pad.

"But how do we get hired?" the Second Man whined. "We don't know anyone connected with filmmaking."

"I do," said the Fourth Man. "This is where my position as postmaster is going to come in handy. I've already contacted the local production agency that's handling the arrangements. We all will be hired as production assistants. And the job pays fifty dollars a day."

"But you forget," the Second Man whimpered, "we're all working. What are we going to do about our jobs? I just got moved up to the checkout counter at the supermarket. It's the longest I've ever been employed anywhere."

"I just hired in at Michigan Bell," said the First Man.

"And at the service station, my boss said if I keep up the good work I can go from pumping gas to the repair department," the Third chimed in.

"Gentlemen," said the Fourth Man, "arrange for a leave of absence. Quit. Take sick leave. I myself am taking my vacation time to be there. Do whatever you have to so we can carry out our plan. Besides, you know, if you're going to be brutally honest, none of you ever holds a job very long."

"Neither would you," the Second Man retorted, "if you weren't protected by Civil Service!"

"Oh, forget it," said the First. "We're pledged to complete our project. We ought to be grateful that one of us holds so influential a position as postmaster. I move that the three of us do what we have to do to take the job as production assistants."

"O.K., I'm with you," said the Third Man.

"Oh, all right; I'm in," said the Second, "but I want to go on record as agreeing reluctantly. I don't know what I'll do if I lose that checkout clerk's job!"

"Good," said the Fourth. "I'll give each of you the address where you can get your papers. I've been assured we can start work immediately." He began to write, then noticed his pen had run out of ink. He shrugged, took a pencil from his shirt pocket and started to write again. The lead point promptly broke. "I'll give you the address later."

"We're still all in this together, aren't we, men?" the Third Man challenged pleadingly.

All agreed the project would have their unanimous participation.

"Why does it have to be so damn dark in here!" the First Man complained. He reached up to pull the light cord, which broke from the fixture and dropped in a useless heap on the table. "Damn!" He strode toward the window.

"Don't!" yelled the Fourth Man.

"The meeting's over anyway," the First Man said, as he tugged at the bottom of the window shade. The shade snapped to the top of the window, clattered in meaningless circles, then fell to the floor.

"I'll have it fixed," said the Fourth Man. "This meeting is adjourned."

Maybe she was a model. Maybe she had been a model.

The central foyer of St. Joseph's Seminary was in a state of chaos. Father Koesler, his back against the rear wall, stood observing the frenetic activity, as people, mostly male, of all ages, milled wall-to-wall. A balding, middle-aged man was shouting through a megaphone. Perhaps he was a director. But not many in the crowd seemed to be heeding or obeying his directions.

Koesler recognized seminarians from both Sacred Heart and St. Joe's. Zimmer, Totten, Wangler, Marks, Doody, and Kulinski, among others. Obviously hired as extras. Koesler smiled. Events such as this continued to prove that things certainly were different from his seminary days. In his day, no one would ever have dreamed that a movie could be made in or about the seminary.

Of course, in his day, faculty members were not assaulted, either.

Of all the people in the crowded foyer, the tall priest had focused on an attractive woman holding a clipboard. She was standing near the large camera and seemed to be trying to assist the director.

She was one of the prettiest women Koesler had ever seen. He wondered again if she was or had been a model. Her glowingly attractive face was framed by shimmering light brown hair. She was almost pencil thin, which led Koesler to ponder about a possible modeling career. He did not know for certain, but he assumed thinness was required of models so the consumer's attention would be drawn to the product rather than the model's figure. He decided he would be surprised if this woman had not done modeling.

At this point in Koesler's musing, the director called for a break. Everyone seemed to migrate centrifugally toward the coffee urns or drinking fountains against the walls or out into the corridors for a smoke. Koesler decided that if he was going to be some sort of technical adviser, he'd better get involved. He also decided he would try to make his involvement as pleasant as possible by talking with the attractive lady rather than the balding director.

"Hello," he opened inventively, "so this is how movies are made."

She appraised him for some seconds. Then she smiled, appearing to have selected that response from many under consideration.

"This is the way a certain kind of movie is made, Father."

"Certain kind?"

"You might call it 'exploitation,' if you wanted to be polite."

Koesler found the world troubling. He did not want to participate in something that could be described as exploiting a situation. He decided he would return later to that point to discover what she had in mind by using that word. "And what do you do, if I may ask?"

"I'm production manager."

"Production manager?"

"Well, for this project. I'm in charge of most of the details of this operation, and generally assist in getting the thing filmed."

"Are you in charge of casting?"

"Not exactly. I hired someone to do that. Is there something special you wanted to know?"

"Well, yes. Who's playing Father Koesler?"

She looked at him searchingly, then consulted some papers. "Chris Lorringer."

"Chris Lorringer." He looked disappointed. "I've never heard of him."

"Oh, Chris is a capable actor . . ." She looked at him more intently, then broke into a grin. "You're him, aren't you? You're the real Father Koesler!"

He nodded sheepishly.

"Mary Murphy," she identified herself, extending her hand. "So that's it: you want to know who is going to play you. Whom would you have picked?"

"Oh, I don't know. Robert Redford maybe."

She laughed. "Father, what we would have had to pay him would be nearly the total budget of this entire project."

He turned serious. "Back to the word you used before: 'exploitation.' Does what you're telling me now have some bearing on your use of that word?"

"In part, yes, Father, I know this is not confession, but I'd prefer this remain between the two of us."

Koesler nodded, though he would have preferred no strings. Treating this as at least a professional confidence would prevent him from acting on what he learned. For instance, he could not back out of his commitment to this project based on what Mary Murphy might tell him; otherwise he would be revealing indirectly that something she said had contributed to his decision. They had been seen conversing and that would establish her as one who could have influenced him.

"You can expect something like this to happen anytime something bizarre makes the national news scene. Could be the eruption of a volcano, fire in a skyscraper, child murder, or, in this case, an attempt on the lives of several priests. Once something like this hits the wire services or network news, you can be pretty sure someone will exploit the situation. For all we know, someone may be writing a quickie book about this right now. But what happened here is that Bruce Lauther heard of these assaults and sold the idea of making a docudrama . . ."

She paused in the face of Koesler's obvious unfamiliarity with the word.

". . . part documentary and part—a big part—dramatic fiction. He sold the idea to one of the major networks. With any luck, 'Assault with Intent' will be a two-hour made-for-TV movie. Without much luck, it will molder on some shelf at the network.

"But you'll find that the answer to any question about why we are doing something this way or that is that it will be the cheapest way of doing it."

"I see."

"You looked troubled, Father."

"It's just that in a weak moment I agreed to provide some technical advice for this film. I'm not exactly overjoyed to be associated with something schlocky."

"Oh, it won't be that bad. Hang in there, Father. You may be able to keep them honest. And," she smiled reassuringly, "of course, you can always demand that your name not be listed in the credits . . . but you'd better get that in writing."

"Thanks for the advice."

"Speaking of getting it in writing, you are one of the real people who'll be portrayed. Has anyone asked you to sign a release?"

"No." It was news to him that any such document was required.

"Damn!" She shook her head. "Pardon my French, Father. I've got a release form here someplace. Would you sign it, please. If *you* haven't been approached, probably none of the other priests has either. I swear, I think I'll need a vacuum cleaner to pick up all the loose ends on this production."

As Koesler signed the release, Mary commented, "Ordinarily, I could offer you some sort of honorarium for signing, but not on this project. I hope you understand, Father."

"Think nothing of it." He grinned. "Come to think of it, I guess you *are* thinking nothing of it."

The man with the megaphone began shouting instructions again, and the crowd reassembled in the foyer.

"Is that the director? I'd better go meet him." Koesler took a step forward.

"No, no, Father." Mary touched his sleeve in a restraining gesture. "That's not the director. That's the first assistant director, Sol Gould. And I wouldn't go meet him now if I were you. The director and the producer are at a script conference. I imagine you ought to be there too, if you're going to be a consultant."

"They ought to make their invitations more clear. They could start by inviting me."

"More loose ends." Mary shook her head.

"Wait a minute: if there isn't a script yet, why are they filming these scenes?"

"They know they're going to need crowd scenes. They're filming now and they'll splice them in later. We're buying time. Remember, Father: always the cheapest way."

The assistant director was shouting at the extras. "No! No! Don't just *walk. Talk* to each other. No! Don't just move your lips. Talk Talk! You do know how to *talk,* don't you? Keep moving! Keep moving!"

The extras, most of whom were not really seminarians, were walking back and forth passing each other in the inner courtyard, just off the foyer.

Leonard Marks and Raphael Doody were walking

toward each other. Each was looking at the camera, fascinated.

"You two, out there in the middle! Don't look at the camera! Just walk the way you normally would. Don't look! I said. Don't—watch out! You're going to run into each other!"

They collided and both tumbled into the fish pond.

"Goddamnitalltohell!"

"Watch the language, Sol," his assistant murmured. "Those two really are seminarians."

Koesler shook his head. They might just have as tough time making this movie as the police were having trying to solve the real crimes.

Leon London stopped at Pete Sands' desk. Sands had just hung up his phone. "Pete, I want you to work up a feature for the Friday entertainment section on that made-for-TV movie they're working on at St. Joseph's Seminary."

At mention of the seminary, Pat Lennon, who had been feeding a story into her CRT a couple of desks away, looked up.

"The governor is forever running off to Los Angeles begging the folks in Tinseltown to make their movies in Michigan—anywhere in the state, even the Upper Peninsula. And here L.A. drops right into our lap within the confines of Detroit. Try that angle."

"Right." Sands, one of whose specialties was covering news angles of entertainment stories, had been thinking about this very event. "Plus there's the angle of added income to the city. I mean, how much does a movie bring in? What can Detroit hope to net from this unexpected windfall?"

"Good idea. The mayor likes to poor-mouth the citizens about how close to bankruptcy we are. Once you determine how much they expect the movie to bring in, you can explore what the city intends to do with it all."

"And there's the obvious lift a city gets when a

movie is made about it. It's great when the film crowd moves in. And it's great when you see the familiar scenes on network TV. All in all, it's quite a kick."

"Yeah. And this is the kind of story that's set off well with photos. People wonder what it's like backstage, behind the cameras. Make sure we get shots from behind the cameras."

"Right, boss!" Sands picked up the phone to start making arrangements.

As London started past Lennon's desk, she stopped him. "Leon, I don't want to appear covetous, but isn't this seminary beat mine?"

"Oh, absolutely, Pat. And if anything additional breaks, you've got it. But this is a different angle: Show Biz. That's why I asked Sands to cover this aspect."

Lennon was confident that she was capable of developing an entertainment feature story as well as or better than Pete Sands. Although disappointed, she tried to conceal it.

"Well, that's your decision to make, Leon. But I have a definite feeling that all is not well with the film. I think it's going to be more trouble than it's worth. Maybe even cause some trouble."

At this point, were she talking to Bob Ankenazy, he would have paid attention. But Leon London tended to discount intuition. "Nonsense, Pat. Why would it cause trouble?"

"Timing, for one thing. It's too early to be making any sort of definitive commentary on these seminary attacks. I just feel in my bones that this business isn't over yet. And if I'm right, then this film company might be contributing to the problem by causing all this hullabaloo and making security all but impossible."

For a moment, the shadow of a doubt crossed London's mind. But he dismissed it.

"No, I'm sure Sands' story will be fine. It's just an entertainment piece. Nothing to get perturbed about. It'll be fine."

Maybe, Lennon thought, but I doubt it. I seriously doubt it.

"I can smell it from here," said Nelson Kane. "It stinks to high heaven!"

"Absolutely," Joe Cox agreed.

"Those Hollywood guys are circling this story like a bunch of goddamn vultures. And the timing is all wrong. It's like making a movie about Mount St. Helens while it's still erupting. How can they start filming when even the cops don't know who did it?"

"That's not all, Nellie," Cox consulted his notes, "they haven't even got a script."

"No script! What are they trying to do, produce a goddamn *cinéma vèrité*?"

"They're relying on their local expert to lead them to the truth."

"Who?"

"Dr. Fritz Heinsohn."

"No shit!" A smile began to play at the corner of Kane's mouth. He was beginning to see the story as it would develop. And he was reveling in the anticipation.

"Yes," Cox affirmed, "the forensic psychiatrist who brought mental health to Detroit's criminal element."

"What's keeping him from issuing his usual statement? The one where he appeals to the criminal to come to him for help. And the doctor will see that the big, nasty policeman will not hurt the poor, troubled lad."

Cox snickered. "They must be keeping the doctor too busy trying to tell them what happened when nobody knows what happened, and what's going to happen when nobody knows that either."

"Damn, Cox, I think we can burn those film guys on this one!"

"If we do, we'll endear ourselves to the cops."

"They're getting in the cops' way, aren't they? Sure; this investigation was running up enough blind alleys as it was without having these out-of-town turkeys mucking up the scene of a crime with equipment, actors, technicians, and extras."

"I've got a friend in the entertainment section of the L.A. *Times*. Why don't I call and see what I can dig up. As far as I know, all the principals on this project are from the West Coast."

"Yeah, Joe, why don't you do just that . . . and let me know what you find out."

As Cox made his way to his desk and phone, Nelson Kane rolled an unlit cigar from one side of his mouth to the other without its ever being touched by human hand. Absently, he wondered how the *News* was treating this story.

"He hasn't got any convictions, Ned," Sergeant Patrick said into the phone, "but he's been brought up on morals charges half a dozen times."

"Morals, eh?" Lieutenant Harris responded. "Boys or girls?"

"Boys."

"Hmmm. How did he beat the charges?"

"Apparently, Bruce Lauther used to carry a lot more clout in Hollywood than he does now. He had just enough markers that he was able to call them in each time he was arrested. The word is, however, he can't do it anymore. His star, apparently, has set in the West."

"Intriguing that he is interested in a story that's set in a seminary populated by young men."

"I hadn't thought of that. Yeah, it *is* interesting."

"How about the others?"

"At least as far as the L.A. group is concerned, nobody is unblemished."

"Oh?"

"Herman Deutsch, the director and scriptwriter? Used to be one of Hollywood's best. Has a string of hits and big moneymakers. Everything but an Oscar."

"What's he doing on this two-bit gig?"

"The bottle got him. Chronic alcoholic. He's been

admitted to almost every hospital in L.A. at one time or another. No criminal record. Works just often enough to keep up the supply of booze."

"Interesting."

"Sol Gould, the first assistant director? Spent time in San Quentin for forgery and passing bad checks."

"Quite a crew you've got there, Dean. The others have similar problems, I take it?"

"All but the locals."

"Locals?"

"Yeah. Mary Murphy, for instance. She's a partner in a local production company. They undoubtedly signed her on because the film's being shot in Detroit and they're using a lot of local people. She's the production manager."

"And she's clean?"

"Yup."

"What's a nice girl like that doing with the French Foreign Legion?"

"Maybe she doesn't know."

"No sense in telling her now."

"Well, with this gang, at least *we* know what to look for."

"Yeah: trouble."

"So, did you get anything from your friend in L.A.?" Kane could tell from a glance at Cox's face that the reporter had, indeed, got something.

"Yeah. Quite a bit."

"This friend of yours, you said he's on the entertainment desk at the *Times*?"

"Yeah. Does reviews, interviews, that kind of stuff. Really in with the Show Biz crowd. In a perfect position to give us the dope we wanted."

"So, what's with whatzisname, the producer?" Kane leaned forward expectantly, his clasped hands resting on the desk.

"Lauther," Cox supplied, "Bruce Lauther, executive producer. Until recently a TV network vice president.

When he was fired, according to my buddy, he joined a large and notable club of canned TV execs. Evidently, when he got wind of our seminary goings-on, he got this idea to do a quickie made-for-TV movie."

"But why now? Isn't it a bit early in the game for a film treatment? I mean, the cops don't even have a handle on who did it yet."

"For the very good reason"—Cox made sharp, cutting gestures with his right hand— "that Lauther got word that another producer was thinking of filming this story. Except that the other guy was wasting his time, in Lauther's view, by researching it."

"Aha! Get it first—who gives a damn whether it's accurate!"

"Exactly. So Lauther gets together a package and sells the idea to a rival network."

"He wouldn't dare go back to his own network."

"Right. Incidentally, my buddy says that selling is what Lauther does best. If he were satisfied to be himself, he'd probably make good money selling anything from TV time to used cars.

"So anyway, he sells the idea and the network puts up the money."

"How much?"

"One point five mill."

"One and one-half million dollars! Is that significant?"

"Not for a big screen movie. But for a made-for-TV movie, it's standard. They get it in time-released increments of one-third each.

"Next, Lauther gets together the second- or thirdstring Hollywood technicians."

"Second- or third-string?"

"The scriptwriter-director? A lush. Nobody's hired him to make coffee in years . . . check that." Cox consulted his notes. "He's been given an advance a couple of times, but he didn't complete either project. He gets a little money and the next time anyone sees him he's in detox drying out.

"Next"—Cox glanced at his notes—"the first assistant director? An ex-con; forgery. The second assistant director? One of the whiz kids to hit L.A. about ten years ago. Everybody predicted a brilliant future. Nothing. Zilch. No ambition. In his thirties and already burned out.

"Want me to go on?"

"Naw, that's O.K." Kane scratched his head. "What's the kicker? It doesn't make sense. A million and a half would appear to be enough to make this movie with a touch of class. Why the bums, has-beens, and never-will-have-beens?"

"A good guess—and this can't be more than a guess —is that if they come in under budget, the producer gets to pocket what's left."

"Aha!"

"Aha!"

"Can you get substantiation for this stuff?"

"Most of it. It's like having the answers and trying to find someone to ask the questions of."

"O.K. Get on it. Get some quotes from Lauther and his crew. Find out how he got the use of St. Joe's while a police investigation was being conducted there. Find out his shooting schedule. See if you can pin down as a fact that he intends to come in under budget. And by how much."

"O.K., O.K., O.K.!" Cox had been scribbling furiously. He began to back away from Kane's desk. "I think I know how to do this." He laughed.

"O.K., but get on it. I want it for Friday—all editions."

Kane sat back, hands clasped behind his head. For the second time he wondered how the *News* was covering the story. Everyone would know soon enough.

By a process of elimination, Father Koesler finally found the room in which the story conference was going on. He had reasoned it would be somewhere within the confines of St. Joseph's Seminary. After searching two of the building's four wings, he located the conference in a small, airy room off the library.

Koesler was not at the moment tasting the milk of Christian kindness. If these guys wanted his help, he thought, the least they could have done was to let him know when and where their meetings were being held.

He knocked on the door. It was opened by Bruce Lauther.

"Am I supposed to be here?" Koesler's voice held a discernible edge.

"Of course you are, Father. My fault entirely for not letting you know about the meeting." Lauther swung the door wide and with a sweeping gesture motioned the priest in.

Koesler had met two of the men in the room; he recognized the third only from having seen him on TV and in newspapers. The two he had met were, of course, Lauther and Deutsch. The third was unmistakably Dr. Fritz Heinsohn, the locally famous forensic psychiatrist.

Heinsohn regularly surfaced in police investigations of particularly baffling cases. He would give a psychological profile of the unknown culprit which usually turned out to be inaccurate and totally off-base, and then make a personal plea for the culprit to give himself up into the good, professional hands of Heinsohn himself.

Koesler could recall no instance of any criminal's taking Heinsohn up on his invitation. Yet the psychiatrist remained a local vogue figure, appearing fairly frequently on J.P. McCarthy's popular radio interview program, "Focus."

Lauther introduced the others to Koesler and the meeting resumed.

Initially, Koesler could not take his eyes off Heinsohn. The priest had seen attire such as the doctor's, but only in ads. A maroon velour pullover with turtleneck insert was topped by a dark green jacket that Koesler guessed was a designer make. He had no possible clue as to which designer. The trousers, in a light shade of brown, appeared to be Ultrasuede. At the base of this sartorial extravaganza were brown Western boots. At the crest was an ample supply of wavy brown, silver-flecked hair, which was definitely tonsorially tailored.

"I don't know whyinhell we have to have this meeting—excuse my French, Father," Deutsch appended.

Koesler guessed quite a bit of French would be spoken at these gatherings.

"Because, Herm," Lauther soothed, "we're pretty much in the dark when it comes to who is responsible for these attacks and, more than that, why he's doing it. That's where the good doctor here comes in. Be patient."

"My God, man," Deutsch protested, "read the accounts in the papers and magazines. You've got enough dope there to cast the part."

"Really, I—"

"He's in his forties, maybe late forties. He tends to go to baby fat. He's got a high-pitched voice. He's slightly taller than Truman Capote . . . my God, man, what more do you need?"

"Motive, Herm. We need the man's motive."

"Bruce, just pray we get this thing in the can and on the network before the cops solve it. That way the network will get in at least one of its two screenings. We don't stand a snowball's chance in hell of solving this thing before the cops."

"Be patient, Herm. Doctor?"

Heinsohn slid his chair closer to the table. He ran his hand through his hair. It fell impeccably back into place.

For the first time, Koesler noticed the oversized gold ring on the little finger of Heinsohn's right hand. But now that Koesler became aware of it, he also became aware that the ring was just the start of something big. There were large gold and silver rings on his left hand, and a gold pendant suspended from a gold chain around the doctor's neck. For some reason, Koesler was reminded of the golden calf of Exodus worshiped by the sinful Israelites.

Heinsohn cleared his throat. "Father and gentlemen. . . ."

Koesler thought he did not care to be identified as other than a gentleman. People were forever putting men of the cloth on generally undesired pedestals.

"I've, of course, been giving this a lot of thought. I believe—am convinced—" Heinsohn corrected himself —"that we are dealing here with a sociopathic personality. . . ."

"Sociopathic personality," Lauther repeated. He liked it. It had a ring. It would definitely play on TV.

"And all this time I thought a guy who assaults priests was as normal as blueberry pie," Deutsch murmured.

"As I was saying"—it was clear Heinsohn was determined to overlook whatever impediment Deutsch might drop in his path—"we are dealing with a sociopath. Consider, if you will, the definition given for such persons by the American Psychiatric Association: 'Sociopaths,' " he quoted from memory, "are chronically antisocial individuals who are always in trouble, profiting neither from experience nor punishment, and maintaining no real loyalties to any person, group, or code. They are frequently callous and hedonistic, showing marked emotional immaturity, with a lack of sense of responsibility, lack of judgment, and an ability to rationalize their behavior so that it appears warranted, reasonable, and justified.' "

Heinsohn leaned back, a smug smile creasing his unseasonably tanned face.

"I must say, Doctor," Lauther found it necessary to say, "that you certainly have done your homework."

"Bullshit," Deutsch snapped.

Koesler took note of the fact that Deutsch was a chainsmoker. He also noticed that the writer's hands were trembling ever so slightly. Like a man who needed a drink.

"If you pause to ponder this definition," Heinsohn proceeded, unabashed, "you will readily reflect that it describes our assailant to a T."

"It does?" Lauther wondered.

"Of course. Thompson, another psychiatrist, commenting on this definition, listed the outstanding manifestations of the sociopath as impulsiveness and a diminished superego."

"Lots of id, eh?" Deutsch asked derisively.

"In a sense." Heinsohn was not about to be provoked. "Consider our assailant. He has attacked four, perhaps five, priests. He has attacked once with a knife; once," he nodded toward Koesler, "with poison; and two, perhaps three times with a gun. From the very nature of the devices he has used, it is safe to assume that he has intended to kill. Yet he has managed to inflict only one wound amid all this violence. And that wound, while not superficial, was quickly healed.

"Does not all this point to a person who is not planning carefully? Who is acting impulsively? Who is learning neither from experience nor punishment?" Heinsohn clearly intended this series of questions as rhetorical.

The silence that followed seemed appropriate.

"Is this not the kind of person who is always in trouble?" Heinsohn pressed his point. "In each case, he acts alone. Does not this reveal a type who has no loyalty to any other person or group? Certainly, his failures indicate a type who is lacking in judgment."

More silence.

"And there, gentlemen and Father," Heinsohn concluded, "I submit you have a parallel between the assailant and the classic definition of the sociopathic personality." He spread his hands expansively as if demonstrating all the cards were on the table.

Still more silence.

"Well," said Heinsohn finally, since no one else

showed any inclination to speak, "what do you all think?"

"I'd say," said Lauther, "that was a pretty impressive presentation. Personally, I'm pretty well convinced that you've nailed it down. I'm willing to go with it. The act of a sociopath. I love it. We're going to have to write in the role of a forensic psychiatrist. Say! With your looks . . . what would you say to doing a cameo, Doctor? Play yourself in the film. You'll be going to the police with your magnificent profile of the killer—potential killer—won't you? By George, I like it. What do you think, Herm?"

"Bullshit." Deutsch lit one cigarette from another.

"If I may say so, Mr. Deutsch," said Heinsohn with a pained expression, "that remark is rather repetitive, unimaginative, and not very constructive."

"And that, too, is bullshit." Deutsch coughed.

"If you don't mind, Doctor . . ." Koesler spoke almost apologetically, as if reluctant to intrude in another's field of expertise. "There may be another side to the coin."

"Oh?" Heinsohn seemed genuinely startled that anyone would question his rhetoric.

"I am thinking specifically," said Koesler, "of the timing of these attacks. I believe it is in the timing which indicates that not only are we not dealing with a sociopath, but we are also not dealing with only one person. In each instance, the attack was made at an optimum moment for the assailant. Father Gennardo, for example, always paced the inner courtyard of this building at the same time each day . . . a time when no one else was likely to be there.

"Then, there's Father Merrit. Each morning at the same time, he leaves the seminary to offer Mass at a parish. It is so early an hour that nobody else is likely to be around. An ideal time for an assailant to strike.

"And," Koesler smiled, "there is my own experience. I dine at the seminary every Friday evening. I always check my mailbox after dinner, as do the other faculty members, for any notes or messages. Early Friday evening was the perfect time to place the bottle in my mailbox.

"You'll find the same conditions true in the other incidents. Father Ward always brought the skull to his classroom the evening before his class would be reading about poor Yorick. And Father Sklarski always took his clothes to the cleaners at the same time each week.

"I think it obvious, gentlemen and Doctor, that, far from acting impulsively or with lack of judgment, the perpetration of these acts was extremely well planned and involved a level of surveillance that would seem to require the participation of more than one person."

Several moments of silence followed Koesler's presentation. Herman Deutsch felt that if it were possible for him to like a man of the cloth, this priest had brought him close to that emotion.

"No offense intended, Father, but let's leave the psychological diagnoses to the professionals." Lauther was obviously reluctant to part with Heinsohn's hypothetical characterization.

"Father has a point," Heinsohn conceded with a slight smile, "but I think you're leaning too heavily on it. It is quite possible for a sociopath to plan—even with as much care as you attribute to him—and yet at the moment of attack to act impulsively and then to fail—as our assailant has on each occasion that we know of. I think there are sufficient indications of sociopathology that I will stick to my diagnosis."

Koesler noted Heinsohn had substituted the verb *think* for the stronger *am convinced* that he had earlier used.

"Fine," Lauther glowed, "now, let's go on to the motive. And I wonder if, at this point, I might introduce the concept of sex."

"Sex?" blurted Koesler.

"It was only a matter of time," Deutsch commented wryly.

"Absolutely! Of course!" said an eager Heinsohn.

Lauther was growing increasingly convinced that he was to going to appreciate Heinsohn even more as time went by.

"In Linder's view," Heinsohn leaned forward and made a steeple formation with his fingers, "sociopathic behavior begins as a function of hatred for the father, which is complicated by an unsatisfactory dependent identification with the mother."

"Excuse me, Doctor," Lauther interrupted, "but what does any of that have to do with sex?"

"I am coming to that." Heinsohn was unruffled. "Don't you see already? It's classic. Hatred for the father. Identification with the mother. It's the classic formation of the homosexual."

"Homosexual?" Lauther blanched.

"Gay?" Deutsch chuckled.

"Yes. To the sociopath, women represent his own mother. To have sexual intercourse with any woman would, for him, be an incestuous relationship. So he turns to other men for sexual gratification."

"This will never do," said Lauther.

"However," Heinsohn continued, oblivious of Lauther's objection, "since the sociopath hates his father, the sexual expression will tend to be violent. So, you see, what we have here is a sociopath as well as a sadistic homosexual. And the ultimate expression of this personality is the murder of his father. Only, in this instance, the victims are the fathers in the seminary. Fathers who, though unmarried, teach young men to become priests Unmarried Fathers who make other unmarried Fathers. What a perfect target for the sociopath!" Heinsohn spread his arms wide. It had been an impressive performance, he was sure. Yet only the priest seemed impressed. Lauther appeared to be fighting some inner battle, while Deutsch was clearly amused.

After several moments of silence, "We are talking," Lauther spoke slowly and deliberately as if instructing a backward child, "about prime-time network television.

About network television in prime time. Nine o'clock Eastern, eight o'clock Central and Mountain. On a commercial network "

This meticulous explanation was obviously for Heinsohn's benefit. But the doctor seemed unaware of its import.

"So?" Heinsohn wondered aloud.

"So," Lauther continued, "when was the last time you saw depicted on network prime time a sado-masochistic homosexual couple carrying on fairly graphically?"

Since he had never seen such a sight, Heinsohn was silent. It was Lauther's turn to ask the rhetorical questions.

"No, Doctor," Lauther continued, "I'm afraid this will never do."

"But why must you include graphic sex?" Heinsohn asked.

"Oh, come now, Doctor! You do watch TV, don't you?"

"Not much."

Although most people, even some addicts of the medium, will not admit to watching much television, Dr. Heinsohn was telling the truth. His TV-less life was due to a crowded schedule rather than to specific choice.

"Well, then, Doctor, let me bring you up to date on the most popular entertainment medium ever invented." Lauther was not sure whether the doctor was being honest in his disavowal of logging TV time but, to be safe, the producer decided to explain, at least briefly.

"Most of the popular prime-time shows feature two elements, violence and sex. Not too much violence and not too much sex. But not too little either. What we are aiming at, to switch media for a moment, is to produce a made-for-TV movie, which, if it were produced for the big screen, would be rated PG, or even better, R— but definitely not X.

"We needn't concern ourselves about the violence.

This is a story of violence The violent attacks on, perhaps attempted murders of, several presumably innocent men. . . ."

Koesler was not overjoyed by the innuendo.

"We've got all the violence, short of actual death, we need. But as yet, we have no sex angle at all, let alone graphic jiggles—neither 'T' nor 'A.' "

"That's the way it frequently is with celibates," commented Deutsch.

"We are relying on you, Doctor," Lauther ignored Deutsch's remark, "to provide us with a credible sexual angle that we can treat graphically but tastefully "

"Tastefully! That'll be the day!" growled Deutsch.

"Take my word for it, Doctor. I know the type of network executive we will be dealing with. A sadomasochistic homosexual relationship simply will not do. But we've got to have sex."

There was a prolonged silence. The ball very definitely was in Heinsohn's court.

"Would you buy a bisexual personality?" Heinsohn ventured.

Lauther silently but deliberately shook his head. Deutsch snorted.

After another pregnant pause, Heinsohn said, "Well, what about an affair for one of the priests?"

"Now, just a minute!" Koesler broke his long silence. "Talk about gratuitous! With the possible exception of myself, the priests who've been attacked are elderly. Not only would they not give serious thought to violating the virtue of chastity, they have devoted many years to the Church in a very dedicated fashion and—"

"That's all right, Father," Lauther interrupted, as he looked pointedly at Heinsohn. "That way lies libel, Doctor. And we're going to stay very clear of any chance of libel. No; you've simply got to think of the assailant in terms of some acceptable sexual manifestation."

It was obvious Heinsohn was most reluctant to part with any segment of his carefully crafted hypothesis.

"Well," he finally said, "I suppose there are exceptions to every rule. I suppose it could be possible that the assailant might be heterosexual." It was also obvious the admission pained the doctor. "But I must insist that even in a heterosexual relationship, this man would physically express himself violently."

"No problem, Doctor," said Lauther, glancing at Deutsch, who nodded. "The violence will make the graphics more . . . uh . . . graphic."

"There is one more thing I ought to tell you about our assailant," said Heinsohn.

All look at him attentively.

"That A.P.A. definition of a sociopath: It says that sociopaths have 'an ability to rationalize their behavior so that it appears warranted, reasonable, and justified.' "

"Yes?"

"The assailant, when the police or I catch up with him, will believe he has been doing God a favor by attacking these priests. It doesn't matter how crazy that sounds; that's the way the man will look at it."

"Perfect!" Lauther tended to think in headlines. "Joan of Arc gone wrong!"

7.

"GET THAT DIRT OFF YOUR FOREHEAD!"

Instinctively, Raphael Doody's eyes rolled upward, as if in so doing he would be able to see his own brow.

"I said get that dirt off your forehead!" Father Albert Budreau insisted.

"But this," Doody pointed at his forehead, "is blessed ashes. Father Feeny blessed them this morning and rubbed them on our foreheads during the Ash Wednesday Mass."

"First of all, Doody, the priest does not *rub* ashes. He *imposes* ashes. Secondly, and more importantly, the sacramental is important only at the moment of imposition. After that, it is just dirt."

"But Sister said—"

"Sister said! Sister said! Sister said!" Budreau expoded. "I don't care what Sister said! This is theology! Now get that dirt off your forehead!"

Doody dabbed at his forehead with a clean handkerchief, checking the cloth after each stroke to ascertain when the ashes would be completely removed.

Doody's forehead had been singled out from among a roomful of ashed heads because Doody's skin always exuded nervous perspiration. Thus, the large cross on Doody's forehead was more mud than ashes.

Budreau was a large man, slightly more than six feet, well over 200 pounds, not particularly fat, built something like a safe. Besides his priesthood, the experience that had most shaped his life was his ten-year hitch as an Army chaplain, including time spent in Europe in World War II.

In addition to "Theology and Morality of Christian Marriage," the course he was teaching at this moment, Budreau also taught "Historical Issues in Moral Theology" and "Moral Principles of the Christian Life." As often as possible, he attempted to slip back into pre-Vatican II theology, where he felt more at home.

"Open your workbooks to page 255."

There were those unspecific sounds that are typical of classrooms. Shuffling papers, students shifting in their seats, coughs, whispers, boredom.

"Now, you can see that I have listed here all the impediments to a marriage, the impeding impediments that make a marriage unlawful but valid, and the diriment impediments that render a marriage invalid. In addition to understanding all of them, I expect you to memorize them."

Muffled protesting noises. One student raised his hand. Budreau did not like it. He favored answers, not questions. He could remember a time when there were no questions. Back then, a student, particularly a seminarian, with lots of questions about Church doctrine usually had an abbreviated seminary career. After which he was encouraged to remain in the ranks of the laity and shut up.

"Maley?" Budreau acknowledged the student reluctantly.

"Father, aren't there many Church marriage courts that will accept marriage cases for many more reasons than just the ones you have listed?"

"Mr. Maley, we are not discussing what individual tribunals do or don't do. That has no significance here. We are dealing with theology, not the vagaries of some young rebel who somehow becomes head of a marriage court before the oils of ordination are dry on his hands!"

"But this list is so restrictive. I don't think any list, no matter how long, can cover all the possible things that can go wrong with a marriage!"

Budreau sensed the soft underbelly.

"Ah, Mr. Maley, but we are not talking about what can go 'wrong' with a marriage. We are talking about whether there *is* a marriage, and that is entirely dependent on how the contract is entered into, not on what happens afterward. There are happy marriages and unhappy marriages, good ones and bad ones. We consider only whether there is a marriage."

"But Father, how can an eighteen-year-old enter into a lifelong contract without knowing what the future holds . . . without knowing how he or she will develop? I don't think anybody can do that!"

"Mr. Maley, that is just what is wrong with your generation: you are incapable of a lifelong commitment. That is why so many marriages are breaking up today! That is why so many priests and nuns are leaving their vocations. What we need today are more young people who, when they put their hand to the plow, will not turn back. People who can take orders. Why, what would happen if the military thought like you?"

Oh God, the class groaned inwardly, not the Army again!

"What would happen if the troops in the trenches were permitted to question orders? Do you think they should take a vote when they are ordered to clear out? The military way is the only efficient way to run an organization. And in the military a commitment is a commitment. Not an agreement to do something until one tires of it or becomes bored with it or until something better comes along. There's no doubt about it, things would be better today if there were more of that old-fashioned commitment. And, Mr. Maley, it is perfectly possible for people to make a lifelong commitment. Just look at the people who are celebrating silver and even golden anniversaries of their weddings or ordinations or religious vows!"

Maley thought that along with some lucky people who found the right lifelong vocation on the first try, he also would be looking at some silver and golden failures and some pretty miserable priests, nuns, and married couples. But he also thought it wise to keep this notion to himself.

The bell rang. The students hurried out, eager to see how the movie, which was being filmed in their very building, was progressing.

Father Budreau strode off in his military gait, left arm swinging stiffly, right arm crooked around his books as if supporting a rifle.

He headed for the chapel for a private prayer before lunch. He recalled only a few years back when the then large student body would daily visit the chapel together for prayer before the noon meal. Now he was the only one to continue the custom. He was a man of custom and habit. Eating, resting, working, and praying each at the same time each day. Days off and vacations, as well as his twice-a-week target practice at the rifle range, were scheduled events that he depended upon for recreation.

He knelt and tried to pray. But he could not rid himself of the thought of how much better than today were the good old days. He thought it fortunate that Edward Maley was not studying for the priesthood and unfortunate that Raphael Doody was. In the old days, both of them would have been dropped—the former as one whose loyalty to the Church would always be in question; the latter as a hopeless incompetent.

He was wondering if there were, indeed, any way of returning to yesteryear, when he finally caught the thread of prayer.

By anyone's standard, the scene in St. Joseph's transverse corridor was chaotic.

The windows had been covered with black plaster-board. A camera track had been laid the length of the corridor. Technicians were everywhere, stringing lights, arranging equipment, looking busy. Makeup people were attending two actors, one of whom was dressed in black cassock and white surplice, the other in dark street clothes.

Father Koseler was observing all this carefully, marveling at the number of people required to make a simple movie. It seemed to him there were actually two crews, one doing almost nothing but trying to look busy.

Sergeants Patrick and Morris stood to the front of a group of bystanders who had come to see how a movie was made. Most of the bystanders Koesler recognized as students of either Sacred Heart or St. Joseph's seminary. Evidently, when on hand, some were hired as extras.

Standing near the large camera were Bruce Lauther and Sol Gould. Nearby, Herman Deutsch, looking much the worse for wear, curled into a canvas folding chair. Mary Murphy stood off to one side with what Koesler thought was a slightly dubious expression. He had found Mary to be both enlightening and refreshingly normal. He decided to stroll over to her.

"Oh, hi, Father." She smiled, crookedly. "If you have prayers, prepare to say them now."

"Things going badly?"

"I've never seen anything like this. We've been rehearsing this scene all morning. If anything more can go wrong, I don't know what it might be."

"People not cooperating?"

"Nothing is cooperating! Actors blow their lines; the track breaks down, tilting the camera; lights pop; we've already run out of film once; three technicians have been fired so far; Herm is hung over, and Bruce is edgy. You can budget for a certain amount of waste and error, but this is phenomenal. And we're just beginning!"

"You're right; a little prayer couldn't hurt."

Koesler looked around casually, then halted his survey to focus on five men who had been occupied in the center of the action. They were now clustered at one side of the corridor. Koesler would not have thought it possible to describe work clothes as conservative work clothes. He realized that he recognized one of the men.

"Excuse me, Mary, but," inclining his head, "those men over there; did you hire them?"

She glanced at the small group. "No, but I hired the person who hired them."

"What do they do?"

"They're production assistants. A rather pretentious title for gofers. They do odd jobs."

"I'll bet they do."

"Something wrong?"

"Oh, no . . . it's just that I know one of them."

"I wouldn't be surprised: production assistants are always locals."

At the same time that Koesler spied the five production assistants, Sergeant Patrick also spotted them. They called attention to themselves by their huddle and by their conservative, almost uniform-like clothes.

"Looka there," Patrick called the five to Morris' attention. She gazed at them for several seconds before recognition crossed her face. "Oh, my God, it's Kirkus —Roman Kirkus!"

"That's who it is, all right."

"How did *he* get on this set?"

"Apparently, someone hired him. I think we ought to find out who."

"Do you think we ought to get him out of here? If he's the one we're looking for, he could be a danger to someone on the faculty here."

Patrick pondered that possibility.

"No, I don't think so. We've got him right out front. I'd rather have him where I can see him than have him skulking about somewhere."

"Quiet on the set! Quiet on the set!" Sol Gould's megaphone blared. "Places everybody!"

It occurred to Koesler that he had not yet heard the first assistant director's normal speaking voice.

"Now let's get this right for a change!"

"What are they filming now?" Koesler whispered to Mary.

"This is the scene where Father Ward gets attacked."

"That's what I was afraid of. That actor playing Father Ward must be in his fifties. The real Father Ward is in his eighties."

"Artistic license," Mary said, with a thin-lipped smile.

The silver-haired actor entered the corridor from an adjoining room. All lights were extinguished but the flashlight "Ward" carried. In his other hand was a human skull. With the exception of the age discrepancy, Koesler thought, so far so good. Then he noticed a flaw that had hitherto eluded him.

"Wait a minute," he whispered to Mary, "that priest should not be wearing a surplice. That's a liturgical vestment, and carrying a skull down a corridor has nothing to do with any liturgical function."

Mary quickly moved forward and whispered to Gould.

"Cut! Cut! Damnitalltohell! Cut!"

The lights went up and the crew went into action. Koesler thought all this effort a bit excessive just to remove a surplice.

Finally, all was again ready. The lights were extinguished. Gould again called for action. The actor once more entered the corridor, this time sans surplice. He walked at an unhurried pace down the corridor as the camera followed silently on its track.

"Father Ward said he was reciting Hamlet's speech about Yorick as he walked down the corridor," Koesler whispered to Mary.

"That'll be done later with a voiceover," she whispered back.

As the Father Ward character neared the end of the corridor, a figure stepped from the rear doorway. Though the corridor was dark, Koesler was immediately aware of the assailant's presence, perhaps, he thought, because he had heard the story from the real Father Ward. So the figure's appearance was not unexpected. Nonetheless, Koesler jumped. He thought of old Father Ward and how frightening the actual assault must have been for him.

What happened next made Koesler disbelieve his eyes. Instead of stumbling and falling all over each other as the real Father Ward had described, the film Father Ward was giving as good as he got. After the initial surprise advantage of the assault, the assailant was slammed up against a wall. Then the two became locked in a frenzied wrestling match.

"Ouch! Oh, damn it! Watch what you're doing with that damn knife, will you!" the Ward character shrieked.

"Cut! Cut! Now what the hell is it?" Gould shouted through his megaphone.

The lights went up.

The Ward character was clutching his left hand. It obviously had been cut.

"Props! Props!" Gould yelled. "You were supposed to get a stage knife with a retractible blade, not a goddam real knife! Whatinthehell's the matter with you?"

"But I did! I did!" A small, agitated man ran onto the set and took the knife from the assailant. He placed his palm beneath the blade and bravely plunged the knife downward. The blade seemed to pass through his palm without appearing beneath the hand. The blade was retracting into the handle. "See!" the man said with an air of vindication.

"Well, it didn't do that a minute ago!" said the actor, displaying a fairly deep slash in his hand.

"O.K., all right!" said Gould, for the first time speaking unaided by the megaphone. "Get him patched up and see if anyone can figure out what happened to the damn knife.

"Listen, on the next take, let's go from the struggle sequence. At least we finally got him all the way down the goddamn hall for a change!"

Mary Murphy returned to Koesler's side. "You see, Father, that's the way it's been going: just one fool thing after another. The knife retracts every time except when we're filming. Then it cuts. I swear, I'm almost ready to believe there's some sinister force at work here."

"I don't know about the sinister force, but what on earth happened to that scene? I mean, the writing of it? According to the only eyewitness we've got, that's not the way the attack took place."

"Oh, you mean the awkwardness, the stumbling, the falling all over each other?"

"Yes—the event as described by the real Father Ward."

"Well, to tell you the truth, Bruce and Herm seldom agree about anything. But they did agree that Father Ward's story was incredible. And it does sort of explain why we needed a somewhat younger actor for the role."

"But it is the truth. He was even quoted in the newspapers."

"Father, think of the millions of people who will watch a made-for-TV movie—the group to whom we have to present a simple, uncomplicated plot. We are not thinking of the much smaller group who takes the time to read a newspaper and grasps the subtleties and nuances. In brief, Father Ward's story might make sense in print, but it won't work on TV."

"But it's the truth. Father Ward wouldn't lie."

Mary simply shrugged.

"Yeah, I know; the same thing happened when Pilate asked Jesus, 'What is truth?' He didn't get an answer either." Koesler's disgust was evident. "Look, Mary, if I'm not needed here, I've got things to do."

"It's all right, Father; they'll be lucky to get this scene wrapped up today."

As he left the set, Koesler noted that Deutsch had sunk deeper into his chair, almost into a fetal position. He also noticed that Roman Kirkus was smiling so broadly he seemed near breaking into laughter. Koesler wondered about that.

He also wondered again, since the movies rejected the verity of this event out of hand, about the peculiar ineptitude of this assailant. Somewhere in that was a message. It just wasn't coming through clearly.

"Pat, are you old enough to remember when there were the big three newspapers in Detroit?" asked Bob Ankenazy.

"The *Detroit Times*? The Hearst paper? Just barely. I was just a kid when the *Times* folded."

"In a way, Detroit has been singularly lucky in its metro newspapers. Most cities that have a couple of newspapers find little, if any, difference between them. Both conservative, or both liberal; both play it close to the vest or both are willing to take chances. The Minneapolis papers for example. Both owned by the same company and hardly a shred of difference between them. Same with St. Paul.

"But in Detroit, it's never been that way. The *News* has always leaned to the conservative, at least editorially. The *Free Press* has been audacious. And the *Times* was sensational."

"I suppose," said Lennon, "you're leading up to today's dramatic disparity in the coverage of this filmmaking." Lennon had on her desk Friday morning editions of the *Free Press* and the *News*.

The *Free Press* carried a page one story by staff writer Joe Cox, exposing the sordid background of the moviemakers and the opportunistic motives behind the made-for-TV film, "Assault with Intent." This contrasted with the *News'* entertainment feature extolling the benefits, financial and moralewise, Detroit could anticipate from the work of the gurus from L.A.

News readers would be left with the feeling that they should prostrate themselves in gratitude before these powerful visitors from the West. While *Free Press* readers might consider running these interlopers out of town on a rail.

This dichotomy in treating the story was an embarrassment to the *News* people, and Ankenazy was responsive to this. He was also aware that had he and Lennon been allowed to develop this story, there might have been no embarrassing gap between the two papers.

"I don't think it's the fault of either Leon or Pete," said Lennon. She knew she had anticipated the angle of the story as it had been developed by the *Free Press*. But she was not in the mood to gloat, nor was she the I-told-you-so-type. "It was just one of those things."

"I can see where, from London's viewpoint, he went with what were his best lights. But Sands should have sensed there was something wrong with this setup. After all, he was on the scene."

"Yes, but," Lennon said loyally, "Pete's specialty is entertainment. This was an investigative story and you simply have to have the nose for that sort of thing." After all, what might have happened had she been insistent that London assign the story to her instead of Sands? They might now be neck and neck with the *Free Press*.

"And look who they sent on the story," Lennon continued, "Joe Cox, the ace of their investigative staff."

"Well," Ankenazy acknowledged, "at least we can kill Sands' account in our later editions and save ourselves some embarrassment."

"There, you've salvaged some silver lining. Want me to get back on the story?"

"Not much to get back to. They're going to make their movie—probably not very professionally—and that's that. But be ready in case something hard breaks: We'll want you on it.

"By the way, Leon wants me to get someone on that new Jerome P. Cavanaugh Memorial Building. Word is the contractors are cutting every corner possible and there might be some collusion with Mayor Cobb's office. Looks kind of promising. Want it?"

"Yeah, I do. But first, I've got a tip on who's dumping the latest barrels of toxic waste all over the city. I've got some good sources rounded up. O.K. with you if I finish the waste story before I tackle the building scam?"

"Fine with me. Personally, I'd welcome the return of capital punishment if for no other crime than the irresponsible disposal of toxic waste."

"Absolutely." Lennon picked up her notepad and totebag and prepared to leave. "When you think of the innocent people in those neighborhoods and the scum who, just to save a few bucks, dump that stuff illegally, it's enough to make your blood boil. They poison the land, the water, the air. And all for a few bucks. And if they're found out, they may get a small fine and an insignificant jail term. But with any luck, we can fry them in print!"

"Go get 'em!"

"Oh, good, here's Tony." Father O'Dowd welcomed Father Gennardo to the luncheon table.

Father Budreau rose to greet his friend and attempted to help seat him.

"Please, please," Gennardo protested, "I'm all right. Just a little slow." He snorted.

"Snow? Snow?" asked Father Dye. "We aren't expecting any more snow, are we?"

"How are you feeling, Father?" asked Father Feeny.

"I'm coming along. It takes time, I guess. I am forced to conclude it is no fun being shot."

"I can attest to that," said Budreau.

"I didn't know you'd ever been shot." O'Dowd was surprised.

"Not I," said Budreau, "but I've seen and ministered

to any number of boys who bought it on the battle-field."

"Ah, yes. In your military career." O'Dowd remembered all too well.

"I just don't want to be treated as a martyr," Gennardo protested.

"Thank God you didn't become a martyr," said Budreau.

"That's an interesting point," O'Dowd observed. "To be a martyr, one must live up to the etymology of the word 'martyr,' and die as a 'witness' to the faith."

"The point being?" asked Budreau.

"It goes back to the motive as, I believe, the police would say. A martyr dies because he or she is witnessing to the faith. The one responsible for the martyr's death kills the martyr because of what the martyr believes."

"So?"

"Why are these priests being attacked? Why was Father Gennardo shot?"

There was a prolonged silence as each elderly priest seemed to consider this question in the light of martyrdom for the first time.

"No offense, Father Gennardo," Feeny broke the silence, "but it could not be because of the faith. That makes no sense in this day and age. Besides, why single out Fathers Ward, Merrit, Sklarski, Koesler, and yourself? Where is the common denominator?"

Again silence.

"Probably somebody who doesn't like priests," Dye observed.

"That's probably correct," said O'Dowd, who, from time to time tried to encourage his friend, who was fighting a losing battle against senility.

"Common denominator?" Gennardo stabbed a large chunk of lettuce from his salad. "I don't see one, outside of the fact that we are all priests and none of us is exactly young."

"And the fact that all are seminary professors," O'Dowd added.

"So far," said Feeny.

"Borrowing from George's earlier observation," said O'Dowd, "perhaps it has something to do with hating elderly seminary professors."

"But why?" asked Budreau.

"I don't know," O'Dowd admitted.

"Maybe the movie will shed some light on it," Dye offered.

"The movie!" Feeny almost spat the words. "Can you imagine bringing all those foreign people into the seminary in the old days! Disrupting the order of the house and making a mockery of the priesthood! It isn't likely those movie people can tell us *anything*."

"Don't they have a psychiatrist with them?" asked O'Dowd. "Perhaps he can shed some light on the matter."

"A forensic psychiatrist? And Dr. Fritz Heinsohn to boot!" Gennardo snorted. "All he will derive from this is more publicity for himself and, perhaps some more pocket money."

"Now, don't be too harsh on him, Tony." O'Dowd slid a morsel of tuna salad onto his fork. "He's a man, has to earn his living. And he is skilled in what he does."

"The best thing you can say for psychotherapy is that it is an infant science," pronounced Budreau.

Gennardo snorted and laughed.

"Has it occurred to you gentlemen," said O'Dowd, "that we have discussed this series of crimes, which the filmmakers chose to call 'Assault with Intent,' many, many times and have come up with no constructive ideas that could lead to a solution? We have fine, trained minds. On top of which—and this we can overlook only at our own peril—each of us is a possible target of this madman.

"Thus, in addition to the Christian charity of trying to help solve these crimes for the benefit of the community, we have a personal stake in their solution. Can we arrive at nothing more positive than the ridicule of a professional man trained in the field of psychotherapy?"

"We don't have the answer," Budreau observed. "The police don't have the answer. What more can we do?"

Father Dye stirred his coffee. "We can be very, very careful."

It was an accident. It could have happened to anyone.

The First Man, while walking by the goldfish pool, accidentally kicked the film containers. The top container fell into the pool. By now, he was more than familiar with the summary justice meted out by the honchos of this film company. He looked about. No one appeared to have seen what he had done. Casually, he scooped the container out of the pool, brushed the water off against his trousers, and placed the container back atop the pile. He then went about his business.

Father Koesler entered the inner coutryard. He had hastened here after teaching his class in communications at Sacred Heart. He never ceased to be amazed at how many people were apparently required just to make a movie. Men and women, technicians and staff were crawling about the set like an army of ants. He located Mary Murphy. Ah, he thought, the sane one. He moved to her side.

"What's going on today?"

"Oh, Father," she smiled, "we're doing a spot where Dr. Heinsohn makes a plea for the assailant to give himself up."

Koesler massaged his ear. "Does that make sense? What if the police have caught him in real life before this film is released?"

"Then we don't use this spot. It was the only way Bruce could get the doctor to collaborate on the film. You and I, as Detroiters, know this will not be the first time the good doctor has made a melodramatic appeal for a criminal to surrender to him. This will just be the first time he has done it in a movie."

"Do you think any disturbed person will ever take the doctor up on his offer?"

Both laughed.

It was an accident. It could have happened to anyone.

The Second Man was dusting the props to be used in the upcoming scene. The props consisted merely of a chair and a desk, on which was a pitcher of water and an empty glass. After he finished dusting the chair, he wondered, not for the first time, what it might be like to be in a movie, facing a camera, waiting for the director's signal to begin action. Impulsively, he sat in the chair. Hard. There was a sharp cracking noise that was lost in the hubbub on the set. The velocity with which he had dropped into the chair, together with his persistent weight problem, had broken it. He did not know what part, but he knew it was broken. Well, at least it had not collapsed. He looked abut quickly. No one appeared to have seen him. He carefully rose and placed the chair exactly where the prop man had placed it, and went on about his business.

"How are you feeling, Doctor baby?" Sol Gould addressed Dr. Heinsohn, who was having makeup applied.

"Fine! Just fine!" Heinsohn looked carefully into the mirror. He was paying close attention to the ministrations of the makeup person. He did not want her to get powder on his crushed velvet jacket. Nor would he allow her to touch his hair, which had been shaped by his hairstylist just this morning.

"Look, sweetheart, they tell me you're going to wing it without a script."

"That's right." The doctor oozed self-confidence.

"Look, sweetheart, it will be no sweat to have my people work up a set of cue cards for you."

"No, no." Heinsohn laughed self-confidently. "You

don't understand. I have been on radio and television hundreds of times. I assure you, I am not camera-shy. I don't need any artificial support."

"Whatever you say, sweetheart." Gould shook his head. He had a premonition there would be a lot of wasted time this day.

It was an accident. It could have happened to anyone.

The Third Man happened to be passing by the large bank of lights. Not only did he accidentally kick the plug out of the wall socket, he stepped on the plug and crushed it. He looked around. As far as he could tell, no one had seen him do it. With his toe, he nudged the crushed plug close to the wall. He hoped no one would notice the plug was no longer in its socket. At least until he was out of range. He went on about his business.

The only person who seemed to have nothing to do was Herman Deutsch. Father Koesler noticed Deutsch seated in his canvas director's chair. He seemed even smaller than he had the previous time Koesler had seen him. His arms tightly hugged his chest; his head hung down. He appeared ready to roll up in a little ball and blow away.

"What is it with Mr. Deutsch?" Koesler asked. "He doesn't seem to be taking a very active interest in what's going on."

"Oh," Mary replied, "he spends most of the evenings writing. But while he writes he drinks. Then Bruce shows the script to Dr. Heinsohn, who always seems to have objections. So, Herm has to rewrite. And when Herm rewrites, he drinks even more. It doesn't leave much of him for the daylight hours. But Sol has been stepping in pretty well."

"All right, quiet on the set!" Sol Gould's megaphone broke through the hubbub.

Deutsch seemed to shrivel even more.

Cameramen and lighting crew readied their gear; others settled back against the wall out of camera line.

"All right!" Gould yelled, "Doc, baby! You all set?"

Heinsohn, seated on the desk, one foot touching the floor the other leg hanging over the front of the desk, nodded self-confidently.

"All right, let's have the lights!"

Nothing happened.

"All right, I said. Lights!"

"I can't, Mr. Gould," said a tremulous voice. "The plug is crushed."

"Fire that man!"

"But—"

"Fire that man and get the electrician to fix that plug!"

The hubbub resumed though no one moved but the freshly dismissed technician and the electrician. Koesler glanced at Bruce Lauther. He seemed to be mentally computing the cost of this delay.

The electrician completed his repairs and moved away from the wall. He was replaced by a grinning technician from the local contingent.

"All right, you ready, Doc baby?"

"Quiet on the set! Let's have the lights!"

The set was bathed in powerful light, which did not appear to bother Heinsohn, who gazed into the camera with an expression of self-confident concern.

A man with a flipboard appeared in front of Heinsohn. " 'Assault with Intent' Epilogue. Take One." The sticks clacked.

"And action!"

"Ladies and gentlemen," said Heinsohn, "you have just viewed a drama of violence. To the layman, this violence would appear to be senseless, but to the forensic psychiatrist, no violence is senseless. There is meaning, sometimes subtle meaning, behind all human actions. Now, I am going to address myself to this man—"

"Wait a minute!"

"What's wrong? What's wrong?" Gould shouted.

"Something's wrong with this film," said the cameraman. "Something's wrong!" He opened the camera and began feeling inside. "It's wet! The film is soaking wet!"

"Fire the loader!"

"But it wasn't—"

"Fire the loader and get another can of film in here!

"And this time, check and make sure it's not goddamn wet!"

There was a babble of subdued conversation while the freshly fired loader retreated in disgrace. Lauther tallied the loss with a mounting sense of panic.

"Quiet on the set! Lights!"

" 'Assault with Intent' Epilogue. Take Two!"

"And action!"

"Ladies and gentlemen, you have just viewed a drama of violence. To the layman, this violence would appear to be senseless, but to the forensic psychiatrist, no violence is senseless. There is meaning, sometimes subtle meaning, behind all human actions. Now, I am going to address myself to the man who is responsible for all this violence. . . ."

Heinsohn rose from the desk, walked nonchalantly behind it and sat down.

"To that man, I want to say—"

With a drawn-out crunching sound, the chair collapsed. Heinsohn's feet shot up and he sprawled backward and downward.

"Cut! Oh, shit! Cut, goddammit, cut!"

The overhead lights went on.

"Someone see if the Doc is alive! Fire the prop man!"

Gould hurried onto the set as a couple of men picked up Heinsohn and began brushing off his clothing.

"You all right, Doc?"

Heinsohn looked decidedly shaken, but nodded nonetheless. Much of his self-confidence clearly was dissipated.

Gould started to return to his position.

"Oh, Mr. Gould," said Heinsohn, "if it's not too much trouble . . . if it's not too late, could we have those cue cards made up?"

"Sure thing, sweetheart."

As Father Koesler prepared to leave the scene, he wondered absently whether this filming might set a record for takes. He wondered if anyone kept statistics on such matters.

"Now, you see, at the beginning of this school year, I told you ascetical theology wouldn't bite you if you gave it a try. And I think our experience last weekend was a good indication that we've learned that ascetics can be both good and useful."

Father O'Dowd addressed his ascetical theology class in the smallest classroom in St. Joseph's Seminary. Perennially, only a handful of students elected to study ascetics. If it were not for O'Dowd's reputation for erudition, kindness, and genuine interest in his students, there probably would be so few signing up that the course would have to be dropped.

They had studied the spirituality of the Church, especially in its Western tradition, with heavy emphasis on its contemplative tradition.

It was O'Dowd's aim to demonstrate to his class that a contemplative approach to life was possible and desirable even in this day and age. Pursuant to that aim, the class had been encouraged to progressively write its own version of the ancient rule of life of St. Benedict. The previous weekend all had lived this rule at a nearby collaborating monastery. Now, each student was attempting to evaluate and put in perspective what he or she had learned from that experience.

"Let's begin," said O'Dowd, "with work. After all, that's 50 percent of Benedict's initial maxim, *Ora et Labora:* Prayer and Work. Did any of you experience any new attitudes toward work over the weekend?"

"Yes?" He acknowledged a volunteer. "Eileen."

"Well, I surprised myself with how my attitude toward work changed in so short a time."

"Tell us about it."

"Well, when I got kitchen duty when we were dividing up the chores, I must confess, I was more than a little ticked off. You know, the stereotype of 'women's work.'"

"Hey, wait a minute," another student interrupted, "we didn't assign jobs. We chose lots."

"I know. But it seemed as if fate were arranging things in a sexist way. Anyway, I started with the all-American kind of resolve to see how efficiently I could organize the kitchen. You know, build a better assembly line. . . .

"But gradually, a funny thing happened. I guess the slower pace of the weekend reached me. There was no hurry. No rush to get things done. So why hurry and try to find the fastest way to prepare food or clean dishes?

"And then I found that I enjoyed seeing the colors and feeling the texture of the raw vegetables and smelling the aromas and odors of the food.

"Now, since we've returned to the real world, I haven't wanted to use any of the automatic gadgets we had in our kitchen. Mother can't get over it."

The students were smiling. All had had similar experiences.

Father O'Dowd thought once again what a waste it was that the Church refused to ordain women. Eileen Schaaf wanted very much to be a priest. But she was not likely to become one. Not in the few years left in his life. Nor even in her lifetime.

"Would anyone else care to share an experience regarding work on the weekend?"

No other volunteers.

"Very well. How about prayer? The other half of *Ora et Labora*. Yes, Richard?"

"It was kind of funny. All my life, I just—prayed." The young man seemed embarrassed in this testimony.

"But by Sunday, something happened. Maybe it was like what Eileen was saying: There was no hurry, no rush. There was no reason to speed through Hail Marys or Our Fathers or Acts of Contrition or anything.

"And the quiet—God, it was quiet!"

Appreciative laughter.

"In the beginning, on Friday, I thought the quiet would drive me bananas. But then I got used to it. Then it happened: on Sunday, I was out early, walking by myself in the woods, and all of a sudden, I can't quite explain it, but I felt as if I were part of the forest. As if there were some common bond between me and the forest and all living things—all of creation."

Silence as others recalled similar epiphanies.

"Yes," O'Dowd acknowledged another volunteer, "Raphael?"

Ordinarily, Doody volunteered for nothing. He philosophized that sufficient unto the day was the evil of being called on, which, when it happened, regularly was disaster. If he ever felt any dram of self-confidence, it was in O'Dowd's class. The elderly priest always treated Doody kindly and with a measure of respect that the young man received from no one else. At least from no one who knew him well.

"While we were out there," Doody began haltingly, "I felt . . ." he searched for a word, "as if we were together."

"You felt a sense of *community*." O'Dowd supplied the term that had eluded Doody. "But you said it better, Raphael. Just tell us about your feeling in your own words."

"Well, when we're in school, say somebody is absent because they are sick." O'Dowd nodded encouragingly; he did not correct Doody's grammar. "And you just take it for granted that they are not well. You don't think about them after you are aware that they are absent.

"But when we were out there, if someone was absent

or late, I felt a real loss. Like part of me was missing. I never felt that way before we went out to the monastery."

"Very good, Raphael," O'Dowd commended. "You have discovered one of the essentials of the contemplative life: the sense of mutual dependence. Now you can better understand and appreciate that familiar quotation from John Donne: 'Any man's death diminishes me, because I am involved in Mankind; and therefore never send to know for whom the bell tolls; it tolls for thee."

O'Dowd was particularly pleased that Doody had survived any number of attempts to dismiss him from the seminary. The law of supply and demand was in his favor, of course, to a degree no one could have anticipated. And to a degree no one could remember. The religious vocation shortage was reaching epic proportions and there was no solution in sight.

But quite apart from the dearth of priests, which contributed mightily to the survival of seminarians such as Doody, with O'Dowd the situation was a matter of principle. Having been intimately involved in the education of seminarians for what was now the majority of his life, he was most lastingly impressed with the caliber of man Jesus Himself chose as His first priests. Very ordinary people: one outcast, one traitor, one prone to doubt; all prone to error, misunderstanding, and failure. Hardly the cream of the crop. Yet somehow this ragtag group had, against overwhelming odds, gotten the Christian religion off the ground and firmly established.

O'Dowd had always believed there was a productive place in the priesthood for people such as Raphael Doody. Only very recently had circumstances offered an opportunity to prove his thesis that the Doodys of this life could be of fruitful service to mankind.

O'Dowd's thoughts flowed to his dear friend, Father George Dye, presently teaching a course in liturgical prayer planning in a neighboring classroom. From time to time, laughter could be heard from Dye's class.

At one time Dye had been a brilliant anthropologist. But with advancing age came the stirrings of senility. And with that, Dye had become the butt of many a barb. Nevertheless, O'Dowd recognized and respected Dye's deep spiritual life as well as his steady humility. Dye was not so senile that he was unaware that some people—especially young ones—tried to make him play the fool. But he accepted all biting remarks and insults in a seemingly unlimited spirit of humility. To O'Dowd, Dye, in his present state, was a further argument that those whom the world tended to discard could be effective servants of God and man.

Besides, every once in a while, old George could fool you.

The bell rang. O'Dowd departed immediately for the refectory where the kitchen staff had prepared his afternoon snack. He would sip his tea and munch his biscuits alone, as was his custom.

"For God's holy Church: that the holy Pope of God may continue to be infallible, let us pray to the Lord." The student looked up from his paper and glanced at his classmates, who returned his gaze with a combination of mild bemusement and disbelief.

"For the nations of the Third World: that they may climb a notch or two and not be so dependent, let us pray to the Lord."

Someone snorted with barely controlled laughter.

"For the Church hierarchy in this country: that the bishops will have a successful meeting in Chicago and all find their way back home, let us pray to the Lord."

Somebody laughed aloud. This seemed to disconcert the reader slightly. But he plowed bravely on.

"For our Archbishop, Mark Boyle: that he will enjoy good health and not have to move from his mansion in Palmer Park, let us pray to the Lord."

Several of his classmates were snickering. Father

Dye, leaning back in his chair behind his desk, contemplated the ceiling.

"For the young people of our parish: that they may make out all right at the Youth Club dance, let us pray to the Lord."

His classmates whooped at the double entendre.

"Young man," Father Dye interrupted, "just what was your purpose when you composed these 'prayers of the faithful'?"

"To have a happy congregation."

Father Dye pushed his small, round body erect and observed his students, who were in varying states of helpless laughter. "It would appear you have achieved your goal.

"Class! Class!" Dye slapped his pudgy hand against the desk. "Class! Come to order!"

Gradually, they settled down.

"You know, young man," Dye knew no one's name, "it is not necessary to attach all those clauses onto the prayer of the faithful. In the earliest forms of this prayer, the leader, the president of the assembly—the priest, if you will—would simply announce the intention, 'for world peace,' for example, and let the congregation form its own prayer. And I would strongly suggest, young man, that you adopt that form. It will be better for all concerned: those who are praying and those who are being prayed for.

"Now," Dye addressed the class, "I believe your assignment was to pick a topic and, following the liturgical formula, compose a suitable prayer for it."

Papers shuffled as the students located their assignment sheets.

"Supposing we start with you, young man." Dye nodded at the first student in the first row to the left. "And then we will continue with you, young lady," he nodded at the second student in the row, "and so on."

"This is a prayer in time of war."

Dye shifted his mind into neutral.

"Almighty and eternal God, our Father, give strength

to the forces of good—us—and turn away from the forces of evil—them. Give us the quick victory that nuclear power deserves. This we ask through our gentle Jesus. Amen."

This August, thought Dye, I'll be ninety. My God, that's a ripe old age. If I'd known I was going to last this long, I'd have taken better care of myself. Who am I kidding? I *have* taken pretty good care of myself. An occasional cigar, a little wine with the meal, maybe a cocktail before dinner; regular medical checkups, and most of all, a father and mother who lived into their eighties and nineties respectively.

"This is a prayer in time of great stress. O dear God, please hurry to help us. Take away all stressful things from our lives. Crush those who would inflict stress against us. Cover us with your protection and make everything come out all right. This we ask through Christ, our Lord. Amen."

The thing you have to remember when you get to my age is not to give anyone a chance to put you on the shelf. Because if anyone gets a chance, he'll do it. And then you are out of sight and definitely out of mind. No family. Few friends. Chaplain in some nursing home until you drop. And judging from what's happened to my cronies, it isn't very long between being put on the shelf and being main attraction at a Mass of Resurrection. Something must go out of a man after he's shunted aside. I hope I never have to experience that.

"This is a prayer in time of drought. O almighty and eternal God, who maketh the rain to fall on the just and the unjust alike, why are you not making it rain on anybody? Shake down thy heavens and make it pour down so that we may have water for swimming, washing, sprinkling, bathing, and drinking. We ask you this through Christ, our Lord, and through our parched lips. Amen."

I wonder if these young people are trying to pull my leg or if they are serious about these silly prayers? It doesn't much matter. They won't have been the first to pull the old man's leg. If they are serious, the saving grace is that they are young and have a lot of maturing to do. I've never understood why my confreres could get so upset over ineffective students. Efficacy may lie just over the hill for them in the maturation that a developing adulthood can bring. Besides, I agree with Charlie O'Dowd: look what Christ started with. In the beginning, the Apostles probably couldn't pray any better than these youngsters.

"I have a prayer in time of flood. Almighty and merciful Lord, please overlook the previous prayer and shut up thy heavens before we all drown. Thou knowest we needed rain. But this is enough already. If you will but hear our prayer today, we solemnly promise we won't ask you to muck about with the weather again. This we ask through Christ, our Lord. Amen.

The bell rang, mercifully ending class.

"Remember," Dye called out as the students prepared to leave his class, "to listen to your NCR cassettes of Father Benedict Groeschel. Next class we will try to integrate pastoral psychology with liturgical prayer."

We might as well, thought Dye, try to flap our arms and fly.

As he did every day but Sunday, he headed down to the crypt chapel for private prayer. The crypts were no longer used. When there had been many more priests on the faculty and before private Masses were set aside in favor of concelebrated community Masses, the crypts had been busy with priests whispering the ancient Latin liturgy. Now, scarcely anyone else visited them.

That was precisely why George Dye favored the crypts. He could pray uninterruptedly. He could be alone with his God.

He called it his aerie. And it was like an eagle's nest. The suite was located in the center of the seminary atop the central inner courtyard. This towerlike structure was several stories taller than the surrounding seminary wings. By moving from window to window, Father Lyr Feeny, rector of St. Joseph's, could see into all the windows on the inner side of the wings. He was aided in this sneakpeep enterprise by a pair of very powerful field glasses.

Periodically, Feeny felt constrained to justify this clandestine surveillance. In the light of some days, the practice of spying on seminarians, other students, faculty, and staff seemed sophomoric. But, after some rationalization, he always arrived at the ultimate justification: It was he, Lyr Feeny, against everyone else.

With few exceptions, everyone was trying to ease him out of his position as rector of Detroit's major seminary. And, as his avid interest in professional football taught, the best defense is a good offense. What better defense than to know what was going on behind one's back?

Besides, times had changed. And with the times, the mores. Gone was the day when seminarians were open and daily confessed their violations of the rules. Good God, there were hardly any rules remaining If one wanted—no, change that—if one's position *required* an intimate knowledge of the students and their behavior, then, by God, a little covert surveillance was more than called for.

He could not decide whether George Dye was asleep in his class again or merely daydreaming. He could see Dye leaning back in his chair, eyes closed, hands clasped over round tummy. Miraculously, his class appeared to be functioning normally. Dye's classes had been known to dismiss themselves halfway through the period while Dye slumbered.

From time to time, Feeny felt he should begin the process of putting Dye on the shelf. But that kind of move could start a chain reaction that might topple Feeny from his seminary position. No use roiling the water when he himself might end up going down the drain.

Father Gennardo's class seemed to be functioning in orderly fashion. Gennardo's stock with the students had risen markedly since the attack on his life. With all the media coverage, he had become somewhat of a hero to many students. Yet, it had been this attack that had finally attracted the film people. God, Feeny would be happy when they got out of here. Nothing but a disruption, and focusing much too much attention on his precariously held fiefdom.

Feeny shifted his field glasses quickly from the window immediately above Gennardo's classroom. He had seen enough to know that a nude woman was standing at that window, and Feeny still believed in the ancient discipline of custody of the eyes.

Still, he had better be sure there was no seminarian in there with her. He moved the glasses back. No doubt about it, as Oscar Hammerstein had expressed it, there was nothing like a dame! But Feeny had put all this behind him long ago. She seemed to be alone. Probably just out of the shower. He would have to remind the students—and her particularly—to be more careful about window shades.

He would shock her, he knew. He always did when something like this came up. The students wondered if he had a private pipeline to God. He seemed privy to their most secret thoughts and actions. And why should he destroy a good thing? It did not much matter to Feeny that the students might be more motivated by fear than by love. After all, "the beginning of wisdom is the fear of the Lord."

There was Raphael Doody flat on his back in bed. Feeny checked the schedule. Just as he suspected: Doody should be in class. In the good old days, a student such as Doody would have been expelled long before he reached his final seminary year.

In the good old days, come to think of it, a female, clothed or unclothed, in any of the residence rooms, would have been unheard of. And if a seminarian had been with her—the Irish bull galloped unnoticed through Feeny's ruminations—it would have been anyone's guess which of them would have been pitched out the front door first.

Doody, meanwhile, was the straw that snapped Feeny's already threadbare patience. He would go to Doody's room and roust him immediately. He knew Doody would, first, be amazed that Feeny knew about his illicit nap, and, second, feel that he was being singled out and picked on.

But dammit, if Archbishop Boyle was going to ordain this silly young man in a few more months, Feeny would do his utmost to make sure Doody would not be napping his afternoons away while his pastor thought the parish census was being taken.

And it wouldn't hurt if Doody was left with the impression that Feeny, in some preternatural way, was able to see every goof-off, no matter how insignificant.

Feeny checked his watch. After getting Doody back on the track, there would be just time for Feeny to go down for his daily workout. It was the only time during the day he could be sure of being alone in the exercise room.

The First Man shifted slightly, thereby nudging the half sandwich off the ledge and into the pool.

"I wonder if peanut butter is harmful to goldfish," the Second Man said, in all seriousness.

"What?" The First Man looked over his shoulder and saw the remaining half of his sandwich sink slowly to the bottom of the pool. "Damn! There goes nearly half my lunch!"

"Here," said the Second Man, "you can share mine."

"Thanks." The First Man helped himself to a Hostess cupcake from the Second Man's lunchbox.

"As I was saying," said the First Man, "how much longer is it going to be before you're going to make your move?"

"Not much longer," said the Third Man as he removed the string from his lunchbag. He opened the bag and looked in. "Damn! I must've dropped my lunchbag in the wastebasket and brought the garbage with me."

"I'm afraid I don't have enough for all of us," the Second Man said.

"Oh, it's all right. I think better on an empty stomach. Anyway, we're getting close now."

"In a way, I find that sort of sad," said the Second Man. "I kind of like this job. It's fun being part of a real movie. I never thought I would ever be able to do anything like this."

"Well, don't get too attached to it," the Third Man warned. "Once we act, this movie will be finished. They couldn't possibly continue over the body of a dead man."

"I wouldn't be too sure of that," said the First Man. "The more I see of this bunch, the more I'm convinced they would stop at nothing to get something—anything—on network TV."

"It doesn't really matter whether they continue. The important thing is that we are closer to actually completing part of our plan than we have ever been."

The First Man concurred. "This has been much better than Phase One."

"You mean because you're not depending on me any longer." The Second Man almost pouted.

"It has nothing to do with that," said the Third Man. "It's just that since we have been able to get inside the building so easily, we've been able to have better surveillance. We've got our target now, and we know he is alone."

"Then what are we waiting for?" the First Man complained.

"The final part of our plan. How you two will best be able to cover for me. Once we fill in these details, we'll be completely ready and we'll act. I assure you, the time is near."

"Oh, for Pete's sake!" The Second Man turned abruptly. During their lunch break, the three had been seated on the edge of the pool in the seminary's inner courtyard. Unbeknownst to the Second Man, his shirttail had trailed into the pool. The water had saturated the cloth until it reached the small of his back. He was suddenly conscious that half his shirt was bedraggled.

"Oh, wring it out," said the Third Man, "it's not as bad as bringing your garbage to lunch."

The set was closed to all but crew members. Sergeants Patrick and Morris were the only exceptions. Everyone else on hand was either a technician or actively involved with the filming.

The camera and other equipment had been relocated to one of the seminary's spacious and empty dormitories, where a set, consisting mostly of flats, was being constructed. When it was completed, they would have a facsimile of three walls and part of the ceiling of a poorly furnished room. A single metal bed, a small desk, and a straightback chair composed the entire furnishings. Technicians swarmed around the room, adjusting microphones and testing sound levels, experimenting with lighting, laying a track for the camera, or merely helping to complete construction.

At one corner of the set, the Second Man was pounding nails into the side flat. His job was to attach the side to the rear flat. Many of the nails he was hammering through the side flat were not entering the rear flat. He didn't worry about this. He was sure enough nails were entering both flats to hold them together.

On the other side of the set, the First Man was carrying out the identical job. Identically. He, too, was certain that enough nails were entering both the side and rear flats to hold the set together.

For a change, Herman Deutsch was out of his director's chair, although barely. He was walking around the set gingerly, as if each step were bringing him closer to some sort of doom.

"This is it, Doctor," said Bruce Lauther. "This is where the money is. Both sex and violence in the same scene. I love it!" He rubbed his hands together.

"I don't know." Dr. Heinsohn shook his head. "I am not at ease with this heterosexuality. It doesn't fit the profile of the sociopath. Not *this* sociopath."

"Don't worry about it, Doctor. After the suggestions you made yesterday and the subsequent reworking of the scene that Herm did last night, we'll have more than enough violence to make up for the broad in his room. It could just as easily be an act of violence against the woman as an act of love. In a word, it will be ambiguous. You can look at it as the hostile act of a homosexual. And if anyone questions it, you can explain it in that light. Meanwhile, we'll sell it to the network as the act of a heterosexual—albeit a wild man who is violent in all that he does, from attacking innocent priests to having intercourse. Perfect, eh?"

"I don't know. Maybe."

"Any of you guys ever work on a set where they were filming a big sex scene?" the second assistant cameraman asked the production assistants, who were huddled in back of the camera after finishing their various tasks.

As one, all shook their heads.

"Wild! Everybody always says it's very professional and nobody notices there is usually a naked broad on the set. That's a laugh! When was the last time any of you guys was in a room with a naked broad and didn't notice her?"

The assistants exchanged glances and shrugged.

"Well, I should say! Look, fellas, I'll make some stills later on. See me tomorrow and I'll have them ready. Eight-by-ten glossies. Just a buck apiece and you'll have some memorabilia to really remember this day. Something you can show your friends. See me tomorrow."

The production assistants seemed very interested in the offer. The cameraman was encouraged.

"I can't believe that little set will look like a real room when they film it," said Morris.

"The magic of television," Patrick responded with a grin.

"I suppose it has something to do with the small screen. I mean, if they were making this for the big screen, they'd probably have to film a scene like this in a real room, wouldn't they? But on the smaller screen, they can get away with a fake set like this . . . don't you think? I said, don't you think? Uh, Dean . . . Dean Patrick?"

"What? Oh . . . sorry, Marge. I was watching Roman Kirkus. He's wearing that evil smile. I keep wondering what's going on in that head."

"You mean besides thoughts of hate for select individuals?"

"Uh-huh; besides that."

Sol Gould was talking to the actor and actress near a corner of the set. They seemed oblivious of everyone else. He played the assailant. She was his girlfriend.

"Know your lines?" Gould asked.

The actress smiled. "There aren't that many." The actor merely nodded.

"Basically, sweetheart, remember: you're a wild man. Even though your girlfriend is willing, this is more a rape than a voluntary offering. So let's see some action, sweetheart. And let's see if we can get this in one take."

Amid shouted jargon and general confusion, the set was cleared and all the preamble rituals to filming completed.

"And action," Gould called.

Lauther stood to one side and began the mental computation of how much this scene would cost.

Deutsch peered into the darkness; the set alone was illuminated.

The actress was seated on the bed. Except for shoes, she was fully dressed. A knock sounded at the door.

"It's open," she called.

He stepped into the set from the darkness. She rose

from the bed and ran to meet him at downstage left. She threw her arms around his neck. He lifted her from the floor. They kissed passionately. While still kissing, he clutched the collar of her blouse at the back and began ripping it.

"Hey, lover," she pulled back, "you don't have to—"

He ripped a strip the entire length of the back of her blouse. He dropped her, stepped back, grabbed the front of her blouse and yanked it from her body.

She looked at him. Something in his eyes brought genuine terror to her face.

He tugged at his shirt; buttons popped. He ripped the shirt off. He was bare to the waist.

Stunned, she tried to step away, but he was too fast. He grabbed her skirt at the waist and pulled her close. With incredible strength, he tore the waistband and ripped the skirt from her. She screamed.

"Do you think they planned it this way?" Sergeant Morris whispered.

"I'm not at all sure," Patrick whispered back, "stay alert."

She half turned and tried to run, but he snatched at her bra strap. She toppled back toward him as the catch broke and her bra flapped loose.

"What the hell!" said Deutsch to Gould. "Did you typecast this bastard? He means it." Deutsch was actually sitting up straight in his chair.

Gould appeared uneasy. "Shit, I don't know Herm. Should I stop them?"

"Hell, no. Film it. We can always cut what we can't use or doctor it so we can waltz along the fringe of bad taste. We can always trim; we can't add."

She crossed her arms over her breasts and backed away; he reached out and yanked her panties down to her knees. Hobbled, she tripped and fell back against the bed. The bed slammed into the rear wall and the entire set collapsed.

"Cut! Cut! Oh, shit! What a time for that to happen! Oh, shit! Fire the prop man! Damn!"

"I don't think they intended that to happen," said Morris.

"Where's Kirkus?" Patrick asked sharply.

"I don't know." Morris looked quickly around the set. "Damn! He disappeared while we were watching that crazy mess. We can't let that happen again. We've got to find him.

"You go this way; I'll go that. Don't lean on him; just find him. But do it fast or we may find a dead body instead."

Pat Lennon glanced about. The Tridentines would have a good house tonight. Business for this ultraconservative group was definitely picking up.

This evening's meeting, announced, as were all previous meetings, through an ad in the *Detroit Catholic,* was being held in the auditorium of Holy Redeemer church. It was one of the largest such structures in the Archdiocese.

Lennon could see that, while the balcony would not be needed, the main floor would be nearly filled. She estimated attendance at approximately four hundred. A large increase from the comparative handful present when she began going to these meetings with Joe.

She had been unable to convince Cox to attend tonight. He was off the assignment for now, and preferred remaining at their apartment to catch up on his reading. She felt strongly that even if there were no specific assignment, nor even a story in this particular meeting, nevertheless it was all building toward a story, and to miss the meeting would be to miss an essential element in the story.

From talking with a sampling of people at these meetings, she had determined that some—relatively few —were dyed-in-the-wool Tridentines. Some, attracted by the publicity, had attended only one or two meetings but found the group too far to the right for their taste; others enjoyed the glamour of being present at a media event. For the meetings continued to receive at least periodic, if brief, TV coverage.

With no registered membership, it was impossible, without inquiring, to know which category people fell into. One sweet little old lady had approached Lennon earlier this evening and shyly asked after the health of her "mister," since Cox was absent. Lennon considered this a distinctly old-fashioned expression and wondered what the lady would think if she knew that they lived together without benefit of any ceremony, civil or religious. On second thought, Lennon knew what the lady would think.

"Look, over there. That's Conrad Nap, isn't it?" Marge Morris asked.

Patrick craned until he could see the man. "Yes, it is. Looks mean, doesn't he?"

"He would have been my leading candidate. But he doesn't have the access to the seminary that Kirkus has."

"Don't count him out yet. Whoever the guy is, he had no special access to Sacred Heart, but seemed to get around all right there. Kirkus might not be our man after all." Patrick had great difficulty crossing his long legs. The architect had left little room between the rows of hard, unpadded theater seats.

"That's right. Speaking of Kirkus, where did you find him yesterday?"

Patrick smiled wryly. "In the men's room."

"The men's room! You mean while all that ruckus was going on, Kirkus went to the john?"

"Well, not exactly. All that 'ruckus' sort of, uh, aroused him, and he went to, uh . . . relieve himself."

Morris turned toward Patrick. "Masturbating?"

Patrick nodded.

"Puberty must have hit that man hard."

Kirkus called the meeting to order. He led the group in a recitation of the Rosary.

It appeared they were again going to experience trouble with the microphone. Lennon wondered about that.

"This evening, instead of having individuals report from the floor, I've asked Brother Alphonsus to put together some of your complaints and make a single presentation."

He did not ask for a motion or put the matter to a vote. Lennon got the impression of opposition to this procedure spreading through the audience. She surmised the Tridentines felt cheated in not being allowed to make their own presentations.

"So, without further ado, let's welcome Brother Alphonsus." The mike was losing about every fourth word.

The tall, thin, conservatively dressed man approached the stage. In height and build he resembled Kirkus. Alphonsus completed his journey almost without incident. He did trip on the top step, but didn't fall.

"Could he be a religious brother?" Inspector Koznicki whispered.

"It's possible," murmured Father Koesler.

Brother Alphonsus arranged his notes, then tapped the mike. It was completely dead. He sighed.

"Ladies and gentlemen," Alphonsus almost shouted in order to be heard, "to show you how terrible things really are, I am not even going to mention the unjustifiable loss of our beautiful Latin Mass."

There was some stirring in the audience. Lennon guessed there were at least some who would very much like to dwell on that loss for a good long while.

"Rather, tonight, let's talk about what's going wrong with the 'new' Church and the 'new' Mass that these post-Vatican II heretics have concocted."

A murmur of assent ran through the audience. Lennon heard someone—could it really have been that refined-looking white-haired woman?—say softly, "Sock it to 'em, Al!"

"These young upstart priests waste hundreds of thousands of dollars needlessly remodeling our churches under the excuse of making them 'fit' for a new liturgy. And that's not just to turn the altar around so the priest can shamelessly face the people instead of standing with his back to us and looking at the crucifix, as the Church has always taught! That's to move the choir and the organ all over the church! And to move the Blessed Sacrament off in a corner where no one will even be able to find Jesus, let alone worship Him! And to remove the communion railing!"

"Yeah!"

"Right!"

"It's terrible!"

"It's the work of the devil!"

He was reaching them.

"Not only will they not let us kneel to receive Holy Communion reverently anymore, now they've taken away the whole communion railing that traditionally separated the sanctuary from the rest of the church."

"Shameful!"

"Oh, yes! They stand up now to receive Holy Communion! They even extend their hands to receive Holy Communion in their hands! And we know what those hands have been busy doing only hours before, don't we!"

"Terrible things!"

"Unclean things!"

"Oh, my!"

"Fooling with their wives!"

"And that's not all! Those priests wanted what they call 'extraordinary ministers'—laymen and women—to distribute Holy Communion. They want us to forget what we learned in school and what the nuns taught us and what the Church has always taught—that only the priest's consecrated hands are worthy to hold the Sacred Host and to distribute Holy Communion!"

"Use them consecrated hands, I say!"

"Shameful!"

"They don't need help!"

"Now . . . now . . . now . . ."

Lennon feared Brother Alphonsus was about to hyperventilate.

"Now, on Sundays, who is the 'ordinary' minister of

Holy Communion? The 'extraordinary' minister is the 'ordinary' minister! While the priest sits over in his rectory and reads the Sunday paper instead of distributing Holy Communion as he should. Or he is counting the collection. Or whatnot!"

"Whatnot!"

"They should be over there working!"

"Who do they think they are?"

"They should be over by the church!"

"And that isn't all!"

No, not hardly all, thought Lennon. I'll bet he could go on forever.

"No, that is not all! The Holy Pope of God has commanded that little children go to confession before they receive their first Holy Communion. But what are our pastors doing? How are they responding to the commands of our Holy Father? They are letting the little tykes receive their first Holy Communion years before they go to confession! Don't they know that at the age of seven, a child reaches the age of reason and can commit a mortal sin? That's why the children must confess before they receive their first Holy Communion!"

"Like the Church has always taught!"

"Don't they listen to the messages of Fatima!"

"Haven't they ever heard of Our Lady of Tumerango!"

"They should listen to Evita, Elena, and José!"

"Let's get 'em!"

Lennon wasn't sure, but thought the last outcry came from Conrad Nap.

"Our priests are getting lazy. Not only do they not show up to distribute Holy Communion, but they are now granting general absolution. You don't even have to go to confession anymore. Just find a priest who gives general absolution to everybody and anybody, go to his church, and get absolved of sin without going to confession! Imagine all those dirty sins that never get told!"

"The Pope doesn't like it!"

"The Church has always taught you gotta go to confession!"

"The priests are getting lazy!"

"Let's withhold our money from the collection!"

"Let's get 'em!"

Conrad Nap again.

At this point, a crew from Channel 2 entered the rear of the auditorium. Evidently, it was the only channel that would provide coverage of tonight's meeting.

Roman Kirkus stepped to the podium and physically displaced Brother Alphonsus.

"We'd all like to thank Brother Alphonsus," Kirkus shouted above the uproar. "Well done, Brother. You certainly touched on some of the outstanding problems we face in today's Church.

"And now," Kirkus took dead aim at the TV camera, which, after panning the audience, had focused on him, "I'd like to bring up another matter that should be of great interest to us and our cause, but which most of us haven't known about.

"It's the seminary I'm talking about—St. Joseph's Seminary. We have already heard Brother Alphonsus tell us about the sex classes they run there and at Sacred Heart Seminary. Well, now, I'm here to tell you of the latest abomination at St. Joe's. They are making," he paused for effect, "a dirty movie!"

"A dirty movie?"

"A dirty movie!"

"How could that be?"

"Yes, my friends, they are making a dirty movie! You may have heard that there is a crew here from Hollywood, that sin city, to make a TV movie of what's been going on in our seminaries. That's what they tell you. But what's really going on is they are making a dirty movie! Now, you may find that hard to believe—"

"That's hard to believe!"

"Are you sure?"

As if it were a flaming torch he had carried from Marathon, Kirkus began waving a pack of photos.

"Here, my friends, is the proof! On behalf of the Tridentines, I have infiltrated that den of iniquity and have had someone in their crew make a series of what they call 'stills.' My friends, these pictures speak for themselves. I will make them available to all of you who wish to witness to this atrocity.

"You will see a man tear the clothes off a woman until she is bare-naked."

Many men in the audience leaned forward.

"And this is the movie they are making at the seminary! At our seminary! For a few thousand dollars, the Archdiocese of Detroit has sold out and let this crew come in and film a dirty movie! What do you think of that?"

"An outrage!"

"The Church never taught that!"

"Shameful!"

"Let's get 'em!"

"Friends, I'm going to make these picture available to all of you in just a few minutes. Right after we finish the meeting. I urge you all to see this scandal for yourselves!

"Now, we'll close with a prayer. And then you can see the dirty pictures. In the name of the Father and the Son . . ."

"You know," Father Koesler remarked to Inspector Koznicki as they filed out of the auditorium, "everything that Brother Alphonsus said this evening was exaggerated way out of proportion. But it was all based on legitimate complaints."

"Well, Father, we have already agreed that things pathological are all based somewhere in the normal sphere."

I'm going to have to do a little research on that crazy movie they're filming at the seminary, Lennon thought. If there's anything at all to what Kirkus claims, it could just make it to page one. Meanwhile, this looks like a good time to interview Kirkus. He's on a high and he's available. The ones who usually crowd around him after a meeting are trying to get a look at those pictures. I can have Kirkus to myself.

She made her way laboriously toward the stage. With the majority of the audience leaving, Lennon's *anabasis* was about as untroubled as a trout's trip to spawn.

"It's a lucky thing," Morris said to Patrick as they made their way out, "that Kirkus was able to get those photos. This way, he doesn't miss out on a thing."

Patrick laughed.

Ordinarily, immediately after these meetings, Kirkus would be surrounded by Tridentines hoping to pass on their horror stories of the "new" Church. But this evening, there were only a few. The majority of those who remained in the auditorium were clustered near the apron of the stage, taking turns at viewing the glossies Kirkus had purchased from the second assistant cameraman.

Lennon waited until the last Tridentine had finally departed. Notepad open, Cross pen at the ready, she introduced herself.

From his expression, she could tell that though Kirkus had certainly heard of the *Detroit News,* he had never heard of her. He probably read the sports and comics, if that. She also was aware that he was ogling her bosom. So that was how it was going to be!

"I'd like to get a little background on you, Mr. Kirkus."

"Call me Roman."

"I'd prefer Mr. Kirkus."

"Suit yourself."

Lennon noticed Kirkus' gaze straying over her head. He occasionally nodded to someone, exhibiting a quick, nervous smile. She guessed all the adulation he got from his Tridentines was, for him, pretty heady stuff.

"Are you a native Detroiter, Mr. Kirkus?"

"Sure am. Born in old Providence Hospital when it was over on West Grand Boulevard."

"And a Catholic from birth?"

"Yup."

"Year of birth?"

He hesitated as if debating whether to answer. Then: "1928."

"Education? Parochial schools?"

His face hardened. "No. Public. My parents couldn't afford Catholic. Graduated from Cooley High. When it was still a decent neighborhood. Before the niggers took over." He studied Lennon's expression to see if his racial epithet had offended. He gauged it had. "Don't bother asking about college. I didn't go. Too busy making the world safe for democracy.

"You were in the war?"

"Two of 'em."

"Two?"

"Just barely old enough to get in on World War II, and just young enough for Korea."

"That's remarkable. Army?"

"Yup."

"What rank?"

"Private."

"Private? Two wars and a private?"

"Private First Class." Kirkus reddened slightly.

Evidently, his military stagnation was a source of embarrassment. Lennon considered it significant he had not been promoted. After a few more general questions, she changed her tack.

"Mr. Kirkus, I'd like your opinion on a few topics." She paused. "Guns."

"Don't be silly. The Constitution guarantees the citizens' right to own guns."

"Do you own any guns?"

"Of course. Automatics, revolvers, rifles, and a shotgun."

"I see. You subscribe to the theory that 'guns don't kill people, people kill people'?"

"Of course not. Guns kill people. People kill people with guns better than with anything else."

"You don't mean you approve of killing?"

"It depends whether you're talking about justifiable or unjustifiable homicide."

"What's your definition of justifiable homicide, Mr. Kirkus?"

"Killing someone who deserves to die."

"And whom would you put in that category?"

"Oh, some."

"Do you know anyone who deserves to die?"

"There are a few."

"Could you kill someone?"

"I have. Two wars, remember?"

"How about the person who attacked those priests in the seminary?"

"He's probably got his reasons."

"Could you think of any reason why he might have attacked them?"

"Hell, you've been attending these meetings. I've seen you. You're so pretty you stick out like a sore thumb. You've heard these people testify. The priests in the seminaries today are ruining the young seminarians with teaching about sex and this new namby-pamby religion that has no relation to the Church of our fathers. And these seminarians are all we have to build for the future of Catholicism in Detroit."

"And do you, Mr. Kirkus, think this is reason enough to kill?"

"Some things are worth dying for and some things are worth killing for." Kirkus' smile was slightly twisted.

"Thank you for the interview, Mr. Kirkus. If I need any more information, I'll be in touch." Lennon shut her notepad and departed.

What a mind-blowing statement at the end. She could throw that into the lead and really grab the readers. Cox would regret he hadn't attended this show.

As she walked away from Kirkus, she could feel his gaze on her hips. Well, what the hell! She gave them an exaggerated shimmy and walked out and down the stairs.

8.

FATHER CHARLES O'DOWD, ALTHOUGH HE TAUGHT A course in ascetical theology that included a healthy measure of contemplative prayer, did not consider himself much of a contemplative.

He could not—would not—permit himself to be swept up past that Cloud of Unknowing into an altered state of consciousness. He had long ago decided to leave that to the Trappists. Many of them were using Zen to attain that altered state which, for the Oriental, was the point of it all, but which, for the Christian, was the vehicle, the means to the most intimate form of prayer. For some reason, though he was most familiar with the vehicle, he was reluctant to take the trip. Perhaps it was because this abandonment of rational consciousness was too suggestive of death. And, if the truth be known, Father O'Dowd feared death to a degree that he was ashamed of.

Of course, as a Christian, let alone a Catholic priest, he believed in a life after death. But O'Dowd's prayer was the same as that of the Biblical father of a son possessed by the devil: "I believe, Lord. Help Thou my unbelief."

Death was the ultimate argument. Every time someone he knew died, O'Dowd's first thought was: Now he knows all the answers—now he is either in heaven, hell, purgatory, is a crayfish, or nothing.

O'Dowd had been forced to reflect on death more subjectively during this scholastic year because some maniac had apparently declared open season on seminary professors. Though O'Dowd was well into his seventies, he was a remarkably healthy specimen. Under normal circumstances, he could be expected to live many more years. And many more years was what he hoped for. But a maniac could change such a prospect in an instant.

It may have been the weather. A dull, chilly, wet, depressing March day when it seemed winter would never let Michigan out of its clutches. A day dreary enough to spawn thoughts of mortality.

No sooner had he finished his afternoon class than he began brooding about violence, suffering, and death. Slowly, he made his way toward the dining area where, assuredly, his tea and biscuits awaited.

It occurred to him how vulnerable he was in this setting. The students, staff, and other faculty members were now all in other parts of the seminary. No one ever visited the dining room at this hour but himself. Even the kitchen crew was gone. They would not need to begin preparing dinner for another couple of hours.

What a prime moment for the assailant to strike. O'Dowd's body would not even be discovered until the kitchen crew returned. More than enough time for the killer to cover his tracks and escape.

He consciously began to use and lean more upon his peripheral vision. He did not wish to turn continually. But he did want to know what was going on around him. He was enough of a contemplative to at least trust his intuition. And his intuition compellingly suggested that someone was watching him, or that something out of the ordinary was about to happen.

He pushed open the swinging doors to the dining room. No one was in sight nor was there any sound other than his own footsteps on the tile floor. On the table at the rear of the room was O'Dowd's midafternoon snack, thoughtfully if routinely prepared by the now absent kitchen staff.

O'Dowd sat at the table in his customary seat. He poured his tea, cut a corner from a biscuit, carefully buttered it, bit into it, and began chewing.

With this nourishment before him and the reassuring comfort that fulfilled routine always brought, he began to relax and consider that he had been overreacting. This nonsense of attacks on seminary professors was very probably over. Besides, why would anyone select him as a target? In all his years as a priest—almost all spent teaching seminarians—he had made no enemies he knew of. In fact, he sometimes chided himself for this. There were those even on this faculty, especially Fathers Feeny, Budreau, and Gennardo, who held that if you made no enemies it meant you were doing nothing. O'Dowd could not recall making any enemies, and, since he did not wish to admit he had done nothing, he sustained himself by denying the hypothesis.

What was that? O'Dowd did not want to believe his ears, but it sounded as if the dining room doors had opened and swung shut.

He cursed himself for having sat with his back to the doors. He had always trusted his intuition before. Why had he not taken the simple precaution of facing the entrance to the dining room? What a fool!

Now it was clear. Footsteps approaching. His heart was in his mouth as he whirled in his chair to face the intruder.

"Bob," O'Dowd's voice betrayed vast relief—"Bob Koesler! You scared the living daylights out of me!"

"Sorry, I didn't mean to." Koesler took a seat opposite O'Dowd.

"What do you mean coming down here now? No one ever does that!" Without intending to, O'Dowd sounded as if he were reprimanding Koesler.

"Hey, calm down, Charlie. I only came down here

to see you because I knew you'd be here now. And that is exactly why I wanted to see you."

"Oh?"

"Well, I've been thinking about these attacks . . ."

"Hasn't everyone?" O'Dowd's heartbeat was just beginning to settle back to normal.

"Well, whoever is doing this has been taking advantage of the routine in our lives. Things like Phil's daily Mass, Ed's dry-cleaning visit, my Friday dinner. That's what I wanted to talk to you about. Of all the faculty members, you are the one who might best see the wisdom of breaking up these routines. And the one the others might be most likely to listen to."

"I'm not the rector." O'Dowd offered Koesler some tea. Koesler waved the offer away.

"Listen, we both know that Ly, Tony, and Al, who, with you and George Dye, make up the older members of the faculty, would never agree to this evasive sort of action. In all candor, no one would listen to George. You are the only one who might consider it."

"You're right, Bob, I might. And that's especially true after this afternoon. I had a premonition something was going to happen. I didn't know the something would be your visit. I, of course, feared the worst, an attack on me. That's why I was so startled when you came in here behind me."

"Well, isn't that enough? I'm by no means the only person who knows you are habitually—and vulnerably—alone here at this hour. What happened just now ought to be the strongest argument possible for breaking up these routines that make you and the others so vulnerable."

O'Dowd smiled. "And what of you, Bob? Will you alter your routines?"

"That's different, Charlie. I've been through my baptism of fire."

"Ah, yes. That is the difference: you have been attacked. I know from talking with the others—Leo, Phil, Ed, and Tony—that you now consider yourselves, in a manner of speaking, immune. You all feel that once having been attacked and having survived, you will not be a target again. But you could be wrong."

"Yes, I suppose you're right."

"Exactly. But how would you enjoy changing nearly everything you do for an unknown length of time? For perhaps as long as you live, even? In effect, live the rest of your life mentally and emotionally in hiding. In fear."

"When you put it that way . . ."

"That's the way it is. It didn't really occur to me plainly until after you walked in here a few minutes ago. At first, the very same thought occurred: I shouldn't be here. I should never take my afternoon tea again. I must examine my life and alter it to find other habits. Do I take a walk at the same time each day? Offer Mass? Pray? Study alone? Visit the library?

"No, Bob, a life like that is not living."

"I must say, I know exactly how you feel, Charlie, and I can't really argue with you. Until recently, I thought it would be impossible for any of us to change our habits, our routines. I could see the wisdom of it but I just didn't think it was possible. But I thought I would at least make the suggestion to you on the grounds that what I found impractical you might have been able to live with. But let's just leave it in the 'nice try' category."

"We will. And thank you, Bob. Now have a biscuit."

Father Lyr Feeny was writing a series of words on the blackboard. Anyone familiar with "sperm," "ovum," "Fallopian tube," "endometrium," and "abortion" would have been able to make an informed guess as to the topic of this medical ethics class.

"Has it occurred to you," whispered one student to his neighbor, "that between Flinty Feeny and Tony Gennardo, we get a lot of information about the female anatomy?"

"Well," whispered the other, "you've got to admit

there's some connection between the theology of human sexuality and medical ethics."

"I was just thinking," whispered the first, "it would save them a lot of trouble and, at the same time, hold our interest better if they brought in a live model."

They laughed just loudly enough to be heard by Feeny, who turned quickly and spotted the guilty pair immediately. His jaw, which seemed permanently set slightly off center, was clenched. A stern-visaged Flinty Feeny, as he was unaffectionately known to generations of students, was acknowledged to strike terror in the hearts of innocent and guilty alike.

"I would like it remembered, both of you," he addressed the two whisperers through clenched teeth, "that a military officer is a gentleman by an act of Congress, whereas a priest is a gentleman by an act of God! And God does not so act in behalf of seminarians who laugh behind a professor's back."

He said it but he didn't believe it. An anachronism, he was a throwback to a former day, and he knew it. In the good old days, any seminarian who dared toy with the displeasure of a rector found his days in the seminary were numbered. Not any more.

Feeny sat at his desk and arranged his notes. He explained the clinical process leading to pregnancy. For most of his students he did not cast any new light on their understanding of the matter. Some few of his students had had more practical experience in matters sexual than Lyr Feeny had had in his long lifetime.

"Now," Feeny continued, "once the egg is fertilized, there is present a human being with an immortal soul. A person with all the rights that are due a human being. Chief among these is the right to life. Now, what is the popular term used in referring to a spontaneous abortion?" He glanced around the class, searching for the student who least wished to be called on. Feeny had a knack for that sort of thing.

"Mr. Doody."

Raphael Doody, startled, dropped his pen. It rolled

noisily down his desk and fell to the floor. In trying to retrieve it he nearly toppled out of his seat.

"Mr. Doody," Feeny repeated, "what is the popular term used when referring to a spontaneous abortion?"

"Uh . . ." Doody might possibly have known, but he was unnerved. "Uh . . . I think, 'murder,' Father."

"No, Doody. No, again, Doody!" Such incompetence! Such a simpleton! Doody's continued presence in the seminary as well as his probable ordination in June was a monument to one shoddy solution to the priest shortage.

As was his wont, Feeny next called upon someone he was certain would know the answer. "Miss Schaaf."

"Miscarriage." She had tried insisting that Feeny address her as "Ms.," but she soon learned that one did not insist on anything with Feeny. Neither did she care for the manner in which Feeny and others treated Raphael Doody. He might be naturally clumsy. But he could do so much better if people were supportive rather than made fun of him. She was sure if people continued to treat Doody with derision, he would become arrested in a state of klutziness.

"And what is the morality of a miscarriage, Miss Schaaf?"

"It's an accident of nature. It is morally neutral."

"Now, a therapeutic abortion, any deliberate expulsion of the inviable fetus, is murder and more. It carries the penalty of excommunication for both the abortionist and all who formally cooperate in the abortion—is there a question, Miss Schaaf?" Feeny's demeanor indicated there should be no question at this point.

"I don't think you can say for certain that there is a human person present at the moment of fertilization."

"You don't." Feenyologists would recognize that Vesuvius trembled inside him.

"No, I think the most one can say at that point, and probably for a much longer time, is that a fertilized egg is present which, left to develop normally, will become a human being."

"Is that right?" The prominent vein in Feeny's forehead had begun to throb.

"It is much like the moment of death. No one really knows when that is. And until recently, it didn't matter that much. Not until the technique of transplanting organs was developed. Then, determining the earliest moment when all could agree death had occurred became crucial. So, a general medical agreement was reached that when the EEG revealed no brain wave, that indicated clinical death, and if any organs were to be donated, that was the moment to permit removal for transplant.

"So," she continued, oblivious to Feeny's barely contained rage, "I think it's unfortunate that the approach to abortion is so black and white. One must be either for it or against it.

"I think that, just as with death so with life: no one knows for certain when it commences. So, why could not the medical and perhaps the theological experts get together and agree when human life begins? Say, the time of implantation in the womb. Or, the third month.

"Before that time, the fetus would be treated with all the respect and care one would give to something which will become human. But grave reasons would allow for an abortion. However, after that time, the fetus would have to be treated as a full human person."

"Are you quite finished?"

"Yes."

"Does it make any difference to you, Miss Schaaf, that the Church has defined the moment of conception as the moment when human life begins? In the Church's liturgy, Miss Schaaf, we pray that from the moment of conception in Mary's womb, that was the moment of the incarnation, the moment when the Son of God became man. And, Miss Schaaf, *lex orandi, lex credendi*—a law in prayer is a law to be believed."

"That is the Church's opinion!"

"Miss Schaaf—"

The bell sounded.

Several students thought that Eileen Schaaf had been saved by the bell.

There was no denying, thought Feeny, as he gathered his books, that Eileen Schaaf had a brain. But it was undisciplined. Fortunately, although she could and might study theology the rest of her life she would never be able to be ordained a priest. The Church had waffled badly in many matters. But it was clear from the attitude of everyone from the Pope to the world's bishops that the barrier between women and priestly ordination would never fall.

He would argue for Schaaf's dismissal at the year's final faculty meeting. He would lose. He'd seen the writing on the wall. Bodies. The seminary must have bodies. Even bodies whose biology kept them from the goal for which a theological seminary is established. But, like St. Paul, he would fight the good fight anyway.

He had time before his period of solitary exercise to return to his room, take up his field glasses, and see what was going on that needed correcting.

In the mood he was in, God knows, he needed to take something out on somebody.

"I don't think you're going to like this, Father."

Mary Murphy stood with Father Koesler near the rear of the film set.

Koesler smiled. "Why, Mary? Is this going to be another of those torrid sex scenes like the one Pat Lennon wrote up in yesterday's *News*?"

"It's not that . . ." Mary seemed apprehensive. "It's . . . well . . . they're going to shoot the attempt . . . on your life."

That wiped the smile off Koesler's face. Then, in an attempt at nonchalance, he jested, "I don't suppose many people whose lives are threatened get to see a reenactment of the event." He brightened. "Well, I suppose if they ever needed me for technical advice, this is probably the time."

Koesler studied the set that had been constructed near the end of a long transverse corridor. The set consisted merely of a series of open, partitioned cubicles resting on a long table that was against the rear wall. Technicians were moving back and forth, bringing business-size envelopes and small boxes and putting them in the open boxes. Others were adjusting lights or microphones. Still others were moving about, appearing to be busy, but Koesler could not ascertain what it was they were doing.

"What is it?" Koesler asked.

"It's supposed to be the mailboxes at Sacred Heart Seminary," Mary replied.

"The mail—? But they're not even close to—"

"We know."

"The mailboxes at Sacred Heart are long, thin, deep boxes of fine, dark, aged wood, joined together and enclosed."

"Too expensive to duplicate."

"Then why couldn't someone have borrowed the real one for a day or so? I'm sure Sacred Heart would have been willing to lend them for a short while."

"Just another release to get. Besides, the way things are getting broken or lost on this project, neither Bruce nor Herm wanted to take a chance on having to replace them. We're running pretty close to the thin red line of our budget."

"But those bright yellow boxes . . . they're obviously plastic. They look cheap!"

"Father, don't forget what I told you in the beginning: The answer to most questions about why things are done this way or that on this project is that this is the least expensive way to do it."

"I'll remember, but I won't like it."

Meanwhile, in a classroom not far from the set, Father Budreau was conducting his morality of Christian marriage class.

"Roma locuta, causa finita." Father Budreau tugged at the cummerbund-like sash he wore over his black

cassock. "Rome has spoken, the question is settled." He seemed quite pleased with himself, as if he had presented the ultimate solution.

Edward Maley, whose query had elicited the ultimate answer, shook his head. "I'd have to agree with you, Father, that the question has been answered, but not by the Church."

"Of course it has, Maley. Go back to Pius XII and his *'Casti Connubii'* address to the midwives in 1951. When he spelled out the principles for utilizing the 'rhythm method' of family planning—"

"Or Vatican Roulette," a student whispered behind his hand.

"—he put to rest for all time the possibility of using any form of artificial birth control."

"But Father, 1951 was more than three decades ago."

"Our Savior lived two thousand years ago! What does time have to do with the eternal?"

"Father, are you saying we must overlook all that mankind has learned in the past thirty-some years?"

"Ha! Why don't you just check with Father O'Dowd about what all mankind has learned in the past thirty years? He'll tell you all the horror stories about how mankind is destroying its own environment!"

"Well, all right, Father. I would naturally concede Father O'Dowd's thesis on how we long ago lost our contemplative approach to life. But I'm talking about the knowledge explosion: mankind's knowledge about itself, about mankind!"

"And I'm talking about the Ordinary Magisterium!"

Meanwhile, on the movie set . . .

"You shouldn't be swinging that around," said the Second Man.

"What's the difference," said the First Man, "nobody's going to drink it." With that, he flipped the bottle of champagne into the air. He reached to catch it but missed. Fortunately, it landed on a large sofa cushion.

"Watch it!" said the Third Man. "We don't want to call attention to ourselves. Now put that bottle on the set where it's supposed to be."

"Cheap," commented the First Man, scrutinizing the bottle's label.

"So is everything else connected with this movie," said the Third Man.

"Has it occurred to you guys that we've been very lucky lately? I mean in holding onto these jobs?" said the First Man. "Just about everyone around us has been fired. And here we still are!"

"That thought has occurred to me many, many times," said the Second Man. "I have taken it as a good omen. God is with us. I think we're going to succeed."

"Don't take anything for granted," the Third Man warned. "As soon as any of us lets up, this whole thing is going to fall apart. So stay on your toes! Be alert!"

"I can't help it," said the Second Man, "I just feel we're going to make it this time."

"Well, one thing's for certain," said the Third Man, "it won't be long until we know."

Meanwhile, in the classroom . . .

"Most Catholics never heard of the Ordinary Magisterium, let alone pay any attention to it," said Edward Maley.

"Then it's up to people like us," said Father Budreau, "priests, seminarians, or a religious education coordinator, as you will probably become, to tell them."

"It's too late to 'tell them,' Father. They have already decided the matter for themselves. All the surveys and statistics say the same thing: The majority of Catholic laity have abandoned the Church's teaching, at least on this issue, and they practice birth control without any guilt."

"Now you know as well as I do, Mr. Maley, that the Church is not a democracy. We don't vote on doctrine or morality. It doesn't matter what percentage of Catholics do or do not follow the ordinary teaching authority of the Church.

"And there is no doubt that this teaching on artificial contraception is part of the Ordinary Magisterium. If you wanted to quibble about the teaching of Pius XII, there is 'Humanae Vitae,' the encyclical of Pope Paul VI, that has been affirmed by every succeeding Pope."

"The people are voting with their feet, Father. They're walking out on antiquated teaching."

"Mr. Maley, remember what Our Savior said when the crowds found him teaching a 'hard doctrine.' He did not call them back. He turned to His Apostles and said, 'Will you, too, leave me?' The problem, Mr. Maley, is theirs, not ours."

Meanwhile, on the movie set . . .

Sol Gould stared at his wristwatch.

Father Koesler stared at the actors standing to one side of the set. Some wore black cassocks. Others wore black clerical suits and roman collars. They were prepared to enter the set, on cue, and go to the mailboxes where the film Father Koesler would pick up his doctored bottle.

The real Father Koesler did not much care for the thespian Father Koesler. The actor, an inch or two under six feet, was not nearly tall enough. But primarily, there was the actor's vacuous look, particularly when he was not on camera. Koesler thought the actor should appear to have something going on behind his eyes at all times. Having made this critique, the priest laughed at his own vanity.

Finally, Koesler noticed the bottle in one of the boxes.

"What's that?"

"That's the doctored bottle intended for the actor portraying you," Mary Murphy explained.

"But . . . but . . . the bottle was a fifth of very good gin," he protested.

"Well, neither Bruce nor Herm thought gin was classy. They decided on champagne."

Koesler shook his head.

The bell sounded, ending the classes that were going on in the building.

Apparently, the sound was what Gould had been waiting for. Get it out of the way so it wouldn't mar the sound track. As soon as the clanging ceased, he called for silence. Everyone, including the many student onlookers, fell quiet.

Meanwhile, in the classroom . . .

Father Budreau gathered his books.

The need for bodies to keep the seminary functioning notwithstanding, he would campaign for the expulsion of Edward Maley at the faculty meeting in June.

Maley's argumentative attitude was disruptive. He was not studying for the priesthood anyway. In point of fact, with his reaction to the Ordinary Magisterium, one might even wonder whether he was actually a Catholic.

Budreau stalked down the hall—quick strides, left arm swinging in a swooping arc. He passed the periphery of the movie set. The corridor was jammed with students watching wide-eyed as the miracle of moviedom unfolded before them.

Budreau shook his head as he strode past the set. Secular nonsense! Nothing like this three-ring circus would have been tolerated in the seminary of old.

In spite of himself, he looked back to see if he could figure out what was going on. He was certainly familiar enough with the story line. Not only had he read it in the papers and seen it on TV, he knew the principals personally.

He saw a group of actors dressed as priests. They were in front of a row of plastic boxes, which Budreau identified as poor substitutes for the ancient, ornate mailboxes at Sacred Heart Seminary.

They must be doing the Koesler episode, Budreau surmised. Fortunately, he thought, I will not be a part of this frivolous affair.

As he passed from the set area through the swinging doors that bisected the corridor, Budreau could not have noticed that the champagne that had been shaken previously was bubbling furiously in its bottle.

Budreau entered the empty chapel, walked about a quarter of the way down the aisle, genuflected, and entered a pew. He knelt and tried to focus on prayer. It was never easy, especially after a long debate such as he'd had with that Maley. The student's stubbornness had irritated Budreau and he needed time to calm down.

He decided to pray, as they had in the old days, for missions and missionaries. And he would pray in the Latin that he so loved and which was becoming a foreign language.

Pro missionibus et missionariis. Pater noster, qui es in coelis . . .

Someone had entered the chapel behind him. Odd. Seldom was anyone but himself in the chapel at this hour.

There was no sound. Again, odd. Whoever was there was going nowhere. They always went to a pew or an altar or somewhere. Not nowhere.

. . . adveniat regnum tuum . . .

Budreau slipped his right hand into the front of his sash.

. . . fiat voluntas tuo sicut in caelo et in terra . . .

To one who had spent as much time around firearms as Budreau, the sound was unmistakable. Whoever was behind him had just cocked a gun.

In one fluid motion that seemed surprising for a man of Budreau's heft, he pivoted to his left, pulling a derringer from his sash as he did so.

BANG!

The cork shot from the champagne bottle and ricocheted from ceiling to wall to floor. Champagne spurted over most of the clerical clothing in the vicinity.

"Cut, cut! Damn!" Gould yelled. "Doesn't anyone here know how to make a movie!"

"What was that?" Patrick asked.

"The cork." Morris seemed surprised by the question. "Someone must have shaken that bottle."

"No, there was another sound. Almost simultaneous with the cork popping . . . where's Kirkus?"

Both looked about quickly. No sign of Roman Kirkus.

"Come on," Patrick snapped, "it came from this direction."

He led Morris down the corridor. They were halted by the swinging doors that were now locked. Patrick kicked repeatedly before the wood splintered, the lock snapped and the doors swung back.

Service revolvers drawn, the two raced the remaining twenty yards to the chapel.

They found only a very shaken Father Budreau still holding his small pistol and giving every sign of being about to slip into shock. After quickly ascertaining that he was unhurt, they followed his trembling finger and whispered "that way," and headed off in the direction whence they had come.

Morris was first to spot the gun with its silencer lying on the tile floor at the rear of the chapel. Slipping a pencil through the trigger guard, she carefully wrapped the weapon in a handkerchief, then followed after Patrick, who had headed back toward the set. She found him just inside the swinging doors, which were now propped open. The floor between the doors was littered with debris from the splintered door and the broken lock.

Patrick had found Roman Kirkus.

"Where were you just now?" the detective demanded.

"In the men's room, right there." Kirkus pointed to the room, which was just the other side of the swinging doors.

"When did you go in there?"

"About five minutes ago."

"You didn't hear anything?"

"Yeah, I heard a noise like someone was busting down the door. So I hurried out. The lock on the swinging door was broken. I figured somebody wanted to get out pretty bad. So I propped the doors open."

"Did anyone see you go in or come out of the men's room?"

"I did." Another of the production assistants stepped forward. "I was in the men's room at the same time he was."

Patrick looked from one to the other suspiciously.

"Look!" Morris showed Patrick the gun she had picked up.

"Good work! Any blood?"

"No." Using the kerchief as a sling, Morris turned the pistol over. "But look at this."

There was a noticeable gouge in the silencer.

"I'll be damned," said Patrick. "He shot the gun right out of the guy's hand."

"Yup. Shades of the old movie Westerns."

"Take it to Ballistics. I'll stay here and see if I can get some answers. Like who locked these doors."

The onlookers were unaware that there was a better show going on in the corridor than the one they were watching on the film set.

"So, they finally got the smoking gun," Bob Ankenazy observed.

"Literally." Pat Lennon was checking her notes prior to programming her story in the CRT. "The cops got to the chapel a few moments after the shooting. When I got there, I could still smell the gunpowder."

"It's a good thing you were on the scene. Talk about being at the right place at the right time!"

"It was a bit lucky. I wanted to follow up on the 'dirty movie' within a movie. I owe it all, including that super interview with Roman Kirkus, to the Tridentines, God bless 'em."

"Yes, your story on the gratuitous sadomasochism in that film got us about caught up with the Freep's story on the cheapie moviemakers. And your interview with Kirkus put us ahead . . . I suppose Cox was there today?"

"Yes."

"Damn! Well, you can't win 'em all . . . what have the cops got?"

Lennon flipped through her notepad. "No fingerprints. The guy had to be wearing gloves. There was no way he could have taken time to wipe the gun and still make his escape."

"That brings up the locked door. Anybody know who locked it?"

"That may just be the key to the whole thing, Bob. As far as I could determine, the cops don't know who locked the doors. They're double doors that swing open or shut. While they're filming, they want the doors shut, of course, but not locked.

"Father Budreau, it seems, walked down the corridor where they had built this simple set and were filming. He pushed open one of the doors and walked through. The chapel is about twenty yards beyond the doors. He went in and started praying.

"Nobody saw anyone go through the doors after Budreau. Everybody was watching what was going on on the set. But at least two other people went through them. One was Roman Kirkus, and the other was another of the production assistants. I've got his name here somewhere. They went to the men's room, which is just on the other side of the doors from the set.

"Apparently, sometime after the two went into the restroom, someone locked the door. They can be locked from either side."

"And you say the cops don't know who?"

"No one will own up to it. You wouldn't believe the number of people who have master keys that fit almost all of the inside doors. Any number of people could have locked the doors from either side."

"What was the idea of locking the doors, anyway?"

"It gave the assailant just enough time to get away. After the shooting, he must've gone down the corridor in the opposite direction from the movie set. It's about thirty or forty yards to the exit and another twenty or thirty yards to Schoolcraft, where a car could be waiting."

"What about the two in the men's room?"

"They claim that after they heard Patrick kick the door open they hurried out to the hallway. They saw the lock had been broken, so one of them propped the doors open.

"So, they can't identify who locked the doors . . ." Someone across the office was trying to get Ankenazy's attention. He signaled that he would be only a few minutes.

"No one admitted it and no one saw anyone do it. It could easily have been the assailant. He could have locked the doors, blocking or at least delaying the cops from following him. Then he could have gone quickly to the chapel, be thwarted in his murder attempt, and run the rest of the way down to the exit."

"What does Pat Lennon think?"

"It was a conspiracy. Somebody waited until the assailant was on his way to the chapel, no matter which direction he came from, the set or outside. When he was ready, his conspirator locked the door.

"It adds a whole new dimension to this thing. Until now, everyone thought the assailant was acting alone. If I'm correct, there's a conspiracy involving at least one other person. And, more important, the motive changes. One person can have one reason for trying to kill people. But a team or a group has to have a motive that is mutual or common to them all. They have to have a motive both or all of them can agree on."

"Interesting. Have they been able to check out the assailant's gun yet?"

"I was just about to call Ballistics on that." She picked up the phone.

Joe Cox cradled the receiver. "Nellie! Ballistics just

finished checking that gun. It's the same one that was used to shoot that Gennardo guy."

"Great!" Nelson Kane looked up. He was seated at his desk sifting through copy.

"That pretty well ties it up." Cox, notepad in hand, crossed to Kane's desk and sat across from the city editor. "I think I've got all I need."

"No prints on the gun?" Kane removed an unlit cigar from his mouth and dropped it in an ashtray in which there were never any ashes.

"No."

"What kinda guy is this Budreau? Carries a gun in his belt all the time?"

Cox smiled. "No, not really. I got most of my information from secondary sources. The cops got first crack at him, naturally. By the time they finished, he looked as if he was going into shock. Some of his buddies hustled him off to the hospital."

"What makes the guy tick?" Kane replaced the cigar in his mouth.

"He's a military freak. Saw some action as a chaplain in the ETO during World War II. Changed his life. Some of his students claim his specialty is teaching how to say Mass on the hood of a Jeep."

"Students are irreverent by nature," Kane commented.

"They say he had a tough time deciding whether to make a career of the army or teaching in the seminary. But the kicker, Nellie, is that once a week, every week, he takes target practice. He's also a gun freak. I guess that goes along with being enchanted with the army. He used to practice with rifles, but lately, he's taken up handguns. Which apparently put him in pretty good stead for today's Shootout at the O.K. Chapel."

"Who was his instructor at that firing range, the Sundance Kid?"

"Whaddya mean?"

"The guy came at Budreau from behind. He had to turn to fire, didn't he?"

"Yeah. And to top it off, he knocked the gun right out of the guy's hand. What a goddamn lucky shot! He admitted as much. Said he heard the guy behind him cock the gun; says once you've heard it, it's a sound unlike any other. Then, he kind of slid to his left while he drew the derringer. He twisted and fired. He admits he was just hoping to hit the guy somewhere —anywhere. But he says about all he could see was the barrel of the guy's gun. Said it looked about the size of a cannon.

"Maybe that explains why he hit the gun; he was looking at it. You hit what you see." He grinned. "That's a little maxim I just made up."

"With all this emphasis on the gun, am I to assume he didn't get a good make on the guy?"

"That's right. Says the guy was back in the shadows, dressed in black. His description runs from very vague to nil. Police said they might try to get something from him with hypnosis. But that'll be later."

"How come nobody but Patrick heard the shot?"

"Got ears for it, I guess. He's heard enough gunshots in his time. Besides, he was geared for something to go wrong. But it *was* difficult to hear. A derringer doesn't make that much noise. Two sets of closed doors separated them from the shooting scene. Then there was that crazy coincidence of the champagne cork popping at almost the instant the shot was fired."

"What was with the champagne?"

"That's too long a story. I've gotta start feeding this in. But the champagne was being used instead of Koesler's famous poisoned bottle of gin. It was a case of Murphy's Law. The only thing that could have gone wrong with that bottle was if the cork popped. So, naturally, the cork popped."

"I can hardly wait to read your story."

"Nellie, I don't know whether they're making a dirty movie on that set, but they sure as hell are making a disaster film."

*   *   *

The shades had been drawn, making the small room nearly dark.

The four darkly clad men had been meeting for more than an hour.

"I simply can't understand it," said the First Man. "When I heard that gunshot, I was sure we had finally succeeded."

"I locked the doors as soon as I saw you enter the chapel," said the Second Man.

"Everything was perfect except for one thing," said the First Man.

"He fired first," said the Third Man.

"There was no possible way we could have known," said the Fourth Man. "We watched him so carefully. He always went to the chapel before lunch. He was always alone there. It was the perfect opportunity. There's no doubt about that, even now."

"We knew about his practicing on the shooting range," said the Third Man. "I even went there and practiced alongside him. He never even recognized me." He seemed to drift off into pensiveness. "You know, it's funny: none of them has recognized any of us . . . and there we've been, on the set, right there in the seminary, every day." He shook his head, as if to bring himself back to the present. "He isn't even that good a shot. That's what boils me. He isn't a marksman. I've seen him miss target after target with pistols and rifles!"

"It was a lucky shot, there's no doubt about it," said the Fourth Man. "Even Budreau admitted that he hoped to hit you somewhere, anywhere."

"As it turns out," said the Second Man, "it was a lucky shot in more ways than one. If he hadn't hit your gun, he would have hit you. You must have been surprised."

"Surprised!" the Third Man almost shouted. "How many priests do you know who pack a gun in their cassocks? I had him in my sight. Then he started to move to the left just after I cocked my gun. I moved my gun too, so I was still aiming at the back of his head. I was just beginning to squeeze the trigger when he turned and fired. I thought my hands were going to fall off. The pain went right up my arms. It wasn't a case of holding onto the gun. The damn thing was knocked right out of my hands.

"Then, all I could think of was the rest of the plan. I knew I had only a few moments at best to get out of the chapel and into the men's room. I didn't have time to pick up the gun. Besides, my hands hurt too much."

"Speaking of the plan, doesn't it seem obvious? The plan is over, finished. We tried to make our statement. We gave it a good try. But we failed. It's as simple as that."

"What do you mean the plan is finished! We have one final victim left. We have not failed unless we fail in this last statement!" The Fourth Man sounded desperate. "What about it, men? We can't quit now!"

There was a brief silence.

"I'm afraid I must agree that we are indeed finished," said the Third Man. "Now, you all know me well. You know I'm no quitter. None of you wanted to carry out this plan more than I did. Only reluctantly did I agree to the original drawing of lots to determine which of us was going to be the Instrument of Justice. It was torture having to sit by while four successive assaults failed." He looked accusingly at the Second Man, who looked away.

"I was overjoyed," the Third Man continued, "when fate finally dealt me the opportunity of being the Instrument of Justice. But now, I've seen the plan fail with my own eyes. I know from having been personally involved with all the planning of this latest effort that our plot was foolproof as far as it is humanly possible to ensure such a thing. And I was there when it fell apart. There is a power higher than we are that is trying to tell us something. And the message is that we should stop now before someone, possibly one of us, gets hurt."

"Yes," said the Second Man, "speaking of a power higher than we are, have any of you been aware of something different about this meeting?"

"Only that some creatures who are talking about deserting the ship are revealing themselves," said the Fourth Man, disgustedly.

"No, no," the Second Man countered, "I mean something different that didn't happen."

He got no response.

"Remember how in all our previous meetings, things would go wrong, accidents would happen. In the past, there has been almost no time when something untoward wasn't happening. But our meeting this evening has been completely without incident."

In the silence that followed, there was tacit if reluctant agreement with the observation.

"I call it a sign from above," said the Second Man, "an omen."

"And I call that poppycock. And I also call for a vote," said the Fourth Man. "All those in favor of continuing with our plan signify by saying 'aye.' "

His was the sole aye.

"All those against—" He spat the last word.

Three resounding nays became part of the record.

"Very well," said the Fourth Man in a resigned but determined tone, "I will take the obligation of our pact on my own shoulders. I should have done so from the beginning. We wouldn't be where we are—which is almost point zero—if I had."

"No, you can't do it!"

"It's not right!"

"We voted! You should abide by the vote!"

"*You* abide by the vote!" the Fourth Man snarled. "You three dissolved our pact with your votes. All right, our plan is finished as our plan. It now becomes *my* plan."

"We can't help you."

"I don't need your help! I don't want your help. All I ask is that you continue to work on the movie. It would be suspicious if they had to hire three new production assistants now. Besides, I can at least trust you not to betray me." He hesitated. "Can't I?"

"Of course."

"You shouldn't have to ask that question."

"What kind of friends do you think we are, anyway?"

"Very well. I hereby declare this meeting closed. And with the closing of this meeting, the Instrument of Justice Society is—reluctantly—dissolved."

As the four men walked out of the small room for the final time, there were tears in the eyes of at least two of them.

Nothing had to be constructed. The Gennardo shooting was going to be filmed in the seminary's inner courtyard, where it had actually occurred. Still, technicians were swarming all over what had become a movie set. Lights, reflectors, microphones were being set up and tested. Tracks were being laid for the camera. The first assistant director and the actors were plotting the action. Herman Deutsch, who had been awake all night rewriting the new scene wherein Father Budreau becomes William Tell, was quietly asleep in his chair, undisturbed by the commotion. Bruce Lauther stood in the center of the set, absorbing all the activity and mentally calculating the cost of it all.

Off to one side, Inspector Koznicki, Sergeants Patrick and Morris, and Father Koesler were conversing. They were forced to speak rather loudly to be heard over the cacophonous babel.

"Father Budreau was not able to recall any more details of his assailant's appearance even under hypnosis?" Father Koesler asked.

"No, it was a complete washout," said Patrick.

"Unfortunate," Inspector Koznicki commented. "If Father Budreau had been able to remember, it might have resolved the mystery of the masks."

"The masks?" Koesler repeated.

"Yes," Koznicki said. "Consider the six times the assailant has acted thus far. Father Ward reported that his attacker wore some disguise, probably a sheer stocking, on his face.

"Father Merrit also said the man wore some sort of mask. Father Sklarski recalled no mask on his assumed assailant, but the man was under attack himself so Father did not get a look at his face.

"You, of course," Koznicki said to Koesler, "did not see whoever placed the bottle in your mailbox. And Father Gennardo did not see the person who shot him. Now, Father Budreau cannot recall any details at all regarding the man at whom he fired.

"We are left, in a manner of speaking, with a headless assailant." Koznicki spread his hands in a gesture of futility.

"The presumed attack on Sklarski was the only one of the six that occurred away from the seminary grounds," said Patrick. "Perhaps that was why he wore no mask that time."

"Well, it was certainly cold enough back then to wear a ski mask," said Morris. "He could have worn a mask without question just because of the weather."

"Strange," said Patrick, "as far as we know, the man has disguised himself each time he has attacked someone on seminary property. Yet the one time he tries something away from the seminary, he is without a mask."

"Perhaps," observed Koesler, "he does not feel the need to disguise himself when he is off seminary grounds."

The other three looked at Koesler attentively.

"If," Koesler continued, "we look at these assaults through the eyes of the assailant, what *modus operandi* do we find? He quite obviously intends to kill his prey, so there is no necessity to hide his identity from the victim. Now, we know, as things turned out, he was fortunate to have been disguised, because none of his targets was killed. But obviously, he did not intend things to end that way.

"That being so, why the disguise *in* the seminary but not out? Why would he fear being identified on seminary grounds but have no such fear when off campus? Could it be that he was afraid of being recognized by people in the seminary other than his victims?"

"Makes sense," Patrick acknowledged.

"But who would be recognized by someone in the seminary?" asked Morris.

"A priest," Koesler replied, "a student, an employee. Or the other side of each of those coins: a former priest, a former student, or a former employee."

His listeners seemed so grave, Koesler felt impelled to lighten the atmosphere. "I realize that, if my hypothesis is correct, I have narrowed the list of possible suspects to a respectable few thousand."

"Not at all, Father," said Koznicki, "your observation is well taken. After all, I asked for your help in this investigation because I thought you could add some singular insights."

"Thank you, Inspector. It's just that I feel so absolutely unqualified to dabble in police work. And yet, at the same time, I feel very close to this investigation. Not only am I personally involved as one of the intended victims, I know the others in this case so well. And I have an inkling that there is only one more block that has to fall in place and everything will be clear. I can't help feeling that this case is so very close to being solved. Have any of you ever felt this way?"

All three officers smiled acknowledgment.

"It's got to be one of the most common experiences that police officers share, especially in Homicide," said Morris. "You work on a case until your eyes cross. You think everything out a hundred times from a dozen different angles. Then there's just one more corner to turn, but it looks as if you'll never get there."

"I'm glad I'm not alone."

"Believe me, Father, you're not alone," said Morris. "But let me ask you about something in your field of expertise. I'm curious; why is the chapel still open?"

"That's right," said Patrick. "An act of violence took place in there . . . almost a crime."

"Some people would maintain that some of the sermons given in some churches are also a crime," said Koesler. "But it's a good question. As a matter of fact, I looked it up last night in the Code of Canon Law. Canon 1172 covers the matter."

"Eleven seventy-two? You've got more than eleven hundred laws?" Morris seemed surprised.

"Two thousand, four hundred and fourteen, to be exact," said Koesler. "Eleven seventy-two is the one that deals with the desecration of a church."

"That's the word I was looking for," said Morris, "desecration."

"We came within a hairsbreadth of having a desecrated church. It seems there are four categories in which a church can be desecrated. The first is a homicide. Thank God that didn't happen, although it almost did.

"The second is an injury caused from which there is an appreciable amount of blood spilled. If Budreau had not been so accidentally accurate, I'm afraid we would have had a lot of blood spilled.

"The third way would be to put the church to a sordid or grossly irreverent use. Like making it a gambling den or hosting an orgy. You will recall Christ's driving the moneychangers from the temple.

"Finally, a church can be desecrated by burying an infidel or a notoriously excommunicated person therein.

"Now, have I told you more than you ever wanted to know about desecrated churches?"

"Not at all," said Morris. "It's fascinating. Even if it does sound sort of medieval. But what would have to be done if, say, Father Budreau had missed the gun and there were a lot of blood?"

Koesler laughed. "Well, to answer your question

seriously, there is a rite in the Roman *Ritual* that would be used to reconsecrate the church. The reason I'm laughing is that it reminds me of a story that is rather famous in seminary circles. Have you got another minute?"

"All three figuratively settled back to hear Koesler's story.

"Do you know what a sacrarium is?"

Koznicki nodded; Morris and Patrick shook their heads.

"Well, all Catholic sacristies are equipped with an object called a sacrarium, which resembles an ordinary sink. Except that the drainpipe of the sacrarium leads, not into a sewer, but into the ground. When the cloths used in Mass or at, say, baptism, are washed, the water is poured into the sacrarium. It's just a reverent way of disposing of water that's been used to wash sacred linens."

His audience appeared to comprehend this explanation.

"Some years back, a seminarian who was about to be ordained a priest was being given his final exams.

"One of his professors posed this problem: 'You are saying Mass. Just after you have consecrated the wafer and the wine, a mouse runs across the altar, takes the host in its mouth and runs off with it. What would you do?'

"The young man thinks this over and finally says, 'I'd burn the church down and throw the ashes in the sacrarium.'"

Laughter.

"Is that true?"

"I can't say that it is, and I can't say that it isn't."

Most of those who came in hopes of seeing today's filming wouldn't. The inner courtyard was confined, especially after the filming equipment, technicians, actors, crews, and advisers crammed in.

Standing in the corridor just outside the courtyard were, among many others, Pat Lennon and Joe Cox.

"Haven't I see you before?" said Cox to Lennon. "In fact," he slipped into his very poor Groucho Marx imitation, "earlier today, didn't I see an awful lot of you?"

Lennon blushed. "Why don't you broadcast it?"

"I'll take out an ad in the *New York Times*."

"Speaking of the *Times,* isn't that . . .?"

". . . their local stringer."

"They're back on this story, eh?"

"Everybody's back on it after Budreau's fastest-gun-in-a-cassock act."

"That reminds me"—for the first time Lennon faced Cox full on—"what was it you called it in your article —"Shootout at the O.K. Chapel? I know they let you get away with that stuff at the Freep, but don't you think that's a bit flip? Someone could have gotten killed. As a matter of fact, that was the idea—to kill Budreau."

"That may have been the idea, but it was not fact." Cox enjoyed her perfume. Indeed, he enjoyed everything about her, even her arguing with him. "The fact is, the guy blew another one. He must be setting a world's record for bad luck. Besides, I thought the line was kind of clever."

"I won't argue clever with you. But I think you'll regret the phrase if there's another shooting here."

"You think there'll be another one?"

"What do you think all these media people from all over the country are doing here? They didn't come to see a movie made. Especially this one!"

"You think the idea is to keep trying until he actually kills somebody?"

"Why are you interviewing me? And worse than that, why are you taking up my time when I could be interviewing someone worthwhile?" Lennon began working her way toward Sergeant Patrick. He saw her coming and began moving toward her. He did not mind one bit talking to her.

Father Koesler moved nearer to the camera. He studied the actor who would portray Father Gennardo. The actor, whom Koesler did not recognize, was listening intently to Sol Gould, who was pointing to various spots in the courtyard.

Although he did not recall seeing this actor in any previous movie, Koesler had to admit that the man bore a striking resemblance to the real Father Gennardo. They were about the same height and build, with dark hair heavily salted with white, and a swarthy complexion. Koesler wondered if anyone had taught the man to snort as Gennardo did from force of habit.

If this actor so resembled the real priest, Koesler wondered if, for a change, the script would more nearly reflect what really had happened when Gennardo was shot.

Technicians seemed to be burying things in the floor, the wall, even in the fish pond. Koesler edged closer to Mary Murphy.

"Excuse me, Mary, but what are those men doing?"

Mary looked up from her clipboard. "Oh, hello, Father. Those men? They're positioning explosive devices."

He looked at her for further explanation.

"You see, nobody actually fires real bullets. The assassin will be firing blanks and those devices will be set off by that machine over there. All they've got to remember is the order in which they're supposed to explode. Otherwise, we'd have the actor in one part of the courtyard and it would look as if the gunman is shooting in some other part of the courtyard."

"Quiet! Quiet on the set!" Sol Gould called through his megaphone. Quiet set in. "Places!"

Mary Murphy assured Koesler he could remain at her side.

The lights were turned up. The black-cassocked "Father Gennardo" began pacing the courtyard. Koesler could see a shadowy figure on the balcony over-looking the courtyard. So far, so accurate.

The assailant aimed his gun, elongated by the silencer, and fired.

The device near "Gennardo's" left foot exploded.

Very realistic, thought Koesler.

The actor dove behind a bench. The device embedded in the back of the bench exploded.

Hey, wait a minute! thought Koesler.

The actor raced from behind the bench to behind a column. The device embedded in the column exploded.

"This isn't the way it happened," Koesler urgently whispered to Mary. "Father Gennardo wasn't really aware of what was going on. He didn't take any evasive action!"

"I know," Mary whispered back. "Bruce and Herm didn't think the viewing public would believe a gunman could miss at this range unless the target was a moving one."

Koesler thought about that for some time.

The actor moved from behind the column and began to move quickly toward the door. Suddenly, he seemed to have been slammed to the ground. He lay very still. Red began to seep from beneath his shoulder and spread across the bricks.

"Cut! Cut! That's a keeper!" The satisfaction in Gould's voice was rare, particularly on this project.

Herman Deutsch woke momentarily. On hearing Gould's exuberant tone, Deutsch, contented, snuggled down again.

Koesler wondered about a sound somewhere in the distance. It couldn't be an echo. It was far too belated to be an echo.

Morris and Patrick knew.

"Gunshot!" snapped Morris. "Where's Kirkus?"

"Right there!" Patrick nodded in the direction of the sound equipment where all the production assistants were gathered. "I haven't taken my eyes off him. Let's go!"

The two ran full-tilt down the hallway.

"Back! Stand back! Make way! Police!" Patrick, service revolver in hand, lowered his shoulder and charged through the crowd with Morris in his wake. As the two headed in the direction of the sound, they were followed pied-piper style by nearly everyone who had been at or on the set.

They reached a turn in the corridor.

Patrick inclined his head to the right.

"The racquetball courts!"

The parade turned right and stampeded toward the courts.

Patrick threw open the door leading to the first court. He and Morris darted through, bringing their guns to firing position.

Then, as the crowd jostled at the door trying to peer into the court, the mouths of both detectives dropped open.

The court had been converted into a firing range.

Father Budreau, whose mouth also hung open, was teaching a student to fire a gun.

"Just what we needed," said Patrick.

"Son of a Billy the Kid," Morris commented.

Father Koesler was distracted. He found it most difficult to pay attention to the parish council proceedings.

It was not unusual for his mind to wander during council meetings. But this evening, the distractions were notably more intense.

Sometimes it was like this when he was reading the paper. He would have to read the same paragraph several times before he would grasp what he was reading. When that happened, there was no remedy but to put down the paper and go settle whatever it was that was distracting him.

He could not apply that remedy now. One does not simply get up and leave in the middle of a parish council meeting. Especially if one is pastor of the parish. He was trapped.

Something was disturbing Bob Bullock. Koesler always thought of him as Sweet Old Bob. Bullock, who resembled a slightly more handsome Sam Jaffe, had taught school and been in politics. He now sold insurance. Bullock combined a strongly conservative viewpoint with a highly irascible temperament and managed to keep everyone near him on edge. Koesler had long ago come to the conclusion that Judy, Bullock's long-suffering wife, was destined to go directly to heaven with no stop at purgatory just for having put up with Sweet Old Bob all these years.

"Bob, we have no choice in the matter." Council president Ty Obermyer, a most civilized man, was trying to be patient. He had not much hope he would succeed. "The superintendent of Catholic schools for the Archdiocese issues salary regulations and we have no alternative but to accept them."

"I don't see how, Mr. President, they can send out directives from downtown that they expect us to follow blindly. How do they know what we can afford?" Bullock declared in that ingratiating way he had.

"The idea is, Bob, if we can't afford to pay a decent wage to our teachers and help, we should close the school."

That was a mistake. Long experience with Sweet Old Bob had taught Koesler that Bullock would lay down two or three smokescreens before getting down to what was really disturbing him. The trick was to resist the urge to argue with him, as well as the urge to throttle him, until he reached the bottom line.

But then the distractions took over. For once, displacing the objections of Bob Bullock, they were welcome.

He recalled what Inspector Koznicki had once told him: that in a series of murders—or, in this case, attempted murders—the assailant usually is making some sort of statement. He is saying something using actions rather than words. The better able you are to under-

stand the statement, the more likely you are to discover who the assailant is.

But what could the statement here possibly be?

Could Dr. Heinsohn's hypothesis be correct: that the
assailant is striking out at a father figure? Koesler considered the victims thus far. With the exception of himself, they all were rather elderly. And even he was
easily old enough in the normal scheme of things to be
a grandfather. Could the man be striking out against a
grandfatherly figure?

"You've got to remember, Bob, that these are different times," said council president Obermyer. "You can't
expect the kids today to be using the *Baltimore Catechism,* or, for that matter, the textbooks we used."

"I don't care," Bullock droned, "I took the trouble
to look through the religion textbooks of both our first
and second graders. Do you know I couldn't find a
listing of the Ten Commandments in either one!"

No, that wasn't it. Sweet Old Bob would know that
no kid was going to get out of a parochial elementary
school without learning the Ten Commandments. Besides, his voice had not yet reached the strident tone
Bullock reserved for the ultimate gripe.

Something was missing from the puzzle of who was
attacking these priests. If only Koesler could put his
finger on the missing piece. It seemed so close, so
tantalizing. As if his brain would recognize it if only
the logical progression of thought would build to one
more level.

How could all these priests have one common
enemy? They did not all teach at the same seminary.
And although he himself did teach at both seminaries,
he had only recently joined the faculty of St. Joe's.
Of course, all the priests knew each other. But that was
not unusual; older priests tended to be a homogeneous
group.

"And I say it's a disgrace!" Bullock brought his fist
down on the table. "Conducting a parody of the suffering and death of our Savior in a Catholic church, mind

you. And during the the sacred season of Lent! What kind of religious instruction are we foisting on our youngsters? I ask you!"

Bingo! Koesler had stepped into the church en route to the council meeting. The teachers of the public high school catechism classes had put together a Lenten penitential rite. They were using three slide projectors to show rather traditional pictures of Jesus, depicting some of the final events in His life. Mostly, the pictures were reproductions of paintings of the Masters. Bullock could have no objection to that.

However, along with the pictures, they had been playing at peak volume a tape of "Jesus Christ, Superstar."

That was it! Koesler had conceded that while the rock version of the life of Christ was not his cup of tea, it seemed most relevant for teenagers. But for Bob Bullock, "Superstar" was hemlock.

If only he had known Bullock intended to stop in at the church during the penitential service, Koesler would have somehow found a way to divert him. As it was, and judging by Bob's current level of dudgeon, Koesler estimated that, for all practical purposes, the council would have little time for futher business this evening.

He drove willingly back into his distractions.

A decidedly festive atmosphere was discernible on the set. This was the final scheduled filming date. With any luck at all, after today, the movie crowd would move out, bag and baggage.

This pleased the movie crowd, at least those from Los Angeles, who had had more than enough of the early part of Michigan's spring, which was late winter. It delighted the seminary crowd, at least the older faculty members, who longed for the return of peace and order. And it relieved those police who had to pursue a criminal investigation through the chaos created by the film crowd.

The setting for this final day was the seminary chapel where Father Budreau had fired the shot heard 'round the nation, thanks to network news and wire services. Earlier, the same Father Budreau had removed the consecrated hosts usually reserved in the chapel.

Present on the seminary scene for the first time was petite brunette Shelley Eden, the *Free Press's* ebullient syndicated show biz columnist. The only woman known to have deliberately postponed a dalliance with Cary Grant, Shelley was interviewing Father Budreau. Until now, no personality connected with "Assault with Intent" had been deemed important enough to attract Shelley's interest. But almost overnight, Budreau had become known as the fastest clerical derringer in the Midwest. Now, although he had been discouraged by both civil and Church authorities from continuing his firing-range class, he would become the leading light of one of the most popular columns in Detroit if not the nation.

Herman Deutsch had spent the entire night rewriting the script. He had developed such alcoholic adeptness that during such sessions he was able to drink just enough at appropriate intervals to remain awake just long enough to finish the last of the dialogue before falling into a drunken slumber. So, once again, he was unable to direct what he had written.

Bruce Lauther stood near the camera, a satisfied expression playing about his face. It appeared that, in spite of everything, they were going to bring this movie in slightly under budget. In a few weeks, after additional scenes had been shot in Hollywood and the editing completed, he would be able to show the finished film to the network brass. Not bad for somebody whose career was supposed to have gone down the tube.

Father Koesler was talking with Mary Murphy, his usual reliable source.

"I don't understand," he said, "how they can be sure this is the final day of shooting."

"We have it on the word of no less than Dr. Heinsohn."

"Oh?"

"He says that when the priest shot at the assailant, it was all over."

"But Father Budreau didn't hit him."

"No, but Dr. Heinsohn says it was the father figure striking back. You see"—Mary didn't know why she was explaining this hypothesis; she scarcely understood it herself—"the asailant had been striking out at you priests as if you were his father figure. According to Dr. Heinsohn—and Bruce tells me the doctor cited lots of similar cases—one of two things had to happen: either he would kill one of you—excuse me, Father, nothing personal—or one of you would have to at least acknowledge his presence by striking back at him."

"I see." In fact, he did not.

"So, when Father Budreau fired at him, the assailant was satisfied. But Dr. Heinsohn still intends to make periodic pleas through the media for the man to turn himself in so the doctor can return him to mental health."

"I see." He didn't.

In one corner of the chapel, Sergeants Patrick and Morris huddled with a dozen uniformed Detroit police who had been assigned to this case just for the day. Evidently, the police department did not put much faith in Dr. Heinsohn's diagnosis.

"This is supposed to be the final day of filming," Morris addressed the group, "so it is more than likely that if our man is somehow connected with this movie, or has been using the filming as a cover for his activities, he probably will make his move today."

"Yes," Patrick amplified, "and it doesn't much matter whether this actually is the final day. The point is, the assailant expects it to be, just as we expect it to be. If he's with this crew, today's his last chance for unrestricted entree to the seminary. In any event, he should be convinced this is his last opportunity for inconspicuous movement."

"Now," Morris picked up, "you've all familiarized yourselves with the premises?" All nodded. "All right. Then spread out around the rear of this chapel."

"And keep an eye on Marge and me," added Patrick. "If we spot anything suspicious, we're going to move fast. And we want all of you with us."

"All right, clear the set!" Sol Gould's megaphone blared.

Deutsch cringed at the sound and seemed to shrivel into his canvas chair.

"Places everyone!"

Father Koesler moved to the rear and to one side of the chapel. Most of those who had come to gawk were, again, relegated to the corridor outside the chapel. For most, merely being in proximity to a movie being filmed was enough, even if all one saw were blank walls and all one heard were shuffling feet and throats being discreetly cleared.

The real Father Budreau watched the film Father Budreau enter the chapel, followed by camera and lights. The actor genuflected, more reverently, the real Budreau had to admit, than he himself, and entered a pew. As the actor knelt, Budreau could see his right hand slip inside the top of his sash.

How narrow it can be, Budreau reflected, that distance between life and death. He relived the original event. An instant's hesitation and he would have been a dead man. An inch in any direction and his assailant could have been the dead man.

Out of the corner of his eye, Dean Patrick thought he saw something move at the right rear corner of the chapel. He spun in that direction in time to see a door silently close. He nudged Morris. The two broke for the door. They were closely followed by the uniformed officers. There was no attempt on anyone's part to muffle the racket they were making.

"Cut! Oh, cut! Damn! Now what the hell's going on?"

The officers piled up at the door. It was locked. Patrick who had obtained master keys for all the seminary doors, but didn't want to waste a minute, motioned a burly officer forward. The latch fixture splintered at his kick, and the door slammed open, almost coming off its hinges.

Led by Patrick and Morris, the officers raced down the stairway. The rearmost uniformed officer remained at the door blocking entry—or exit—to anyone else.

"The crypt chapels!" Patrick knew where these stairs led.

"Father Dye!" Morris knew who would be there.

As they neared the bottom of the stairs, the sound of a shot reverberated through the vaulted rooms. They took the final steps three at a time.

"Drop it and freeze!" Morris hit the landing, revolver held with both hands at eye level.

"Drop it or you're dead!" Patrick, too, drew a bead.

He did not drop his gun immediately; it would be unmanly to obey the command of a woman. The only thing that saved him was that he did not move. A few seconds after Patrick's command, he let the gun drop to the tile floor.

"So," sad Patrick, "Roman Kirkus after all."

Morris knelt next to Father Dye. He had fallen from the kneeler. She turned him over. There was a bullethole in the rear of his bald head. She could find no exit hole. She checked for vital signs.

"He's gone."

Several officers had spread-eagled Kirkus against a wall and shaken him down for weapons. As they handcuffed him, Patrick read him his rights.

An officer called in to report the arrest. Inspector Koznicki, who was in a mobile unit in the vicinity, was immediately informed. He phoned Patrick and had Kirkus taken to an office in the seminary. Koznicki wished to question Kirkus before he was taken downtown and booked.

Koesler, along with everyone else in the chapel or its vicinity, wondered what had happened. Especially after hearing that shot. But the police were withholding all information until receiving clearance from the Inspector.

An hour later, few of the original bystanders had left the scene. Indeed, their number had been augmented by media people, particularly local TV crews.

There was much activity in and around the office now occupied by the police. From time to time, someone would enter or leave. But no one would say what was transpiring.

Finally, there was a significant flurry, as several large officers hustled someone out of the office, down the stairs, and out of the building. Even on tiptoes and craning, Koesler could not tell who it was.

A policeman came out of the office and repeated in a loud voice, "Is there a Father Koesler here? Is there a Father Koesler here?"

Koesler stepped forward, identified himself, and was ushered into the office. Koznicki, Patrick, Morris, and several uniformed officers were there, all looking quietly pleased.

"It's over, Father," said Koznicki.

"Over?"

"Yes."

"Who is it? Who did it? Was it—?"

"Roman Kirkus."

"Kirkus?"

Something was wrong. It didn't fit.

Koesler had a feeling of extreme frustration. As if he were trying to pound a square peg into a round hole.

"Yes, it was Kirkus," Patrick echoed. "He made a full statement of responsibility for all the attacks. We've got our man."

"The bad news—and it is very bad," said Morris, "is that he was successful with his final victim."

"Successful?"

"He actually killed one of the priests. I'm sorry, Father."

"Who?"

"Father Dye."

"Old Father Dye?"

Now that made no sense at all. It was as if all the pegs were square and all the holes round.

Then, slowly, as in a sunrise, it began to become clear to Koesler. The final piece fell into place. All the rationalizing he'd gone through recently began to make sense. It was not that something was missing; there was *too much* in the equation.

But, if all this was wrong, what was right?

Rapidly, Koesler put the puzzle together again, using what he believed to be the correct pieces.

Koznicki grew concerned. He wondered what was wrong with his friend, who seemed dazed. It was shocking news, of course, but he thought it odd that the passing of Father Dye would affect Koesler so deeply as to strike him dumb. After all, Father Dye was almost ninety; it was not as if he had been taken out of due time.

Koesler checked his watch, then paused to let this latest information sink in.

"Oh, my God, no! Inspector, I could be wrong, but if I'm right, there's not a moment to spare. Quick!"

Koesler ran out the door, followed closely by those in the office, then by those outside the office. No one had the vaguest idea where the priest was headed or why.

When they reached the chapel, Koesler ran to the left rear door instead of to the right, which would have led back to the crypt chapels.

He flung open the door and raced down the stairs.

"The exercise room!" Patrick yelled as realization hit.

"Father Feeny!" Morris, checking her watch even as she ran, knew only too well who would be there at this hour.

At the bottom of the staircase was another door. Koesler put his shoulder to the door and shoved, as he turned the knob.

It was unlocked. Koesler, almost catapulted through the doorway, collided with a man standing just the other side of the door. The two tumbled down the several steps that led to the balcony railing that demarcated a twenty-foot drop to the exercise room's floor. Fortunately, the railing halted their headlong progress.

At Koesler's impact, the man's gun had been jarred from his hand and had fallen harmlessly to the balcony floor.

Morris retrieved the gun.

Koznicki untangled the two men.

Koesler began brushing off his black suit. It was an almost hopeless task. But his expression was the one he wore when one of his hypotheses was confirmed.

Koznicki turned the frustrated assailant around.

"Well," he said, "if it isn't Brother Alphonsus!"

"Who's there? Who's up there?" shouted Father Feeny. He felt naked without his field glasses.

The Blue Plymouth left I-75 where the freeway ends at Gratiot, and turned right. It was only a few blocks to police headquarters at 1300 Beaubien.

"One problem with the Miranda warning," Patrick was saying, "is that some suspects take it seriously and, while they do not remain silent, they do refuse to answer any questions."

Marge Morris smiled. "So it was with Al Wiedeman, a.k.a. Brother Alphonsus. And if it hadn't been for Father Koesler, we still wouldn't know about those other three. How do you suppose he found out that those two students knew about the others?"

Patrick chuckled. "I've heard some of his explanations before. They can get fairly convoluted, but they usually make sense eventually. He has a knack for glomming onto little things and tying them together."

"Just what a good detective should be doing."

"Hey, don't get down on yourself or us or the department. Koesler would be the first to admit that in these 'Catholic' investigations we get involved in from time to time, he is privy to more information than we are. He's just got more going for him. Though, to give him his due, he does well with what he picks up. It's undoubtedly why Koznicki calls him in from time to time."

"Well, thanks to him, we're booking four instead of one."

"Five," Patrick corrected.

"That's right! How could I forget Kirkus, the only one who actually killed somebody?"

"Easy. He doesn't belong to the gang—what is it they call themselves?—the Instrument of Justice Society. Kirkus was booked earlier. Our Gang of Four probably just got finished being processed."

Patrick drove into the huge police garage.

He and Marge could scarcely believe their eyes. There had been a collision, a significant collision, involving at least three police vehicles. Fluid was leaking from two.

"What happened, Barney?" Patrick asked the garage supervisor.

"Incredible," was all Barney could say as he shook his head.

"What happened?" Morris repeated.

"I keep telling myself it was an accident, but I still don't believe it. I was able to dispatch three marked cars to St. Joseph's Seminary to pick up the four suspects—to try to separate them so they couldn't communicate with each other en route.

"Well, the three cars got here about the same time. One went that way. Another went this way. And the third circled this car here and went down the middle. You can see where they met!" He shook his head again.

"Anybody hurt?" asked Patrick.

"Three drivers had badly wounded pride and when

the brass hears about this they're going to have their asses in slings."

Patrick and Morris headed for the garage elevator.

"You'd better use the inside elevator," Barney warned, "this one's stuck."

En route to the fifth floor, the two discussed the unusual three-way collision.

As they walked toward Homicide, they encountered Sergeant Cartney, who, many thought, resembled a young Sean Connery. This ordinarily smiling, buoyant detective appeared harassed.

"Those four you had brought in," said Cartney, "what are you booking them for—black magic?"

"They give you a rough time?" asked Morris.

"Not them so much. But bad times seem attracted to them like rock fans to a Cobo Concert. I'll give you a quick tour."

Cartney exhibited a series of squadrooms that had been used to interrogate the four-member Instrument of Justice Society. Though the normal state of these rooms was anything but neat, neither Patrick nor Morris had ever seen them in such disarray. Here a typewriter had fallen to the floor, the roller snapped off. There several filing cabinets were overturned. Even the door to the microwave oven hung loose.

They were impressed.

"And that's not all. Let's go upstairs," Cartney said. "No, not by the elevator. The stairs. The elevator is stuck, fittingly, on the ninth floor, along with your Instrument of Justice boys.

As they trudged up the remaining four floors, Cartney remarked, "I don't know how they did it. Hang around with those guys long enough and you'll be walking *into* doors as often as *through* them.

"C'mere." Cartney led the way to the property room. An obviously harried officer was mopping his brow, though the building certainly was not overly warm.

Patrick cautiously leaned over the Dutch door and

gazed into the property room. The floor was nearly covered with piles of large manila envelopes, many of which had ripped open, spilling their contents. Each envelope normally contained—with the exception of small change and cigarettes—all the personal property brought into the building by prisoners now held in either a bullpen or a holding cell. It would be the responsibility of the officer in charge to return each liberated item to its proper envelope. The officer mopped his brow with good reason.

Next, Cartney led Patrick and Morris to the fingerprint units against the side wall. The two had anticipated this would be the next exhibit. They were quite sure they did not want to see it, but at this point they had no choice.

Black smudged fingerprints had blossomed in the most unlikely places. Up the walls, on the floor, on the underside of the shelf. The officer who had supervised the fingerprinting seemed stupefied. "Sometimes it would happen when things fell on the floor and they would reach down to pick them up," he murmured. He appeared to be explaining the ubiquitous prints to no one but himself.

"Are those four plagues your collar?" the large black officer in charge of the ninth floor demanded.

Patrick grimaced. "I'm almost ashamed to admit it. But, yes, I'll try to hurry along their arraignment and get them out of your hair. Where are they now?"

"Holding cells. We managed to get them spaced far enough apart so they can't communicate with each other. Come on, I'll show you."

He hefted his bulk off his high stool and led them to the door leading to the holding cells.

"I've got one of them in the end cell and—"

At that moment, the trio entered the longer corridor and came in view of the end cell. A man stood behind the bars. His trousers were lowered to his knees. Water was gushing out of his cell and down the corridor toward the officers, filling the other cells like tidal channels along the way.

"I just sat on it. . . ." The prisoner was almost in tears.

"Oh, my God!" the officer exclaimed, "he musta tore the crapper right off the wall!" He could not appreciate why the others were convulsed in laughter. For them, it was merely the last straw. For him, it was a major catastrophe, the cleaning up of which was his responsibility.

It was serendipitous that both Father Koesler and Inspector Koznicki had worked up hearty appetites and that both fancied Italian cusine this evening. This pair of coincidences led them to Mario's, a quality Detroit restaurant unaccountably situated in a poverty-ridden high-crime neighborhood not far from downtown.

They arrived early enough to be seated at once without a reservation.

Ordinarily, a priest in clerical garb entering a restaurant draws some attention. Not this evening. Seated alone at a corner table was a small bald man in a toga. On his head was a laurel wreath. Koesler reasoned that Mario's, engaging in some promotional advertising, had probably filmed a TV commercial. Either that or the neighborhood was going daffier than usual.

After studying the anachronistic Roman for several moments, Koesler turned to Koznicki. "Can't you just picture that man in the toga saying to his waiter, 'What do you mean, what kind of salad do I want!' "

They laughed, then glanced cursorily at the huge menu. Each knew what he would order—spaghetti. Koesler had, in the past, frequently ordered veal, an Italian specialty, until Koznicki had informed him, in stomach-turning detail, that veal was the result of maltreated calves. That had marked the end of veal in the priest's diet.

They ordered drinks, after which the busboy brought bread and butter.

To the best of Koesler's knowledge, all Mario's waiters were male and Italian. They seemed singularly lacking in deference to him as a priest. He took that as merely another manifestation of a general Italian-male anti-clericalism. But whatever the reason, Koesler welcomed being treated as an ordinary person.

"Well, Father," Koznicki broke off a piece of crusty bread and presented it to Koesler as if bestowing a trophy, "tell me how you did it. Once again, I am in admiration of your deductive powers."

Koesler reddened. "There wasn't anything special about it, Inspector. I simply knew a few things that your people had no way of knowing."

"You're too modest. How did you know that Kirkus was not really the one we were looking for? And how did you know that the final victim was supposed to be Father Feeny? Among many other questions I have. . . ."

"It's a little difficult to explain. There were just too many pieces in the puzzle. The other night I was thinking about the whole thing during a parish council meeting. . . ."

Koznicki looked surprised.

"Well," sheepishly, "a person has to think about *something* during parish council meetings. I was trying to find a common denominator in all these victims. Each time I looked for the common feature I was forced to exclude myself. I couldn't fit myself in.

"But, if I excluded myself, there was more than one common denominator. All the others were considerably older than I am. They were all roughly the same age. All of them had taught in the seminary for many years. And all of them had a well-earned reputation for being strict, even harsh, with their students. It was common knowledge that many of the students who were cut from the seminary in the past owed their expulsion or termination to one or another of these particular priests."

Drinks were served and meal orders taken.

"So," Koesler continued, "for the sake of argument, I excluded myself. I had to suppose that someone other than the assailant had given me that doctored bottle of gin.

"Now, with me out of the picture, the picture was much clearer.

"Then, when Kirkus killed poor old Father Dye, that was the second, and telling error in the equation. The assailant was being very selective about who he —or they, as it turned out—selected as victims. Why had Fathers Burk, Martin, Grandville, Smith, O'Dowd and the others not been singled out? Some of them, like Smith, did not fit the pattern because they were too young. Others, like Burk, Grandville, O'Dowd and yes, Dye, did not fit the pattern because they had the reputation of being almost infinitely patient with and tolerant of the students.

"So, when I learned that Father Dye had been attacked, I was sure it was the wrong man. If my reasoning was correct, it should not have been Father Dye, it should have been Father Feeny, who shared with the other victims that harsh, strict image. And if we had the wrong victim, we also had the wrong assailant.

"But it was the perfect time to attack. It was the final scheduled day of filming. After this, it would be easier to make the seminary more secure, and infinitely more difficult, if not impossible, for an outsider to operate unnoted. Now, with everyone thinking the case had been solved, and almost everyone gathered around the office where you were interrogating Kirkus, and this being the hour when Father Feeny habitually was alone in the exercise room—now was the best moment for the real assailant to act."

"And so you led us to the exercise room."

"And ended up colliding with Brother Alphonsus, or Al Wiedeman."

Salad was served. Like the toga-clad gentleman in the corner, they had Caesar salad.

"Did you have some special reason for assuming

that Father Feeny would be the final victim?" Koznicki broke off another piece of bread, this time for himself.

"Symmetry. Excluding me, there would have been three victims at each seminary. Ward, Merrit, and Sklarski at Sacred Heart, Gennardo, Budreau, and Feeny at St. Joe's.

"You see, when we older Catholics become psychically disturbed, we frequently take on compulsive obsessive behavior. Even those of us who pass for normal frequently become obsessed with numbers; thus it's easy to turn to them when we lapse into abnormality."

"Numbers?"

"Yes. You remember: seven sacraments, Ten Commandments, nine first Fridays, five first Saturdays, fourteen Stations of the Cross, forty days of Lent, three persons in the Trinity, two natures of Christ, five processions of the Trinity, seven deadly sins—"

"Wait!" Koznicki held up his hand. "You're overwhelming me!"

"I could go on—like the traditional penance after confession: five Our Fathers and five Hail Marys—but I won't."

Koesler caught the waiter's eye and ordered Chianti to accompany the entree.

"Well, I do not know that anyone told you, Father, but we, too, wondered about your bottle of gin. If all attempts up till then had been made with guns, we would have wondered even more. But the first attack was made using a knife; the next two were guns. Once a *modus operandi* is changed, it no longer qualifies as an inflexible M.O. So, our culprit could logically have tried poison since he had already tried a knife and guns."

"I wasn't thinking of that. All I could see was that I didn't fit in with what I felt was the assailant's plan."

"Ah, yes, the plan. I know the motive was revenge, only because Wiedeman confessed that. But—revenge for what?"

"The members of the Instrument of Justice Society

were very bitter men, Inspector. They were all semi-narians at one time, although not all in the same grade. In fact, they were just a few years behind me. I didn't know them because frankly, none of them was around long enough to make much of a mark. They were expelled, records indicate, because each was so inept. Sort of classic Catholic klutzes.

"I almost tumbled to them when Mr. Deutsch, the scriptwriter, kept altering the way in which the attacks were made in real life. He had Father Ward fight off his assailant, and Father Gennardo dodge the bullets. The filmmakers thought the TV audience would find it impossible to believe that a knife-wielding assailant couldn't stab a helpless, defenseless old man. Or that an assailant could miss his target four times at close range.

"In reality, these were incredibly inept attacks by in-credibly inept men on priests who had discharged these same men for being incredibly inept. And, as you can see by the way they hopelessly botched their assaults, time had done nothing to improve their luck . . . which makes one wonder whether the priests weren't correct in their assessment and in expelling them."

"But why such a terrible revenge? It would seem out of proportion," said Koznicki.

"I agree. But it helps if one can understand their sense of loss when they were cut from the seminary. In all probability, each originally had a strong spiritual motive for wanting to become a priest. But they could not have been unaware of the special benefits that the priesthood would provide them.

"In a word, they would be secure. Now, Inspector, don't for a moment think I am denigrating the priest-hood. You know better; you know what I think of the priesthood and how I feel about it. It is one of the truly great vocations in the world. Many, many men have lived heroic, even saintly, lives as priests. As for me personally, I still feel exactly as I have all these years: the day I was ordained was the happiest day of my life.

"But, God knows, there is a security in the priesthood that is, perhaps, unmatched in this world. Granted, a priest may be transferred from parish to parish or even country to country. But no matter how badly he bungles things—within the limits of Church law, of course—he remains a priest, with all the perquisites inherent in that office.

"Just think of these men we are speaking of . . . imagine how men like these, particularly, would prize that sort of security. And all that eventual security went down the drain when they were thrown out of the seminary. They must have known all they had lost even then. And they must have been bitter even then.

"Then think how they feel now. Things are so much different than in their day. Today we need priests so desperately that even the Instruments of Justice might make it through to ordination. I recall a conversation I had with Father Ward. He was commenting on Leonard Marks—"

"Yes, I wanted to ask you about him," Koznicki interrupted.

"I knew you would. He and Bill Zimmer are two of the most interesting aspects of this case.

"But to get back to Father Ward. He said of Marks: 'He simply cannot do anything right. Years ago, he would not have lasted more than a semester or two.' And that's true.

"So, our klutzes were doubly bitter. Bitter that they had been cut from the seminary, denied their cherished vocation, and denied that storied security. And bitter that today, young men like themselves are given more leeway, more of a chance—the chance they were denied—and, as often as not, even ordained. So, they planned to strike out at the type of seminary professor, if not the actual specific priest, responsible for their expulsion.

"Their motive was revenge, and also they wanted to

make a statement. That's why they called themselves the Instrument of Justice Society."

The spaghetti was served and the Chianti presented with just the hint of a flourish.

Koesler took fork and spoon and began winding spaghetti.

"Of course, I've never even met three of the four men. Have they, do you know, had a difficult time holding down jobs, finding some sort of security?"

"We have not had much time to check, but thus far it does seem so. That is, with the exception of Wiedeman—Brother Alphonsus. It seems he began a career with the post office and stayed with it, until now he is a suburban postmaster."

"That's hard to believe."

"But true. It was through the good offices and civic connections of Wiedeman that the four were hired by the film company. Kirkus, also."

"Kirkus too?"

"Indeed. Even though Kirkus was not a member of their secret society, the four were all acquaintances of his. Originally, Kirkus had wanted to be on the scene of the moviemaking to keep an eye on the seminary for his own purposes as well as on behalf of the Tridentines. Obviously, his aims, although not initially formulated, were very similar to those of the Group of Four.

"You'll recall that Kirkus was in the men's room when the attempt was made on Father Budreau's life, or, rather, when Father Budreau's shot foiled the would-be attempt on his life. Whether or not he heard the shot, Kirkus must have known something was up when one of the Four dashed in, undoubtedly agitated and breathless and most likely favoring his numbed hand. And then when Sergeant Patrick questioned Kirkus and that same man stepped forward, seemingly to provide *him* an alibi, Kirkus must have realized that the man was in reality providing an alibi for himself. But, what with one thing and another, he felt it best to keep mum.

"The tragic thing about Kirkus is that if any of us had figured out that any assailant was a former seminarian, we could have solved the case in time to keep Kirkus from committing murder. I believe it was Patricia Lennon in the *News* who wrote of Kirkus that he had never attended even a parochial school, let alone a seminary.

"What about Kirkus, Inspector. Do you think he just got swept up in all this?"

"Oh, absolutely. He was a creation of the media. We saw him come to life when the cameras moved in at the Tridentine meetings. I think by the time he shot poor Father Dye, he actually believed he was the one who had attacked the other priests."

Koesler, who had paused in his eating, seemed pensive.

"What is it, Father?"

"Oh, I was just thinking of poor Father Dye. So much has been happening so fast, I haven't really had an opportunity to grieve for him."

"That is understandable, Father."

"I was also thinking about something Dr. Heinsohn said: People who commit crimes like these have an ability to rationalize their behavior so it appears to be warranted, reasonable, and justified. Imagine feeling justified in killing a sweet old man like Father Dye!"

They had finished dinner. Used utensils were removed and coffee served. The two friends were silent for several minutes. Koesler prayed for the happy repose of Father Dye's soul, and thanked God that the old priest had been granted such a long and fulfilled life. He then shifted mental gears to ponder again the whys and wherefores of Kirkus' actions. He found it cathartic in the psychoanalytic sense to verbalize his thoughts.

"I suppose Kirkus' statement was unlike that of the Four. He wanted to expose what he considered the sinfulness in today's seminary. So he would kill a member of the faculty of that seminary, a pillar if you will, of that establishment, as a way of making his point. By that time, his judgment was so muddled that all he could see was the collar and the cassock—not the fact that he was destroying one of the oldtime members of the clergy who could well have felt as he did: that the goings-on in the seminary were a sin—or at very least an error."

Koznicki rarely smoked. Only an occasional cigar in celebration of some unusual event. Tonight, he lit up. In the absence of an after-dinner cigarette, ex-smoker Koesler had to find some occupation for his hands: he toyed with a spoon.

"Well, Father, there remains one question: the two seminarians. How did you you discover their involvement?"

Koesler smiled. "Zimmer and Marks? From the bottle of gin. Once I removed myself from the category of intended victim, it seemed clear that whoever was trying to kill me was not the same person trying to kill the other priests. But, nonetheless, someone put a drug in a bottle of gin and intended it for me. Why?

"I couldn't think of any motive. But giving me that doctored bottle had had an effect: I had gotten involved . . . immediately and very personally. Could that possibly have been the effect the perpetrator intended? Mind-boggling. But if—and this was almost building a house of cards—*if* it was the desired effect, then it followed that it was also the motive. But why would someone choose such a devious means of involving me? Why Antabuse?

"Well, the perpetrator was in a no-lose situation: if I had drunk it, it would have made me deathly sick, although, we've pretty well ascertained, not killed me. However, it certainly would've gotten me directly involved in the investigation. A pretty extreme method, I grant you. But, as it turned out, the perpetrator knew it wasn't fatal.

"And what if I had noticed the tampered seal? Wouldn't I have wondered about the contents of the bottle and had it analyzed? Which is exactly what did happen . . . and which immediately involved me in the investigation.

"You see, either way, the perpetrator would have his desired effect.

"But even so—even if this were the desired effect—who would possibly want me involved in the investigation?"

"Me?" said Koznicki, puffing out a cloud of uninhaled smoke.

"Yes, you." Koesler chuckled. "But you would not stoop to such a prank. You would just bully me.

"No; eventually, I recalled a party we had at Sacred Heart, during which Bill Zimmer made it a point to ask me how the investigation was going. When I told him I was not involved in any investigation, he seemed inordinately disappointed. In retrospect, it seemed evident he wanted me to get involved in this investigation. But why? And if so, why wouldn't he just come right out with the suggestion?

"Once I boarded that train of thought, a series of up-till-then unrelated incidents began to add up.

"At the scene of Father Ward's assault, you yourself, Inspector, noted that the patch of floor where the attack had taken place had been scrubbed.

"What if someone had known when and where that assault was to be made and had tried to prevent it by, say, waxing that patch of floor, thus causing all that slipping and sliding, which, in effect, saved Father Ward's life?"

"You see, Zimmer was doing the best he could—or what he thought was the best he could—at the time. He even, I discovered, hid in a nearby closet with the door ajar, thinking to physically step in if it looked as if the murder attempt were going to be successful. But, you see, he had his reasons, misguided as they were, for not wanting to become identifiably involved.

"Anyway, afterward, he washed the wax from the floor, and you noticed that spot had been cleaned.

"When Father Merrit was attacked, he was headed for his car to drive to St. Gregory's and say Mass. If he had actually reached his car, he would have found it was unstartable because the battery had been removed. In which event, he would have phoned the parish and told them he could not make it.

"Now, what if someone knew Father Merrit was to be assaulted that morning, but presumed the attack was to take place at the parish? In an effort to forestall such attack, he removes the battery from Father's car so he cannot drive to his death. And to camouflage his action, he also removes the batteries from four of the six cars standing near Father Merrit's car, thus making it appear to be ordinary looting.

"Of course, when the attempt was made on Father Merrit before he even reached his car, Zimmer should have realized what he was up against. But it did put him further on his guard; he was determined that nothing be left to chance in the future.

"When Father Sklarski was scheduled to be shot, 'someone' put the word out on the street that a white man, probably dressed in black, would be on a certain corner at a certain time carrying a gun that could easily be taken from him.

"What happens? The would-be attacker is mugged, and Father Sklarski escapes injury. But here again, Zimmer was taking no chances. He told me that he had stationed himself nearby and was ready, if events required, to step forward and physically prevent the assailant from firing at Sklarski. He would have made it seem as if he were a disinterested bystander who had just happened along at the time.

"So far, so good.

"But now, two things happen. The scene of the crime —or crimes—moves to St. Joseph's—outside Zimmer's realm, and even worse, Zimmer has received no input on who will be next, or when any future attacks will be made.

"Now, bear in mind, Inspector, some of what I am telling you is conjecture, some hypothesis, and some I have learned post factum.

"So, when the assailant moves the action to St. Joseph's Seminary, no longer do any of these diversionary tactics occur. Now, failure is due to an astounding combination of ineptitude and execrable luck . . . if this hypothetical, self-appointed protector I have theorized does exist, his influence does not extend beyond Sacred Heart.

"And whom do I know at Sacred Heart with the ingenuity and capability to accomplish all this? Bill Zimmer, of course. And from what source would Mr. Zimmer get information? Is he in on these attacks, or involved with whoever is carrying them out?

"Again I remembered threads of past conversation. During a luncheon at Sacred Heart, Father Ward remarked how all the students seemed to confide in Zimmer, and further, that Zimmer probably knew more about what went on there than the entire faculty put together.

"But what, or rather, who, was his specific source?

"Somehow, Zimmer and Leonard Marks had become close friends. Now, Leonard is a nice young man, but he is every bit the klutz that our assailant is. Had Marks been in the seminary in our day, as Father Ward correctly observed. he would not have lasted more than a semester or so.

"Is it beyond the realm of possibility, I asked myself, that birds of a feather might get together? Whoever was attempting these assaults was proving himself awkward enough to be a clone of poor Leonard. Could Leonard himself be the assailant? That could well explain Zimmer's involvement.

"But no; if Leonard had even thought of attempting such a thing, Zimmer would have known and would have talked him out of it. No; it had to be someone else—someone enough like Leonard to feel rapport with him—rapport sufficient to confide in him to some extent. Or if not to confide, at least to verbalize threats, in his presence, against seminary professors who had tormented the assailant in the past—the same professors who were presently tormenting Leonard. Like the saying, nothing makes better friends than having the same enemies.

"As it turns out, the Instrument of Justice gang, assuming that because Leonard was a fellow klutz he would share their feelings, tried to recruit him and involve him in their plan as a surveillant. Of course it would never occur to a bitter, warped mind that Leonard, even though he was being picked on by his professors, might not feel the same ill will.

"Bewildered and upset, Marks confided in his buddy Zimmer, who promised he would try to ward off the attacks, or at least prevent them from succeeding. Which he did, as far as he could. But when the four moved their theater of operations to St. Joseph's, Leonard Marks was no longer in the picture. All Zimmer could do, at that stage, was to pray—which he and Lennie both did—and to hope that Murphy's Law, combined with the ineptness of the assailant, would continue to protect any prospective victims.

"As a matter of fact, once the operation moves to St. Joe's, that whole element of advanced intervention is noticeably absent. It just disappears. I mean, you could suppose the Instruments of Justice might have tried to find a counterpart to Marks at St. Joe's. Then again, since Marks proved no help to them, they may have discarded that part of the plan. I would venture to guess, Inspector, that when you are able to interrogate those four more thoroughly, you may find that after their experience at Sacred Heart, they imposed an embargo on any further discussion outside their group.

"Of course, as I say, I knew none of this for certain, but I think it made a fairly tenable hypothesis."

"Amazing," said Koznicki, who appeared to be searching for something. "A spectacular hypothesis, on your part, the beautiful part of which is it proved to be true."

"It's always nice when one's hypothesis comes up true. But tell me, Inspector, will there be any charges against Zimmer or Marks?"

"The only possible charge would be against Zimmer for adding Antabuse to the bottle of gin he gave you."

"Oh, I don't intend to press charges against him for that. Talk to him about it, yes. But I was referring to possible charges for not informing the police before the fact."

"No; oddly enough, that is not a crime. Just grievously poor judgment. I would predict that after Sergeant Patrick gives them a tongue-lashing, both the prosecutor and the precinct police will bawl the living hell out of both of them."

"As well they should. I wouldn't argue that. But I am glad there won't be any charges filed. You see, Inspector, because he's very competent and talented, there's a tendency to expect more of Zimmer than is reasonable. He's a very young man—just twenty-one. He's got a lot of maturing to do. This whole thing nearly overwhelmed him. I know that now from talking to him. He didn't know how to handle it. Granted, in his youthful pride, he used very poor judgment; but remember, he was also trying to work things out so no one would get hurt. Not the priests, not the unknown assailant, whom he pitied, and most of all not his friend Lennie.

"He was afraid if he went to the police or to the rector, Lennie would get into trouble. And one more speck of trouble for Lennie and it could easily have been the end of his seminary career, a fate that Zimmer felt Lennie didn't deserve.

"And if this was more than Zimmer could handle, it goes without saying that Marks was at a complete loss in trying to cope. His only recourse was to confide in his friend, confident not only that Zimmer would take the burden from his own shoulders, but that Zimmer would know what to do.

"By the time everyone gets done reading them the riot act, I'm sure they both will have grown up considerably."

Koesler noticed that Koznicki was paying scant attention to him. "Uh, Inspector, is there something—"

"Well, I could use a little more bread."

Koesler waved a napkin until he caught the waiter's eye. "We could use just a bit more bread, if you don't mind."

Obviously, providing bread was a menial function one step removed from the lofty level of the waiter. He snapped his fingers at a busboy who was changing the cloth on a nearby table.

The busboy, easily a decade or so older than the waiter, at length looked up from his work.

"Eh! *Pane!*" the waiter commanded, pointing at their table.

The busboy unhurriedly continued to dress his table. The waiter stood, leaning heavily on one foot, hand on hip as he watched the busboy carefully positioning the salt and pepper.

At long last, the busboy, his table setting completed, picked up a full breadbasket from a serving table and placed it before Koznicki.

At which point, the waiter derisively applauded, and critiqued sarcastically, "Bravo! Bravo!"

One didn't merely eat at Mario's; one participated in a slice of history.

9.

MICHIGAN SUMMERS COULD BE OPPRESSIVE. MICHIGAN winters sometimes brought on cabin fever. But Michigan springs and autumns were worth the price of admission. People of the southern states could have their perpetual warmth; northerners prized their change of seasons.

The only word for this spring day in early June was glorious. The temperature was in the mid-70s under a cloudless sky.

Insects were buzzing, automobiles were humming, and a power mower was making paths in the spacious lawn in front of Sacred Heart Seminary. Inside the faculty lounge on the seminary's second floor, the final faculty meeting of this scholastic year was taking place.

Much had happened in the two months since a series of arrests had marked the end of the assaults on seminary professors. Roman Kirkus had been found guilty of murder but mentally ill. He had been turned over to the Department of Corrections and incarcerated in the world's largest walled prison, the state penitentiary outside of Jackson, where psychiatric therapy was being provided him.

All four members of the Instrument of Justice Society had been convicted on charges of conspiring to commit murder. They also were incarcerated at Jackson.

In the vaults of a major TV network rested the film of a made-for-TV movie entitled, "Assault with Intent." The film company's contract and optional extension with the Archdiocese of Detroit had run out and had not been renewed. The company had been forced to vacate; filming had been completed on a sound stage in Los Angeles. A gaggle of network vice presidents had termed the finished product unacceptable. That is what they termed it when they were being polite. Undoubtedly, it would never be exhibited for anyone else.

Dr. Fritz Heinsohn was keeping, for him, an extremely low profile. But everyone knew that, like MacArthur, he would return.

William Zimmer and Leonard Marks had suffered a verbal barrage from almost every quarter, or so it seemed to them. Zimmer's prior flawless record saw him through the bombardment with comparatively little trauma. Marks, on the other hand, was all but devastated. He had been on the ropes even before the emotional pummeling began. He managed to hang in at the seminary by the skin of his teeth, and by leaning for succor on Zimmer. His tenuous position was, at this very moment, being judged. The question before the faculty was whether to pass Marks on to St. Joseph's Seminary for theological training, or whether to terminate his ecclesiastical career here and now.

The unique scholastic year had given seminary faculties throughout the civilized world much food for thought. The story of the assault against six faculty members by a bizarre group of maladjusted former seminarians had been disseminated by international news services. But Detroit was where it had happened. Such events would have to have made a profound impression on the faculties of Detroit's two Catholic seminaries.

The assembled faculty was almost finished ruling on this year's crop. The argument had been long, hot, and heavy with regard to William Zimmer. But when all was said and done, the bottom line was that although he had been guilty of egregious misjudgment, he was not culpable. His flawless, indeed outstanding, record testified to his general excellence. With some misgivings —a few expressed; others unspoken—Zimmer was promoted.

Then came the final case: Leonard Marks. All present recognized that the Marks case was pivotal. Much more than the normal amount of time and discussion had been given to the pros and cons of the matter.

Father Phil Merrit had spoken emphatically on the necessity to preserve the highest possible standards for candidates for the priesthood. He acknowledged the problem the shortage of vocations was causing. But he insisted it was a dilemma that could and should be laid at the very feet of God.

He quoted Jesus' address to His Apostles: "You have not chosen me; I have chosen you." These same words applied today, Father Merrit maintained. Jesus still chose His priests. Young men did not unilaterally choose the vocation.

It was the responsibility of the present faculty, Merrit argued, to weed out those who did not qualify for the priesthood and who could not fulfill its obligations and duties. He further argued that it would be craven of the faculty to be swayed, indeed cowed, by the show of violence that had been directed against certain faculty members during this scholastic year. As a faculty member who had actually been attacked, he made his point rather forcefully. Merrit concluded by asserting that Leonard Marks clearly was unfit for the priesthood and, in all mercy and justice, should be terminated now.

Both Fathers Burk and Grandville spoke movingly about the multiplicity of roles in the priesthood. They contended that it was impossible to set a uniform standard of excellence for candidates to the priesthood. They cited the words of St. Paul when he wrote of how different are our various body parts but how all of them contribute essentially to the bodily integrity. So, too, there are so many ministries possible to a priest, the faculty members might well think twice lest they unjustly impede a young man who sincerely desired the priesthood and whose main shortcoming was that he was unlike others, was awkward, or was not brilliant.

They cited the Apostles as being as unlikely a group of candidates for the priesthood as any seminary faculty could possibly consider. Undoubtedly, not a man among that original priesthood would have survived the scrutiny of a modern seminary faculty. Yet they had become the foundation of the Christian Church.

Both Burk and Grandville posited, in conclusion, that it was not cowardly, but wise to learn some crucial lesson from the deplorable assault attempts of the past year.

Not a few faculty members kept their own counsel, speaking neither for nor against; each merely tried to find his or her personal way through to a just decision.

The debate concluded, voting had begun. Now, at this point, the votes for and against Leonard Marks were even. Only three votes remained uncast; it was up to Fathers Sklarski, Koesler, and Ward.

There was no doubt in Sklarski's mind: he would turn thumbs down on Marks, a rabble-rouser who would go no further. Koesler too had no doubts: Marks' sincerity far outweighed his awkwardness.

Father Ward, with whom this chain of events had started, had been silent throughout this final discussion. No one felt more strongly than he that clerical standards should never be compromised, no matter the circumstances. Now, all too aware that he held in his hands the future of a young man to whom, in effect, he probably owed his life, and aware that he, like that young man, would have to live with this decision for untold time to come, Father Leo Ward bowed his head and fervently prayed for divine guidance.

For three weeks now, he had been Father Raphael Doody. It had been the happiest three weeks of his life thus far. And he could think of nothing the future might hold that could make him any happier.

He would never forget his ordination. He had wanted to bless everything and everybody. He had to be content with blessing only the things and people he had encountered that day. His last thoughts before retiring that night had been: Well, now that I really am a priest, what can I do for myself that I could not do before? Finally determining there was nothing special he could do for himself, he said his night prayers and fell asleep.

He made a few mistakes during his first Mass. But that largely had been due to nervousness. He had done all right at daily Mass since then . . . pretty much . . . for him.

Then he had been assigned as associate pastor of St. Ambrose parish. He had been thrilled to enter into parochial life. Of course, there had been a few small problems, but nothing of any consequence. Like the first new family he had registered in the parish. He had given them children's collection envelopes instead of adult envelopes. But that was easily remedied. Besides, they hadn't taught that in the seminary.

Then there was the wedding. He had come to the altar completely vested but had forgotten the ritual book. He had sent a small altar boy back into the sacristy to fetch it.

The bride and groom and their attendants had reached the altar and still no boy nor prayer book. Red-faced, he had had to go into the sacristy to get it himself. Funny thing, from that day through this, he had not seen that altar boy again.

Now he was headed to Verheyden Funeral Home to lead the Rosary for Mrs. Ventimiglia, an elderly par-

ishioner who had died two days ago and would be
buried tomorrow from St. Ambrose parish.

He reached the corner of Outer Drive and Mack.
There was Verheyden of Grosse Pointe Park. It seemed
a suitable edifice for the President of the United States.
But it merely contained lots of rooms for the dead.

An earnest undertaker led him to the proper "slumber room," a large parlor packed with mourners.

Father Doody attempted to work his way toward
the bier. He was almost felled several times by rela-
tives, friends, and benefactors of the deceased, who,
at sight of his roman collar, were trying to escape
before they were trapped by the Rosary.

He was stopped dead in his tracks by an ample
woman who identified herself as Mrs. Ventimiglia's
daughter. She wished to go to confession. They found a
small adjoining empty room. Father Doody sat in a
straightback chair. The woman knelt on the floor beside him.

"Bless me, Father, for I have sinned. It's been, let's
see, oh, a lot of years since my last confession." She
waited, flinching, for the diatribe that would be directed at her many years of lapsed Catholicism. When
it didn't come, she assumed the priest was holding it
for delivery after her confession. "Well, I missed Mass
lots of times. I yelled at the kids, oh, all the time, it
seems. And my husband and I . . . we . . . uh . . .
practice birth control!" Now? She tensed

"Is that all?"

"Yes, Father. You gonna bawl me out now?"

"We're just happy you're home again. We'll all pray
for your good mother, who, I'm sure, is with the
Lord. And for your penance, why don't you offer the
Rosary we are going to say for your mother? Now,
make a good act of contrition."

When they finished, there was a tear of surprised
gratitude on each of the woman's cheeks.

"One more favor, if you please, Father. When you
say the Rosary for my mother, would you use the

rosary my aunt, her sister, who was a nun, God rest her, gave my mother?"

"Of course. Where is it?"

"It's on the coffin, Father."

He returned to the proper slumber room. This time, it was far easier to make his way to the bier. A goodly number of mourners had made good their escape.

It was not difficult to find the late nun's rosary. It was the kind sisters wore in the good old days. Fifteen decades of huge wooden beads. As he removed the rosary from the coffin, one end of it fell heavily to the floor, almost pulling him with it.

Father Raphael Doody led the Rosary with most of it on the floor most of the time.

"What's that priest's name?" Mrs. Ventimiglia's daughter asked her neighbor.

"Father Doody."

"He from St. Ambrose?"

"Yes."

"He's a good priest. I'm gonna start going to St. Ambrose from now on."

"This meeting of the Tridentine Society will come to order!" Conrad Nap banged his gavel on the lectern.

"In the name of the Father and the Son and the Holy Ghost, Amen," Nap intoned.

Rosary beads rattled.

"I believe in God, the Father Almighty, creator of heaven and earth . . ." The trouble with Roman Kirkus was that he talked a good fight but never did anything worthwhile. Of course he did shoot that priest, but he was an old man doing nothing to anybody. And the court did say Kirkus was nutty.

"Our Father, Who art in heaven, hallowed by Thy name . . ." Kirkus was not the leader the Tridentines needed. Just look how attendance had fallen off. Why, there can't be more than fifteen people here tonight.

"Hail Mary, full of grace, the Lord is with thee . . ." I've got to find some way of getting those TV cameras back here. That'll draw the crowds. Always does. Gotta get those crowds or the Mayor of Tumerango'll never come back. And we won't hear about the children and their visions. How to get those cameras back again?

"Glory be to the Father, the Son, and the Holy Ghost . . ." The Klan gets TV coverage. The Nazis get it; the abortionists and rioters always get the cameras. We've got to stage some rallies. But first, I've got to get these passive people to get up off their duffs and *do* something. And to do that you've got to get them to hate. That's it: I'll teach them to hate. Then we'll get some action. Then the TV cameras will be back. And then the reporters will be asking Conrad Nap what he thinks about things.

"Oh, Jesus, forgive us our sins, save us from the fires of hell, and lead all souls to heaven, especially those who are in most need of Thy mercy . . ."

About the Author

William X. Kienzle, author of three best sellers, *The Rosary Murders, Death Wears a Red Hat,* and *Mind Over Murder,* was ordained into the priesthood in 1954 and spent twenty years as a parish priest. For more than twelve of those years he was editor-in-chief of the *Michigan Catholic.* After leaving the priesthood, he became editor of *MPLS* magazine in Minneapolis and later moved to Texas, where he was director of the Center for Contemplative Studies at the University of Dallas. Kienzle and his wife Javan presently live in Detroit, the setting for all four of his novels, where he enjoys playing the piano and organ and participating in sports as diversions from his writing.